Volume 11

Secrets

Satisfy your desire for more.

On Jennifer Probst's story: "Jennifer Probst has chosen the perfect setting for this short erotic tale of sexual fantasy. What better way to lose your inhibitions than at a Masquerade party when everyone is in costume and concealed!"

—*The Road to Romance*

On Jess Michaels' story: "Jess Micheals keeps you on the edge of your seat with this highly sensual adventure to die for! Can't wait to hear more from this unique author."

—*The Belles & Beaux of Romance/Reader To Reader Reviews*

On Kimberly Dean's story: "*Manhunt* is the most erotic of the four novellas and will have you wishing that it was longer. I cannot wait to see what Ms. Dean comes up with next."

—*The Best Reviews*

On Angela Knight's story: "You are going to love this one! Angela Knight can get you steamed up in a hurry with her erotic tales."

—*The Belles & Beaux of Romance/Reader To Reader Reviews*

Reviews from Secrets Volume 1

"Four very romantic, very sexy novellas in very different styles and settings. ... The settings are quite diverse taking the reader from Regency England to a remote and mysterious fantasy land, to an Arabian nights type setting, and finally to a contemporary urban setting. All stories are explicit, and Hamre and Landon stories sizzle. ... If you like erotic romance you will love *Secrets*."

— *Romantic Readers* review

"Overall, for a fan of erotica, these are unlike anything you've encountered before. For those romance fans who turn down the pages of the "good parts" for later repeat consumption (and you know who you are) these books are a wonderful way to explore the better side of the erotica market. ... *Secrets* is a worthy exploration for the adventurous reader with the promise for better things yet to come."

— Liz Montgomery

Reviews from Secrets Volume 2
Winner of the Fallot Literary Award for Fiction

"*Secrets, Volume 2*, a new anthology published by Red Sage Publishing, is hot! I mean *red hot!* ... The sensuality in each story will make you blush—from head to toe and everywhere else in-between. ... The true success behind *Secrets, Volume 2* is the combination of different tastes—both in subgenres of romance and levels of sensuality. *I highly recommend this book*."

— Dawn A. Long, *America Online* review

"I think it is a fine anthology and Red Sage should be applauded for providing an outlet for women who want to write sensual romance."

— Adrienne Benedicks,
Erotic Readers Association review

Reviews from Secrets Volume 3

Winner of the 1997 Under the Cover
Readers Favorite Award

"An unabashed celebration of sex. Highly arousing! Highly recommended!"
— Virginia Henley, *New York Times* Best Selling Author

"*Secrets, Volume 3* leaves the reader breathless. Each of these tributes to exotic and erotic fiction offers a world of sensual pleasure and moral rewards. A delicious confection of sensuous treats awaits the reader on each turn of the page. Sexy, funny, thrilling, and luscious, Secrets entertains, enlightens, and fuels the fires of fantasy."
— Kathee Card, *Romancing the Web*

Reviews from Secrets Volume 4

"*Secrets, Volume 4*, has something to satisfy every erotic fantasy... simply sexsational!"
— Virginia Henley, *New York Times* Best Selling Author

"Provocative...seductive...a must read! ★★★★"
— *Romantic Times*

"These are the kind of stories that romance readers that 'want a little more' have been looking for all their lives without crossing over into the adult genre. Keep these stories coming, Red Sage, the world needs them!"
— Lani Roberts, *Affaire de Coeur*

"If you're interested in exploring erotica, or reading farther than the sexual passages of your favorite steamy reads, the *Secret* series is well worth checking out."
— *Writers Club Romance Group* on AOL

Reviews from Secrets Volume 5

"*Secrets, Volume 5*, is a collage of lucious sensuality. Any woman who reads *Secrets* is in for an awakening!"
— **Virginia Henley,** *New York Times* Best Selling Author

"Hot, hot, hot! Not for the faint-hearted!"
— *Romantic Times*

"As you make your way through the stories, you will find yourself becoming hotter and hotter. *Secrets* just keeps getting better and better."
— *Affaire de Coeur*

Reviews from Secrets Volume 6

"*Secrets, Volume 6* satisfies every female fantasy: the Bodyguard, the Tutor, the Werewolf, and the Vampire. I give it Six Stars!"
— Virginia Henley, *New York Times* Best Selling Author

"*Secrets, Volume 6* is the best of *Secrets* yet. ...four of the most erotic stories in one volume than this reader has yet to see anywhere else. ... These stories are full of erotica at its best and you'll definitely want to keep it handy for lots of re-reading!"
— *Affaire de Coeur*

Reviews from Secrets Volume 7

Winner of the Venus Book Club
Best Book of the Year

"...sensual, sexy, steamy fun. A perfect read!"
— Virginia Henley, *New York Times* Best Selling Author

"Intensely provocative and disarmingly romantic, Secrets Volume 7 is a romance reader's paradise that will take you beyond your wildest dreams!"
— *Ballston Book House* Review

"Erotic romance is at the sensual core of Red Sage's latest collection of short, red hot novels, *Secrets, Volume 7.*"
— *Writers Club Romance Group* on AOL

Reviews from Secrets Volume 8
Winner of the Venus Book Club
Best Book of the Year

"*Secrets Volume 8* is simply sensational!"
— Virginia Henley, *New York Times* Best Selling Author

"*Secrets Volume 8* is an amazing compilation of sexy stories discovering a wide range of subjects, all designed to titillate the senses."
— Lani Roberts, *Affaire de Coeur*

"All four tales are well written and fun to read because even the sexiest scenes are not written for shock value, but interwoven smoothly and realistically into the plots. This quartet contains strong storylines and solid lead characters, but then again what else would one expect from the no longer *Secrets* anthologies."
— Harriet Klausner

"Once again, Red Sage Publishing takes you on a journey of sexual delight, teasing and pleasing the reader with a bit of something to appeal to everyone."
— Michelle Houston, *Courtesy Sensual Romance*

"In this sizzling volume, four authors offer short stories in four different sub-genres: contemporary, paranormal, historical, and futuristic. These ladies' assignments are to dazzle, tantalize, amaze, and entice. Your assignment, as the reader, is to sit back and enjoy. Just have a fan and some ice water at your side."

— Amy Cunningham

Reviews from Secrets Volume 9

"Everyone should expect only the most erotic stories in a *Secrets* book. ...if you like your stories full of hot sexual scenes, then this is for you!"

— Donna Doyle, *Romance Reviews*

"*Secrets 9*...is sinfully delicious, highly arousing, and hotter than hot as the pages practically burn up as you turn them."

— Suzanne Coleburn, *Reader To Reader Reviews/ Belles & Beaux of Romance*

"Treat yourself to well-written fictionthat's hot, hotter, and hottest!"

— Virginia Henley, *New York Times* Best Selling Author

Reviews from Secrets Volume 10

"*Secrets Volume 10*, an erotic dance through medieval castles, sultan's palaces, the English countryside and expensive hotel suites, explodes with passion-filled pages."

— *Romantic Times BOOKclub*

"Having read the previous nine volumes, this one fulfills the expectations of what is expected in a *Secrets* book: romance and eroticism at its best!!"

— *Fallen Angel Reviews*

"All are hot steamy romances so if you enjoy erotica romance, you are sure to enjoy *Secrets, Volume 10*. All this reviewer can say is WOW!!"

— *The Best Reviews*

Reviews from Secrets Volume 11

"*Secrets Volume 11* delivers once again with storylines that include erotic masquerades, ancient curses, modern-day betrayal and a prince charming looking for a kiss. Scorching tales filled with humor, passion and love. ★★★★"

— *Romantic Times BOOKclub*

"The *Secrets* books published by Red Sage Publishing are well known for their excellent writing and highly erotic stories and *Secrets, Volume 11* will not disappoint. "

— *The Road to Romance*

"*Secrets 11* quite honestly is my favorite anthology from Red Sage so far. All four novellas had me glued to their stories until the very end. I was just disappointed that these talented ladies novellas weren't longer."

— *The Best Reviews*

"Indulge yourself with this erotic treat and join the thousands of readers who just can't get enough. Be forewarned that *Secrets 11* will wet your appetite for more, but will offer you the ultimate in pleasurable erotic literature."

—*Ballston Book House Review*

Satisfy Your Desire for More... with Secrets!

Did you miss any of the other volumes of the sexy Secrets *series? At the back of this book is an order form for all the available volumes. Order your* Secrets *today! See our order form at the back of this book or visit Waldenbooks or Borders.*

Jennifer Probst

Jess Michaels

Kimberly Dean

Angela Knight

Volume 11

Secrets

Satisfy your desire for more.

SECRETS Volume 11
This is an original publication of Red Sage Publishing and each individual story herein has never before appeared in print. These stories are a collection of fiction and any similarity to actual persons or events is purely coincidental.

Red Sage Publishing, Inc.
P.O. Box 4844
Seminole, FL 33775
727-391-3847
www.redsagepub.com

SECRETS Volume 11
A Red Sage Publishing book
All Rights Reserved/December 2004
Copyright © 2004 by Red Sage Publishing, Inc.

ISBN 0-9754516-1-8

Published by arrangement with the authors and copyright holders of the individual works as follows:

MASQUERADE
Copyright © 2004 by Jennifer Probst

ANCIENT PLEASURES
Copyright © 2004 by Jess Michaels

MANHUNT
Copyright © 2004 by Kimberly Dean

WAKE ME
Copyright © 2004 by Angela Knight

Photographs:
Cover © 2004 by Tara Kearney; www.tarakearney.com
Cover Models: Jake Stone
Setback cover © 2000 by Greg P. Willis; email: GgnYbr@aol.com

Printed in the U.S.A.

Book typesetting by:

Quill & Mouse Studios, Inc.
www.quillandmouse.com

Contents

Masquerade

~❦~

by Jennifer Probst

To My Reader:

I loved writing *Masquerade*. Start with a delicious concept: masked strangers and a bargain to be truthful. Add in the mystery of never revealing their faces, and the stark intimacy of sharing every secret fantasy. The result is a steamy romance that breaks down all barriers. I feel that readers can relate to this couple who have to battle their fear of vulnerability in order to win the ultimate prize: love.

The setting takes place in the sensual world of Italy, Lake Como. I remember looking at the eccentric mansions around the lake and spinning this tale. I truly hope you enjoy the journey and I look forward to sharing more stories. Please go to my website, www.jenniferprobst. com, and write to me. I welcome all feedback from readers.

Chapter One

Hailey Ashton closed the door to her best friend's office and sat down on the chair opposite his desk. Her fingers trembled slightly with excitement as she slid the gold embossed invitation across the polished wood. "I'm going to meet the man of my dreams."

Michael Rivers raised one brow at her declaration and picked up the invitation. "I didn't know you were looking for one." His chocolate brown eyes held a gleam of intrigue and his fingers raked through wheat strands of hair. One lock fell stubbornly over his forehead in rebellion. It was the only part of his appearance not ruthlessly groomed and neat.

She gave a sigh. "Who isn't? Women were raised on stories of knights and dragon slayers. No wonder we get depressed when a man can't do his own laundry."

He grinned and glanced at the card. "A masquerade ball?"

Hailey leaned over. "It's the annual party our boss sponsors. I've heard stories about them but I've never gone."

"Yeah, I remember seeing one of these in my mailbox. It's more like a weekend event than a party. Employees are invited but mostly the rich and famous attend. He picks a different theme each year. This one's being held in some private villa in Italy. Must be nice." Michael narrowed dark brown eyes. "Don't tell me. You've targeted some Duke of England to take you away from all this."

"Very funny. I don't care about money and you know it. I just thought this would be different." She paced the lush wine carpet. "Sometimes I feel like my life is closing in on me. I do everything right. I exercise at the gym, I don't eat red meat, I make sure I get eight hours sleep. Even the men I date are boring. Do you know I can't remember the last time a man kissed me good night and my knees buckled? Usually I can't wait to get back to my own apartment.

Lord, I have more fun with you watching a DVD and eating popcorn. Isn't that sad?"

"Tragic," he said wryly.

"Sorry, I didn't mean it like that." She sighed and pushed back her heavy mane of red hair. "I want to break out of my routine and meet someone I've always wondered about."

Michael studied her, then shifted in his chair. The leather creaked gently beneath his weight. "Are you looking for a general man of your dreams, or have you narrowed the search to one?"

Unfortunately, he knew her well enough to realize she was hiding something. "I'd confess but you'll probably yell."

He muttered something under his breath. "Tell me."

"Promise you won't lecture?" she asked.

He groaned. "I promise. Spill it."

"Our boss."

His face plainly showed his disbelief. "You're kidding me. Ciro Demitris? He's not only the boss of this company, Hailey. He owns a software empire all over the world and he's richer than Midas. You've never even met him. Hell, most people in the organization never caught a glance of the guy."

She raised her chin. "I've seen his pictures in magazine articles! I'd know what he looks like if I saw him."

Michael shook his head. "You think this man is the answer to your rut? He'd eat you for breakfast and not look back."

Her voice turned to ice. "Thanks for the confidence in me."

"Oh, hell, you know what I meant. The rumors about him should make you think twice. Why do you think he throws these parties each year? He's an eccentric who likes to play with people's minds. He does this for his own entertainment."

"You know nothing about him personally, and neither do I. But this party can change that. I know you don't think I'm glamorous enough to hold my own, but with a mask on I can be the woman I always wanted. I can be beautiful and exciting and mysterious."

His tone softened as he stared at her. "You are, Hailey. You just don't see it."

She stopped pacing and looked down at her sensible oatmeal colored business suit and pumps. As always, she dressed to be a businesswoman, and she realized that somehow, along the way, the real woman inside had gotten lost. How could she explain to anyone, even her best friend? She walked back over to the chair and sank down. Then tried to put her feelings into words.

"I'm thirty years old, Michael. I've never been married, never had children, and until lately, I never thought I'd miss it. But I feel trapped. I'm afraid to do anything different if it doesn't fit with my daily schedule. I live for my work, but I know there has to be more out there. This is my chance. And even if nothing happens between us, at least I know I tried. Can you understand?"

A strange array of emotions passed over his carved features, then cleared. He smiled. "Yeah, I think I understand. But these parties are way out of your league. Demitris is known for his erotic themes. I've heard stories about drunken orgies, people playing out their sexual fantasies. Anything goes when a person steps through the door. He's made a reputation of being entirely discreet, and offering his guests the same." Michael paused. "I'm worried."

Hailey faced her best friend and realized she couldn't tell him the whole truth. He was the only man she felt close to, but she had never confessed her upbringing to him. She wasn't one to blame her sexual repressions on her parents, though their deeply-held belief sex was wrong had created problems since her teens.

She'd spent most of her life being reminded of her mother's mistake. Namely her. One drunken night had produced her parents' only child, and after they were forced to marry, they turned to religion. Sex was wrong. Sex meant loss of control. Sex meant diseases and pregnancy and a man controlling every part of a woman's existence. Sex meant fewer choices. Her parents made sure she would never have an opportunity for any reckless behaviors. Of course, she had rebelled.

Then realized her parents were right.

Hailey firmly shook off the memories and refocused on Michael. She ached for an experience to finally propel her out of her rut. She wanted to be free to express her sexuality without fear. The idea of shedding her clothes and her prim ways left her with a tingle of heat that bloomed in her belly. An odd combination of wanting and shame mingled together. She battled with an inner voice that taunted, its familiar sensual tone urging her to throw away constraints.

The voice came sometimes in the middle of the night, a swirl of sexual images of naked men sucking at her breasts, thrusting their fingers deep inside of her as she screamed for release. The last three months the dreams were relentless. She would wake in the middle of the night, bucking her hips upward into empty space, the tension pounding through her body until she moaned in agony and waited for the feeling to pass. With an iron willed control, she never let herself go, never pleasured herself. She believed in controlling her life to the last detail, which included her sexuality. Much easier to deny the wanting than pass over the edge of no return. Because the voice that came to her deep in the darkness always reminded her once she plummeted into her sexual fantasies, she'd never come back.

But the voice was growing stronger. She had always been able to keep the echo to a low murmur. Now, the roar crashed through her mental barriers at night and left her aching for so much more.

She admitted to obsessing a bit over Ciro Demitris. Once she had seen his picture, looked into those deep, brooding eyes, something had happened to her. The article in *Fortune* magazine sketched him as a private eccentric who lived an isolated life. She wanted him to be the one to do all the things she fantasized about. She didn't want to be afraid anymore of losing control.

The thought teased at the fringes of her mind for weeks, and when she received the invitation, she knew the time had come to take a chance.

Her life was perfect on paper. Strong financial background. Solid career. The ability to choose any path she craved. Yet, she felt unfulfilled and empty as she moved through her days. She admitted she was now more scared of being trapped in her ideal life than she was of embarking on a reckless affair.

No, she couldn't tell Michael, her sweet, supportive friend.

"I'll be fine." She said the words firmly but a quiver in her belly screamed she was a liar.

He nodded, obviously deciding to accept her decision. "Okay. So, what's the plan?"

"I already know where I can rent my costume and mask. The party starts Thursday night, and ends Sunday. Everyone unmasks at dawn on the final night. The map was enclosed with the invitation so I know how to get there." She brightened. "Why don't you come with me? This party could help you, too."

He winced. "Boy, you're full of complements this morning. I happen to be satisfied with my dull life."

"You need a woman, old friend. I think your last date was six months ago, almost the same time mine was," she teased.

"Sorry, the Bulls game is on. No glamour queen can compete."

"You're still hung up on her, aren't you?" she asked softly.

He stiffened, then consciously relaxed his fingers around the invitation. "My faithless ex-wife is off having a grand old time with her boyfriend. I never give her a second thought."

"It's been two years, Michael."

He gave a lopsided grin, full of his usual charm. "She never let me watch the basketball games. How could I possibly miss her?"

She let him coax a smile from her. "Okay, I give. I should know by now you'll never be one of these tortured heroes like Heathcliff in *Wuthering Heights*. I've got to stop forcing that role on you."

"Deal," he said. He glanced at his watch. "I've got a meeting at ten. Davidson has a new software program he's still working kinks out of and my head's on the block. Our charming boss will fire me in a heartbeat if I don't get it working. Hmmm, maybe if you two hit it off you can put in a good word for me."

"Cute, real cute." She paused, then bit her lip as she tried to broach the subject. "Michael, I've got to ask you for one small favor."

He rubbed his fingers against his temple as if anticipating a headache. Wheat colored strands of hair ruffled under the motion, then settled back into place. "Why am I afraid to ask?"

"Well, since it's a masquerade ball, and you so intelligently pointed out I don't really know what our boss looks like, I need to know what he'll be wearing."

He blinked. "There will be hundreds of people in that mansion. All in masks and costumes. How am I supposed to get this information?"

"Oh, come on, you've got the inside on all the top people in this firm. We both know this party is presented as a social occasion, but it's still about business. Executives are going to want to get the ear of Ciro Demitris. I bet there are people who'll know exactly what his costume is. I just need you to be one of them."

"You don't ask for much. Got any money to grease their palms?"

She grinned cheekily. "Just use your charm. That's why you've been promoted to director, isn't it?"

"And your smart comebacks are why you're still a lowly manager."

She made a face, then rose from the chair and walked towards the door. "So, this wonderful manager can count on her best friend to do a little detective work, right?"

The phone beeped insistently and interrupted his comeback. He reached for the receiver and mouthed, "You owe me."

She laughed and left the office.

❧❧❧❧❧

Hailey stared at the woman in the full length mirror and caught her breath. It was her. But it wasn't.

The woman's hair had been left loose instead of fastened into her usual tight bun. Gleaming red strands poured wildly down her shoulders. Her blue eyes were framed by dark, lush lashes and took on a hint of mystery behind the brightly colored peacock mask. Her lips had been lined and colored with deep red lipstick, making them appear full and enticing. Her conservative suits and baggy sweat pants had been replaced with a midnight blue silk dress. The material covered every inch of her body but slashed down the front in a deep V, exposing the ripe white curves of her breasts. Delicate high heeled sandals enhanced her height. A simple strand of diamonds clasped around her neck, and the light caught and shimmered on the stones, emphasizing the smooth naked skin beyond.

The longer she stared at her reflection, the more she felt as if a change was taking place deep inside of her. Tonight was the opportunity to explore hidden parts of herself she had denied. She dated many men before, but always approached the relationship with a brick wall firmly erected to hide her feelings. Usually after the third date, the man realized he wasn't going to get "lucky" and moved on. Hailey admitted a portion of fault. She never gave them a chance to get to know her. She offered intelligent conversation, occasional humor, and a simple elegance that was part of her nature. Never any raw emotions or vulnerability. God, how she wanted that now. How she wanted to experience a man who could think of nothing but touching her skin, giving pleasure. A man who was so forceful there would be no thought to holding back. Poised on the edge of a cliff, Hailey wanted more than anything to take a deep breath and jump. But she was still afraid.

Therefore, Ciro Demitris was the perfect man. A man who might give her the push she so desperately needed.

After she read his biography in Fortune, Ciro Demitris had visited her every night in her dreams. Nights filled with darkness and passion and release. Erotic adventures that caused her to wake up in a tangle of damp sheets. She realized this party was the opportunity of a lifetime.

She intended to find the man behind the public image. He was confident about his abilities and could have any woman he wanted. He showed a cool demeanor to the world, but Hailey suspected he felt a number of things kept carefully hidden.

The magazine article painted him as a corporate mogul who traveled the globe and dated a variety of beautiful women.

Hailey was more interested in the private man, the one who gave to charities and avoided long term commitments, possibly because of a broken heart. Like Michael.

The thought made her glance nervously at the phone. She needed to leave within the hour and he still hadn't called. There was no way her plan could work if she didn't know what her boss wore.

The phone rang.

She snatched it up. "Did you get the information?"

A deep laugh rumbled over the receiver. "No hello? No singing 'Hail to the Hero' when I risked my life to get you the identity of his top secret costume? No payoff?"

She sighed impatiently. "You're impossible. I promise when I come back from the weekend I will personally fall before your feet and thank you. But first give me the information."

"Hmmm, this sounds too good to pass up. Will you clean my house, too?"

"Michael!"

"Okay, okay. Our little tycoon will be the Phantom of the Opera this evening. Fitting, too. The guy seems to be part mystery, part monster."

"Thank you. You don't know how much this means to me," she said.

The line hummed with sudden silence. When he spoke, his voice was quiet. "I think I do. I hope you find what you're looking for."

"I hope so, too," she whispered. "Bye. I'll call you on Sunday when I get back."

"I'll be waiting."

The phone clicked.

⁂

Michael replaced the receiver and glanced at his packed suitcase. Tension twisted his gut when he realized there would be no turning back. The plan was set. He had imparted the identity of the costume, and now Hailey was poised to meet the man who would turn her sexual fantasies into reality.

The only thing she didn't know was, the man would be Michael Rivers, not Ciro Demitris.

The thought of finally touching her the way he craved made him grow hard. Yes, he was her best friend. But he wanted so much more, and every time he dared to push the line, he watched her back off with a polite wariness that stopped him like a bucket of ice water. She would never give him a chance. He had lived with the knowledge for almost a year now, and he finally had the opportunity to change his future. Their future.

Two years ago, they were working on the same project together and formed a tentative friendship. An attraction always zinged beneath the surface, but he had been married, and committed to his wife.

Until his wife left him. Admitted to an affair and walked off without a glance back.

Things began to fall apart at work and in all aspects of his life. He refused to admit he needed help, but Hailey had saved his ass on many occasions and never asked a question. Before long, they were spending more time together. Drinks after work; planning sessions spent in the dim light of the conference room; long lunches over a bottle of wine. He finally opened up and told her everything. She held his hand as he cried for the first time. She supported him through lonely evenings and made him laugh again.

Michael took a deep breath and thought over the past year they spent together. He couldn't pinpoint the moment he fell in love with her. He believed it was a gradual deepening of emotion, like a warm summer breeze rather than a crashing thunderstorm.

Before long, they were having movie nights together with a tub of popcorn, feet propped up on the table clad in comfortable sweatpants. They took tennis lessons and teased each other over their bumbling inaccuracies and lack of coordination. He didn't remember when he stopped grieving over his wife and looked toward the future. A future he wanted to share with Hailey.

He'd watched her date a variety of men with a knot in his gut, but she never stayed away too long. The man would always demand a certain level of intimacy, and Hailey would come back to Michael, her safe, comfortable friend. But whenever he felt courageous enough to take their relationship to the next level, the walls would come up, and he always backed off.

He knew she would never let him be her lover.

She was too comfortable in their routine and too afraid of taking a chance and ruining their friendship. He knew she enjoyed the safety of their relationship and the guarantee she'd never be asked for more. But now he wanted Hailey enough to take a leap—even if it meant losing her forever.

Michael knew she was afraid to let go. Her body screamed sex, but her aura kept men firmly away. He wanted to be the man to tap into those hidden aspects of Hailey, but he'd had no way to get what he wanted.

Until now.

He'd noticed a change in her the past few weeks. A restless gleam within those Carribean blue eyes, a distraction in her work. He watched her talk with other men and found she was more open, more flirtatious. Like a juicy fruit on the vine, Hailey was ready to be picked…savored…licked. And now, after all the years of celibacy, she had finally reached her explosion point. Rage wrenched at him when he heard of her plan. He knew he would lose her. She was finally ready to take a chance and explore her sexuality. And she had not chosen him. She had picked out a stranger with a heartless reputation who would use her and throw her away.

Michael did not intend for that to happen. If his lady wanted to be seduced, he planned to give her exactly what she wanted.

On his terms.

The stage was set. He'd studied Demitris' photo and carefully changed enough of his appearance to his satisfaction. Contact lenses turned his brown eyes to a mossy green. A dark rinse turned his hair black, and he'd slicked the strands away from his face in the style that made Ciro famous for female fantasies. One diamond earring now pierced his left ear. His cloak and mask would cover the rest.

He knew more than his appearance needed to be changed.

Michael shook his head when he thought of the past year and his behavior. He always played the protector, not the seducer. This weekend would give him the opportunity to slip into a more dominant role. Demitris was a loner. Probably a control freak. Used to getting women and weary of the games they played. He would take all of those emotions and use them for the role. Hailey confessed she wanted to be free to become a different woman.

He intended to be a different man.

Hailey expected the millionaire and wouldn't search for similarities to her safe, dull friend. He felt confident she wouldn't recognize him. The rest he'd leave to fate.

He got up from the bed and switched off the lights. He knew Hailey would never give him the opportunity to please her. The need was always a distant glimmer in her blue eyes, a need he intended to satisfy tonight. And when it was all over, and he unmasked, if she turned him away at least he would have the memory of her to warm the cold nights ahead. The memory of her breasts in his mouth, his penis thrust deep inside her heat, her cries of pleasure echoing in his ear. Anything was worth that.

Anything.

He turned and closed the door behind him.

She reached the mansion after sundown. White washed stucco gleamed under the first splash of moonlight. Hailey breathed in the fragrant air and lifted her head to catch the warm breeze scented with roses and a hint of lemon. Two decks hooked around the first and second story, offering visitors an enthralling view of Lake Como. She picked her way over the cobblestone pathways. The sounds of laughter and music caressed her ears and called to her as if in a dream. She paused and took in the scene before her.

People gathered on the decks and throughout the gardens, sipping champagne. Exotic masks and brilliant costumes filled her vision and added to the dreamlike quality. And she realized for the first time, she could explore the real Hailey Ashton, who was safely hidden behind her mask and would not have to be exposed until the final night.

She grabbed a glass of champagne and made her way deeper into the gardens, seeking a moment to gather her composure. He could be anywhere, and she wondered where to start her search. Maybe she'd make her way through the crowds on the first floor, then move to...

Someone was watching her.

Hailey spun around. She searched through the thick shadows of the garden. Her skin tingled and burned, as if touched by the sun. She heard the music in the background, the dim shouts of laughter and gaiety as people swarmed around the villa, and then her eyes caught on a flash of white which pierced through the darkness.

He stood on the balcony overlooking the garden. A black cloak covered his body. His hair was slicked back from his forehead, the strands inky black and blending with the darkness. Catlike eyes gleamed through the carved holes of the stark white mask.

Hailey sucked in her breath as a current of raw, sexual energy sizzled in the air. Most of his face was covered, leaving only his mouth and eyes exposed. But as her gaze met his, Hailey felt his isolation as he stood alone, watching her. Dressed as the Phantom, he was a man who kept to the shadows, presenting a civilized veneer to the world which masked the violence. Hailey knew then she gazed upon Ciro Demitris.

Minutes ticked by. Frozen by the sheer power of the electricity stretching between them, Hailey waited, torn between the need to flee and the need to stay.

Then he turned and disappeared from the balcony.

Hailey shuddered. The tension eased, and she began to re-gather her control. This was what she had come for, but the reality of his presence shook her to the very core.

Without pausing to think, she headed determinedly through the garden. She found the staircase and made her way to the second floor, assuming he would still be up there. She passed couples lounging on the steps. A woman with her gown pulled down to the waist laughed as the man beside her dribbled champagne over her breasts and licked at her nipples. Her moans mingled with the strains of the music. Hailey rushed past them, her face burning, and walked down the dimly lit hallway. The chattering voices and music grew faint when she finally found the balcony where her host had stood. The doors were flung open, and Hailey glimpsed the twisting pathways of the garden in the distance. The bedroom was decorated in wood and burgundy tones. A king size bed dominated the room. A dozen plump pillows set off the sheen of wine satin sheets, and cherry wood antique furniture subtly blended into the background.

A vivid tapestry hung on the far wall, a naked Venus offering her body to an array of suitors. Her breasts and belly gleamed as she thrust her head back, her lips parted, her eyes greedy with need as she was pleasured on a soft bed of grass.

He wasn't there.

Hailey sighed and turned away. Maybe he decided to join the party in the ballroom. She still didn't know how she would approach him, what she would say...

"You shouldn't have come."

A deep masculine voice cut through the air. Steel sheathed in silk. Satin dragged over skin. A gravelly tone, yet oddly familiar. Vivid images flashed before her as Hailey felt that voice pour over her ears like warm honey. Her body responded as if the heavy liquid had been dripped over the naked breasts, hips, thighs...

Her hand paused on the knob. Halfway tempted to flee, she forced herself to turn and reminded herself this man was whom she had traveled miles to meet.

He stepped out of the shadows. His black cloak whispered around his body as he moved toward her. Hailey ignored her rapidly beating heart and strove to sound cool and confident.

"I'm sorry, I didn't know anyone was in here," she said as he drew closer. "I was so intrigued by the villa I decided to do a little exploring."

Those eyes narrowed, and Hailey realized they were not just dark brown, but also green, an odd combination that made his gaze even more haunting. His lips turned downward in something that resembled a sneer. "Forgive me for assuming we'd start by being honest. I've forgotten how easy it is for women to lie."

She flinched in both surprise and embarrassment. Hailey forced her chin upward. "I don't lie. And I resent your assumptions about my character. You don't even know who I am."

"I know you came looking for me," he said softly. "I know we're about to start the game a man and woman play when they're attracted to one another. But it's not time yet." He turned as if to dismiss her. "I'm not ready to join the others. You shouldn't have come," he repeated.

An outraged squeak escaped her lips at his raging arrogance. "You flatter yourself, Phantom. I came up here for my own reasons. Now that you've satisfied my curiosity, I can leave." Hailey spun on her heel and opened the door. The music drifted through the crack and filled the room.

"So, you did lie."

She stiffened. "I suppose I did. But you're safe from me. I'm not interested in playing games."

His voice was rough and demanding. "Then what did you want?"

Hailey refused to turn around, refused to meet those mocking eyes. "I saw a man who was lonely, separate. I came up here to find out what could cause someone to feel like that." She paused. "Now I know."

She shut the door behind her. On the stairs, the bare breasted woman thrust upward to receive the ministrations of her lover. The man flicked his fingers over one juicy red nipple, then bent his head.

Hailey rushed past them and stopped in the ballroom. Tears burned behind her eyelids but she refused to give in. She had been wrong. She'd wanted to meet Ciro Demitris, but he was way beyond her, too ensnared in these wicked sexual games that she couldn't play. Michael was right, she thought. She was way out of her league.

Hailey grabbed a glass of champagne and took a few healthy swallows. Though repulsed by his arrogant statements, the pounding heat between her thighs was still too real. He excited her, his command, his masculinity, the raw heat shimmering in those brown-green eyes.

He wouldn't frighten her off. She would stay and use the party to force away her repressions and allow her to express some freedom. She tried to fight the vivid picture swirling in her mind of what she could do with the Phantom. Tried to ignore how badly she wanted to be the bare breasted woman being pleasured.

Her heels clicked on the highly polished floors as she explored the mansion. A twelve piece orchestra took up the front part of the room, and couples danced to the music of Glen Miller and Frank Sinatra. Men in dark suits and tuxedos escorted women dressed in black velvet and red satin, hidden by a variety of masks that enticed as much as they concealed. A mingling rush of perfumes filled the air.

A crystal chandelier shimmered above marble floors and illuminated the rich tapestry and paintings that framed the walls. A circular staircase reminded her of the old Southern style in *Gone with the Wind*, when Rhett Butler first spotted the beautiful Scarlett.

The champagne helped. As the sweet fire of alcohol swept through her blood, Hailey relaxed. One man's arms led to another's as she danced with a long line of suitors, and looked into faces hidden by masks. Another stranger drew her into his arms and led her onto the dance floor. She opened her mouth to protest, but as the music swelled, she gave herself to the moment. Something inside of her loosened and broke through her normal reserve. As the hours ticked toward midnight, the music changed to a Salsa and pounded and pulsed in a more demanding rhythm. Hailey swung from partner to partner. She threw back her head and relished the freedom of the moment, and then she was pulled toward a broad chest and held in an iron grip.

His gaze burned with a masculine demand behind a gleaming white mask. Hailey stumbled, and her fingers gripped the sleek folds of his cloak as she fought for balance. He drew her closer until every carved muscle of his body pressed against hers, the thrust of his erection against the softness of her belly. Her breasts felt suddenly heavy, tender. Her nipples rose against the blue dress in a demand to be freed. Hailey shuddered.

A smile touched his lips. His jaw held rough stubble and gave him a more dangerous air. The diamond in his left ear caught the light and glimmered with icy brilliance. "Why did you come?"

"Curiosity. You haven't satisfied it yet." Fear flamed to life. Hailey wondered if he spotted the emotion in her face. "I'm not part of your fantasy, Phantom. I'll dance with you, but I won't play your games."

"Then you're lying to yourself, my dear. The moment you put on the mask and stepped through the gates you told me you wanted to play." His fingers trailed the length of her spine in a gentle caress, which contradicted the hardness in his eyes. "That's why you're here."

"And why are you here?" she asked. "You sit in judgment, hiding behind a cloak and a mask while you watch and wait. It's easy to be cynical of life when you refuse to be in it, Phantom. Perhaps that's your own secret fear."

Another man reached out to grab her. Demitris twisted her around to avoid the outstretched arms, and his black cloak swirled around their legs as she was led to the other side of the room.

"You've got a sharp tongue," he said.

"And you're arrogant."

Did his face reflect surprise or was that a trick of the light? Hailey wondered if there was anyone who surprised him. Had he lived so long in the shadows, he didn't know anything else existed?

"I don't know if I believe you," he said. "It could be clever words and a clever act. Lies mesh too easily with truth when people play games, and women know that better than anyone."

"You're also a chauvinist," she told him pleasantly.

"Maybe you decided to play with fire because you feel safe behind a mask."

Hailey nodded. "Maybe you're right."

"Who are you?" he demanded.

She stared at him, trying to see past through the carved mask. She had come tonight to learn to be a different person, but suddenly, she wanted to give him the truth of who she was. For once, safe behind her mask, she wanted to reveal herself to him in a way she never had before. The possibility of such surrender made fear curl and tighten in her stomach. Along with excitement.

"My name is Hailey."

"What do you want?"

She took a deep breath and plunged. "I want to know you. The person behind the mask, the person inside. And I want you to know me."

"People never reveal their true selves. They conceal and lie until they don't know who they are anymore." His tone held distance, pain. "They only want what they perceive, and when they find the truth, they leave."

"I want to know you," she repeated.

He gripped her arm and dragged her off the dance floor. He turned her around and pointed to a couple on the stairs who writhed in delight. The man had shoved up the woman's gown, and her legs lay open to any observer, her sex pink and wet as the man slid his finger over her. Her cries were swallowed up in the roar of the crowd.

Hailey felt the strength of his rock-hard penis strain against her buttocks. Felt his fingers clamp around her arms. She tried to mask her response; her mind fought the knowledge her body already embraced. She wanted this man, wanted to be claimed by him.

"Do you see them, Hailey?" His voice sounded like roughened gravel. He slowly pulled her back against him. Lifted her up an inch. Then rocked into her with slow, subtle motions. "That's what you came here for tonight. And I intend to give you everything you want. But first we must set up the rules of the game."

"What rules?"

"You'll tell me everything. No lies, no half truths, no denials. You must lay yourself open as that woman's legs, and let me do whatever I want to you. You'll answer every one of my questions. Obey my every command for the time you're here. And on the last night, I'll let you choose. You can walk away without ever seeing my face. Or you can unmask and I will do the same."

Her body shook. Her gaze was trained on the couple. She struggled to draw air into her lungs. "I have to give you everything?" Hailey repeated.

"Everything."

She paused. Then craned her head around to face him. "Why make a bargain with me? There are plenty of women here who'll do whatever you want without hesitation."

A half smile settled on his full lips. "Because you came looking for me. You made me want you."

She closed her eyes and tried to clear her head. Tried to think of the implications of such a bargain. "I did no such thing and you still didn't answer the question. You want more than just one night of sex. You want..."

"I want it all."

Her eyes flew open. He pulled her harder against him and forced her to feel his erection. Forced her to breathe in the masculine scents of musk and spice and soap, to cradle his iron hard thighs. Forced her to imagine his lips taking his pleasure over her body, imagine each demanding thrust of his tongue.

"Aren't you tired of hiding? When was the last time you exposed yourself to a lover—gave him a glimpse of your inner soul without the fear he'll walk away? One year ago? Five years ago? Ever?"

She tried to turn away from the raw words but he grasped her chin between his fingers. "I want to know who you are. Use your mask to hide your face and feel safe, but give me the truth. I'm tired, too." His voice grew weary, distant. "I want to see beyond the surface just this once. We have the opportunity of a lifetime right before us. We can both be ourselves and still be safe."

"And you?" Hailey met his gaze head on. "What about you, Phantom? Am I to remain vulnerable while you give nothing?"

"I will answer any question you ask. Give you every fantasy you have ever wanted. Isn't that enough?"

Still, she hesitated.

"I promise I won't hurt you. Everything we do together will be for your pleasure. But there will no halfway. All or nothing."

At that moment, everything broke free within her. Her fantasy had been granted. She could explore the hidden parts of her sexuality with a man she desired. She could open herself up to this person in all the ways she had hidden over the years. Another man would finally know who she was—her body and soul. After being locked away in emotional isolation for her whole life, Ciro Demitris had offered the key to freedom.

But, God, what a price.

An icy chill raced down her spine and threw her into a panic. The taunting voices of her parents took hold—warning her to step back before it was too late. The image of her own night of personal heartbreak passed before her eyes. She would get hurt. He could use her and laugh and she would be alone again, except this time without pride, steeped in humiliation. What if she showed him everything she was and it wasn't enough? What if he played a cruel game for his amusement? He could strip both her body and soul bare, and she'd be helpless against him.

The thoughts tangled in her mind like a whirling cyclone.

Then, Hailey realized she had nothing more to lose.

She was already alone and afraid to venture into any intimate relationships. This was her time to take a chance and believe in herself. She was so tired of being fearful of every twist and turn life tossed her way. She had done everything her parents had asked; she had been a good girl. But tonight was an opportunity to let her body fly, to selfishly take pleasure and revel in it. She could not walk away from this gift thrown at her feet.

"I need your answer. Will you give yourself to me until the masquerade is over?"

His hips continued the slow rocking, and liquid heat pulsed between her legs. She arched backward in a blatant invitation, and gave him her answer.

"Yes. I'll do what you ask."

His breath hissed behind her. Without words, he took her hand and led her up to the bedroom she had found him in. He shut the heavily carved door, shutting out the noise of the party, and in the sudden silence, stared at her.

She was stunningly beautiful, Michael thought. She stood in the center of the room, her shimmering blue dress reaching to the floor, fiery red waves of hair spilling down her back. Her long white fingers clenched and unclenched in both anticipation and fear. With her he could satisfy the burning craving in his loins, knew his desire would finally be sated. She was his for the next three nights and would obey his every command. He would not have only her body, as he dreamed of, but he had a chance to touch her inner soul.

"Do you want me to undress?"

A smile touched his lips at her faintly trembling voice. "I'd like to ask you a few questions first. When was the last time you had a man take you?"

"It's been a few years."

He lifted an eyebrow in surprise, then took a few graceful steps toward her. "Your choice?"

"Yes."

"Why?"

She hesitated, and then continued, "My parents believed sex was wrong. I grew up on the notion that the act was something behind closed doors, something to be ashamed of."

"Go on," he urged, taking the time to light a cigarette.

"I heard stories from others, stories of wild encounters that left women helpless for more. I was scared. I never wanted to lose any control over my life, afraid I'd become a man's play toy and then be left behind. I decided it would be easier to ignore sex and go after the things that were safe."

He took a deep pull on the cigarette and blew out the smoke in a lazy circle. "Do you ever pleasure yourself?"

A blush stained her cheeks. "No."

"But you'll leave these reservations behind for our bargain?"

She nodded. "If you command me to."

He smiled then, a dangerous, masculine smile that promised every temptation and satisfaction she had ever dreamed of. "Good. I admire control in a woman. The proper control can extend sexual pleasure for hours on end. Take your dress off."

Her fingers fumbled slightly on the back zipper. The tab slid down and the hiss cut through the silence. The material pooled at her feet. She wore a black garter belt and sheer black stockings with heels. A black lacy bra molded her breasts. Her breathing became heavier, but she managed to stand quietly before him. The smoke drifted through the room and mixed with the remnants of incense. "I want you to keep your gaze on me at all times. Listen to what I ask. When you hear the bell signaling the end of the night, you'll put your clothes back on and leave without another word. I'll meet you back here tomorrow night. Agreed?"

"Yes." She barely whispered the word.

"Take off your bra. I just want to look at you." She unclasped the garment and dropped it on the floor. Her white breasts were heavy and ripe, tipped with pale pink nipples. Minutes ticked by as he drank his fill. A delicate flush washed over her body, almost as if she felt his hot gaze on her like a touch. "You were made to have a man love you. Take your hands and caress yourself. That's right, feel the pointed tips of your nipples. Now imagine my own hands upon you, my tongue licking at them, biting them. I would spend a long time just working your breasts, Hailey, refusing to touch any other part of your body. Now slide your underwear down and leave your garter and stockings on."

He watched her chest rise and fall in tortured breathing. Carribbean blue eyes blazed at him, a mixture of shame, anger, and wanting, but she never took her gaze from his. The panties slid down her legs. Fiery red curls beckoned him from across the room, and his cock throbbed to thrust inside her tight, wet heat. He stroked himself lazily as he watched her, enjoying the anticipation of what was to come.

"Now slide your hand down your belly. That's right. Place your palm between your legs. Do you feel the heat?"

She hissed out a yes.

"Are you aroused?"

She shuddered. "Yes."

"Good. Let's test this will power, shall we?" He paused in front of her and studied the graceful curve of her neck, the slight color on her cheeks. Her lower lip trembled slightly, as if hating to give up her control but determined to stick to the bargain.

He softened his tone. He knew she was afraid and wanted to calm her. "You remind me of one of the paintings on the wall, with your red hair and lush body. I need to see more of you, baby. You belong to me for the next three nights, and I intend on enjoying every inch of you. Part your legs."

She paused for one moment. Then widened her stance.

Michael sucked in his breath at the sight of her delicate pink lips, slick with moisture. He ground out his cigarette and forced himself to stay where he was until he gained control. God, how he wanted to stick his tongue up her wetness and taste her. Spread her legs wider and thrust into her clingy heat until her screams echoed in his ears. He laughed low with pleasure. And he would. But not tonight. Tonight was about foreplay, and he intended to enjoy the torture. He had waited over a year for her; one more night would only heighten the climax.

Slowly, he closed the distance between them. Like a predator in flight, he circled around her and let the folds of his cape brush against her naked buttocks. He watched her shudder, watched her fight for the control she was so proud of, and knew the lesson she must learn tonight was surrender.

He stood behind her and placed both palms on her shoulders. Breathed in the scent of vanilla and sweet smelling soap, breathed in the heady scent of female arousal. He let his fingers slide through the thick strands of her hair with slow, easy motions, letting the waves brush gently against her bare back.

He did this for a long time, until he sensed her muscles begin to relax. Then he cupped a fistful of the silky fire and used the ends like a paintbrush over her body, as if preparing a canvas. With quick, teasing strokes, he touched her nipples, then moved away. Caressed the side of her breasts, then traced her cleavage. Tickled the sensitive underside of her neck. Then let her hair drop from his fingers as he placed his palms on her naked skin.

"There are times for control, and times for surrender. Your stubbornness has become your prison. Do you remember how good if feels to have a man's hands over you?"

He kept his touch light as he studiously avoided touching her nipples. Following the path he had traced before, now he used his own fingers to caress her body while he kept up a slow, circling motion that urged a moan from deep in her throat. Her head slipped back to allow him more access. "That's it, let go and let me touch you any way I want, let me show you what you've been missing..."

Hailey felt like she was slowly going out of her mind. Her nipples grew taut and swollen, aching for the touch of his fingers. Her heart thundered like a pack of thoroughbreds, and a honeyed warmth throbbed between her thighs, and made her knees grow weak. Her lids slid closed as she allowed herself to sink into the sensation. Long, tapered fingers touched her breasts, then gently plucked at her nipples, circling round and round as he urged her arousal to climb higher. She craved his tongue on the hard tips of her breasts, craved his fingers plunging inside her dampening heat. Yet, still he continued to only softly touch, lingering briefly, before moving on.

Warm hands slid down her stomach, explored her belly button, the crease of her thigh, the curve of her hips. They stroked over her buttocks as his foot urged her legs further apart for his exploration. Seething tendrils of sensation nipped at her control and left only the touch of him and the need for more. For years, she had been able to fight her desires, but tonight, as she felt his hot gaze on the private part of her, the wildness was unleashed. His fingers separated the cheeks of her buttocks and slipped between them to test her heat. A rush of wetness met him, and Hailey bit down on her lower lip to keep from crying out. Still, he didn't stop there, didn't allow her a moment of sanity, but pushed her further as he whispered in her ear the things he would do to her, with his tongue and lips and teeth and cock. The cool folds of his cloak swirled around her open legs until he stood before her, his gleaming eyes taunting the control she had built for herself. Never pulling his gaze from hers, he knelt, dragging his palms from her buttocks to the V between her legs. With gentle motions, he parted her swollen lips and exposed her completely.

"What do you want?"

She shook her head hard, as if to deny her own wanting. "Oh, please," she gasped. "I need..."

"Not yet. You're not ready enough."

A choked sob rose from her throat. Every part of her throbbed, and she let herself beg him for more as her hips rocked forward in a demanding motion. He soothed her with his voice, but his touch stoked the fire, as his index finger slid over the swollen nub just once, then stretched inside of her, the tight channel making way for him as a rush of wetness met his entry.

Hailey knew she had never wanted anyone as badly as she wanted him in that moment, and within the loss of control came surrender, an acceptance of her female sexuality she had never felt peace with.

Michael was overcome by the need to possess her completely. The fantasies he had spun over the past year faded away, replaced by the reality of her sheer beauty and honesty. He knew then it was not only Hailey being taught a lesson in control. He ached to end the masquerade right now and make love to her without his mask. Instead, he pressed his face to her stomach until the impulse passed.

He murmured against the smooth skin of her belly, breathed in the musky scent of her as he removed his finger. Her entire body pulsed like an instrument about to be played, and he felt stretched to the limits of his control. Her blue eyes were wild, drugged with passion. She gasped for breath, her nipples hard little points straining for his mouth, her clitoris so swollen just a brief touch of his tongue could make her come.

He couldn't remember another time he had wanted a woman more, couldn't remember when he'd reveled in such an abandoned response from just his touch. Halfway tempted to rip off his clothes and take her right now, he hesitated a moment.

A bell rang out.

Silence filled the room, broken only by the sounds of their breathing.

Michael struggled, wresting back his control. "You may put your clothes on." He paused. "We'll meet again tomorrow."

Hailey blinked at him in confusion. Now? He wanted her to leave now when she was consumed with passion, so close to fulfillment? Was this torment part of his game? To make her crave him more?

She pulled her clothes back on and dressed without a word. Then she walked past him and out the door.

She followed everyone through the massive archways and waited her turn to board the ferry. The damp, musky scent of her arousal rose to her nostrils. The other guests bumped against her as they obeyed the rules of the party. At dawn, every guest was escorted back to their various hotels. No one was allowed to return to the villa until the following night.

Hailey felt eyes upon her as she was about to step off the dock. As she settled down in the boat, she looked up and directed her gaze to the second floor balcony off the right corner of the villa.

A masked figure was barely visible, but she caught a glimmer of white which gleamed from the distance. The shadows closed around him and fought to reclaim their territory. When the ferry chugged through the calm waters, the figure turned and disappeared from the balcony, and Hailey wondered briefly if the whole night had only been an illusion.

But as the ferry headed towards her hotel, she realized she had been flung over the edge of her sexuality. There was no going back. The thoughts of what her Phantom was going to do to her burned through her body with shame and hard edged desire.

There would no sleep tonight.

Only anticipation for tomorrow.

Chapter Two

"Good evening."

She stepped into the room and shut the door behind her. Her palms dampened with nervous perspiration. Her stomach slid and rolled like she was on a roller-coaster, the sensations caused by excitement—not fear. She forced herself to return his greeting. "Good evening, Phantom."

He wore the black cloak. His mask tonight was smaller, still blinding white, but of a smoother material that fit snugly over his eyes and nose, and left more of his mouth free. His lips were full and perfectly sculpted, with a savage curl to the lower one that told her he could be cruel when he chose. "Did you dream about me, Hailey?"

"Yes."

He walked towards her then, with a slow, masculine grace. Moss green eyes gleamed with sexual appreciation as he took in her figure. The long tight sheath shimmered with gold sparkles, emphasizing the curve of her hips and the thrust of her breasts. "I'm glad," he said softly. "Will you walk with me?"

She drew back in surprise, then nodded. "Of course."

He led her through the party and out to the garden. The sweet scents of citrus and roses saturated the air with a potency that made her feel slightly drunk. Hailey maneuvered her way over the cobblestones and when she stumbled, he reached for her hand. His fingers interlaced with hers in a union that staked his claim. She expected a rush of intimidation. Instead, she experienced more excitement.

He allowed the silence of the night to soothe and relax her. The faint sounds of Frank Sinatra's *Summer Wind* stroked her ears as he stopped at a stone bench hidden within the lush tangle of trees and flowers. She sat beside him. He turned her hand over and his thumb began to press and massage the sensitive skin of her palm. An involuntary sigh whispered from her lips.

He smiled. "Where do you live?"

"New York, born and bred."

"And what do you love about New York?"

She gave a chuckle. "Never ask that to a native. We love a good bagel, good baseball, and a good argument."

"So, you never wanted to leave?"

A memory teased the fringes of her mind and brought a touch of sadness. Almost as if he felt the change in her, his touch moved to each of her fingers, rubbing and pressing, soothing from the base to the fingertip. She opened her mouth to make a lighthearted remark and move on, but then she remembered her promise. Hailey took a deep breath and started talking.

"I almost left once. After my parents died, I found myself wanting to experience a different life. One of my own making. I had no other relatives so I was alone. The crowds I was accustomed to made me even more lonely. I almost packed everything up and moved down South, but then I remembered an old friend of my father's who worked in Manhattan. I decided to look him up."

"You didn't want to run away. You were strong enough to try and find who you were in the same place where you lost yourself."

His statement made her head swing around to face him. The words touched something deep within her. "Yes. That's exactly what I wanted."

"Did you father's friend help you?"

She nodded. "He was kind. He worked for a small computer firm and got me a job. I took the opportunity to learn everything about the business and made my way to manager. Now I have security. Money. Safety."

"Do you have everything you were looking for?"

Hailey thought of the long nights alone, staring out at the city chaos and longing to be one of them. She thought of Michael, her best friend, whom she used to protect herself from the unknown. "No," she said softly. "But I'm still trying."

His thumb pressed into the pulse at her wrist and felt the slow steady beat of her heart. Then he trailed his fingers up and down her arm, brushing the sensitive area behind her elbow. Comfort blended with sensuality and caused an inner battle within. His voice spun an intimacy of longtime friends. His touch spun a web of raw edged desire and pure want.

"Sometimes it's easier to blame your past. Parents seem to have this control over children. And when they're gone, we realize there are no more obstacles to stop us from what we really want." He paused. "What did your parents keep you from?"

She sighed into the night and let the words spill from her lips. "Everything. Life. My mother got pregnant young and my father was forced to marry her. They never let me forget I was a mistake. Especially after they found religion." She shook her head at the memories. "My weekends were spent in church and confession. I was never able to date, or go to parties, or be a normal kid. I always dreamed of making my own choices. I wanted freedom so desperately, but when I didn't have my parents anymore, nothing made sense."

"You have to find your own sense."

Something changed in the air. She sucked in her breath as she felt the comfort twist to desire, and his fingers tightened around her arm. Their brief talk had pulled down the barriers she erected last night, and the trembling began deep in the pit of her belly as she realized tonight her Phantom would stake his claim.

"I want to ask you a question," he said softly. "Were you excited when you thought of what we had done in that room?"

He accepted her nod as an answer.

"And did you pleasure yourself in your bed last night?"

Her voice came out in a whisper. "No."

His fingers reached out to touch her face. Slowly traced around the gold mask she wore. His thumb roughly pressed over her mouth, parted her lips, and dragged his flesh across her lower teeth. She tasted his skin and wanted more. He lowered his head. His warm breath caressed her as he continued speaking. "Before I take you back upstairs, I want truth. What stops you from taking your own pleasure? I can't believe you'd turn away from your own sexuality for all these years. Your parents are gone, Hailey. What else are you afraid of?"

She didn't want to answer, but his fingers gently stroked her cheek, her hair, her jawline. She was vulnerable to him when he was kind, and the knowledge gleamed in his eyes, reminding her that at the end of the masquerade he would have more of her than any other man.

She had never spoken of that night to anyone. But now, with her face safely hidden, she decided to tell the truth. "My parents didn't allow me to go away to school, so I went to the local community college so I could live at home. I was nineteen when I met him. He was in my Biology class and I found him beautiful. Blonde hair, blue eyes, and a smile that made me melt. I had never strayed from my parent's rules, but that weekend when he asked me out, I couldn't say no."

She took a deep breath and continued. "I lied to my mother and snuck out to meet him. We went to one of those college parties I heard so much about. I remember the drinking, and the pot, and the wild sex going on in the rooms. I was overwhelmed but excited. I felt ready to take a chance and try to experience being a normal teenager.

"After a few drinks, he took me into one of the rooms. We just talked at first, then started kissing. I never felt like that before. All geared up and wanting something I was so afraid of. But then he started moving faster, and too soon his clothes were off, and I was confused. I just wanted to kiss, but he kept going and…

She trailed off. Raised her chin. Then forced the words out. "We had sex. I didn't want to, but don't really remember fighting him. Things happened so fast and it was over and I felt…used. He put on his pants and thanked me for the good time. Then left the room.

"I heard laughter from outside and knew he was telling his friends how he got lucky. I ran all the way home and never saw him again."

His hand was gentle as he stroked her hair. There was a protective gleam in his eyes she found comforting. "So your first experience confirmed what your parents had been telling you all along."

She gave a bitter laugh. "Yes. I was afraid to go back and run into him. I was afraid I would be pregnant and end up exactly like my mother. That's when I decided they were right. Sex took away control, and I promised myself I would never feel like that again."

The emotions warred inside of her, until every secret fear she battled spilled helplessly from her lips. "Don't you see?" she whispered. "I don't want any man to have that power over me. At least I'll be safe."

"You'll be alone."

"But safe," she repeated fiercely.

Warm hands cupped her cheeks. His lips stopped inches from hers. "Turning away from your womanhood is giving you a false sense of control. You let that asshole win. You've let your parents win.

"Use me and fight back, Hailey." His words dripped over her like hot molasses. His eyes dared her to meet his lips halfway. "You're a beautiful, sexual woman who had a horrible experience. I can show you how to take your pleasure from a man without feeling shame. When I'm done with you, you'll beg for more, as a woman to a man. And you'll feel empowered—not degraded. Do you want me?"

Her voice broke. "Yes."

"Come with me." He stood and put out his hand. He was cloaked in darkness; a phantom image outlined sharply in the light of a full moon, almost a mirage of the dream that had come to her night after night. But his eyes glittered hard with passion and need, the cruel curl to his lip softened as he urged her to make the choice. And she saw so much more in that moment. She saw the man who would give her everything she had looked for if only she had the courage to go with him.

She didn't hesitate as she stood and took his hand.

He led her back through the garden, up the stairs, into the room they shared the night before. Shut the door. Then faced her. "Do you want me?" he asked again.

The dam broke open. Hailey stumbled two steps and reached for him, standing on tiptoes to meet his lips. She repeated her answer with a deep sense of hunger, her rush of breath mingling with his. "Yes."

"Kiss me."

His lips took hers, his tongue slid within the damp, honeyed cave to engage in a sensual game of plunge and retreat. He tasted of smoke and fine brandy and hot male wanting. His tongue tangled around hers, his lips closing in a gentle suction as he took her fully into his mouth. They drank of each other with greed. His teeth sank into the plump lower lip and bit down carefully. A hot wave of sensation seized her between her legs. A sob caught in her throat. She wanted him to take her like an animal, wanted to open herself up to every fantasy he ever had; and as if he knew what she was thinking, he drew back slightly and lowered the zipper of the gold sheath.

The fabric pooled around her feet. She wore nothing underneath.

Hot eyes devoured every inch of her skin. Plump white breasts were swollen, tipped by tight pink nipples. The smooth skin of her belly trembled slightly, sloping into a mass of fiery red curls that hid her lips from him. Cherry red toenails curled into the burgundy carpeting in anticipation of what was to come.

Michael swore softly under his breath. All the questions had been answered. He fought the need to rip off his mask and take her in his arms to give her comfort. He fought the rage that urged him to find the man who had hurt her and make him pay. But he did none of that. He knew this was a chance to give her something back—something that had been taken from her too young. And he knew in that moment he had never loved anyone as much as he loved Hailey Ashton.

He wanted to give her an ecstasy she had never experienced before. He wanted to free her of demons and watch her smile. He wanted to possess every part of her body and soul—and still knew when she met his unmasked face she might turn away. This woman had shared painful truths about herself. He respected her strength, and her honesty, and swore by the time she walked away, she would never deny her sexuality again.

"Come with me." He led her over to the window and positioned her in front of him. The sleek folds of his cloak caressed her naked buttocks and thighs. She felt his erection press against her, and she gripped the edge of the windowsill as the waves of heat sliced through her body. Her gaze blindly sought out the lights in the distance. The balmy night air washed over her skin, and the sounds of the party rose upward in waves of music and laughter and moans of satisfaction. In other rooms tonight, other sexual games were being played out. Hailey felt the sheer excitement of being one of them, reveling in her nakedness and in the man who was about to take her.

"Close your eyes," he demanded in a low, gravelly tone. "I want you to feel everything I do to you. You're not allowed to turn around or to touch me. Do you understand?"

"Yes."

Large hands slipped around her waist and skated upward to cup her heavy breasts. His thumbs rubbed over her nipples, and the sensitive peaks tingled, pearling into hard points. One foot nudged her legs apart, widening her stance, so she was open to him. He spoke into her ear. His teeth pulled at the lobe as his tongue darted around the sensitive shell in hot, quick licks.

"I'm going to do everything to you tonight. I'm going to make you beg and plead and cry for me before I give you what you want."

Every part of her body was being touched, tasted, his tongue in her ear, his fingers on her breasts, his hard cock rubbing against her buttocks in a teasing motion that made a moan spill from her lips. His palm slid down her belly and cupped the junction of red curls. He separated her plump lips slowly, and she felt the rush of air against her hard, throbbing clitoris in a maddening caress. His thumb caressed the miniature bud with a slow, steady rhythm, then stopped when her hips bucked upward against his hand in a plea for release. His teeth bit her neck, sucked hard, and one finger entered her, his flesh soaked by her wetness. She felt the excitement within her build, and she craved an orgasm, but every time he brought her to the edge he stopped, until she begged him in broken pleas.

Pleasure. Pain. Wanting. Need.

"I won't let you come until I'm inside of you, baby. Not until you scream for me to take you."

Both of his hands slipped down her body and pried her legs further apart. While one thumb teased her pulsing bud, he used his other hand to plunge three fingers into her, moving in and out with a ferocious pace until she did as she asked, screaming wildly for him take her, and then his rock-hard penis was freed from his cloak as he bent her forward and rammed his organ into her tight, clinging heat.

She climaxed immediately. Multiple waves of ecstasy washed over her, through her. She felt her breasts sway freely in the night breeze, and her head arched upward as her hips rocked against the hard swell of flesh that invaded her body. He pumped himself in her over and over, not letting her first orgasm pass until another one took hold, and then she sobbed for the pleasure to stop, it was too much, but he kept going on and on. His member was long and iron hard, and he slid himself almost all the way out before pounding back, so deep inside she felt her G-spot tickled and teased until she came again. Then he let himself go, and he exploded deep inside of her. Hailey sobbed with pure release, and he held her and stroked her until she quieted. He closed the window and guided her over to the bed.

Like a child, he laid her upon the burgundy satin sheets, and stripped off his own cloak to rest beside her. Silence bathed the room. She listened to his deep breathing, her head on his chest, his arms pulling her tight against him.

She finally felt able to speak. "That wasn't fair."

A deep chuckle rumbled through his chest. "You had about forty eight orgasms. How wasn't that fair?"

She lifted her head to look at him. His eyes gleamed behind the white mask. "I didn't get to look at you. Touch you. Am I going to get a shot at torturing you?"

The distant air he normally exuded faded away. His hands played with her long red curls and his face softened with humor. "I don't think that was in the agreement."

"Maybe we need an amendment."

"Ah, but then you wouldn't get the final goal. I get your full cooperation. Then at the end you can make your own decision."

She felt him distancing again, and she wondered why she felt so sad. She was a grown woman and knew this game was about sex. Then why did she feel as if she wanted to know this man, not as the Phantom, but as Ciro Demitris? She dismissed the thought as foolish but still felt compelled to launch some inquiries.

"You said you believe people only show the surface. Do you know why?"

The corner of his lips twitched slightly. "Do I get a guess or do you just tell me the answer?"

"Wise ass," she muttered.

He laughed then, and pulled her back into his embrace when she would have grouchily turned away. "Tell me."

"It's so much easier to give people what they expect. Do you remember what it was like to be a child, Phantom?"

"Barely."

"I do. I remember I used to run everywhere because I was so excited to see what part of life came next. Then my mother told me it wasn't ladylike to run. People expected me to behave a certain way, and I got a reward when I was quiet and dignified. So I became what they wanted."

He stroked her hair back from her forehead. His voice was thoughtful. "Do you miss running?"

She gave a deep sigh. "I miss the other part."

"What part?"

"Wanting to see what happens next. After a while, it became so much easier to walk. There was nothing exciting to run for."

They were silent for a while, but his hands soothed and stroked. His body heat comforted and Hailey relaxed deeper into the smooth, cool sheets. "Once you stopped running, what else gave you pleasure? Do you have anything you're passionate about in life?"

The faint sounds of the orchestra drifted through the window. The flickering of the candle lent an air of intimacy as she spoke. "I enjoy many things. Reading, movies, good food and good wine. Opera."

"La Traviata."

She rolled over to face him and laughed in delight. "Yes, my favorite. A little dramatic for a man, I always thought."

"Now who's being a chauvinist?"

She placed an impulsive kiss on his lips. "You're right."

"Have you ever been married?"

"No."

"Children?"

"No." She felt a twinge of sadness.

He seemed to catch her response. "Do you want children?"

"I want a dozen. But I want the whole picture, including the husband and house and happy marriage."

He reached out to touch her cheek. "Why do women always want to settle down and men always want to run away?"

Hailey smiled. "I don't believe that. I think everyone wants to meet his or her true soul mate. Once that happens, a person makes a choice to either take a chance or stay safe. Women sometimes settle for somebody less than a true love because they're afraid no one else will come along. And men just get scared of what will happen if they do meet their true love."

"Not fear, Hailey. Maybe some men realize the real thing isn't out there."

She let his words simmer for a moment before answering. "Do you do this often, Phantom?" she asked. "Bargain with a woman for everything, then walk away?"

He stiffened beneath her. "No."

"Why did you?"

"Maybe I was tired of running myself." She opened her mouth to respond, but he continued, his words growing fierce. "You say you want a husband and children. A soul mate. You may want these things but they come at a price, Hailey. Are you willing to lose this control and take a chance? Or is it still easier to just live in the fantasy?"

She wondered at his anger, but he suddenly rolled over and pinned her beneath him. Within moments, his face cleared. The humor was back. "Why do I feel we switched roles? Are you using my temporary weakness to plunder my secrets?"

Her eyes widened. "I don't think your weakness was all that temporary." His erection demandingly pressed against her inner thigh. "I thought men needed a little bit more, er, time."

He grinned wickedly. "You were lied to. Your education about a man's true abilities has just begun. But first I want you to drink something for me."

He left the bed and brought back a glass of sparkling white liquid in a heavily cut glass. She looked at him questioningly.

"It's a slight aphrodisiac," he explained. "Quite harmless. The drink will heighten your senses and lengthen your pleasure. Here, let me," he murmured.

He filled his mouth with the liquid, leaned over, and slowly let the spiked wine trickle from his lips into her mouth. The sharp, fruity essence slid down her throat in a sensual caress, and she felt her body quicken again. He put the glass on the bedside table, then rose from the bed.

Hailey watched him with heavily lidded eyes, enjoying his nakedness. He moved with a muscled grace uncommon to men, his chest and shoulders broad, his buttocks firm, his legs long and lean. His heavy erection jutted out before him with dominant pride, and the remembrance of feeling him pulse inside her made her hot again. Whipcord strength rippled from every carved muscle as he made his way through the room. When he returned to the bed, he had a corded silk rope, and two vials of oil. Already the effect of the wine coursed through her. The cool satin sheets slid over her naked skin. She made a noise low in her throat as she stretched out on the bed.

Her sex throbbed with slow, heavy pulses and her flesh felt hot as she watched him approach.

He knelt between her thighs, his erection brushing against her tight red curls. She moaned and opened her legs, inviting him to take her again. Her lips were flushed pink and wetness gleamed in the dim glow of the light. "Phantom," she whispered urgently.

A sharp longing cut through him. Damn it, he wanted her to say *his* name, wanted her to know it was him giving her such intense pleasure. He pushed the thought away and concentrated on the moment. For now, she belonged to him, and he intended to enjoy their time together. He knew she was already feeling the effect of the wine, and anticipation shot through him at having her at his will. "What do you want, sweetheart?" he asked.

"I want you to take me again. I want you deep and hard inside me."

"I intend to. But not yet. I have some other plans." He took the rope and gently tied both of her wrists to the bedpost, so her arms were bound above her head. Her breasts arched upward in a gift he intended to enjoy slowly.

"What are you doing?"

He smiled at her sultry tone. "I want to enjoy every inch of your body, Hailey, in every way possible. I intend to taste you and play with you a little more. This will be our second episode of the evening."

She tugged at the silken ropes, and he knew her absolute helplessness only added to her desire. He reached over and uncapped a small vial of oil. The heady scents of incense and herbs rose in the air. Slowly, he poured the oil onto his fingers. Then he coated the tips of both nipples with careful precision, avoiding the heavy weight of her breasts. When each point gleamed, he placed a dab on the swell of her belly right above her pubic hair. Then his knees widened her legs further apart. He took the vial and tipped it right above her clitoris, watching the golden liquid coat the tiny throbbing member and slide over her pink lips.

She moaned and tugged at her restraints.

"The oil will make your body even more sensitive. You should get a tight, tingling feeling. The special herbs will bring a focus to certain parts."

"I'm so hot." Her head tossed back and forth against the pillow. "Everything feels so strange. I'm floating, but my body is on fire. God, what are you doing to me?"

"I'm going to pleasure you." He settled over her, intending to enjoy every inch of her body before he took her again. His mouth settled over one breast, and his tongue slowly licked at the strawberry pink tips which gleamed wetly with oil. Her breasts swelled against him, but he kept the pace slow and easy, knowing she would be wild by the time he thrust inside her. His teeth scraped against her nipple, then he took the whole tip in his mouth and sucked hard. She tugged at her restraints as he palmed her other breast, then moved his mouth to its twin to continue the torment. He licked and sucked for long, long minutes, until her engorged nipples were so sensitive, even the slight rush of his breath against her made her cry out. Still, he continued his love play, while his thumb made lazy circles around the creamy mounds of flesh, his tongue flicked at the tips with the lightest of caresses.

She became a creature of basic, primal needs. Low, animal noises rose from her throat. Every part of her flesh burned to the touch. Her cleft felt tight and tingly, and she became frantic under his hands, her only thought of him and his rock hard penis taking her, possessing her...

He feasted on every inch of her. Nipped at her belly button. Ran his tongue along the path of her pubic hair.

Hailey cried out as he pushed her knees up so she was open to his mouth. He blew gently on the red curls, parting them so her throbbing wet lips were exposed. The hot warmth of his breath against her vulva, the tingling heat of the oil, the tight constraints of the rope rubbing against her wrists, all became a whirl of exploding sensations until she felt herself pushed toward the edge. Her head tossed back and forth on the pillow. Then a sob rose to her lips as she let go.

He chuckled with satisfaction, then lowered his head once again. This time his tongue separated the fold of her sex and found the throbbing knob. He licked at it, then let his tongue slide in and out of her in tiny little motions. "You're so beautiful," he said against her. "Like a flower opening to the sun. What do you want me to do to you? Tell me."

Hailey gasped as the second orgasm threatened to explode. Every muscle clenched. He gave a low chuckle. "Perhaps this is what you want to ask me for." He wrapped his lips around her and sucked. Another cry spilled from her lips. "Or perhaps this?" His tongue plunged in and out of her channel. Hailey let out a scream and exploded around him.

He drank greedily, loving her taste. Then with one swift movement he brought himself up and over and thrust into the swollen heat of her sex.

He took her hard, driving his penis deep, until it was buried to the hilt in her wet, clinging flesh. He slid easily in and out, the stinging oil making every movement more intense, the rubbing motions of his hardness against her clitoris throwing her into another orgasm. He let himself go and they both came together.

He collapsed on top of her. She reveled in his heavy weight. Her spread legs cradled him, their juices sticky and warm over her body. He untied the ropes, and she buried her hands in the crisp ebony strands of his hair.

Something within her rose in fierce waves of protective need as she held him to her. A connection had been formed that went beyond the physical. He had reached a part of her that she had kept locked up for so many years.

Her surrender did not make her feel weak. Her Phantom made her feel the strength of her sexuality, had helped her reclaim what she had feared, and revel in her freedom. And throughout their encounter, even though she was the one who was supposed to give everything, she never felt alone. Emotions warred within her, and she started to wonder what her feelings for him were. Could they be more than just about sex?

Could her feelings have something to do with love?

The bell rang.

He lifted his head. Their gazes locked. A question burned between them, unanswered, unspoken. He rose from the bed and watched her get dressed, then slipped on his cloak. Seconds slipped by but he made no other move toward her.

Hailey turned from him and ducked her head. Her voice was husky when she finally managed to speak.

"Good night, Phantom."

"Good night."

She opened the door and left, wondering what the next night would bring.

⁂

The heavy four poster bed was quite comfortable, but her mind was focused on another bedroom, one with satin sheets and a masked Phantom.

Hailey tossed and turned, her thoughts troubled. Where had the idea of love come from anyway, she wondered. Logically, she understood her body had finally been freed from bondage, and she was a little vulnerable. She had confessed something in her past that no one had ever known, not even Michael. Perhaps, almost like a therapist, she had developed feelings for the man who helped her. She knew those years of controlling her sexuality were over. She could now be a full woman who embraced her physical desires, and not be shamed by them. Ciro Demitris had taught her that. She would always be grateful.

The phone rang.

She jumped and grabbed at the receiver. "Hello?"

"Hailey?"

She smiled when she heard Michael's voice. "I'm fine."

A sigh of relief echoed in her ear. "Good. I was a little worried. He didn't eat you for breakfast then?"

"No. It's been—wonderful. Everything I wished for."

"I take it you finally met the man."

"He's not what you think. He may have a lot of money, but he's lonely. I feel like we connected."

"Did you kiss him?"

She hesitated. Odd, she should feel almost guilty by telling her best friend. "Yes."

A pause. "Your knees buckled?"

Hailey laughed. "Yeah, they crumbled right beneath me. But I'm scared of unmasking the final night. What if he sees I'm just this ordinary woman beneath all the makeup and costume?"

"What if he does?"

She sighed. "I guess you're right. I've come too far to stop now.

How are things on the home front?"

"The Bulls lost."

"See, you should have come with me," she teased.

"And cramp your style? Nah, someone has to get their full eight hours sleep."

"Then why are you up at 6:00am on a Saturday?" she asked.

He made a gruff noise over the phone. "I wanted to make sure you were still intact."

His voice in the dark was oddly comforting, and she thought once again how lucky she was to have a friend who cared so much about her. "Thank you, Michael."

"For what?"

"For always being there. For putting up with my moods and making me laugh. For being my best friend."

"Man, are you in a mushy mood tonight," he grumbled. "I only called to say good night."

Hailey laughed. "My romantic hero. You always run away when I get emotional."

"Yeah, yeah. How are the overnight accommodations?"

"Beautiful. He blocked a whole bunch of inns on the island for his guests. I'm staying at this little bed and breakfast with a huge four poster bed. I thought I'd need a ladder to climb up."

"Just don't break a leg getting down." He paused. "Hailey, did anything else happen between you two tonight?"

An array of erotic images flashed before her. Images of the Phantom thrusting inside her, his tongue deep inside her mouth, his arms pinning her against the bed. She shuddered with the memory and opened her mouth to tell her friend everything.

Then realized she couldn't.

Michael would never understand the dark, secret part of her who longed to be a sexual being. He supported her and kept her safe. He was sweet and kind. After his heart had been broken by his ex-wife, he had closed a part off. Hailey knew they had connected so well because she had done the same thing. Now, she wanted to be free.

But he was still trapped.

No, Michael was better off not knowing the truth. Hailey took a deep breath and lied. "Nothing else happened."

Silence hummed over the line. When Michael spoke his voice was tight with emotion. "I'm sorry I couldn't make you feel like that. Good night, Hailey."

"Good night."

She gently replaced the receiver and stared out into the darkness. A strange ache lay heavily around her heart and she wasn't sure why. Something in her friend's voice made her miss him. Almost as if he was as lonely in the darkness as she, and wanted to feel a connection. His last words were so odd. How could he possibly know how she felt about Ciro Demitris?

Thoughts of Michael whirled with images of her Phantom, until she closed her eyes to avoid the tangle of feelings and fell into a deep sleep.

Michael stared at the phone and fell back on the pillows. Hands clasped behind his head, he thought of her voice and what she had shared with him tonight.

For the first time, there was no barrier between them. Clothes had fallen away; skin touched against skin, but even more powerful was her gift of self. He understood now all the moments she distanced herself from him, afraid of the past, afraid of wanting something that could fly out of control. He needed to use these last nights to burn himself into her so deeply she could never run away again.

The masquerade had been successful so far. He always stayed behind as the guests left, waiting in the same bedroom where he had first spotted her in the garden. He had paid for his own private ferry to pick him up at the mansion a half hour past dawn, so she would never suspect he wasn't Ciro Demitris. Every last detail had been arranged, yet he still feared the final unmasking. He was the one who had set her free, but was she ready to accept the terms of a real relationship, or would she be driven to experience everything she had missed out on? Would she turn away from him to embark on affairs? He had set up his plan in order to claim his lady. Yet, he now realized by setting her free, he might lose her forever.

Chapter Three

He watched her walk in the room, her step halfway hesitant as she closed the door behind her. Tonight she wore an ebony dress that tied around the neck in a halter style, then plunged low in the front and left her back bare. Her mask was held together by vibrant feathers, making her blue eyes even more mysterious.

As she stopped before him, he didn't speak. Just looked at her. The sheer beauty of her presence made his heart pound faster. He'd dreamed of her last night. Their conversation haunted him, along with his troubled thoughts, and his weakness for her suddenly made him angry.

All those evenings they spent together, talking long after the sun set about their lives. She called him his friend, but never told him about her past. She believed him to be safe, but when he made the slightest move to deepen the relationship, she backed away. Yet here she was before him, thinking he was a stranger. With Ciro Demitris she revealed everything—underneath her clothes and into her soul in a way she never let him in.

He had slipped into the role of the tycoon with an ease that surprised him. When he donned the cloak and mask, he decided to let his own secret fantasies take hold. He became dominant and demanding with his pleasure. He knew Hailey wanted intrigue and fantasy, and he intended to give it to her. What he didn't realize was the emotions he used to be the Phantom were quite real. He was lonely and isolated. He longed for sexual freedom and a woman to fly in his arms. Everything he spoke to her as Demitris was the truth.

And that scared the hell out of him.

He didn't want to play the game anymore. He wanted to tell her the truth, and watch her reaction when he revealed himself to her. He wanted to hear his own name echo through the air instead of the false Phantom.

Jealousy bit through him. His eyes narrowed with a cruelty he no longer wanted to hide. "I'm not in the mood for elaborate games tonight. You've begun to bore me. I won't be requiring your service."

She flinched at his tone, knowing something had changed. She hesitated and watched him for a sign of his feelings, but he only walked to the dresser to take a cigarette and light it.

Hailey tightened her arms around her breasts in a protective gesture and watched him from under heavy lidded eyes.

The moment she had seen him, her body quickened, but her mind was now unsure. Tonight, he wore his cruelty like his cloak, but still Hailey remembered the first minute their gazes met. Anticipation had gleamed within his mossy brown depths. Along with a tendril of fear. The emotion was easy to recognize; she felt the same mixture.

He smoked his cigarette with leisure, refusing to turn and look at her. His shoulders remained stiff and unyielding. Hailey turned to go, half relieved at her dismissal, but paused with her hand on the knob. Her Phantom was not invulnerable to the game. Somehow, feelings had begun to develop, and Hailey refused to cower before them. She had made her bargain. Truth at all costs.

She moved toward him. Reached out and laid one hand over his upper arm. The muscles jumped beneath her touch, and he spun around in a whirl of black, his mouth turned down in a sneer. "Why are you still here? I told you, I don't desire you tonight."

"Then I will wait until you do."

"What are you doing? I'm the one who makes the rules of this game. You must obey me."

Hailey lifted her chin high in the air. "I will. Because we made a bargain, Phantom. We're supposed to tell the truth to each other, but you retreat from our pact. You're acting like a coward."

He grabbed her and lifted her up hard against him. His warm breath struck her lips. "You dare to call me a coward? Perhaps, you don't want to hear your own truth. That I don't desire you any longer. That you now bore me, and I crave another woman."

Her hands clenched around the folds of his cloak as she hung on. Hailey prayed her bluff would work. "Then I call you a liar. And if you must prove something to yourself, I will wait while you take another woman, and join you after. Because I made a promise. I want to be with you tonight, no matter what the cost."

He cursed under his breath. "Damn you!"

His mouth stamped over hers. With one quick thrust, his tongue parted her lips and conquered her with dominant, hard strokes, exploring every damp, hidden crevice, claiming her for his own.

She gave it all back to him. Her fingernails dug into his shoulders as she wrapped her legs around his waist and hung on. He thrust his fingers into the heavy weight of her hair to hold her head still, as he took more of her, his tongue battling with hers. His taste and the male scent of him swamped her senses. He nipped at her lower lip, then drew it deep into his mouth to suck her hard. When he finally pulled away, she struggled for breath.

Slowly, he allowed her to slide back down his body until her feet once again touched the floor.

"Phantom?"

He closed his eyes in defeat. Then took her gently in his arms. "I'm sorry, Hailey." She glanced up at him. Disgust carved out his features. "I wanted to hurt you."

"Why?" He remained silent. She pulled away and looked into his face. Then ran her fingers over the sculpted curve of his lower lip, his chiseled jawline, his cheekbone. "You didn't hurt me. I hear your voice and I become aroused. I close my eyes and all I can imagine are your hands on me. I want you all the time. But tonight you seem so angry at me."

"I was angry at myself."

"But you're not going to tell me why."

"I've never wanted a woman as much as I want you. I've never enjoyed a woman's company as I do yours. I hate when you leave at the night's end, and I wish I could sleep with you and awake to your smile. That's why I'm angry."

Hailey felt her heart lighten. A husky laugh escaped her lips, and she reached up to kiss him. Her lips moved over his and savored the taste of smoke, the sting of cognac, and the arousal of male hunger. Her tongue slipped inward, touching the tip of his tongue in a teasing caress, then drank deeply of him. When she finally raised her head, she couldn't hide her delight.

"Let me give you some advice. When a woman hears words like that from her lover, she becomes overjoyed. To know I've made an impression on you, especially after such a long line of women, gives me great pleasure." She paused. "I feel the same way about you."

"We shouldn't complicate matters." His hand cupped her jaw. "We've made a bargain. But there are no guarantees for a future unless we decide to unmask. Are you ready for the fantasy to end?"

The light died within her eyes, but she forced a smile. "I intend to enjoy these last nights with you. You make me happy."

Her simple words made him stare at her in astonishment. Her honesty humbled him. She constantly challenged him. And tomorrow night, she would know the truth, and reject him. He may never see her again after the fantasy ended.

He pushed the disturbing thought aside and cradled her in his arms. "How does one argue with a woman? Especially when she's so direct?"

"Why, have you met many who aren't?"

"Yes. I've met women who lied and betrayed me. Women who see what they want to see."

She heard his slightly bitter tone and tried to ease him out of his mood. Her hand traveled down his chest, over his muscled abdomen, and stroked the hard ridge between his legs. With one quick movement, her fingers grasped his jutted member. She squeezed carefully, felt the pulsing strength, and heard his quick indrawn breath. "Darling, I'm not lying to you. What I see before me is exactly what I want."

He laughed. "And I want to give it to you. Over and over in as many different ways as I can. But I'm confessing more of my secrets. It's time to get back to our bargain."

Within moments, he had undressed them both and laid her on the bed. She climbed on top of him, her fingers exploring his penis with gentle, curious strokes. He lay back and enjoyed her ministrations.

She smiled as she worked her palms up and down his ridged length and watched him grow longer. "A few more minutes and I'll be able to make any bargain I want."

"You're probably right. I better get my information fast."

"What do you want to know?"

"Name one guilty pleasure you never told anyone about."

She groaned and covered her face with her hands. Then peeked through her fingers. "I love art. I suck at painting and I can't draw a thing. I even tried to become an art investor but even my taste seemed awful. So I bought a coloring book and a huge box of Crayola crayons. When I'm stressed I color."

He drew back in surprise. "I never knew you did that."

She laughed. "Of course not, you don't know me."

Her remark seemed to throw him off guard and she caught an almost guilty expression. Then he seemed to recover and forged on. "One thing you hate."

"The New York Yankees."

His lip twitched in the need to smile. "Isn't that the team that wins the most World Series in baseball?"

She made a face. "I like the Mets. The Yankees are too perfect and I'd rather root for the underdog."

"You admit this to people?"

"Not really. I wore my Mets t-shirt once and got heckled. Almost got in a fight so now I just keep it safely in my closet."

"Sexual fantasy?"

In one swift motion she straddled him. She arched her back, her breasts thrust forward, crowned by rosy nipples. She still held him within her hand, her fingers teasing the tip of his rock-hard sex, eliciting drops of moisture. Red fiery waves fell down around her shoulders, and she gave a low laugh, her eyes full of secrets and passion and mystery.

"My sexual fantasy, Phantom?" She smiled slowly. Her tongue slid over her ripe bottom lip as if she imagined how he would taste. His breath hissed through his teeth as desire ripped through him. "This is my fantasy. What I'm about to do right now. I want to take you in my mouth and make you scream my name. I want you inside me, so hard and fast that you forget every other woman you've been with. Since I promised I'd do anything you want, I'm begging for permission." Her voice dropped to a husky purr. "Will you let me pleasure you?"

He swore and clawed for control. His member throbbed against the soft skin of her fingers as she continued teasing him, running her thumb over the turgid flesh. She had become his own personal sex slave, and now he was at her mercy. The excitement built as he gave her his answer. "I think I can allow it."

"Good. Now shut up."

Her breasts pressed against his chest as she lowered her head, and her tongue delicately licked at his flat male nipples. They hardened into little points, and then she used her teeth to gently pull. His low moan urged her on as she moved downward.

Michael groaned as her taut-tipped nipples caused a delicious friction against his skin, and he suddenly knew what it was like to be helpless under a woman's power. This was no longer his innocent, guarded Hailey. This was a sexual witch who used her nails and teeth and tongue to explore every inch of his body, as if crazy for the scent and taste of him. Her hands cupped his hips as she settled over his hard length, and then knelt between his legs.

She looked up once from her position. Gave a smug, half smile. Then lowered her head.

Her warm breath struck him first, and she opened her lips to take him in the slick, satin depths of her mouth. She teased him mercilessly, never taking in his fullness. Her tongue swirled around the tip, gathering the drops of moisture that spilled, then moved up and down the ridged underside as if he was a sweet lollipop she had discovered and decided to suck slowly.

Just as if he was about to go mad and force her to take him completely, her hands cupped his balls and her lips opened wide to plunge him to the back of her throat.

He cursed.

The pleasure was too intense. Her tongue swirled around him as her mouth held him tightly, moving in and out with a steady pace that tested his control. Her name spilled from his lips in a chant, and her suction grew even harder, luring him over the edge. She made hungry sounds in the back of her throat, as if she couldn't get enough of him, and his pulsing, pounding member throbbed within her wet mouth, the pressure building to a screaming point until he exploded in a sharp burst. She took it all. Her hair formed a silken curtain that swung back and forth over his thighs. Her tongue licked every last drop, until he swelled again and damned her to eternity.

He reached for her, but she avoided his movement. His head pounded with desperation and want.

"Tell me what you want."

He cursed, recognizing his own little game had been switched on him. His voice came out in a raspy groan. "Take me now."

She laughed low and a mischievous gleam lit her eyes. "Beg me."

With one swift movement, he lifted her up and plunged into her hot, slippery wetness. She gasped.

"I'm begging you," he said.

Then he began to move.

She took him to the hilt, her legs wide to accommodate every throbbing inch of him. She cried out and arched upward.

She rode him in a wild frenzy. Her hair streamed down her back, her heavy breasts lifted up and down as she took everything he could give her. Her body clenched around him each time he drove inward, then clung madly in a rush of dampness as he withdrew.

He felt her climb towards the ultimate release and decided to tease. As he thrust into her, he kept his sex away from the throbbing nubbin that would give her what she needed. His hands pulled and rubbed at her nipples, rolling the tips in his fingers until she begged him in low, frantic tones of arousal.

"Please, help me."

"How bad do you want it?" Again he plunged deep, keeping her inches away from the edge. He loved the way she looked as she took him in her body, loved the way she gave him everything she had and demanded he keep up with her.

She rode him faster and her hips shimmied against his engorged member. "I need you." She panted, her blue eyes dazed with passion. "I need you."

The words reached out like a fist and tore into his gut. He knew this woman had changed him in some way, had opened him up, and he wondered if he'd ever be the same. With that last thought, he reached up and slipped his thumb over the hard nubbin covered by her fiery curls, then rubbed.

He drove inside of her. Again. And again.

Hailey screamed. He felt her drench him, and he came again with her, emptying himself with a shout. She collapsed over his body like a rag doll, her hair spilling over his chest, her breathing rough and uneven.

"Damn, woman," he finally managed. "Any time you have another sexual fantasy, I'll be glad to help you out."

She laughed. "Donating your body to charity, huh?"

"It's a tough job but someone has to do it."

"I don't think I'll be able to walk tomorrow," she said.

He frowned. "Are you sore?"

"My thighs are still trembling."

He caressed her with soothing strokes. "As soon as I can get up, I'll run us a bath. That will take the aches away."

"I'm not complaining."

"It's for my own selfish pleasure. I want to show you the amazing things you can do underwater."

"I'll need a cane tomorrow."

He didn't answer. The realization of the end of their affair dangled before him with haunting urgency. Almost as if she knew his thoughts, she interlaced his fingers with her own and studied their hands. Fingers touching, pale skin against ivory. A man and a woman. Entwined.

"I don't want this to be over," she whispered.

Hope bloomed within, but he fought the emotion back. He refused to wonder what the last night would bring. The only thing in his power was to give her as much of himself as possible, and hope it was enough.

"I'll run the bath." He got up from the bed and disappeared into the bathroom. Hailey lay back on the pillows. His departure after her confession reminded her this was a game. A game for sex, a game for freedom. But to bring this masquerade into the real world may never work. She needed to face that fact. She was falling in love with him, but he could view her as a novelty which could pass. How could she be sure of his true feelings? At least, if she chose to walk away, she would have the memories to take with her instead of heartache.

She got up from the bed and followed him into the bathroom. The scents of jasmine and lavender rose to her nostrils. The mirrors steamed deliciously and wrapped them both in a world unto their own making. She quietly shut the door behind her and stood before him, naked.

He looked up. Caught his breath. She was beautiful. Her body peaked to attention just from his look, and he knew she was already aroused.

He reached his hand out. With a smile, she took it, and they stepped into the tub. The sharp sting of the hot water made her gasp. He positioned her so she lay over him, her buttocks pressed between his spread legs, her back against his chest. She sighed in deep contentment as he took the soap and rubbed it between his hands.

Slowly, he began soaping her shoulders, digging his thumbs into the sore muscles. A moan rose from her lips. His hands were slippery with bubbles as he worked on the tendons in her neck and moved downward—the line of her spine, her upper arms, and slid around to cup her breasts. He played with the soft mounds, cupping bubbles and allowing them to float through the air, grazing the tips of her breasts like a wet, dainty kiss. He washed every part of her, lingered on every curve with a tenderness that made tears sting against her lids. Her eyes closed with dreamy pleasure as she gave him her body, the gift he had asked for.

And he knew her body hadn't been the only gift. She had given her heart. To Ciro Demitris.

Long, supple fingers slid around her hips and lingered over the full curve of her buttocks. Her cheeks tightened in anticipation as she felt him gently explore the cleft, parting her pubic hair and softly touch her. Hailey floated in the water. Her muscles melted like warm, sticky honey, helpless under his spell.

"Phantom, what are you doing to me?" she asked in wonder, her eyes still shut as she drank in every sensation. The bubbles teased her taut-tipped breasts and sloshed over her quickening muscles. Her cleft felt swollen, and the warm water mixed with her own juices until her thighs floated open and her sex was exposed to his gaze.

"God, you're stunning," he muttered. His fingers clenched into the full cheeks. "I just want to look at you." He drew her knees up so she lay open to him. "I want to take you again. I can't get enough of you, Hailey."

"And I want you again and again," she whispered. "I want you to take me every way possible. I want to belong to you completely."

"You already do." The words slipped out before he could stop them, but he knew they were true. "Don't you?"

"Yes."

She arched her back. Her pubic hair was wet and allowed her pulsing inner lips and vulva to be exposed to his hot gaze.

"I have to taste you. Get on your knees and hold on to the edge of the tub."

She moved. Her fingers gripped the cold, white marble as she knelt. Her flesh quivered as the cool air rushed over her. She felt his hard hands part her legs and urge her forward so her buttocks rose in the air, awaiting his next move.

Her skin was rosy and dripping. She felt his gaze on the curve of her buttocks, the hot pink of her cleft. He leaned over her and blew gently, and she jerked back in response, a half moan caught on her lips.

He lowered his head, and his teeth bit into her firm cheeks, testing her. He moved inward, squeezing, cupping, while his tongue snaked out to take quick, sharp licks. She wiggled helplessly against him but he only laughed and drew out the anticipation. The tip of his tongue slid into her cleft and licked with slow strokes. Her swollen flesh became sensitive to every stroke, and then he flicked his tongue against her over and over with hard, quick motions. Hailey cried out, but he still held back. His fingers pushed the firm globes of her flesh apart so he tasted all of her. His hot tongue teased her clitoris again, and again, until…

She exploded against his lips, and then he pushed himself up and plunged into her.

Heat.

Fullness.

Possession.

The convulsions seized her body and ripped through her. She felt caught in the wind of a cyclone, helpless to do anything but ride out the wild wave of pleasure until she calmed.

Then he started to move.

She took every inch of him up her warm channel of flesh. She felt tight and hot as he pushed even deeper, and she met him all the way, her body arched like a bow, quickening in response to his fierce thrusts. Water slapped over the tub in gentle waves. Bubbles floated through the air. And then her last orgasm took hold like a savage fist that scooped her up and hurtled her toward the stars.

This time when he held her, she didn't allow herself to think of tomorrow. She laid her head on his damp, muscled chest, spent for now, and wrapped her arms around him. His heart pounded in a steady rhythm against her ear.

The clock ticked. She roused herself enough to speak, still greedy to learn everything she could about the man in her arms. "What were you like as a boy, Phantom?"

"More secrets?"

Hailey smiled against him as she heard the teasing note in his voice. "I want to know a little bit about you. As a man, you certainly know how to give a woman pleasure. Tell me about the boy."

The memories flickered past his vision in a series of taunting images. He waited for the usual wall to keep the emotions separate. Instead, he felt the dull ache of pain, and realized he wanted to share with her. Hailey already knew about his failed marriage. What he never shared was his upbringing, and what made him who he was today. He was so like her. He kept that part of his past buried deep where no light could ever stream in. She waited patiently, secure in his arms. And for the first time, Michael decided to tell her everything.

"I grew up very poor," he said. "My father ran out on my mother when I was seven. He found a local girl with no baggage, and they took off. That was the last time I heard from him. I was almost glad to see him go. Even at seven, I remember him yelling at my mother, hitting me occasionally. Telling me I was useless."

She kept her voice low and soothing, even though her heart squeezed in pain. "What did your mother do to support you?"

"Waitressed. Cleaned up after people in hotels. Anything to keep food on the table. I helped as much as I could, but it was years before I could earn any decent money."

She felt the coldness within him envelop the man who had shared the last three nights with her, the man who had laughed and teased and held her close. She held him tighter as if her body warmth could ward off the chill. "What did you like as a boy?"

"Things I could fix. Things I could control. Math, science, cars, computers."

"What business did you decide to embark on?

"Computers. One of my mother's boyfriends was decent to her, and loved to fool around on a laptop. He taught me a few things and something clicked."

"What?"

"I could finally control something. A computer has no emotions, and does what it's told. I decided I would learn everything." He shifted in the water and his hand played with the wet strands of her hair. "Eventually, I found a job at a computer firm and worked my way up. Just like you, I took my opportunity and made the most of it."

"Do you ever think about your father?"

"No."

She picked up her head and gazed into his eyes. The gleaming white mask covered half of his face, but the burning light in his eyes confirmed he was a liar. Hailey stroked his hard cheek, traced the full line of his lower lip, then cradled his jaw. Tenderness bloomed within her.

"I was invited to the senior prom when I was eighteen," she said. "I had never been asked to a dance before, so I was beyond excitement. I spent hours looking through magazines for a dress, talking to my friends about which party we'd attend. When I told my parents I was invited, they refused to let me go." She paused, wrestling with the memories. "They informed me most teenagers lose their virginity during prom. I was better than that. I would not barter my body for a chance at a solid, successful future. So, I called my date and told him I got sick. I watched out my window as the limos pulled out of the driveways with kids dressed in gowns and tuxedos. And I hated them. I wished I could just be a normal teenager and kiss a boy for the first time on the night of prom. I was so tired of trying to be good, of trying to follow my parents' rules. I actually had a rebellion that night and screamed. Told them how much I hated them and their stupid restrictions. I went to sleep that night and wished they were dead." She took a deep breath and angled her head so he could see her face. "Years later they died. I was finally free. So I turned my back on the past and vowed to never think about them again. I wanted to build a new life for myself."

"So, you won."

"Ask me, Phantom. Ask me if I think about them anymore."

"Do you?"

"Every day."

Understanding took hold and blossomed. The chill eased, and Hailey lowered her mouth to his and kissed him. Her lips eased over his as gently as the first hint of a spring breeze strokes a flower petal. Her tongue slipped inside to give and share and receive. He tasted of male hunger. He tasted of her essence. And she knew in that moment she loved him.

Hailey broke off the kiss as the realization shook her. Their gazes locked, and then the ringing of the bell in the distance cut through the air, and the moment was gone.

She eased away from him. God, she didn't want to leave.

He allowed her to slip out of his arms. God, he didn't want her to leave.

"Phantom?"

"Yes?"

"Besides computers, what did you really love when you were little? What made you happy?"

He studied her face. Damned if she didn't know how to reach into a man's chest and rip his heart out. With that simple question, instead of focusing on the rage and pain of his childhood, he remembered something he thought he'd forgotten. A smile played about his lips as the memory took hold. "Roses." He shook his head, almost embarrassed. "We had this neighbor who used to garden. She had fruits, vegetables, herbs. And flowers, incredible rose bushes in red and pink and yellow. She was nice to me. When my mother was entertaining her boyfriends, she would invite me to her house and fix me peanut butter and banana sandwiches, and I would stare out at the roses."

His vision blurred as vivid colors and fragrances danced before him. When his gaze re-focused, he realized she had given him a precious gift.

His one good memory.

She smiled, then leaned over to kiss him good-bye.

"Until tomorrow," she whispered.

Then she rose from the tub and shut the door behind her.

Michael sat in the cooled water for a long time after she had gone and thought about her smile.

Thought about tomorrow, when he unmasked.

Jennifer Probst

Chapter Four

He watched her walk up the twisting pathway. Her dark cloak welcomed her into the shadows, and hid her fiery red hair as she made her way into the house. The music and laughter were deafening; the sexual orgies and encounters flooded through the rooms as they approached their final encounter.

He paced the room with long, graceful strides. His black robe flowed behind him. He still wore the mask, would wear it until the final hour of the clock, and then she would know his identity. Would she draw back with shock and disgust? Would she throw away the moments they experienced these past nights because he was flesh and blood, and not her millionaire fantasy? Did she want to continue this relationship? Did she have feelings for him—the real him—her best friend Michael?

He cursed violently. One last night to touch and taste her sweet body. To kiss her lips and claim her for his own. One last time until the truth was revealed and she made her decision.

The door opened. Her scent beckoned him, a musky, vanilla fragrance that swirled around his senses and got him hard immediately. She stepped in and closed the door behind her.

Then loosened her cloak and let it fall to the floor in soft, velvet folds.

He sucked in his breath.

She was naked. Her glorious red hair tumbled down her back and shoulders, playing peek-a-boo with rosy pink nipples. Her breasts were full and creamy white. Her long legs framed an inviting center of curls that hid her sex. Beneath the musky scent of her cologne he caught the undertones of female arousal.

She wore no mask.

His gaze greedily took in every familiar feature. The graceful curve of her jaw and cheek, the arching red brows, the red lips. Her Carribbean blue eyes flickered warily but she stood before him in all her glory, daring him to turn away.

He closed the distance between them. Thrusting his fingers within the fire of her hair, he lifted her face up and gazed deeply into her eyes.

"You're beautiful."

Then his mouth took hers.

It was a kiss of raw hunger and demand, a need to possess and be possessed, a vow to give pleasure and to take. Her lips opened under his, her tongue tangling, thrusting as they drank from one another as if they had discovered a cool drink of water in the hot desert sun.

Her hands slipped around her shoulders as his lips closed around her tongue and sucked, drawing her very essence into him. His teeth sunk into her ripe lower lip, taking love bites, and he trailed kisses across her cheek, exploring every feature that had been hidden by the mask.

When he lifted his head, her eyes burned as if with fever. Her nails dug fiercely into his shoulders.

"Take me, Phantom. Take me now. I belong to you."

He lifted her up and they tumbled to the bed. There was no teasing, no love play as she ripped off his robe and ran her hands over his long, lean body, loving the feel of his hair-roughened skin contrasting deliciously with her silken limbs.

They were ravenous for each other, hands and tongues and lips tangled together. He cupped her buttocks and sucked on her nipples as she reached down and took his throbbing erection between her fingers and squeezed, reveling in his masculine power, desperate to have him inside of her. She wrapped her legs around his hips and they rolled over in the cool, satin sheets. She climbed on top of him and impaled herself on his rock-hard flesh with one smooth thrust.

He groaned.

She gasped.

She arched back so he buried himself to the hilt in her tight, clingy heat. He sat up on the bed and wrapped his arms around her so they were face to face, flesh buried within flesh, gazes locked. Her nipples pressed into his chest. His lips hungrily took hers and plunged into the honeyed cave of her mouth as deeply as his penis was inside of her. He rocked his hips. Once. Again.

She cried out as convulsions shook her body. He lifted her up and over him and guided her hips up and down, pumping furiously inside of her as he rode the wild wave of hot pleasure to the edge. The orgasms overtook her, and still he pounded his penis into her body while her inner muscles clenched around him in a silken, wet fist.

He shouted her name as he exploded in a hot rush, and she fell over him. Her teeth savagely sunk into his shoulder as she held him to her.

Hailey slid down from the pinnacle with his member still buried inside of her. Her flesh pulsed and quivered in tiny vibrations and she turned her head to press kisses over his mouth, enjoying his ragged warm breaths against her mouth. Her fingers gentled and stroked back his silky, black hair, then lingered over the gleaming smoothness of his mask which still hid him from her full view.

"I can't get enough of you," she whispered, then nipped at his bottom lip. "Would you like to know another one of my fantasies?"

His mouth curved upward in a smile, a deep chuckle rumbled in his chest. "If it's anything like the last one, they'll be carrying me out on a stretcher."

She licked at his jaw and tasted clean soap and the salty tang of male sweat. His rough stubble prickled against her tongue.

"Never. You're my new superhero. No Viagra ever needed. Hours of pleasure guaranteed, until the woman begs for mercy."

"What is this superhero called?"

"Studman."

He laughed. "Batman. Superman. Spiderman. Now Studman."

"Exactly. Still want to hear my fantasy?"

"Go ahead."

"I lock you in a room and take away your clothes. You're at my command every hour of the day, completely at my mercy, and you'll do anything I ask. The only way to escape is to please me, so you work very hard at it."

"Hmmm. Sounds like what we're doing now except I'm the one who has to obey."

"Exactly."

"Hailey?"

"Yes?"

"That's my sexual fantasy, too."

She laughed with him, snuggling into his arms, her fingers playing with the swirling dark hairs on his chest. "There's one other part in my fantasy I forgot to mention."

"You have whips and chains."

"No, but I may have to add that one in later."

"What is it?"

"You have no mask."

He grew silent. The sounds of the party drifted up the stairwell and reminded them of the short hours left. "Once I remove my mask, the game is over. I want a little more time with you."

She blinked back sudden tears, and concentrated on the moment, wanting to pull every second of pleasure from the man beneath her.

"Then take it, Phantom. Take me over and over until the bell rings."

His eyes blazed with promise. "I intend to."

He rained kisses over her face, naked from the removal of her mask. She shook slightly and knew no other man had ever taken her body and soul like her Phantom.

"Give me a little more on our last night together, Hailey," he said.

She tossed him a wicked smile. "I thought I already did."

He chuckled. "I mean truth. Tell me what you want from your life. Tell me what you still fear."

This time, when she spoke she had no mask to hide herself. This time, she didn't need one. She spoke to the man she loved, and refused to hide anything. Hailey wanted to tell him the only thing she wanted was him, but he seemed to ask the question with the assumption this was their final meeting.

"I want to build something that lasts," she said softly. "Don't all people want the same thing? Someone to remember them. If I can't do it with children or the love of my life, I'll pick friendship. I'll pick rewarding work that makes a difference."

He waited a while before answering. "If you had a chance to have this love of your life, would you be strong enough to reach out for him?

"Yes." She spoke the truth. Ciro Demitris had given her that gift.

"And your fear?"

"You already erased my fears, Phantom. The only thing left to be afraid of is being without you."

He turned from her then, as if he couldn't bear the emotion of looking into her face. Hailey took the time to ask her own questions. "And you? What do you fear?"

His voice came from a distant place. "I fear the truth," he said. With one quick movement, he rolled over and pinned her to the mattress. "But you're here now. Mine for the next few hours. That's all I need."

Then his mouth took hers.

The evening slid by with slow strokes of the clock, as they roused one another to make love through the night. He took her places she had never been before. She showed him a tenderness and emotions he had never felt before. The bed became their escape from the world beyond, as the full moon shimmered in the sky and the sounds of the party rose and fell through the rooms. And when the bell finally chimed at dawn, when the music and laughter and screams grew to a crescendo, he sat up in bed and looked at her naked body.

"It's time, Hailey."

His eyes were filled with resolve, and another emotion she couldn't put a name to. A glint, a glimmer, something she needed to hold onto but was too afraid to demand from him. Did he love her? Would he walk away without a second thought? Was she just another woman involved in his masquerade, a rousing distraction to never be thought of again?

He watched her as she sat up. The sheet fell to reveal her creamy breasts. Emotions shuddered through him. He knew he loved her, knew they had formed a connection over these past nights, but did she love him in the same way? Had this been a pleasant distraction and a way to get what she wanted? Would she walk away without a second thought?

The questions whirled through his mind in a dizzying rush.

He reached up and with one savage motion, ripped his mask off.

Hailey sucked in her breath as she stared at the man before her. The man she knew. The man who had played a game and betrayed her trust.

Michael Rivers.

She watched in shocked silence as he dipped his head and popped out the contact lenses. Then he reached up and rubbed his fingers through his hair. The strands fell over his face as they had so many times in the past. The diamond in his left ear winked like a beacon signaling his deceit. His brown eyes gazed into hers with a steadiness that prevented her from turning away. And suddenly, his voice and scent and touch made sense, and she gasped as the pain shook through her body.

"Why?" she moaned. "Michael, why would you do this to me?"

He flinched at the accusation. His voice was low and urgent. "Hailey, listen to me. If you decide you never want to see me again, I can accept the consequences. But this was my only chance, a chance of a lifetime, and I'll never regret taking it."

Her eyes widened at his words, and she bit down on her lower lip to stop from crying out. She forced herself to remain on the bed and listen. Even if it was for the last time.

"When we first met, I only wanted your friendship. I was still recovering from my wife, from the breakup of my marriage, but you filled a part of me I've never really known before. I felt comfortable and accepted with another woman for the first time. But as our friendship developed, I fell in love with you. Every part. I loved seeing you in baggy sweat pants and no make-up. I loved watching the ballgames and taking you out to dinner. I even love all those habits of yours no one is supposed to know about. You sing opera when you clean, and panic if you don't brush your teeth four times a day, and insist on walking in the back door instead of the front because you're superstitious."

"Michael—"

He put up a hand and forged on. "I watched you every day with an ache in my gut because I knew you wouldn't give me a chance. I listened to you complain about your looks when all I wanted to do was yank you in my arms and prove how beautiful I thought you were. And I wanted more, Hailey, so much more. I wanted to give you pleasure until you screamed my name. I wanted to explore every deep fantasy you ever had and some of my own. But whenever I made a move, you backed away."

He took a deep breath and continued. "When you told me about the masquerade party and Demitris, I knew I could lose you. So I took advantage of the opportunity of a lifetime. Finally, you would see me as a man, not your best friend. I wanted to be both. I needed you to see all of me, because I already loved all of you."

"Michael—" she tried to say more but he was at the edge of desperation, knowing everything was over with the next tick of the clock.

"I want to marry you. Have babies. Work together, play together, I want it all. I want to take you to bed every night and make sure your knees buckle every time I kiss you. Everything I said this weekend was the truth. I only hid my face. My heart's been open to you."

Her body trembled helplessly from the onslaught of words and emotions. She drew in a ragged breath, trying to make sense of what he had told her. This was Michael, her best friend and confidante. But he was also Ciro Demitris, a phantom figure who kissed her breathlessly and set her body on fire.

Hailey closed her eyes. A rush of images whizzed before her. The comfort in his presence. The way he made her laugh. The burning edge in his eyes when he looked at her. The facts were all there, had always been there, but she had refused to face them.

A blinding flash of realization shook her to the core. This was what she had been afraid of. She had chased after a strange man this weekend and convinced herself she had been lacking excitement and adventure. In reality, Michael had always been the one she ran from. The man she could share her life with. She stubbornly built a wall around the possibility there could be more between them, afraid of the truth.

This was the man she loved.

Hailey opened her eyes. Her best friend stood a few inches away, his familiar features twisted with an agony that tore at her heart. Tears spilled over her lids as the knowledge sunk in. He had always loved her. Loved her enough to take the risk of losing her completely by setting up the entire charade. Loved her enough to wait until he thought she was ready.

With a low mutter, he closed the distance between them and took her into his arms.

His mouth took hers and claimed her for his own. Her arms came up to receive as she gave it all back. When he finally lifted his head, he smiled.

"You forgive me for not allowing you to meet your rich tycoon?"

She laughed in delight and threw her arms around him. "Who needs a tycoon? He probably has no idea how to do his own laundry."

Dark brown eyes gleamed with intensity. "This wasn't just a weekend fling, Hailey. All the things I did to you, with you, I intend to continue. And I have a long list of fantasies."

She laid back on the bed, naked, and slowly parted her legs, then smiled. "How long?"

"Oh, enough to last the next twenty years."

"Maybe we should get started."

"Maybe we should."

He leaned over her and pressed his body to hers. Put both hands on the inside of her thighs to open her wide to his gaze. Then deliberately thrust into her wet heat, while he watched her face gain the dreamy expression he had enjoyed the last few nights.

"Michael."

She watched his eyes darken with pleasure as his name echoed through the air. And Hailey gave herself completely over to the man she loved.

About the Author:

I've always wanted to be a writer, and I knew my calling was romance from the time I was thirteen years old. My life took on an edge of excitement I never experienced before, and as I grew older, I learned valuable lessons from those feisty heroines and alpha male heroes.

I live in upstate New York, in the beautiful Hudson Valley. I have a deep love for the mountains, chocolate, Frank Sinatra, and a good book. My first novel, Heart of Steel, was the beginning of a long and satisfying journey through the world of romance. I loved writing Masquerade, and look forward to many more stories with Red Sage Publishing.

I share my life with my wonderful husband and our two canine children, Bella and Lester. They've all suffered through late nights with me as I work. I look forward to hearing from all of my readers, so please check out my website: www.jenniferprobst.com.

Ancient Pleasures

by Jess Michaels

To My Reader:

A Victorian woman searching for the truth, an American tomb raider looking for treasure, and a tomb with a sensual curse. The Egyptians never had pleasure this potent...

Chapter One

Egypt, 1897

Isabella Winslow fingered the artifact in her bag and smiled at her Egyptian maid. "This is it, Anya. This is the place."

Anya shoved a lock of coal black hair from her shoulder and looked nervously around the barren desert. She'd made it no secret that she didn't want to leave the safety of Cairo for the wilds of the sand dunes and the unknown adventures of tomb raiding. Or that it was inappropriate for two unmarried ladies to be in the unescorted company of their handsome Egyptian guide.

"Yes, ma'am. This does seem to be the place described on your late husband's map, but are you sure we have to go inside Merytsat's tomb?"

Anya glanced at their guide out of the corner of her narrowed eyes. He was standing a few feet away from them at the top of the stone steps that lead to the round tomb door. His arms were folded in waiting, his long silky hair tied back from his face to reveal a black tribal tattoo that curled around the back of his neck. His brown eyes were always focused, though. Mostly on Isabella's maid.

Anya wrung her hands as her eyes darted away from his pointed stare. "Surai has told me stories about the curses placed on these ancient burial grounds. And I've heard the tales about English archeologists who haven't made it home after their adventures in dark places."

Isabella laughed at the superstitious drivel. "Surai only tells those stories to make you sit closer to him by the fire." Though the maid tried to deny it, Isabella had seen the spark between her two servants. It was one she chose not to discourage. She had too many other things on her mind. "If we don't go inside, we'll never finish Hiram's work.

Or find out exactly what drove him to the way he behaved after he returned from the dig in this…" She looked around at the two worn, rock statues that guarded the tomb entrance, two half naked women who brandished sharpened spears and wore fox headpieces. "This strange place."

Anya's eyes narrowed. "I don't think you need to sneak away from polite society and come searching tombs to find out why a man would stray from his wife. Or die in bed with two Egyptian whores."

Isabella forced her thoughts away from the ugly facts. Facts she'd tried to soften with all her might since that horrible night so many months before, but to no avail.

"That's enough, Anya," she snapped. She turned away from her servant and switched from English to Egyptian to address their male companion. "Surai, open the tomb door and lead the way inside."

He nodded and descended the steps into a shallow, sandy pit where a thick door awaited. The sand storms had long ago turned the identifying hieroglyphics to mere scratches, but the outline of the door was still clear. He crouched to his haunches to run tanned fingers around the edge in order find the best place to pry open the door.

They'd been lucky Hiram had visited here first. He'd not only mapped their journey to the tomb, but his team had done much of the excavation of the site. Still, she knew the door had been resealed when Hiram departed and she expected they might have to stand in the blazing sun and swirling sands for a while before their guide managed to pry it open. But to Isabella's surprise, the covering opened with ease, as if the gods wanted her to come there, to find the answers she'd sought since she'd been widowed.

"Madam," Surai whispered in his native tongue. "The door is already open."

"This is not a good idea, mistress," Anya said as she clasped Isabella's arm with both trembling hands. "There is something foul about the tomb being open. Anyone and anything could await us inside."

Isabella shared her maid's fear, but shook off her feelings. This wasn't the time to have the vapors. She needed to go inside. Something called her to enter. And it was something she refused to deny.

"Light the lanterns," she ordered as she pulled away from Anya.

She spoke with far more bravado than she felt. "If you two are afraid, then I shall lead the way."

Surai opened his mouth as if to protest but Isabella gave him the icy expression her mother had always utilized with servants in London and he grew quiet. After a few moments of shuffling, he handed her a glowing torch and let her take the first few steps into the tomb of Merytsat.

The air was hot and dry, dusty from millennia of being shut up. As far as she knew, only her husband had entered this place with his men since it had been sealed thousands of years before. The idea gave Isabella a shiver. The last man who had entered here was now dead.

With slow steps, she made her way inside. The low glow of the torch allowed her to see the intricate carvings on the walls. Prayers for the dead.

She had gone into the dim tomb about a hundred yards when a sound made her stop in her tracks. Had that been a laugh? And not just any laugh, but the sultry laugh of a woman? No. She had to be imagining things. No one should be in this place but her and her servants. No one else even knew it existed.

When only silence met her waiting ears, Isabella took another step. The dim corridor before her split in two directions and she hesitated as she lifted the light to peer down each one. Which way to go? Which way had Hiram gone?

"Who the hell are you?"

With a start, Isabella pivoted and found herself looking down the short barrel of a pistol. It was aimed at her by the most handsome man she'd ever seen. He had tousled brown hair and stubble that indicated he hadn't shaved for at least two days. His eyes glittered in the torchlight, reflecting back an intense blue fire that almost had her turning away. Only she found she couldn't. She was too drawn in, despite the threat he posed.

Swallowing, she managed to find her voice. "Who the hell am I?" she asked. "I think a better question is who the hell are you?"

"I'm the guy who's laying claim to this place, lady," he said in a decidedly American drawl. He inched the gun away from her face, though he didn't holster it as he shot a side-glance toward Surai.

"Laying claim?" she repeated as shock and anger wiped away

some of the sharp desire she'd felt when she first met this stranger's gaze. "You have no right, sir. My husband found this tomb and it is rightfully his to harvest its findings for the British Museum."

The man motioned his head toward Surai, who had taken up a battle stance in front of Anya. He looked every inch the ancient warrior. "That your husband?"

She blinked. "No. My husband is—well, he's dead."

The blue eyes widened and then the man had the audacity to laugh. And not a chuckle, either, but a low belly laugh that seemed to fill and shake the narrow corridor in which they stood.

"And just what is funny about that, sir?" she asked with as much dignity as she could muster when her cheeks were flaming with a blush.

"If your husband is dead, then he has no claim to anything in this world." The man's intense gaze lingered on her for a long moment. "Anything at all."

The knot that had closed Isabella's throat when she'd first seen this rude stranger now filled it again. She knew a man's desire when she saw it, and it was clear in every part of the unknown outsider before her. Worse was that her nipples hardened in answer to his pointed stare and her thighs clenched.

Obviously she'd been too long without a man's touch if she was considering this…this lout to be an object of lust.

"You still haven't told me your name," she said coolly.

He grinned as another man appeared from the narrow corridor behind him. Now the odds were worse for her party, though she strangely felt no fear. She wasn't sure why, but she knew without a doubt that these men wouldn't hurt her or her servants.

"Jake Turner at your service, my British lady." He jerked his head toward his friend. In the lamplight she could see he had blonde hair and coal gray eyes. Eyes that were focused not on her, but behind her at Anya and Surai. "And this is my partner in crime, Rafe Christian."

"Very nice." She thinned her lips to a frown. "Now, Mr. Turner, Mr. Christian, I'm going to have to ask you again to leave. This tomb is under the jurisdiction of the British Museum. Marauders are not allowed."

Turner gave his partner a look before let out another low laugh.

This one raked over her senses and made her ever more aware of her reacting body. What was wrong with her? It wasn't like she'd never seen a handsome man before. Or heard a deep, throaty chuckle like his. But her body was behaving like a sex-starved wanton. She hadn't been so wet in...well...ever.

"Are *you* a representative of the British Museum now?" he asked. He leaned closer and the heat of his breath warmed her skin. "Because I'd like to see your papers."

She opened her mouth in outrage, but he held up a hand to silence her. "I'm sorry, lady, but this tomb is free to the public now. And my friend and I have our own plans for it. You and your crew are certainly welcome to whatever spoils it is you're looking for. I'm sure there's more than enough booty to go around."

He turned to walk away, but she caught his arm. Instantly heat and electricity shot between them. With a gasp, she yanked her hand away and he reeled back a few steps as if he'd felt the same reaction.

She struggled for equilibrium. "You mean to raid the tomb?"

"That's what treasure hunters do," he said, though his eyes moved over her again. "We ravage and pillage."

She shut her eyes as an image of this man ravaging her entered her mind. His broad shoulders gleaming in the pale lamplight as he entered her inch by inch. Though she shook the fantasy away, she couldn't pretend that a telltale tingle hadn't begun between her heated thighs.

"You know." He stepped closer. "You never told me *your* name."

She stiffened at the reduced proximity between them. He was invading her personal space, trying to intimidate her with his presence. It was working, too, though she'd be damned if she'd allow him to know it.

She straightened her spine and used her most proper and refined tone. "My name is Isabella Winslow. My husband was the late archeologist—"

"Hiram Winslow."

She jerked back in surprise. Her husband's death had been chronicled in the newspapers, but she was still stunned that a man like this would know Hiram's name.

Jake's eyes narrowed. "I'd heard of the circumstances of his death.

I am sorry, Mrs. Winslow. But that doesn't change the fact that I don't accept your claim to this tomb. As far as I'm concerned we have equal right to the spoils here. So why don't we just try to stay out of each other's way."

"Mr. Turner!" she cried in outrage.

"Mistress," Anya snapped from behind her. "The walls!"

Isabella turned around. She'd been so caught up in arguing with the handsome tomb raider she hadn't noticed that the corridor was shaking.

"Oh my God!" she cried out as she stumbled back. She came in hard contact with Jake Turner's solid chest.

Clasping her arm, he began to drag her through the dim hallways away from the entrance. She pulled back against him, but he refused to let her go as he ran. "The tomb isn't stable. We must get closer to the center!"

"But the door!" she screamed as dust and years of cobwebs clouded her eyes and blocked her throat.

"It's the most unstable place of all!" he insisted just as a loud, ugly crash echoed through the passageways around them. Throwing all his weight on top of her, Jake hurtled Isabella to the floor and covered her with his body as a hail of stones and dirt settled around and on top of them.

Followed by a dark and sinister silence.

⁂⟨ＣＣ⟩⁂

Isabella Winslow was yielding and warm beneath Jake's hard body. Though rationally he knew that was the last thought he should have been having, he couldn't help that he was a virile man and the supple body pinned beneath his own made his cock throb with powerful need.

But virile or not, the dust was settling in the total darkness and he had to get up to investigate how much damage had been done to the structure. And ascertain if anyone in either party had been hurt by flying debris.

As he shifted his weight in preparation to rise off Isabella, she let out a low moan. The sound was rich and throaty and made his blood run even hotter than it had been.

"You all right?" he asked quietly as he reluctantly shifted off of her and got to his knees at her side. He wished he could see her, but without the torch lights and the sliver of daylight from outside of the tomb door, he could only tell her location by touch and sense.

Still, he was sure if he could see her that her wide, brown eyes would be glazed with fear.

"I'm fine except for being crushed by you," she said, though her voice trembled and lacked the heat of her sarcastic quip.

"Well, better me than the walls," he answered as he pawed around on the ground for the torch he'd been holding when the tomb collapsed around them. He smelled the sharp tang of kerosene on the torch's rag nearby and finally managed to grasp the end. Using his cigarette lighter, he set it to flame again and held it up to look at her in the wavering circle of light.

She'd risen to her knees beside him, mere inches separating them. With a gasp, she skirted away, but not before he saw the fear he had predicted in her stare. Along with a surprising amount of desire. Isabella Winslow wanted him.

With a triumphant smile, he stood and dragged her up by her elbows. Immediately, she snatched her arms away and stumbled back a few steps. He frowned as he looked around through the dust. Everyone seemed to be getting to their feet. "Was anyone hurt?"

One by one Isabella's two servants and Rafe all answered in the negative. Mopping dirt from his face on his shirtsleeve, Jake surveyed the damage done in the tomb. In the dim glow of the torch, he couldn't see much of anything, but the walls around them seemed to have remained solid, despite all the dust and rubble that now littered the floor at their feet. Still, the deafening rumbling they'd heard indicted far worse should have befallen them.

What had set off the avalanche of debris? He'd been arguing loudly with Isabella, yes, but that shouldn't have been enough to make the very walls shake. Jake had raided plenty of tombs that were far older and in worse shape than this one. None had ever threatened to bury him with the long-dead mummies and their priceless treasures.

"Well, don't just stand there," Isabella said as she crossed her arms. The action forced Jake's gaze to her breasts. Even under the loose fitting man's shirt she wore, it was obvious they were round and perfect. They'd probably overflow his hands when he cupped them. He wondered what color her nipples were.

He shook his head. What the hell? Where had those thoughts come from? And why did the corridor seem to be growing ever hotter and closer.

"Come on," he whispered in a voice made harsh by desire. "We need to go back to the entrance. If the tomb isn't stable, we should go outside. At least until we can get a crew to reinforce the walls."

Her brown eyes grew wide. "Go? No, I have to stay. I must find out—" She broke off the sentence with a suddenly panicked stare. "I just can't leave, that's all."

"Whatever it is you need to find here, it isn't worth your life," Jake barked out. "Now, come on."

When she shook her head in protest, Jake reached out to grasp her arm. Heat whooshed through him and set him off balance. She seemed to feel it too, for she pulled away from him with a squeal of protest.

"Surai!" she cried.

Jake turned to ready himself for battle against the large and menacing Egyptian guide, but was surprised to see that the two of them were now alone in the corridor.

"Rafe?" he called into the misty dark. "Where the hell are you?"

He waited for a response, but only his own voice answered him as it bounced along the walls in the maze of the tomb's many twisting corridors. It rang back at him, distorted from ricocheting off countless doors and around corners.

"What did your man do to my guide and maid?" Isabella asked with all the haughty attitude of a British aristocrat. It set Jake's teeth on edge.

"Look, lady, I have no idea where any of our friends are. But if they're smart, they aren't arguing in the corridor. They're heading toward the entryway and safety." With a growl, he pulled her closer and caught a whiff of the rich spicy scent of her hair and skin. It dizzied his mind. "Come on, your highness, let's go."

Her protests died on her lips as she stared up into his eyes. But then she shook away his hand and said, "Fine. But don't think that just because I'm going with you means I agree with you."

He rolled his eyes and used the flickering light from his own torch to find another for Isabella. With a curse, he brushed it free of dirt and lit it. Dim, sickly light finally emanated and Jake shoved the torch into her hand as he motioned for her to follow him.

"Stay close," he ordered. "We don't know what kind of debris may be in the path now and the torches have very weak light."

She muttered a sarcastic response, but did as he'd ordered and slipped up behind him. Her body heat warmed him through his shirt and he could have sworn he felt the brush of those full, lush breasts pressed against the plane of his back. With a shiver, he headed toward the entrance. Once they were out of the tomb, he hoped these strange desires would go with them. He didn't think he'd ever been so full of a need for a woman in his life. Especially a woman like this.

"It's so quiet," Isabella whispered. "Why can't we hear the others?"

Jake shook his head. That was what he wondered, too. If their friends were anywhere close by, they would have heard their echoing voices and footfalls.

"Maybe they've already gone into the desert and are waiting for us," he offered though he didn't believe it himself. Still, there was no use getting her even more upset than she already was.

"Anya wouldn't leave me alone," she answered quietly.

Jake was silent. Neither would Rafe. The two of them had been friends for over five years. They'd raided tombs and avoided authorities and enemies alike. Rafe had never left him before.

"What if they were hurt in the accident?" she muttered with a tiny catch in her voice.

Jake stopped in his spot and turned back to her. The tough woman she'd tried to portray since he'd first leveled his pistol in her face was gone, replaced by a fragile beauty. He set the torch in a sconce on the wall and drew her against his chest.

She stiffened at first, but within moments she relaxed in his arms. Her chest flattened against his, her legs molded to his own. Every tantalizing inch of her splayed across him like out of some erotic dream. But this wasn't a dream. It felt too good.

He struggled for words. "They each said they weren't hurt," he reminded her as his erection inched harder and longer. There was no way she couldn't feel him pressed against her thigh, yet she didn't pull away. "They just roamed off."

She looked up at him with cloudy, unfocused eyes. Her tongue came out pink and wet to slide across dusty rose lips. With a groan, Jake pulled her closer and slammed his mouth down on hers.

He half expected her to pull back and give him the slap of his life. Instead, she wound her arms around his back and returned his kiss with an equal intensity. He drove his tongue between her lips and she sucked it. His cock twitched. He was going to have this woman. One way or another he was going to enter her heat.

In a few long steps, he crushed her back against the nearest wall and pushed her legs apart with his thighs. All the while he continued to plunder her mouth, bruising her with his out of control need. Yet she whimpered in desire, not a request for him to stop. Already her nails raked along his back and he felt her hard nipples through several layers of fabric.

"Yes," she moaned as he grasped a handful of her skirt and thin silky underskirt. He yanked them up in jerky movements. She arched against him until her pelvis ground against his cock and he nearly spent himself there and then.But just as she pried a hand between them and found the top button of his trousers, a sound pierced the echoing silence around them. A sound that brought them both up short.

A woman's moan.

For a brief moment, Jake thought it must have been a trick of the corridor that had sent Isabella's cries of encouragement back to them on the hot, dry air, but then the moan came again, this time even louder.

"Is that Anya?" Isabella whispered as she shoved back against Jake's chest. "Is she hurt?"

Jake cocked an eyebrow at her. That was not the sound of an injured woman. It was the sound of a woman climaxing. The sound of a woman being well pleasured. Isabella's cheeks darkened as she met his gaze. She knew it as well as he did.

"We need to...go," she choked out as she turned away from his scrutiny with a red face. "We need to find our friends and get out of this place."

His erection jolted in protest, but Jake managed to nod. "This way," he muttered as he grasped the torch from the wall.

The outer door to the tomb was only a few hundred feet away, but with the moans and cries echoing around them in the oppressive darkness, it seemed to take an age to reach it. The sounds taunted him, reminding him that he could have been plunging inside Isabella's willing body right now if they hadn't been interrupted.

They rounded the last corner, but instead of being greeted by the filtered sunlight of the desert streaming in through the doorway, they were met by ominous darkness. The cavern door was shut, blocked by a pile of debris.

"Damn it!" Jake cried as he hurried toward the entrance. He thrust his torch in Isabella's direction and she took it wordlessly, then watched as he dug at the rocks and dust. Despite his best efforts, he was only able to free a few smaller rocks.

"We're trapped," she said behind him in a strange, low voice that made him turn. Her face had paled two shades and her eyes glazed with tears she was fighting to control.

He straightened up and tried to look optimistic. "For now. But you know that many of these tombs had more than one entrance. If we can't find another way out, I'm sure Rafe, Surai and I can dig our way out of the main corridor."

"But we can't find the others," Isabella whispered.

He reached out to her and was surprised when she took his hand without argument. "Well, we will. Come on, let's go back the way we came and see if we can work our way out of this maze."

Chapter Two

Isabella fought the urge to grasp the back of Jake's dusty linen shirt. Touching this man wouldn't help anything, especially considering how their last innocent contact had lead to that animalistic display up against the corridor wall. Her body tingled with just the memory of the way his erection had pressed against the junction of her thighs, encouraging the wetness that still lingered inside her.

She swallowed hard. Her fear and desperation had led to that moment of surrender, nothing more. She wouldn't let it happen again. And she wouldn't show a scoundrel like Jake Turner that she was afraid either.

She peered over his shoulder. Their two torches cast a sickly light up the ever twisting corridor ahead, revealing the beautiful carvings on the tomb walls. Isabella wanted to stop to chronicle them in her little notebook, but they had to find their friends before she did anything of the kind.

They rounded a corner, but this time instead of the never-ending passage, an open doorway came into view at the end of their circle of light.

Her heart leapt. "Is that a chamber up ahead?"

Jake lifted his torch higher and squinted into the dimness. "I think you're right." He half turned to face her. "Do we dare try it?"

Now that she was looking up into those amazing blue eyes, Isabella temporarily forgot her capacity to speak. Swallowing hard past sudden desire, she nodded.

"A-Anything is better than roaming around in the dark," she managed to whisper.

His breath rasped heavy in the echoing chamber, bouncing off the walls and making her ears and body tingle with the knowledge that looking at her made him want her. Made them both forget the fear associated with being trapped.

With a shiver, he turned away and began walking again. They passed through the chamber door and her fear returned, laced with a strange, dizzy sensation. One that wasn't entirely unpleasant.

"Let me raise the light in here a bit," Jake muttered as he crossed to a few torches on the walls. He lit them with his own and the chamber blazed forth in firelight.

Enough light that the hieroglyphics on the walls were clear. Tombs often contained sayings or stories of the departed's life written on the walls. But these weren't the usual symbols for words. These pictures were of men and women engaging in sex acts.

Isabella gasped as she took a step forward to put her torch in an empty sconce. She instinctively reached out to brush her fingertips along the long jut of an animated penis as it plowed into the waiting mouth of a woman.

"What is this place?" Jake muttered under his breath as he stared both at her and the walls.

"You're raiding this tomb, but you don't even know whom it houses?" she asked with purposeful superiority in her tone.

Still, she couldn't seem to take her eyes from the pictures drawn with paint thousands of years before. This one depicted a woman enjoying two handsome men. One suckled her breasts as he buried himself deep within her womb, the other pressed into her bottom. No detail was left undone, including the tell tale droplet of moisture that trickled down the woman's inner thigh. Though the position was foreign to Isabella, it excited her. She actually had to will her hands from straying up to stroke her own breasts.

"If you know so much," Jake said in a strange, choked voice from behind her. "Then why don't you fill me in on the details. All I know about this tomb is that it was rumored to hold riches."

Isabella continued to stroll along the wall's parameter, pausing to look up at the detail of a man gliding his pointed, red tongue along the nether lips of a woman in the heights of ecstasy. The wet heat between her own thighs increased and she had to labor her breathing to speak.

"This is the burial place of Merytsat. She is unique in that she was only a pharaoh's mistress, yet she was buried with the wealth and glory of a queen," she whispered as she found herself looking up at a picture of the beautiful Egyptian herself.

Merytsat was straddling the prone form of a well-endowed lover, riding his cock with fervor. Isabella could have sworn if she lowered her lids a fraction, she could almost feel the animal heat of that man between her own legs. Could almost hear Merytsat's moans of pleasure and power as she rode him to orgasm and took his hot seed deep inside her.

"Why?" Jake asked. His rough voice cut through the air and the timbre of it made Isabella shiver. He wanted her. And it excited her to turn him on with her every word.

"She was a very accomplished mistress. One who learned the art of sex with a zeal that put all other concubines to shame. Some say she had powers only making love could awaken, but I've never believed that." She leaned closer to the wall. "Still..." She reached out a trembling finger and stroked it along Merytsat's slit. "Looking at these hieroglyphics, you can almost feel her power. Her passion."

"Isabella," Jake murmured.

She turned to face him and found she'd unbuttoned the first three buttons of the shirt she had taken from her husband's dresser before departing Cairo. Her hands were inside the warm heat of her thin chemise and she was stroking her own breasts, teasing the nipples with her fingers and kneading the sensitive flesh.

Propriety dictated she be embarrassed by this stunning slip. That she apologize and cover herself decently. But somehow she felt no shame. Instead, a stir of the power Merytsat herself must have possessed began in Isabella's very center. In place of shame, she felt elation. Freedom.

And the need to have this man touch her. To make him groan as the men in these pictures around her had their mouths open in moans of pleasure. The pleasure she would bring.

Jake continued to stare at her and she was finally so bold as to meet his gaze full-on. "Would you like to watch me touch myself?" she asked softly. Her voice wasn't her own. Her hands weren't her own. And this moment was just one out of time. There were no consequences. Only sensation.

He shut his eyes for a brief moment, but she didn't need words to know the answer to the question. The hard outline of his jutting member was already clear through his trousers.

"Oh, yes," he finally breathed as his lids came open.

With a boldness she'd never known she possessed, she slipped the remainder of her buttons open and tossed her shirt aside. Then she slipped the slender chemise straps off her shoulders and bared her breasts to him. He mumbled something unintelligible under his breath, then gasped when she cupped her herself again.

"Then watch," she urged as she stroked her thumbs across her nipples. Her nerves sang as she fondled her skin with soft palms.

Normally her ministrations were limited to a few shy caresses in a bath or in the darkness of her lonely bed. A woman of her station was told over and over that sex was dirty. Isabella had touched herself, but it was always fleeting and had brought her shame. But now, to bring herself pleasure in front of a stranger, in the blinding light of a chamber filled with ancient erotic art, was exhilarating.

She unfastened her skirt and removed it, along with the remainder of her underclothes and boots. She stood before him naked, without even her long hair down around her shoulders as protection from his eyes.

"Isabella," he breathed as he reached for her.

"Not yet," she protested while she skirted his reach. Then she snaked her hand to the blonde curls between her legs and slid a finger along her wet slit. The slippery heat intensified with the touch, dampening her fingers and sending a flash of powerful pleasure through her. With another long sweep of her finger, she brushed the hardness of her clit and couldn't hold back a moan.

Without breaking eye contact with Jake, she lifted her finger to her mouth and licked it, tasting her own juices before she returned to touching herself.

He let out a low moan and moved toward her. "I want to taste you. I want to taste your desire."

Her knees almost buckled as he dropped down before her and placed a rough hand on the inside of each her naked thighs. Slowly, he backed her legs open until she stood splayed before him. With a grin, he leaned up and took a deep whiff of her woman's scent before he slipped his tongue across her.

"It's been so long," she murmured as she gripped a fistful of his hair.

"Then I'll make the wait worthwhile," he promised as he pulled her down to her knees to face him. He leaned down to kiss her and she tasted her own earthy flavor on his lips just as she'd tasted it on her finger.

With a groan, he laid her back on her discarded clothes. She bent her knees and spread her legs further, offering her feminine secrets to him without hesitation. He took them with equal determination, stroking his tongue first across her outer lips, just teasing her pulsing body with light nips and long strokes.

She rose to meet each flick of his hot tongue, writhing with the need for more of him than just his mouth, but wanting the moment to never end. Hiram had certainly never loved her like this. It was exquisite.

Jake finally delved his tongue deep inside her, plunging it in and out in a slow, languid rhythm that mimicked the one she knew he'd set with his cock later.

His cock. The hard, hot one she'd felt pressed against her earlier. The long length she'd seen jutting against his confining trousers.

"I want to see you," she whispered.

His head came up in surprise, but then he shook it. "Not yet. I want to lick every drop of need from your body before I create even more in you."

She shivered as he nuzzled his nose back against her. "No, I don't want you to put yourself inside me yet. I want to taste you as you're tasting me. I want to suck you."

She had no idea where that request had come from, but the desire was overwhelming. Blue eyes met hers with a heat that was burning hot and full of dangerous promise. He stood and shucked his shirt and trousers, revealing his nakedness to her. Her eyes widened. This man had both length and girth. He was far bigger than Hiram had been, and looked like he would fill her to the brim when he finally did enter her.

He looked delicious.

"Lay on your back," she ordered as she crawled to her knees.

He followed her command, laying across their discarded clothes in the soft sand. With a purr of satisfaction, Isabella straddled his mouth, then bent to take just the head of his magnificent erection between her lips. Jake let out one low groan before he went back to work on her pussy with renewed vigor. She mimicked his every action. When he sucked her clit, she sucked the head of his penis. When he ran his tongue down her slit all the way to the tightness of her bottom, she ran her mouth up and down the long, turgid length of his cock. When he drilled his tongue inside her, she filled her mouth with his length.

The pressure and pleasure was building, and by the way he twitched against her tongue and moaned into her body, it wasn't just nearing culmination for her. He was going to come, and she was going to drink every drop of his essence even as he lapped up the last bit of hers.

With a shift of her hips, she began to grind in slow circles against his unyielding mouth. Her clit rubbed just right against him, causing a delicious friction that would allow her a release she knew would go on for ages. She also increased the speed of her mouth, alternately sucking him and taking him down as deep as he would go.

Finally, in a release so powerful it actually made her scream against his cock, Isabella came. Her hips jerked wildly, only prevented from injuring Jake by the fingers he dug into her skin to keep her in place as he continued to lap at her mercilessly.

Just as she exploded, he joined her, pumping hot into her mouth and down her throat. Like he had, she continued her torture until he was spent and softened a fraction in her mouth.

Isabella blinked as she lay exhausted on his sweat-slick stomach. Slowly, reality set in. What had just happened? She and Hiram had been married for nearly three years. In that time, she'd never even considered the possibility of taking his member into her mouth. Of sucking him dry.

She shivered as a fresh, insistent wave of desire washed over her. What was driving her to do these things with a man who was nothing more than a stranger? A tomb-raiding, overbearing, American stranger.

Briefly she flashed to an image of Hiram. When he'd returned from Merytsat's tomb, he had behaved differently, too. He'd demanded things from her in their bedroom that he'd never wanted before. When she hadn't been able to provide him with those desires, it had driven him away. Driven him to his death.

And now she was experiencing the same powerful longings.

Her hands began to tremble with that association. With a start, she rolled off Jake's body and yanked her shirt from beneath his muscular backside. She was *not* going to end up like Hiram had. She wasn't going to let herself be driven by her suddenly awakened sexual desires.

Jake sat up on his elbows to watch her dress with unhidden interest and the flash of what she knew was desire. She ignored it, and her body's unwanted, wet response.

"From the look on your face, I'd never have guessed you got as much enjoyment from that as I did." His grin was wicked and intoxicating. She almost wanted to return the smile, even though she was terrified. "As unexpected as it was."

She turned her back on him to avoid the distraction he posed. Shoving her arms through her sleeves, she whispered, "Well, unexpected or not, I hope you don't think it will change anything." She struggled to button her shirt with clumsy fingers. When she'd managed to cover herself decently, she finally dared to face him. "And I hope you don't expect me to give into your charms again, Mr. Turner."

The amusement on his face was gone. "It's a bit late to call me Mr. Turner, isn't it?" he asked in a dry voice. "And it wasn't as if I held you down and forced myself on you. If I recall, you started this little encounter. And you were the one straddling me, riding me to your pleasure."

She blushed, hating that he was saying exactly what she knew to be true. She *had* started this. And she wanted more. Looking down at this man, with his tousled dark hair, his stubbly cheeks that she'd felt brush against her most private areas and his broad, utterly naked body, she wanted nothing more than to fall back into his arms. But this time his mouth wouldn't be enough. She wanted that strong thrust of cock she'd held in her lips. She wanted it inside her, rocking against her.

With a shiver, she looked away. Even when she was dressed, he was still far too dangerous a draw.

"I'm not like this," she muttered. "I am not the kind of woman who throws herself at a man. Especially one like you."

He laughed long and hard at her insult as he rose to his feet and pulled on his trousers. "Yes, that's probably true. Perhaps it's this place."

"What do you mean?" she asked as she allowed herself a glance over her shoulder. He was already buttoning his dusty, wrinkled shirt, covering up the body that had given her so much pleasure. And could give her so much more if she only asked.

And how she wanted to ask. She wanted to beg for more. Shaking her head, she steeled herself. She had to fight these strange desires no matter how hard it was.

He shrugged. "There have been many tales of explorers and tomb raiders who've encountered much more than history or treasures in Egyptian tombs. Some say these places held curses, as well. Warnings to invaders to take at their own peril. Maybe this place has a curse, too. One that involves the sexual skill of the woman who was buried here."

She pursed her lips. "I believe in science, Mr. Turner." Even if science couldn't explain what she'd seen her own husband do. Or how her aching body was betraying her at that very moment.

"Jake," he interrupted. "If you're going to let me give you the most intimate of kisses, Isabella, I'm going to have to insist you call me Jake."

Her breath hitched as he took a step closer. She could smell his skin from the short distance. A tantalizing mixture of sweat and man…and now sex. The new addition only made her all the more aware of the power he could hold sway over her.

"I assure you Mr.—" She sighed when he arched an eyebrow. "Jake, that what happened between us a moment ago will never happen again. And it had nothing to do with a curse or an enchantment or any other superstition."

"Then why?" He reached out a hand to brush across her face with gentle pressure. The challenge to her resolve was nearly overpowering. "Or are you admitting that you simply wanted me and against every regulation you would usually follow, you gave in to those desires?"

Her teeth sank into her lip as she contemplated a good answer for that question. If she admitted she'd given in to her desires of her own volition, that would be opening up the door to saying she still wanted more of this man's touch. Something that completely went against her every fiber. Even though it was true. She wanted what they'd shared again and even more, despite everything that told her not to touch him.

But saying their joining was possibly caused by something in the tomb went against her scientific instincts. And also took away from the sweet moments she'd found in Jake's arms.

"I—" she began, but then she stopped. In the distance, she heard a low, feminine moan. "Did you hear that?"

He looked around with a nod. "Yes. The same moan we heard earlier in the corridor."

"Perhaps it's a trick of the tomb," she whispered.

She shut her eyes as the sound came again, this time louder. It sounded like Anya. But not like she was in pain. It sounded like a woman being pleasured. Like the moans she, herself, had uttered while Jake suckled and teased her to orgasm. Her pussy clenched in response and her nipples puckered.

"Perhaps," he said quietly.

"I have to look for my friend." She shook her head to cast away whatever spell came over her when this man was so near. "I need to find Anya and then we can begin our work while you and the other men start digging us out of the tomb."

As she turned to leave the chamber, Jake's hand snaked out and caught her arm. He spun her back around to face him. His body heat hit her like a wall, then surrounded her in an embrace.

"Now wait just a damn minute, Isabella. There's no way in hell I'm going to dig you out of this tomb while you go sifting through the chambers looking for the secrets of a dead concubine. It's utterly ridiculous that you're willing to risk your life for some historical relic."

She yanked on her arm, but he wouldn't set her free. His touch burned, clouding her mind and awakening her senses. "I'm not looking for *her* secrets, I'm looking for my husband's!" she snapped without thinking.

Immediately he released her and she stumbled back, covering her mouth with a trembling hand. What had she done? Why had she revealed the truth to this man?

He stared at her with a hooded gaze. "What the hell are you talking about?"

"Nothing," she mumbled as she cast her eyes down to the dirty floor. "I didn't mean anything."

He frowned. "I'm not stupid. Just what are you doing here really? And don't tell me finishing your late husband's work because I didn't buy that the first time you said it. There are plenty other archeologists at the British Museum who could take on that task. And you certainly didn't come equipped with the right tools for a dig." His fingers curled around her shoulders, this time gently. "Tell me the truth, Isabella. Maybe I could help you."

She gazed up into eyes so blue she was reminded of the ocean on a clear day. She could almost believe in him. Almost.

"And why would you want to help me?" she whispered.

His head dipped lower, moving ever closer to her lips. "I have no idea."

Just as their mouths met, the moan cut through the room as if the owner of the voice were right outside the door. Isabella jolted back.

"Anya," she said as she skittered away from Jake's grip. "I must find Anya."

Gathering her skirt into one hand and a torch in the other, she hurried from the room. Away from the man who drew her in such powerful and puzzling ways.

The moans told her which way to turn, which way to go. She followed them blindly until she stood outside another chamber. She could only pray Anya was inside. Once she found her friend, she knew she could fight the undeniable attraction that drew her to Jake Turner. If only she really wanted to fight it.

Taking a deep breath, she stepped inside.

"An—" she began, but then stopped dead at what she saw.

Her friend was there, and so were Surai and Jake's friend Rafe. But they were engaged in an activity that guaranteed they cared very little about who came into the room.

Anya was leaning back against a pillar, Surai kissing her deeply, while Rafe slipped the last of her under things from her smooth, round hips.

Chapter Three

Why the hell was he chasing this woman?

Jake ducked under a low beam and skidded around a corner as he continued his search to find the wily Isabella Winslow. She didn't mean a thing to him. She'd been a hindrance to his plans for the tomb, then nothing more than a fellow prisoner. Now she was something more. A sensual partner in a game he had no idea how to win.

He paused at a crossroad in the winding tomb and licked his lips. God, he could still taste her there. Heady and warm like her thighs had been as they clenched and she screamed out release. He still throbbed from his own orgasm, the one she'd brought with a skillful mouth. But he wanted more. He wanted to plunge into the warmth of her body, to feel her womb contract around him as he plundered her.

He wanted to fuck her until she shuddered beneath him and came as hard as she'd come when he sucked her clit.

He shook his head to make those images go away. This wasn't like him. He'd known plenty of women, had more than his fair share of their warm and willing bodies over his years of world travel. None had ever distracted him so completely.

This was an emergency, for God's sake, not some party. Here he was, trapped in a tomb, his friend and partner missing, and all he could think about was bending Isabella Winslow over the nearest pillar and making her scream his name.

Ridiculous.

And completely exciting. He adjusted in the hopes his throbbing cock would settle down.

"Jake."

He came to a complete stop and looked around. The dim corridor was empty as far as he could see in every direction. Only the hieroglyphics kept him company, yet he knew he'd heard his name.

"Jake."

There it was again, echoing around him in the darkness. It sounded like Isabella's voice far in the distance. Soft and low like a whisper in a bedroom.

"Isabella?" he called out, only to have his words bounce back off the tomb walls to his ears. She didn't respond. Jake hurried down the corridor in the direction of the voice and came to a stop again when he heard the moan that had been taunting them since the cave-in.

A woman being well-pleasured he had told himself, right before he and Isabella had lost all control and pleasured each other. Were the two things connected? Isabella claimed to believe in science, not superstition like curses, but even she'd admitted she didn't normally allow a man she hardly knew to bring her to shattering orgasm on the floor of a tomb.

Jake believed in science, too. But he also believed in his instincts. They were telling him there was something more going on in Merytsat's tomb than met the eye.

"Jake."

Isabella's voice was more urgent now, filled with a need that tingled through him to harden him even farther. He rounded a corner through the empty door of a new chamber and came to a sudden halt. The three people he and Isabella had been searching for stood against the back wall. They weren't hurt as feared. In fact, Anya, Surai and Rafe looked anything but injured. All three were naked and it was obvious they'd begun the process of making love.

Anya's dark hair had fallen over her exotic face, but by the way her hips ground against Rafe's lips, Jake had no doubt she was enjoying every moment of what was happening to her. Meanwhile, Surai, the huge guard who'd given Jake pause when he'd first encountered Isabella's party, was standing behind Anya, massaging her breasts as he sucked along her slender neck.

Jake couldn't move or say a word, even though he knew he should either stop the threesome and insist they all exit the tomb, or leave to allow them their privacy. Instead, he stayed, fixed in that spot and unable to look away until a soft whimper grabbed his attention.

Isabella.

He turned and saw her leaning one hand against the nearest pillar. Like she had been in the room filled with erotic images, she was staring at the threesome with wide, glazed eyes. Shocked, yes, as any good Victorian woman would have convinced herself she should be, but there was something more. She was aroused. It was clear by the way she licked her lips as Rafe dragged his tongue away from Anya's glistening slit and glided it up the long length of her body.

And when Surai urged Anya to her knees and slowly, gently parted her legs to enter her from behind, Isabella's hips lifted along with her friend's. Jake moved closer, but Isabella didn't seem to notice. He positioned himself so he could watch both the threesome in the corner and her reaction to her voyeuristic pursuits.

Surai thrust into Anya with long, smooth strokes, ones she met with little gasps and moans. Then the maid looked up at Rafe with a smile and wrapped her hand around the hard shaft of his erection. Slowly, she glided her tongue around the head, only stopping from time to time to moan out her encouragement to Surai as he pumped into her with a slow, lazy rhythm.

Finally, Anya took Rafe's cock entirely into her mouth and matched Surai's pace as she sucked him. Jake's friend tangled his fingers into her dark hair, gently urging her to suck faster or harder with just the flick of his wrist. She followed his silent orders with the expertise of a woman who took two men at once all the time, but Jake knew that couldn't be true. This had to be new to Anya, as it was to Rafe and probably Surai. Yet, like what had happened to Jake and Isabella in the chamber a short time before, they seemed to be swept away, their inner desires and pleasures awakened by something in the tomb. Nothing seemed shocking to any of them, and none seemed uncomfortable with their decadent acts.

Jake shivered as Surai grasped the long, silky coils of Anya's hair and eased her up into a standing position. He continued to thrust into her even as he backed up to sit down on a huge fragment of a shattered pillar.

He found himself moving, too, edging ever closer until he stood just behind Isabella. She was getting more and more excited as she watched Anya lift off of Surai's cock and position herself differently. The guard spread the soft cheeks of her rear end, bending to tongue her there for a brief moment before he spread her wider and eased his cock into the tight, little hole. Anya writhed, gripping Surai's arms as he nudged further and further inside her, stretching her gently and allowing her plenty of time to get used to this new invasion.

Reaching around, Jake found the buttons of Isabella's shirt and slowly slipped them open. He eased his hands beneath her silky chemise. She gasped in surprise, but didn't pull away. Instead she leaned back, pressing her body against his and grinding her backside against his throbbing erection until he could have exploded at that very moment.

As he massaged her breasts, flicking the hard beads of her nipples to elicit a little gasp of pleasure from her, he watched the threesome in the corner. Now Surai had completed his entry into Anya. He reached around to spread her legs, opening her like a flower to Rafe's eyes. As Surai pumped against her, Rafe dropped to his knees and began to lick Anya's clit. Even across the room, Jake could hear the sucking sound as he rolled it with his tongue and let it slip in and out of his mouth.

Anya wailed, thrusting back against Surai as she tangled her fingers in Rafe's thick, blond hair. Just as she was about to orgasm, Rafe stood up. Bracing himself against her legs, he eased inside her until she was sandwiched between the two men. Anya didn't seem to mind. In fact, her wail became a scream as she thrashed out an orgasm that had both men gripping at her as they thrust in time.

As the grunts and moans from the other group bounced off the walls behind them, Isabella turned her head and sucked Jake's lower lip. Her mouth was hot on his skin, burning him, making him mad with desire. Desire he chose not to fight anymore. With a groan, he shoved her skirt up around her waist. As he fumbled with the fly of his own trousers, he slipped his opposite finger between her lips. Isabella sucked the digit obediently, rolling her tongue around him as if his forefinger were his cock. Every time she sucked, his penis twitched, longing to fill her anywhere, everywhere.

He withdrew his finger from her mouth and rubbed his hands over her behind, reveling in her soft skin before he slowly parted the globes and ran his damp finger along the cleft of her rear end. She gasped, but didn't pull away as he slowly eased the finger inside her. He pumped in and out, slowing when she moaned louder and increasing the rate when she strained against him.

"Please," she whispered and he could almost hear the tears in her voice. "Please just take me. Take me."

She didn't have to ask twice. Gripping her hips, he guided his throbbing erection to her wet entrance. He felt her humid heat against his tip before he drove up into her. She enveloped him like they were made to fit together, and was as hot and tight as he'd envisioned since the first moment he'd seen her wandering the corridors of the darkened tomb.

"Yes, yes, yes," she moaned as she braced herself against the pillar.

He withdrew until he nearly left her body, then surged forward again. She practically purred as she writhed against the stone, digging her fingers against the sandy rock, her breath coming in little pants and moans.

He plunged into her again and again, loving the way she arched and screamed with each thrust. Loving that she didn't give a damn that her cries were surely being heard by the copulating group across the room. She was his, and for the moment there was no one else.

Finally, with an ear-shattering cry, she came. Her pussy gripped him, milking him with wet heat as she convulsed around him. It was too much to take, even for the most controlled of men and he pumped hot into her, filling her with everything he was. Then he sagged against her to lean on the pillar with a satisfied groan.

"Mmm."

Even though Jake was pinning her against the hard pillar, Isabella felt nothing but satiated pleasure. He wasn't rock hard anymore, but he was still buried deep, filling her entirely and leaving her with a sense of…completion.

It had been a long time since she'd had a man inside her, and she'd certainly never experienced such bliss from her husband. Hiram had stayed in the safe territory of the missionary position. Not unpleasant, but never explosive, never addictive.

Her eyes fluttered open at that thought. What was she doing? Back in the chamber with the erotic art, she'd convinced herself that fear had driven her to such wild abandon with Jake. She'd sworn privately and even to him that she wouldn't allow it to happen again, yet here she was with his cock buried inside her. With her body twitching around him with the remainders of her pleasure.

Twice she had surrendered to needs she'd never even known she had. She could no longer pretend that surrender didn't mean something more than just fear. She'd abandoned all her standards, thrown away her inhibitions. In the outside world, coming upon her friend having a threesome with two men would have shocked and even horrified her. Here, it had made her an animal of lust. Out of control.

The thought was terrifying.

Jake nuzzled her neck and her body lurched back to the ultra-sensitive state he always inspired.

"Am I hurting you?" he murmured against her skin.

No, he wasn't hurting her yet, but it was obvious how easily he could do just that. Whatever was driving her to find sexual release at every turn was also driving her to Jake Turner. And not just because he was the nearest man available. While watching Anya with her men, Isabella had wanted to feel a man inside her. But not just any man.

The only person she'd wanted was Jake.

"Isabella?" he repeated.

"No, you aren't hurting me." She shook her head and the stubble on his chin rasped across her neck to set off an explosion in her nerves. She had to find a way to fight these urges, and the only way she knew was to escape the tomb.

She peered around the pillar to the rest of the large, open room. She fully expected to see Anya and the two men. It would be difficult to behave normally around her friend after what she'd witnessed, but to get out of here alive and with her sanity intact, she was willing to pretend she hadn't watched those erotic things. Hadn't been able to move until Jake touched her.

But the room was empty except for a few broken pillars and ceremonial tables. There was no sign of Anya, Surai or Rafe. Nothing but the heady scent of sex that now filled the air.

She jerked away from Jake, separating their bodies in an instant that left her empty before she shoved that emotion away.

"Anya is gone!" she cried as she motioned across the room.

Jake blinked, seemingly still lost in the haze of desire and whatever else kept driving them together. When her words finally registered, he lurched. "Gone?"

He yanked up his trousers and buttoned just the first few buttons. Coming around the pillar, he stared at the place where the threesome had been having sex.

"How is this possible?" Isabella wailed as desperation and frustration loomed up in her, threatening to overtake her with as much force as her lust had. "If we could see them…see them…"

"Fucking like animals?" he offered mildly.

She turned on him, shocked by his harsh language, and even more shocked by the images it conjured. Did everything the man said and did have to make her pant for him?

"Yes. They must have been able to see us, too. Why would they leave?"

Jake stared at her without answering and she slowly became aware of the fact that her skirt was still hiked up around her thighs and her shirtwaist was open. With an exasperated sigh, she yanked the fabric close to her chest.

"Is that all you can think about?" she snapped with more anger than she felt.

He arched an eyebrow. "You don't have to pretend like it isn't all *you* can think about, too. I haven't exactly been raping you, you know." He stepped closer and ran his hands over the fists she clutched around her shirt. "In fact, you've been most willing."

She swallowed, unable to combat the truth. She had been willing. In fact, standing so close to him and looking up into his eyes, she knew if he pushed her hands aside to touch her, she'd spread herself open for him again. There was something addictive about their joining. Something…magical.

"Why is this happening?" she whispered, unable to keep up the façade of bravery she'd shown him until that very moment. "We've been stuck in this tomb for hours, yet until we came upon them making love, we haven't seen or heard anything from our friends. And every time we spend more than five minutes in one spot together, we can't keep from tearing each other's clothes off." Her eyes stung with tears as she thought about Hiram and his behavior in Cairo. "Are we going crazy? Is this some kind of madness?"

For the first time since she'd met him, Jake's face softened. He didn't look like a man who wanted to ravish her, he looked like he wanted to take care of her. It made her heart lurch with sudden emotion and she wasn't sure which option was more dangerous.

"It isn't madness," he reassured her. "But I don't know what it is. You say you don't believe in magic or curses, but this isn't normal behavior for either of us." He smiled and her blood heated. "Not that I'm complaining."

"I don't know what I believe anymore," she admitted with a sigh as she leaned back on a pillar.

He wrinkled his brow. "Do you mean you're beginning to agree with me that something unnatural is happening in this tomb?"

Her bottom lip quivered uncontrollably as she lifted her gaze to his. She had to put a great deal of trust in this man, and trust was a gift she'd been punished for giving in the past. Still, staring up into the Mediterranean blue of his eyes, she felt...safe.

"Yes. There's other no explanation for why we can't find our friends or another door even though I've studied the plans for this tomb in detail." She sighed and tried to regain her composure. She failed and the tears flowed freely. "There's no reason why Anya would disappear with your friend and Surai, then show back up only to be indulging herself with both men."

Jake nodded. "So this isn't her standard behavior?"

"No." She sighed. "Anya has had feelings for Surai for months and never acted on them even though I know she's had ample opportunities. Is your friend Rafe the kind of man who would..." Blood heated her cheeks. "Do that?"

A small smile turned up one corner of Jake's mouth. "No. At least not under these circumstances."

She let her gaze drop to the dusty floor. Even the scientific use of deduction was leading her to a supernatural answer, no matter how she tried to pretend it wasn't possible. She ran a hand over her hair absently. "Besides, I know Anya wouldn't leave me once we'd found each other again. No matter what."

Jake reached out and brushed a tear from her cheek. Slowly, he raised his damp finger to his lips and licked the tear away. "And what about you and me?"

She shivered because his gaze had transformed from the kind and comforting one to one of desire. A desire she felt growing in herself, despite their predicament.

"I don't know what is drawing us together in this explosive way," she said on a sigh. "I can tell you I did find you handsome and was drawn to you, even when you leveled your gun in my face. But until the entrance to the tomb caved in, I was able to control that attraction."

"Are you sorry you can't anymore?" he asked softly as he slipped an arm around her waist to pull her closer. His breath heated her face, heated her blood. Made her want.

"I don't know," she whispered as her tears subsided. What he was asking her was so dangerous to her heart, but she felt as drawn to tell him to the truth as she did to take his body into hers. "Being with you has been...amazing. I'm not sure why this is happening, but I don't think I'd want to take it back."

He rewarded her honesty by dipping his head for a kiss. "You're not alone," he murmured as he probed his tongue between her lips. She arched against him. "I've never been this out of control with any woman before. I like it."

She shook her head, but was unable to break away from his kiss. How could being out of control, being unable to direct the longings of their bodies, be a good thing?

Finally, Jake managed to pull away. His face was flushed with need and his eyes sparkled. She nearly went down on her knees with the power of her disappointment, even though she knew keeping her distance, denying whatever was driving them together, was the only way she could hope to overcome this power and find a way out of the tomb.

"Isabella." His voice shook. "You told me in the cavern before you ran away that you weren't looking for Merytsat's secrets, you were looking for your husband's."

She nodded weakly, still reeling from her body's powerful drive to feel him. "Yes. I came here to find out what happened to him and why."

"Tell me more." Jake reluctantly moved away to one of the few broken pillars that littered the chamber and sat down on the stone. "Perhaps it can help us figure out what's happening to us."

She sighed. It was so humiliating to talk about Hiram and his death. But Jake was right. Her mortification was a small price to pay for her escape and her life. She stared at the handsome man she hadn't known just a day before. Though he was little more than a stranger, she knew he wouldn't judge her on Hiram's indiscretions. He wouldn't mock her.

With that thought relieving her, she began to tell her tale. "Hiram and I were married a few years ago. We had a good marriage, even though we had little in common but our love for the Egyptian culture and history. I was more than happy to relocate from London to Cairo. And although I wasn't allowed to join him on his digs, I enjoyed the tales he told me and the artifacts I was allowed to research after his return."

Jake nodded, but she thought she saw a flash of jealousy darken his eyes to nearly midnight. Then it was gone and she was wondered if she'd imagined it. She must have. This man hardly knew her, surely he couldn't be jealous of her dead husband. Her eyes strayed down to his lap. Even if he was, he certainly didn't have anything to fret about. He was far superior to Hiram in so many ways.

"Something must have changed," he said quietly.

She shrugged and looked at the room around them. "Hiram came to this tomb. That's when everything changed. He was supposed to be away from Cairo for just two weeks. That stretched to a month with no word on his whereabouts. I was worried enough that I contacted the officials for the British Museum in Cairo. After reviewing the facts, they sent out a search party. Before they'd been gone for three days, they all returned to the city together. Apparently they met my husband and his crew along the road. Hiram scolded me for being such a worrying wife." She shivered. "But he was different right away."

"How?" Jake leaned forward with his elbows draped over his knees.

"He'd always taken his findings immediately to the Museum field offices in the past. We would do our examinations there and properly catalog the relics. This time, he illegally smuggled artifacts into our home. He was secretive and distracted. He went out at all times of night without explanation. And in our bed—"

She swallowed as Jake's eyes widened. Was this something she really wanted to share?

"Go on." His voice was choked.

"H-Hiram had always been a courteous lover to me," she stammered with a fierce blush. "He treated sex like a business that had to be done and the sooner, the better. But when he returned, he was different. He was rough with me. Not hurting me, but like an animal. Like he hardly saw me at all."

Jake didn't say anything, but the look of rage on his face was plain. The idea of Hiram taking her like that obviously bothered him.

"He told me I was unsatisfactory in bed." Her voice caught on the embarrassment she still felt. "And his passions for me faded, which I admit, was not an entirely bad thing since he was growing more and more aggressive. He began to find his pleasure elsewhere, and made no effort to hide it."

"He publicly cuckolded you?"

She hesitated a long, awful moment before she managed one short nod. "I caught him being pleasured by a parlor maid in my own bedchamber. When he saw me standing there, too shocked to say a word, all he did was tell me to shut the door."

Jake murmured a curse beneath his breath.

"Later, at a party at the Ambassador's mansion, he snuck off with the ambassador's wife. I went searching for him with some of the museum staff and we found him tied to a bed, with her riding him. Word of that indiscretion went all the way back to London and he nearly lost his job. I was utterly humiliated, yet nothing I said or did impressed upon him the seriousness of the situation. He was risking both our marriage and his career with his out of control behavior."

"And apparently, his life," Jake muttered, though his eyes never left hers.

She shivered. "Yes, apparently."

She drew in a shaky breath and readied herself to continue with the last and most humiliating part of her story. "The night he died, he told me I should find a less demanding lover to fulfill my small needs because he no longer intended to waste his pleasure on a woman too cold to enjoy it fully. He left our house and went to buy two Egyptian whores. He died in their arms before morning. The doctor said something about his heart giving way, though he'd never had any troubles with his health before."

Jake flinched. "Your husband was an idiot not to see what a passionate creature you are. The fact that you weren't enough for him speaks volumes about his lack of taste."

She couldn't help a smile at his defense. It warmed her heart after so many embarrassing months alone. "I appreciate that."

"So what made you decide his personality changes had to do with this tomb?" he asked. "I mean, a woman like you, one who's dedicated to scientific explanation, would surely explore other options before organizing an expedition and heading out for a dangerous trek across the desert to a place like this."

"Yes." Her heart lightened as she winked. "You never know what kind of scoundrels might be waiting for you in abandoned tombs."

He laughed and the rich, deep sound touched some part of her. It made her tingle with sexual energy, but there was something more. In all the years of her marriage, Hiram had never listened to her with the kind of focused attention Jake used. He'd never watched her every move, hung on her every word. Laughed at her jokes.

"So what did make you come?" he asked, neatly interrupting her troubling thoughts.

"When the circumstances of his death came to light in public, the officials at the museum came to raid the house. They found all kinds of items from this tomb. His name was pulled through the dirt in our professional circles. He was called a robber and—" She paused apologetically. "And a tomb raider. When I began to clean up the mess from their search, I found Hiram's diary. It detailed his trip to Merytsat's tomb. And I also found something else. An artifact he'd hidden so well that the museum hadn't found it. He talked about it endlessly in entry after entry in his book. He said he was drawn to it, obsessed with it. So I took the artifact and came here, hoping to find out more."

She sighed as she finished her story.

Jake rose from the shattered pillar. "You have the artifact with you now?"

She nodded and grabbed her bag. Reaching in, she wrapped her hand around the piece and felt its power throb through her, just as she had every time she touched it.

"Yes." With a sigh, she pulled the item from her bag and held it out to him.

He gasped as he stared at it. A stone phallus, perfectly carved to mimic a man's fully erect member.

Chapter Four

Jake had visited many foreign lands on his archeological digs. He'd seen sex toys of all kinds both in person and in pictures. Still, the sight of Isabella holding the stone dildo took his breath away.

What made the piece special were the delicate carvings etched with painstaking detail on every side of the stone shaft. Engravings of Merytsat, whore of a pharaoh, bringing herself pleasure. It was evident she had been as talented at that as she'd been rumored to be with the men of her time.

Reaching out, he ran his hand along it and was greeted by a rush of erotic energy. Had it come from the sexual power that snapped between Isabella and him, or the toy itself? He wasn't sure. He did know he was beginning to feel that low ache in his belly. The one that told him he was going to lose control and need Isabella again.

Her eyes gleamed as she looked up at him. Her wants were clear there. Hot desires, the kind her husband had been unable to spark in her.

That thought gave him more pleasure than was healthy.

"You believe finding this artifact was what made your husband so out of control?" he asked, his voice rough as he tried to rein in his body.

She nodded slowly. "A bit like us, don't you think?"

He continued to stare at the dildo, wondering if it could possibly be true. Could something such as this make a man mad with desire? So out of control that he would kill himself with sex?

She blushed. "I-I know it looks like a...a..."

"A cock," he supplied, watching the flush of her skin darken in the dim glow of the torches. "Fully erect and ready to service a woman in heat."

He knew that was unnecessary, but watching Isabella's nipples tighten beneath her shirt was worth the crude words.

"Yes." She smiled, the look a little feline and full of lusty power. "If you're wondering, you stack up nicely against it."

He grinned despite the shot of almost painful pleasure that worked through him all the way to the twitching head of his cock. "Thanks."

She shook her head, trying to clear it. Jake knew it wasn't going to be that easy. Once they started down this road of lust, it didn't seem like it was possible to go back. One thing would eventually lead to another and they'd be joined, experiencing the power of each other's touch.

He ached just thinking about it.

She let him hold the phallus as she turned her back to look around the large, open room. "I've been studying ancient artifacts for years, even before my marriage, but I've never seen anything like it. Perhaps that's why it draws me."

He nodded, though she couldn't see him. Sure. That was why the hard thrust of a stone cock enthralled her. The novelty. Still, if that made her feel better, he wasn't going to debate the point.

He examined the sex toy carefully. "I've read about the sexual customs of the Egyptians, but I admit, I've never seen anything like this, either."

She turned, but avoided his eyes. "What—" She licked her lips. "What do you think it was used for?"

Jake reeled back. This woman who had straddled his eager tongue while she sucked him to oblivion...the same woman who had watched a threesome and allowed him to fuck her until he was nearly comatose...she didn't understand what a woman in any time would do with an object such as this?

He was more than happy to show her.

Taking a step forward, he invaded her personal space. "You can't guess?"

She drew in a harsh breath, but shook her head slowly.

Jake dropped to his knees on the sandy floor, taking his time so he could watch every inch of her. She made a soft sound of pleasure in the back of her throat and it nearly unmanned him. Using the stone phallus, he stroked along her leg, still wrapped in the heavy cotton of her long skirt. With his other hand, he inched the fabric up and up, revealing her soft, pale skin to the firelight.

"Jake," she breathed and dropped her head back as she gripped his shoulders with both hands for support.

He leaned forward and blew a hot burst of air through her skirt, right at the apex of her thighs. Her knees buckled and he caught her with one hand to ease her to a sitting position on one of the broken pillars behind her.

"Relax," he said softly as he pushed her skirt all the way up. She splayed out before him, spread wide for his greedy eyes. He could have done anything his heart desired and the power of that increased his passion tenfold.

Gliding the stone artifact up her inner thigh, he measured his breathing. He wanted to be careful, slow and let her get all the pleasure she deserved, especially after she'd been forced to admit her darkest and most embarrassing secrets. He knew her candidness about Hiram had cost her.

He pushed her outer lips apart to reveal her sex. It gleamed in the light, wet with a combination of the juices he'd spent in her earlier and the ones made by her own desire when he touched her.

"This is what the ancient Egyptians used to do with these," he whispered. "What modern women still do in the privacy of their bedchambers and for the pleasure of their men."

With that, he stroked the stone phallus across her slit. She responded by lifting her hips with a sharp cry.

"Cold?" he asked as he watched her slick skin darken with increased desire.

"A little," she gasped. "But good, so good."

"You could tease yourself with this like I just did," he said as he breathed in her womanly scent. "Or if you get it wet, you could put it inside you like you would a man's cock. Either way, you could pleasure yourself with it. But judging from what you told me about her, I'd wager Merytsat pleasured both herself *and* her lovers with it."

"How?" she asked breathlessly, keeping her head dipped back as he stroked her.

"By letting them watch while she did this."

"They watched?" Her voice wavered and he was surprised that her skin had flushed even deeper. Apparently he had touched on one of Isabella's own hidden fantasies.

With a nod, he stroked her again. His excitement ratcheted up each time he fondled her. "Or by letting them please her with it as I'm doing to you now."

"It arouses you to do this to me?" she panted as her fingers curled around the edge of the pillar, clutching for a hold as she fought to keep her orgasm at bay for as long as possible.

"More than I could tell you," he answered, just inching the head of the phallus inside her. When he pulled it back out, it was dark with wetness. "She might have also let him use it on her while he was inside her. Kind of like making love to two men while remaining true to one."

She shivered and he knew she was thinking of what they'd witnessed between Surai, Rafe and Anya earlier. Her body contracted around the sex toy, trembling wildly as she danced on the edge of her explosion.

"Jake."

He looked up into her face to find her staring down at him. Her eyes shone as she glided her hand down to cup his cheek. The gentle gesture, so kind and loving when he knew she was feeling the burning heat of an orgasm, threw him off guard. His own reaction shocked him all the more.

Even in the midst of his lust-addled responses, her touch brought something even stronger to the forefront of his mind. A burst of tender emotion he'd never felt for a woman before, for anyone before. It was so powerful that he rocked back away from her, withdrawing the dildo and pulling away from her caress.

"Jake?" she repeated, her hand still outstretched as her expression changed to one of confusion. "Is everything all right?"

His fist contracted around the stone phallus and his heart raced. Was this some new trick of the tomb? These feelings, these wants that had nothing to do with sex? If they were, then why didn't they feel like a manipulation? Why did they feel so real?

"Jake?" Isabella's voice was filled with real concern and her eyes sparkled with more than just lust.

"Nothing," he stammered as he leaned back toward her.

With a relieved smile, she reached to cup his cheek again, but he dodged her. Instead, he took her hand and guided it to her breast, encouraging her to touch herself while he finished what he'd begun.

He pressed the dildo back against her clit and she let out a soft cry, one that made his cock ache and his heart swell with those strange emotions again. The complications he didn't need and hadn't wanted until that very moment.

Jake shut his eyes. This was only desire. Nothing more. He would give Isabella release. He would make her scream out his name, but he couldn't give her a piece of his life or his heart.

With that intent, he ground the head of the stone phallus against her clit. She clutched at her breasts with a keening cry then shuddered uncontrollably as she came. Jake watched her face as she moved through ultimate pleasure into relaxed satiation. She was so beautiful, so pure despite all the carnal pleasures they'd shared since being trapped together.

She let out a long sigh of satisfaction, then gave him a sensual smile. "Why don't you come down here?" she whispered on a short breath. "I want to feel you inside me."

How he wanted that, too, but his feelings were too raw, too close to the surface. He was afraid if he let her take him into her arms, he would do or say something stupid. Something he couldn't take back. Something that could only hurt them both once they'd escaped the tomb and the curse was lifted.

"No," he muttered as he pushed to his feet and shoved the damp sex toy into her hand.

She took it with a jump of surprise and slowly rose, smoothing her skirts down as she did so.

"What's wrong?"

"We-we don't have time for this," he muttered. Even as he said it, he knew it sounded like a cold lie. After all, he had been the one who'd stalled them when their friends had disappeared. But he could think of no other excuse when his body was still pounding hot and his mind was running scared. "We should look for the others. Come on."

With that, he grabbed a torch off the wall and motioned to the corridor. Even though he didn't look behind him, he felt her follow him.

He also felt confusion and hurt emanating from her, but he couldn't bring himself to comfort her. If he did, he knew he wouldn't be able to escape the strong feelings that had begun in his heart. A place no woman had ever touched.

⁂

Isabella fought tears as she stumbled along the dark corridor behind Jake. She could only just see him in the circle of light from his torch and he seemed in no mood to wait for her. He didn't want to talk, either. When she tried, his response had been mere grunts.

What had happened to change his attitude? They'd been so close to making love. Her body still throbbed with the incessant need to have him inside her. Yet his face had twisted with…what was it? Horror? Fear? Disgust?

He'd pulled away, leaving her empty in more ways than one.She hated herself for it. Hated herself for coming to need this man in such a short period of time. She'd depended on a man before and he'd let her down. Hiram had promised to be there for her, but in the end he'd tossed her aside like so much refuse. A man like Jake could be no different. In fact, he had to be worse. He was a scoundrel. A tomb raider. A seducer of women.

She looked up the corridor at his broad back. It was so much easier to think of his unappealing qualities when she wasn't looking into his eyes. Now if only she could believe her condemnations in her heart.

With a sigh, she hurried forward to keep up with his long strides. She'd almost reached him when a noise echoed in the corridor around her.

The moan again. That rich, feminine moan that seemed to come from nowhere and everywhere all at once. The one that had her dripping wet in an instant, longing to be touched. To be filled to the hilt by a man. And not just any man. By Jake.

"Did you hear that?" she called out in the darkness.

His sigh echoed back toward her. "Hear what?"

"The moan." She stopped in the pathway and closed her eyes. It came in the distance again. "There it was."

"I didn't hear it," he insisted as he glanced over his shoulder at her. Just as quickly, he looked away and her heart stung with rejection.

"Come on, maybe we should try this path."

She ignored him as she continued to listen intently. An undeniable urge to follow the sounds of passion persisted, even if Jake didn't want to listen. She shut her eyes and moved away from him. She found her way by hearing, sensing along the corridors with only her touch and ears to guide her.

The moans seemed to increase in intensity as she moved forward, pulling her toward something, making her body quiver with the anticipation of what that something might be.

This was madness. She knew it even as she followed the phantom groan. It was enough to make her believe Jake was right. This place was cursed. Haunted by the ghost of a concubine who had risen to the status of goddess.

Then, as quickly as they had begun, the sounds of pleasure faded away to nothing.

Her eyes fluttered open and she realized she'd entered another chamber in the tomb. It was large and open, lit by torches that couldn't have burned for so many hundreds of generations, but still glowed nonetheless. In the center of the room was a raised platform that held a large, square pool of water.

Moving closer, she climbed the first few steps of the platform. What she saw made her gasp and she stumbled over a missed step. The pool still held water, even after so many years beneath the dry sands. Even more outrageous was that the water was perfectly clean, as if the pool had been filled that very hour.

She looked down into the crystal waters at the cool marble that shone up from the depths. After so many hours of being trapped in the dusty tomb her muscles ached for a soak and her body screamed out to be washed.

"This is crazy," she murmured, but she found her hands moving up to her loosen bun as if by their own volition. One by one, she found the pearl pins that held her locks in place and her blonde hair fell in a fragrant wave around her face. Her scalp tingled as the air hit it, releasing the heat that had been pressed against her skin all day long.

"Isabella!" Jake's voice echoed just outside the chamber door.

She wanted to answer him, but the draw of the pool was a much stronger one. She *had* to climb into the water. She needed it more than she needed her next breath.

She unbuttoned her shirtwaist next and shimmied out of her skirt. Her mind emptied as she dipped a toe into the waters. They were cool on her sore feet and parched skin and she released a hiss of pleasure as she let her entire leg dip over the marble edge. When the juncture of her thighs hit the water, she nearly collapsed. It felt like the cool touch of a man's lips on her hot and throbbing body, but then the sensation was gone, snatched away as Jake had snatched away his body earlier.

"Isabella."

It was Jake's voice again, but this time he was inside the chamber. With effort, she turned her face toward the door and saw him as if she were looking through a fog. He stared at her, his mouth open just a fraction, but he no longer called her name. It was as if he, too, was controlled by the powerful forces in the chamber and could only watch her.

She lounged back against the smooth marble, enjoying the feel of her hot skin cooling in the lukewarm waters. She let her head dip under the surface, slicking her hair back as she emerged for a gulp of air.

Isabella began to smooth her hands over her skin. Even without soap, she was able to wipe some of the sandy grime from her body. She smoothed over her arms, her face, and finally her fingers brushed over her breasts.

Her nipples hardened to the touch, throbbing until she couldn't resist another swipe over them. The water allowed for no friction, just the glide of skin on skin. And the little beads seemed even more sensitive than usual, puckered from being suckled and rubbed so many times by a man's hands.

Leaning back against the marble, Isabella shut her eyes and simply caressed her own skin, imagining a lover's hands drifting over her, lazily arousing her in preparation for lovemaking.

She pictured her imaginary lover's body, hard from years of work, sculpted by muscle and strong, yet gentle. Then she pictured his face. Jake's image danced into her mind.

At the same time, she heard him take a sharp breath from the chamber door. When she looked at him, he had gripped his hands into fists at his sides. The jut of his cock was perfectly outlined on the front of his fitted beige trousers and his eyes were focused on her. Watching intently as she glided her hands over her breasts and tugged at her nipples.

She started at the look of desire on his face, sending a splash of water over the edge of the tub to slap against her bag. With a curse, she leaned over the marble edge and snatched it up. She reached inside to insure nothing important had gotten soaked and her hand found the stone dildo.

When her fingers clutched at the stone, that same thrill rushed through her. A thrill of desire, of sensual power. Of need. She let the bag fall and pulled the phallus into the tub with her.

She wondered what it would feel like to plunge this into her body. Jake had only teased her, refusing to enter her with it or with his own cock. It had left her aching and curious. And not just about the feel of the toy. When he'd told her about what women did to pleasure themselves and their men with objects such as this, it had given her a burst of sexual curiosity. Especially the idea of a man watching his woman pleasure herself with the stone phallus.

With a smoldering glance for Jake, she let the sex toy dip under the water. When she rubbed the unyielding stone against her stomach, her body crackled with awareness and need. She rasped it against her nipples and couldn't hold back the sigh that escaped her lips.

Across the room, Jake groaned. A surge of power moved through her. She was torturing him just as he'd tortured her earlier. He wanted her, but couldn't have her. And while she brought herself pleasure, she would also be bringing him to a fever pitch of desire.

She spread her legs wide and teased the head of the phallus along her inner thigh and up across her opening. Her sigh turned to a moan as she brushed along her clitoris. It swelled beneath the touch, hardened to exquisite sensitivity. She knew just a few strokes would bring her to completion, so she only teased herself with it. She rubbed the phallas along her outer lips, spreading herself with its head. When her fingertips brushed her slit, she was slick with desire.

Her hand seemed to move of its own volition now, swiping up and down, rolling along her clit just enough that she cried out with ecstasy, then backing away before she could find release.

Knowing Jake was in the room, panting out breaths in time with her, only made her desire more potent. Her need to come all the more intense. When she was writhing, sending bath water sloshing over the edge of the pool with a smooth rhythm, she plunged the stone cock into her body. She exploded around it, wailing and thrusting wildly as her orgasm consumed her, overtook her, so strong that it nearly made her lose consciousness.

She released the sex toy with a sigh as she slumped against the side of the pool, but didn't withdraw it from her body. She liked the way its unyielding hardness felt inside her.

Shutting her eyes, she let herself relax for a moment. She blocked out her worries about Anya and the others. Forgot her obsession with the truth about Hiram. And most of all, pushed away thoughts of Jake Turner and the fact that the pleasure he had brought her with his body far eclipsed anything she'd ever given herself.

꙳ঌ৻৻৩৶ৣ৵৵

Jake's body hummed with need. It coursed through every nerve, every fiber of his being, at once insanely erotic and intensely painful. He'd never wanted a woman more, but something in the room, something in the air kept him from taking her. He was forced to watch, motionless, as she pleasured herself with the ancient sex toy.

God, how he wanted to touch her. To fill her. But those other emotions, the ones that had sent him reeling, were still present. If anything, watching as she arched up in the pool of water just out of his reach only made those emotions stronger. He wanted to be inside her, but not just for his own pleasure. He wanted to give. To be the one that made her writhe like that, and the one who set her free from the fever of passion. After she shivered in release, he wanted to be the one who held her.

His mind spun. He'd pushed her away because of those deeper desires, but now it was as if the tomb was calling him back, forcing him to see what he would lose if he didn't face his emotions.

Isabella cried out as she came, thrashing water over the floor around the elevated pool before she slumped back against the marble.

Jake's cock throbbed in time with her gasps, pressing against his trouser front, but still he couldn't find the ability to move, neither to walk away nor give in to what his heart and body wanted most and join her.

Her eyes fluttered open. Unlike earlier, when she hadn't seemed to truly see him, they were clear now. Filled with questions, as well as needs.

She sat up straighter and locked gazes with him. Her voice was husky, sultry, when she asked, "Like what you see, Mr. Turner?"

The sound of her voice shattered the spell that had restrained him. He took one step toward her as her gaze moved over every inch of him with clear intent. She wanted him as much as he wanted to be inside of her.

But her expression also reflected another emotion. The same emotion he'd seen and felt when she had caressed his face before. It told him she could curl into his life forever, if only he'd ask.

Even more stunning was that he could see himself asking for just that. He had a brief, but clear image of comforting her, learning about her life the way he'd learned the needs of her body.

"Are you going to just look?" she asked, then slowly rose from the water like a goddess.

The dark blonde strands of her hair curled around her wet breasts, framing the pale skin and making the pink circles of her nipples even more pronounced and beautiful in the torchlight. Water droplets rolled down her skin, cresting over the hills of her curves and dipping into valleys that Jake longed to taste. He wanted to lick her dry, then caress her until she was sopping wet again.

She smiled as if she'd read his mind, then snaked her hands down between her legs. He watched wide-eyed as she eased the stone sex toy out of her body and set it on the edge of the marble tub. "Or perhaps you want to join me?"

He realized he now had a choice. He could run again. If he did, he had no doubt Isabella would fight the influence of the tomb as hard as he had, to keep her heart from being broken.

Or he could go to her. He could take everything she offered, from her lush body to her fragile heart.

But he had to choose now.

He didn't say a word, just shucked off his boots and clothes as fast as he could. He stepped into the water and for a moment was distracted by how good the cool sensation was against his overheated skin.

"That's right," she whispered, moving over to his side. She placed a hand on each shoulder and gently shoved him to a sitting position. "Relax. I'll wash you off."

She straddled his body and he reached for her, eager to enter her, to claim her. But she pushed him back.

"We're trapped," she said with a wry smile. "We've got all the time in the world. Let's enjoy it."

He bit back a moan as her hands began to slide down his body. She moved slowly, almost reverently, rubbing over his arms, his sides. She shifted closer until he could feel the entrance to her body rubbing against the head of his erection, but she didn't take him inside as she continued to touch him. He couldn't remember when a woman had spent so much time focused on his pleasure and his pleasure alone.

She glided her palms down the muscles of his chest, tangling her fingers in the soft hair before she flicked a thumb across his nipple.

His penis twitched against her in reaction. For a brief moment, she shut her eyes on a moan, then smiled. "You like that, do you?"

"I do." He lifted his hips until he brushed her slit again. "And I like that, too."

"So do I," she groaned. "But I'm not finished yet."

Her hands continued to move, spending time caressing his nipples, then moving down his stomach. She paused when she brushed against the scar that traversed his side.

"What is this from?"

He opened his eyes and gazed up at the ceiling high above. If he was truly surrendering to the effects of the tomb, to the effects of Isabella, he would have to give her some of his past. To his surprise, the reality of that wasn't as terrifying as he'd thought it would be.

"A dispute over rights to a tomb. Two years ago." He smiled. "You should have seen the other guy."

"How long have you been raiding tombs?" she asked as she adjusted her position and began to stroke her fingers along his legs. He stiffened when her hand closed briefly around the length of his cock.

"Five years," he said with effort.

"And do you enjoy your 'work'?" she asked, rubbing her wetness against him once more.

He locked gazes with her. "Some days more than others."

"What do you do with the antiquities you find and steal from the tombs?" she asked softly as she let the head of his cock enter her. He longed to surge all the way inside, but held back. She flexed her inner muscles around him, squeezing him rhythmically until she elicited an unbidden groan.

"What do you do with what you take?" she repeated.

"I sell some to museums or private collectors," he ground out as she let him slip into her another few, precious centimeters. "And some I donate."

She paused. "You donate?"

"Yes." He tilted his hips and she slid onto him even further.

Her gasp was a reward, as was the way she latched her legs around his waist.

"Why?" she asked, though her voice trembled.

"Why what?" He struggled to maintain his thoughts now that she had taken him into her almost to the hilt. Only a few more inches and he would be home.

"Why do you donate the things you find?" she asked. "I thought tomb raiders were motivated by the money they could make."

He shrugged as he glided his hands around to cup her rear end. The motion slid her forward and he filled her completely. A long groan issued from some deep, primal place inside him.

"Some treasures were meant to be shared," he whispered as he dipped his head to lap her nipple. She arched back and ground against him, whimpering in need.

Her reaction threw him over an edge and he responded by thrusting into her. The water allowed him leverage and a range of motion he didn't normally have. He stood up to wade into the deeper waters. He pushed her hips away, then yanked them back, using her to thrust as he pressed his mouth to hers.

She told him the rhythm she wanted by plunging her tongue into his mouth. She thrust slowly, pushing her tongue between his lips in soft time. But as her excitement grew, her mouth's movements grew quicker, more erratic. Jake kept up, taking her fast and hard as the water sloshed around them.

He loved every whimper, every moan she breathed against his skin.

Loved that he was giving everything he had to bring her pleasure. The fact that he wanted to give her more no longer terrified him.

He cupped her chin with one hand and tilted her face until she looked into his eyes. Searching, he slowed his rhythm, gentled his pace. Her eyes clouded with tears, but he knew they weren't tears of pain. He had reached her in that most emotional place, the center of her heart.

With a smile, he slid a hand between their wet bodies and found the hard nub of her clitoris. With a sweep of his finger and thumb, he drove her over the edge. Her legs latched around his waist like a vice and her spine straightened, lifting her up and against him as she cried out her pleasure and her release.

He tried to hold back, wanting more than anything to maintain control. To keep tormenting her until she came again and again, but the look of pure pleasure and the joyful tears that cascaded down her cheeks did him in. He dug his fingers into her backside and poured himself into her.

As they'd stood, locked together for what seemed like a blissful eternity, she looked down into his eyes. When he grinned at her, she gave him a wicked smile that stirred his blood, then she slithered down his body until her feet touched the bottom of the marble pool. Leaning up, she gave him a gentle kiss.

"That was amazing," she whispered as her arms came around his waist and she rested her head against his chest.

Jake looked down at her, so comfortable leaning against him, and slowly let his arms come around her waist. It was amazing. And so was this woman.

Chapter Five

Isabella rested her head on Jake's shoulder as the water in the pool lapped against their bodies with a gentle rhythm. She dragged her fingernails down his arm and loved the way the muscles bunched beneath her hand and his body tensed with pleasure.

"Do you think we'll ever get out of here?" she asked softly. "Or are we trapped forever?"

Jake drew back so he could see her face. When he looked at her, she knew he saw her fear. Fear she wouldn't have shared with just anyone.

He caressed her back, and she leaned into him, gathering strength from his warm touch.

"I'll get you out of here, Isabella. You and your friends. I promise you that," he whispered, but the power of his statement was in his words, not the level of his voice.

She knew it was a promise he might not be able to keep, but hearing him say those words helped her nonetheless. Until Jake gave up entirely, she would keep looking for a way out, too.

"You know, if I had to be trapped in a tomb that might be cursed, I'm glad I was trapped with you."

He smiled. "Me too."

He captured her cheeks between his hands. His gaze was so intense, so full of emotion that it brought tears to her eyes.

When he finally leaned down to kiss her, the reaction was even more powerful. The kiss was deep, but not possessive, not filled with the overpowering lust that had always accompanied his touch in the past. No, this was comfort, this was...

Love?

What did she know about love? She'd never felt that kind of powerful emotion for anyone or had it returned, even in the best of her days with Hiram.

Yet there it was, swelling in her heart, filling her with equal measures of joy and terror. Perhaps she had imagined it in Jake's kiss, but she didn't imagine it in her own soul. Somehow lust wasn't all she felt when she looked at this man. She felt love.

"You okay?" he asked as he slipped a damp lock of hair behind her ear.

For a moment, Isabella struggled for words. This wasn't the time for confessions of such complicated feelings. Not while they were trapped. Not while the powers in the tomb held such sway over both of them. For all she knew, the new emotions were just part of the game Merytsat was playing with them.

Only they felt so real.

"I'm fine," she whispered as she leaned up for another kiss. "I'm fine."

With reluctance, Jake ended the kiss, though he kept her pressed flush against him in the water. "So, now do you believe this place is cursed?"

She shrugged. It seemed crazy to talk like this, but she couldn't lie either. Not to him.

"There are things happening here that can't be explained by science. Like the woman's moan that keeps guiding us to each room. Or this pool, which should be dry or filled with rancid liquid. Instead, it's clean and filled with water that could have been pulled from a spring today. Even after we've made love in it, bathed in it, it's still fresh."

He nodded. "When you wandered away a while ago, I thought I heard your voice, but it couldn't have been you. And when I came into this room, I couldn't do anything but watch while you pleasured yourself in the pool. It was as if something was forcing me to stay in place."

"It was the same for me," she sighed as she drew small circles on his back with her fingertips. "I wanted to look at you, to call to you, but some force drove me to Merytsat's artifact and made me play out my fantasies around it. And my fantasies about you watching me."

His smile was hot and filled with desire as his hand slipped beneath the water to caress her thigh for an all-too-brief moment.

"So, what kind of curse could it be?" he asked in a voice thick with the same passion she felt when he touched her. She admired him for continuing to focus on the problem at hand. From her own experience, she knew how difficult that was. "You're the expert between the two of us. What kind of curses do tombs like this one hold?"

She shrugged. "That's the trouble. There's not another place like this that anyone knows of. Normally, these elaborate burials were left to royalty, but Merytsat wasn't a queen. She was a common girl who raised herself up in society by using her body. She gave pleasure and demanded it in return. She brought one of the most powerful Pharaohs to his knees...literally if you believe some of the writings about her."

He pondered that for a moment. "The curses that are detailed and warned of for a member of the royal family are meant to protect the riches they buried with them. The gold and jewels were what was important to those people. That's what they wanted waiting for them when they reached their final destination after death."

She nodded, amazed by his grasp of Egyptian history. "Yes. That's what folklore tells us."

"So what if Merytsat's curse protected what *she* held dear?" He cocked an eyebrow toward her and motioned his head toward the stone dildo Isabella had rested on the tub's edge.

"Her sex toy?" she asked with an incredulous laugh.

"Not the toy itself. What it represents. Her sexual power. Her hunger. Her life force."

Isabella rose out of the water in surprise. Jake's hypothesis made perfect sense. If there were such a thing as a curse, the woman who was buried in this place wouldn't have cared about her riches. She'd care about the things that could bring her power.

And those were the exact things Hiram had taken with him when he'd removed the artifacts buried with Merytsat.

"You know, you're much more than just a pretty face," she teased as she climbed out of the water and grabbed for her shirtwaist. "You are very smart."

He grinned. "Well, I was educated, you know. I went to university."

She stopped dressing. "You did? What did you study?"

"Archeology," he said without a hint of teasing to his voice or his face.

"What?"

He gave her a sad, fleeting smile. "In Boston. My parents wanted me to pursue medicine, but history and archeology enthralled me."

"You have a degree, but you raid tombs?" she asked with a shake of her head. "Isn't there a more official post you could take with a university or museum?"

His face tensed. "I went to university, but I don't have a degree."

She buttoned her shirtwaist before she sat down on the edge of the pool. She'd never seen Jake's emotions so clear on his face before. Anger, betrayal, but mostly hurt. Whatever had happened to keep him from completing his education was still a raw spot. And it inspired a need to comfort in her.

"What happened?" she asked.

His mouth thinned and his hands gripped into fists as they rested on the marble. "In my last year, I wrote a paper about my theories on the building of the pyramids. I proposed a field expedition to study my theory which was to be overseen by my mentor, Dr. Phillip Grasier, but conducted by me. Grasier read over my work and told me flat out that my ideas were incorrect and if I turned in the proposal I'd be laughed out of the university. I disagreed, but I appreciated his attempts to protect me."

The blood drained from Isabella's face. "But Phillip Grasier…"

"Did an extensive field study of the building of the pyramids five years ago, putting forth some new theories about how they were built." Jake's voice was harsh and tight, as if he were forcing the words past his lips. "When I found out he had put forth a proposal to the committee and what that proposal contained, I confronted him. He'd been my friend and mentor for four years and I couldn't believe he would really steal my ideas, my work from me. But Grasier not only told me I wasn't welcome on his expedition, he put me on academic probation. When I protested, he had me kicked out of school and put such a stain on my record that I wasn't allowed to finish my degree anywhere else."

"Oh, Jake," she whispered as she covered his hand with her own. He was still naked, powerful like the statues of gods she'd seen so many times. Yet he was a man. And there was more to him than she'd let herself believe. Much, much more.

"Is that why you became a tomb raider?" she asked, wiping a line of water from his cheek.

He nodded. "No one would let me work anywhere legitimately, but I didn't want a man like Grasier to take away what I'd dreamed of for so long. I wouldn't let him."

She blinked back sudden tears as she looked down into the face of this man who had been such a distraction and a savior to her since they'd met. She had judged him for the job he did, the job that so went against her academic sensibilities. But all along he'd only been trying to find a way to do the thing they both loved. The thing neither was allowed to do because of society. Her for being a woman, him for his lack of credentials. For the greedy robbery of a man he had revered and trusted.

"You and I are more alike than I ever thought possible," she whispered before she leaned down to brush a kiss along his jaw line. "And I believe that if any two people can figure out what's going on in this tomb, it's you and me."

"Are you saying you want to be partners with a dirty American grave robber?" he asked with a teasing smile, but in his eyes she saw the real need to hear her answer.

"More than anything."

She kissed him, pulling away only when the spark of lust between them began to grow again. As much as she wanted to sink back down into the water and worship his body, she knew their time was running short. They still had no idea where their friends were or what they were going through. They needed to find a way out.

"The key is finding Merytsat's burial chamber," Isabella said, breathless as she went back to dressing, fingers fumbling with the task. "If there was a curse put on this tomb, that's where we'll find the details of it. And maybe be able to figure out how to break it."

He grinned, a crooked smile that made him look younger and less harsh. A smile that touched her in those deep places in her heart she'd believed had gone cold.

"Where my lady leads, I shall follow."

He rose out of the tub in one smooth motion. Droplets of water cruised down his naked body and she had to force herself to look away as he dressed. It was far too tempting to push him back into the water and have her wicked way with him again.

As he buttoned the last button on his shirt, he smiled at her. "Or actually, I'll lead since I have the gun. But you get the point."

She laughed as he pulled a torch from the wall and followed him from the chamber and into the darkness of the hallways once again.

"How long have we been walking?"

Jake scrubbed a hand over his face. "Time is hard to judge here, but I'd guess about an hour."

Silence came from behind him and he didn't even have to look at Isabella. He knew he'd see the fear in her eyes and it was fear he couldn't ease. He'd promised to get her out of the tomb, but he didn't really know if that was possible.

"Should we stop to—"

She froze.

"Stop to what?" He finally turned to face her, hoping she meant stop to give into passion one more time. It was what he'd been aching to do for most of the last twenty minutes.

"Shhh." She held up a hand. "Do you hear it?"

He strained, hoping to hear Surai, Anya and Rafe. They needed all the people they could get to figure this riddle out, even if it meant interrupting their sex play. He went rock hard just thinking about it and willed himself to concentrate.

"There."

In the distance the low, needful moan floated through the corridors and sent a jolt straight to his cock. With a shiver of pure desire, he nodded. "I heard it. I think it came from this direction."

He motioned down one pathway and they followed it at a near run. When they'd gone a few steps, he felt Isabella move closer. Then her soft hand slipped into his. The shock of emotion that accompanied such a simple gesture surprised him. Just one touch from her and he was filled with desire, tenderness, but mostly pride. Her touch meant she trusted him to get her home. It meant she depended on him to keep her safe. Having her put that much faith in him was astounding and humbling.

He stopped and turned to her. The pride faded into the background, replaced by the lust that flared between them whenever they stopped for more than a moment.

Her eyes were soft in the torchlight. With the woman's moans echoing around them, Jake's desire filled him. He could tell Isabella was reacting similarly. Her chest lifted and fell on short breaths and her body swayed in his direction. He wanted her. Against the wall, on the floor, it didn't matter. He just wanted to be inside her.

He shook his head. "I think we're heading the right way."

"Yes. I want…well, I want to feel you inside of me. That seems to happen when she's trying to lead us somewhere." Isabella blushed.

"God, don't tell me what you want, sweetheart or we're not going to get very far," he groaned.

She nodded. "Just keep moving. Think about ugly things while we walk and maybe we can stave this off long enough to find what we're looking for. Then we can make love."

"Isabella!" His eyes grew wide with shock. He'd never expected her to say those words. Or expected it to be such a source of excitement for him.

"Okay, sorry," she stammered. "Ugly things. The sooty air of London."

"You think *soot* is going to tame my hard-on?" he asked as he dragged her down the hall. "All I think about is dirty and dirty makes me want to lay you down in the sand right here, right now—"

She made a strangled sound at the back of her throat. "Uh, war. War is ugly. You can't make something sexual out of war."

He sighed. Yes, he could. "There's a war raging inside of me right now. I'm fighting the urge to unsheathe my…saber."

"That's reaching a bit, isn't it?" she asked, but her voice was barely more than a squeak.

"Yeah, but you've got the image in your head, don't you?" He winked even though his erection was actually throbbing.

"Yes. The image in my head is of you and me—"

He let go of her hand to cover his ears. "Don't tell me. We're almost there and if you say one word I'm not going to be able to stop myself from ripping your clothes off and taking you."

"Wait," she said and the desire in her voice had faded a bit. "Wait, look at this doorway."

He shook away the image of Isabella stretched out naked and ready on one of the preparation tables in the chambers around them and stared where she was motioning wildly. It was a stone door, one of the first sealed chambers they'd found in their search. It had a painting on it, done in the same style as the erotic hieroglyphics in the first room where they'd made love. This one was a picture of a woman holding a dildo above her head. She wielded it like a sword.

"Merytsat's burial chamber," Jake breathed. He glanced at Isabella. She seemed mesmerized by the strong image, unable to do anything but stare up at the picture on the door. "Stand out of my way. I'll see if I can get it open."

She backed against the wall behind them. Jake was able to block her presence out for a moment while he dug into his bag and drew out a short stick. He slid it into the space around the door and pushed, hoping the leverage would assist him in getting it open. The door didn't budge.

"Can I help?" Isabella asked from behind him.

He shrugged. The extra weight couldn't hurt. "Just be careful."

She stepped into the circle of his arms, positioning herself in front of him. Her hands found a spot in the places where he didn't hold the wedge.

"Uh," he mumbled, suddenly finding concentration much more difficult with Isabella's scent filling his nostrils and her body heat permeating his clothing. "One, two, three…"

Before they even began to push against the door, it made a creaking noise and then rolled open. Without the wedge bearing their weight, Isabella and Jake fell backward into a pile. Isabella landed on top of him on her back, her legs splayed open. He couldn't help but imagining making love to her in this position.

Apparently, she thought of the same thing, for she pressed her backside against him with a little moan. He grabbed for her hips, pulling her up even more firmly against him. For a few moments, they lay that way, grinding against each other in slow circles that had him dancing on the edge of madness.

He was ready to hike up her skirt and just take what they both so obviously wanted when the throaty sound of a female laugh taunted them from the chamber they'd just opened. Both froze, then Isabella scrambled to her feet.

"Do-do you think she's...in...there?" she stammered and began to shiver.

Jake got up, ignoring the throbbing pain in his groin, and put an arm around her. "This isn't a ghost story," he reassured her softly. "We're going to be fine."

She nodded, but he could tell she was still scared. Hell, he was scared, even though he'd never admit it to anyone. They were about to go into the deepest chamber in the tomb. The chamber where Merytsat's body was buried. Where her presence would surely be the strongest.

They moved forward in tandem, with Isabella clinging to his arm. Inside, the chamber was dark.

"L-light the torches," she whispered.

He had to gently remove her fingers from their death grip on his shirt to do just that. When light softly filled the room and Jake's eyes had adjusted, he looked around. The space was enormous, as all burial chambers were. It was also filled with riches, things that the Ancient Egyptians believed Merytsat would want in her next life. Jewels and gold, tablets and exotic oils.

The sarcophagus sat in the middle of the room on a slightly elevated platform. Isabella moved toward it as if she were in a trance and gasped when she reached it.

"What is it?" Jake asked as he moved to her side, but he became immediately aware.

Egyptian sarcophagi almost always had the likeness of the person mummified within carved into the wood. This was no different. Merytsat stared up at them, her beautiful Egyptian face done up with colorful paints and beautiful carvings. But it was her body that was different. Instead of being memorialized in her finest gown, the artist who had done the concubine's coffin had carved her entirely naked. Only a few jewels adorned her body, including a dangling diamond that accentuated a swollen, aroused clitoris.

Isabella ran her hands down the carving. "She was beautiful. So exotic. So sensual."

Jake swallowed hard. What was sensual was watching her caress the carven image of a naked woman. He was distracted from their task by the lengthening of his penis. If he didn't have Isabella soon…

"Jake, look!"

He pushed back his desire and stared in the direction she pointed. A large statue sat a few feet away. It matched the hieroglyph that had guarded the door. A statue of Merytsat, her hands above her head, but the dildo that had been in her hand on the seal was missing.

Jake and Isabella stared at each other.

"The artifact," she breathed. "Hiram took it from the burial chamber. From the statue."

"Perhaps she wants it back," Jake offered as he examined the statue's face. Like the sarcophagus carving, it was done in exquisite detail. Merytsat had been extraordinarily beautiful, with a fierce warrior's face and a fine body.

"Perhaps." Isabella dug the stone sex toy from her bag and stepped forward. She looked up at the motionless, stone face. "Is that why you've trapped us here? Is that why Hiram died? Because he took this from you?"

She stood before the statue and lifted up on her tiptoes, but she couldn't quite reach Merytsat's empty hands.

"Want a boost?" Jake asked.

She nodded silently, stepping onto the hand he offered. She had perfect balance when he lifted her, and he had a great view up her skirt as she leaned up and slipped the stone phallus back into the hands of its rightful owner.

The moment the artifact was firmly attached, there was a huge crash in the distance. Once he'd lowered Isabella back to the floor, Jake spun on his heel to face the door. Had the tomb collapsed even further? Or had Merytsat shown them a way out?

"Look at this."

Isabella seemed oblivious to the noise that had rocked the tomb. She was on her knees on the dusty floor, wiping sand away from the foot of the statue with a little brush she'd produced from her bag.

"What is it?"

She smiled up at him, looking every bit the excited explorer. "It's the curse. It's Merytsat's curse." Taking a deep breath, she translated the words to English. "'Take my secrets, but not my power. Use them for love or...'" She faltered.

Jake frowned. "Use them for love or what?"

Her face was pale when she lifted it to his. "'Use them for love or suffer the consequences.'"

Chapter Six

A heavy silence hung in the air between them and for the first time, it wasn't because of desire. Isabella wondered what Jake could be thinking. Probably that the curse had killed one man in her life and he could be next.

But instead of turning away from the danger she posed to him, he took a few steps in her direction. Covering her hand with his, he gave her a squeeze.

"Your husband tried to steal Merytsat's power. Then he used that power in the wrong way. He could have come home and brought you enormous pleasure. He could have built your love with it. Instead, he grew greedy with lust. And it killed him."

She nodded slowly. "But do you think that returning the artifact will break whatever spell we've been under since we were trapped?"

Even as she asked the question, she wondered...did she really want that? If the spell was broken, that would be the end for them, wouldn't it? No more passionate encounters where their desires raged out of control. No more ravenous matings where caution was thrown to the wind. And if they escaped the tomb and returned to Cairo...no more Jake. The tomb raider certainly wouldn't want a permanent place in her staid life.

He let go of her hand, but continued to search her face intently. "Sure. It should, shouldn't it?"

By the wavering question in his tone, she knew he was asking her about more than her take on the tomb's curse. He was asking what she wanted. An answer she wasn't sure she had. But she knew she didn't want to let go of whatever had driven them together. She had to take a chance.

"Then why hasn't it?" she stammered with heat flooding her

cheeks. "At least not for me."

Jake's eyes widened. "What do you mean?"

"I-I-" she struggled for words. How could she explain that she'd fallen in love with him? How could she tell him the feelings she had were real? There was no way he would believe her.

"Are you saying you still want to be with me?" he asked softly when she didn't answer him.

She squeezed her eyes shut to ward off the tears that pricked her. With a little shiver, she nodded. "Yes, I still want you. And it's more than just wanting you. I have—I have powerful feelings for you."

She heard him draw in a sharp breath. Drawing one of her own, she forced her chin up to meet his gaze. She had to be strong. And honest. If he turned her away, at least she could live the rest of her life knowing she'd given herself the best chance possible at love.

"But perhaps those feelings are just a trick of the tomb, too. After all, how can a person fall in love in such a short time?" she whispered, then held her breath for his reaction.

Unlike when he'd confessed his professor's betrayal, Jake's emotions were cloaked. All he did was search her eyes with a gaze so piercing she was sure he saw everything she'd ever felt and done from the time she was a girl.

"You think your feelings and desires are still a trick of the tomb, even though we've returned Merytsat's stolen artifact?" he asked in an even, unemotional tone.

She shrugged. "Perhaps."

"Let me ask you something. Do you want me right now?"

With her body trembling, she looked him up and down. Her breath hitched at just the sight of him in his rumpled clothing, wet dark hair, startling eyes and the body that had pleasured her in so many ways. "Oh God, yes."

He smiled and the expression relaxed her a little. "But do you have to have me?"

"I-I don't understand," she stammered.

"I mean, under the curse you couldn't stop yourself from making love with me. Even when you knew you shouldn't, you had to. Do you feel that way now?"

She considered the answer, then shook her head. "No. I feel the same way I did when I first saw you. I want you, but I can fight it. The difference is now I don't want to fight it. I just want you."

"So the curse no longer forces your body to follow its every desire," he said.

"No. It doesn't."

He took a step closer and reached out to cup her cheek. Isabella let out her breath in a low hiss as pleasure spread from his fingertips throughout her body. Pleasure and powerful emotion. How would she go on if he didn't return her love?

"Then doesn't it make sense that if the tomb no longer controls your desire that it no longer controls your heart? If your desire is real, doesn't that mean that your love is real, too?" His face swayed ever closer to her own, but he didn't kiss her.

Her bottom lip quivered as she nodded. "Yes."

"Because my love for you is real." With his opposite hand, he caught her waist and pulled her closer until she molded against his body.

Her knees shook as his words sank in. "You love me?" she whispered as tears began to fall down her cheeks. "Did you tell me that you love me?"

"I love you," he repeated slowly as he finally let his lips touch hers.

For a moment the kiss was gentle, filled with the love they both felt and the joy that rushed through Isabella as she realized her feelings were not only real, but returned. Then the passion and desire began to build, only this time, those drives weren't overpowering. For the first time, she knew she could pull back if she chose. Only she didn't want to pull back. She wanted to give this man her body, her heart, her everything. Forever.

He pulled away reluctantly. "We should find the others," he whispered in a harsh, desire-filled tone.

With a small smile, she shook her head. "No," she murmured as she took his hands and led him back through Merytsat's burial chamber toward the preparation table behind the sarcophagus and statues. "I don't want to find the others just yet. I want you. Without a curse. Without fear. Just you and me. As if it's our first time."

She backed up until her rear end pressed against the table, then released his hands to hoist herself up on the ancient stone surface. The table was the perfect height. She wrapped her legs around his waist and felt the heat of his erection against her core.

"The first time?" he repeated.

"Yes. Because it's like the first time for us." Slowly, she began to unbutton his shirt. "The first time where making love is just between you and me. The first time *she*—" Isabella motioned her head toward Merytsat's statue. "Has nothing to do with it."

Slipping her hands against the warmth of Jake's chest, Isabella let out a little sigh. Touching him was like coming home again, a home she never wanted to leave. And she wanted more. She wanted it all.

Whatever resistance he'd had melted away as he leaned into her and clutched her closer. She shoved the shirt off his shoulders and let it fall into the sand at his feet as he plundered her mouth with kisses that stunned and awakened her at the same time.

He pulled her to the edge of the table as he stroked his tongue into her mouth and began to inch her skirt up her leg with little slides. With every bit of skin he revealed, he caressed her with rough hands. By the time he had hitched her skirt up to her thighs, she was writhing with anticipation and need.

But before he touched her in the place that ached for him the most, he stopped and instead went to work on her shirt buttons. He met her eyes as he popped them open one by one, revealing more and more to him. It wasn't until he had her shirt entirely open that he actually looked down and took in the sight of her naked body.

"My God," he mumbled, almost more to himself than to her. "You are so beautiful."

She blushed like it was the first compliment a man had ever paid her. "It's the torchlight."

He shook his head as he bent to swirl the tip of his tongue around one taut nipple. "Torchlight." He sucked the little bead between his lips and suckled until she arched up with a cry. "Daylight." He switched his attention to her other breast while he kneaded the first with firm strokes of his palm. "Gas light. It doesn't matter. You would captivate me no matter where we were."

He glanced up when he made the last statement and Isabella drew in sharp breath. In his eyes she saw his love, as stark and pure as her own.

With a wobbly smile, she bent her head and took his lips as his hips collided with hers. Her moan was lost in his mouth as he released her breasts and instead let his fingers travel down her body between her legs. She broke the kiss as his hand cupped her sex, then he slid a finger inside.

"Yes," she hissed as her head dropped back against her shoulders.

He placed a hand against her belly and urged her to lie down as he continued to glide first one, then two fingers in and out of her in a gentle rhythm that soon had her bucking her hips in time. She actually felt her orgasm coming, building in some deep place inside her. It rose up and billowed as he added a thumb to her clit.

"Please, I want to feel you inside me when I come," she whispered as she braced herself back on her elbows to look up into his face.

He shucked his pants down in one smooth motion and before she could ask again, plunged his cock deep inside her. Immediately, she spasmed out an orgasm so intense it bordered on the thin line between pleasure and pain.

It was made even more powerful by the way he caught her hands and pulled her to a sitting position. He wrapped her arms around his neck so they were face to face, eye to eye. As he thrust into her with deep, long strokes, he never broke eye contact. Never stopped holding her. Even when she stiffened in release a second time. Even when his own face contorted into a mask of ultimate pleasure. He held her gaze steadily until the last of his essence had filled her, until her last tremor of pleasure had passed and then he kissed her, deep and gentle.

"I love you," he whispered against her lips.

She smiled. "And I love you."

"Mistress!" Anya's voice echoed in the hallway.

Isabella pressed another kiss against Jake's throat before she allowed him to pull away from her and begin dressing again.

In another time, she might have pushed him away like they were children being caught by a schoolmarm, but now she didn't care if her maid found her in such a compromising position. Not after all she'd seen, all she'd done and all she'd come to feel.

"Mistress!" her friend called again and this time her voice was much closer.

Isabella buttoned the last of her shirt and grinned as Jake put his warm hands around her waist and set her on the ground from her perch on the preparation table. As she smoothed her skirt one last time, she called out, "In here, Anya!"

In a burst of fluttering hands, dark hair and colorful gown, Anya flew into the room. She hardly looked at Jake as she hurtled herself into Isabella's arms and gave her a hug so tight that Isabella almost couldn't breathe.

"I'm so glad I found you!" her friend panted. "After everything that..." She blushed. "Happened."

Isabella smiled. "I don't think we have to talk about that. What happened in this tomb was meant to be." Jake's agreeing smile warmed her. "I regret nothing I saw or did or felt."

Her servant's face softened with relief. "Mistress," she said. "Light. We see light. We've found a way out of the tomb."

"Go then and tell Surai and Rafe that we're on our way," Isabella ordered as she slipped her hand into Jake's. Anya looked from her to him and her face slowly widened into a bright smile.

"Yes, I'll do that." Her friend scurried from the room.

Jake wrapped an arm around Isabella's waist as they headed for the chamber door and the corridor that led out of the tomb.

"I'm almost sorry to leave," she said as they took the last few steps out into the cool evening air of the desert.

He looked over his shoulder at the tomb, then back at her. "Well, we'll do things differently than Hiram did. We'll use what we saw and did here for love, so we'll always carry a bit of Merytsat's treasure inside us." She looked up at him with unhidden love and he returned that love freely. "Come on, Isabella. Let me take you home."

About the Author:

Jess Michaels' dreams of becoming a writer began in grade school. The voices in her head started muttering then and have muttered ever since, even when she tried to ignore them. Eventually, her husband encouraged her to listen to those characters that kept harassing her in her sleep and she has been writing ever since. You can find her at http://www.jessmichaels.com.

Ancient Pleasures is for Johanna, who made me send it. For my parents who instilled a deep love of the written word in me. And for Michael, who always believed...even when I didn't.

Manhunt

by Kimberly Dean

To My Reader:

Those of you who read my story *Wanted* in **Secrets Volume 9** must be thinking that I've got fugitives on the brain. Well, you're right. When I finished *Wanted*, questions kept running through my head. What if I turned everything around? What if this time, instead of a bad girl/good boy combination, it was the opposite? What if instead of one hunter, the whole world was after him? And what if nobody—absolutely nobody—was running? The answer to all my questions was *Manhunt*. I hope you enjoy it.

Chapter One

It was freezing! Taryn felt the bite in the air the moment she stepped out of the shower. Teeth clattering, she reached for her towel.

"The furnace." She sighed. With the fall air turning from crisp to bitter, she'd meant to turn it on, but with so many other, more important, things on her mind she'd forgotten. She was tending to do that a lot these days—forgetting things, letting things slide, not caring... Briskly, she rubbed the terrycloth over her skin, trying to generate some warmth. She felt cold from the inside out. Unfortunately, she knew that had little to do with the lack of heat in her house.

Betrayal could be bitter, too.

Water dripped from her hair, and she shuddered as it ran down her spine. She couldn't remember a worse day in her career. She'd told the Diazes that it wasn't necessary for them to show up at the arraignment, but they'd insisted. They'd wanted to look their son's accused killer in the face as he entered his plea. The entire family had sat in the front row, faces full of pain and fists clenched. Poor little Benny had looked like he could be sick all over his new tennis shoes at any moment.

She'd known how he felt.

Not guilty.

The words were still bouncing around in her head. They sounded right. They rang strong and true. It was what she'd wanted to believe, what she'd been desperate to believe when the accusations had first been made. Not guilty had been the only option...

Until the evidence had convinced her otherwise.

Not guilty. Now the words turned her stomach. She rubbed the towel almost viciously over her dripping hair. She hated drug dealers. Hated their cockiness, their power, their sliminess. They were among the vilest creatures she faced—especially those that targeted kids.

But this one...This one had been a coworker. And a friend.

Or so she'd thought.

Her shoulders slumped. She needed to forget about all that and accept that it was going to be a long, difficult trial. The only way she'd ever get through it was to distance herself emotionally. If she was going to be firm, decisive, and dispassionate, she had to pull back. Way back.

And she would, but tonight...Tonight she had to allow herself a little slack.

Dejectedly, she wrapped the towel around her body and opened the bathroom door. First thing, she was going to turn on that heat. Then she was going to curl up on the couch with a weepy romance novel and a glass of wine.

Maybe a bottle.

A cold whoosh of air hit her skin, and she shivered anew. It was like the Arctic. She stepped into the hallway, but stopped before she'd taken two steps.

The hallway was dark.

She knew she'd left the light on.

Her muscles tensed, but before she could move, an arm circled her waist. A scream leapt into her throat, but a hard hand covered her mouth. Her heart nearly exploded when she was pulled roughly against a big body hidden in the shadows.

"Hello, A.D.A. Swanson."

Fear swamped Taryn's system when she heard the low voice. It couldn't be. *It couldn't be!* She *knew* that voice.

Darkness magnified the danger. With a muffled cry, she began to fight. She clawed at her assailant's face and kicked out, aiming for anything she could hit. She heard a sudden expulsion of breath and felt a second's worth of success until the man hauled her closer. Hard hands circled her wrists and twisted her arms behind her. The position arched her back and flattened her breasts against the man's chest. Her fear took on an edge. He was all around her. His arms encircled her, his belly rubbed against hers, and his legs...They'd gotten tangled with hers during the short struggle.

The forced intimacy was almost sexual.

Unbidden, her nipples started to stiffen, and Taryn's conscience screamed at her. He was evil. Malevolent. Heartless. She knew the truth now.

She tried to squirm away, but his whipcord arms held her immobile. The ease with which he held her alarmed her. If he could subdue her this easily, he could do anything he wanted to her. Anything. His breath brushed her neck, and she flinched.

"You smell good," he growled against her ear. "Let's see how you look."

A whimper escaped her lips. This couldn't be happening!

He pushed her towards the bathroom. Moist air hit her back, and she trembled. *What was he doing here?* Her feet touched the linoleum floor, and she slipped when he unexpectedly let her go. He caught her before she could fall and, for the first time, she looked up into his eyes.

Michael Tucker.

Her heart began to pound double time. He wasn't supposed to be here. He was supposed to be in a holding cell!

She jerked when he reached out and touched her hair. She backed away quickly, but he followed and trapped her against the wall. He hovered over her, big and ruthless. Taryn shrank from him. They'd always been equals before. No more. Helplessly, she watched as he wound a blonde strand of her hair around his finger.

"I see why you always wear it up at work," he said. "You look like a sex kitten with it down."

She swallowed hard. He was trying to rattle her. She needed to concentrate and keep her senses about her. It was her only chance of coming out of this situation unharmed.

Or at least alive.

"What are you doing here, Tucker?"

One dark eyebrow rose. "Why am I not behind bars?"

She nodded slowly.

He stroked the soft tips of her hair against her chin. He watched the movement with an intense expression on his face. He seemed to be considering his own question as he moved the caress up to her lips. "I had a little problem with that plan, but nobody seemed to want to hear my side."

Goosebumps rose on Taryn's skin as he brushed her hair down to the pulse in her neck. The light caress was at sharp odds with the harshness in his voice. His touch might be gentle, but his temper was barely tamped.

"You had your day in court."

"Yeah, one of many to come, I'm sure." His dark gaze locked with hers. "You know what, Swanny? I'm still pissed about that."

Her stomach knotted. She'd never been afraid of Tucker before, but then again, she'd never seen this side of him. There was something about the tone of his voice and the bleakness in his eyes. He was angry—not just with the trial, but with her. "I'm an Assistant D.A.," she said cautiously. "I'm just doing my job."

"Just doing your job?" he repeated. His teasing caress stopped, and his hand fisted in her hair. "I expected a hell of a lot more than that out of you."

"More? I…I don't understand. I have to prosecute the case. What more do you want out of me?"

"A little thing called trust, Taryn," he said in a low voice. "Out of everyone, I expected *you* to have more faith in me."

The accusation hung in mid-air. Taryn stared in disbelief at the man she thought she'd known, the man she'd thought she'd *liked*. She couldn't believe he was turning this on her, trying to make her feel bad—and that it was working. He abruptly turned her loose, but she hugged the wall for support. Uneasily, she waited as he paced the tiny room.

He was wet, disheveled, and dirty. A day's growth of stubble covered his chin, and dark circles underlined his eyes. A too-small trench coat strained to span the breadth of his shoulders, but the dull gray material managed to cover most of the bright orange jumpsuit he wore. She didn't know where he'd gotten the coat, but it had obviously managed to hide him from detection. Her gaze dropped to his feet. His boots were wet. He'd shoved the pant legs of the jumpsuit into them to try to hide more of the jail uniform, but they, too, were wet and muddy.

"You've escaped."

His lips twitched. "You always were quick."

Taryn desperately tried to make sense of her predicament. The county lock-up was on the other side of the city. How had he managed to get all the way here, and why had he made this his destination? What did he have in mind? Revenge?

Oh, God.

She hadn't really known him at all, had she?

Her gaze flew to the bathroom door. If she ran, could he catch her?

Yes.

Tears burned in her eyes, but she fought to stay calm. He was bigger, stronger, and faster than she was. The only area where she matched him was brainpower. She couldn't allow herself to fall apart, couldn't let her emotions cripple her. She might not be in control of the situation, but she could keep control of herself.

She focused. Information was power. She needed to approach this situation like she approached a case. Logically. Straightforward. Observant for any loopholes.

She desperately needed to find a loophole.

"Why are you here?" she asked.

"To talk to you. Alone. Just the two of us."

She watched as he raked a hand through his thick, dark hair, rumpling it even further. He looked around the room, and she got the vague impression that he didn't know what his next move should be, that he was acting on instinct now—a hunted animal trying to avoid its pursuers.

It made him all the more dangerous.

"What are you doing?" she squeaked when he suddenly moved.

He looked up from his crouched position. "I'm grungy, stinky, and cold to the bone. I'm going to take a shower and see if I can get my head on straight."

A shower? He'd come all this way for a shower? Her focused mind started sliding down the slippery path towards panic.

Calm down, she told herself. If he got into the shower, she might have a chance to escape. A slim chance, but a chance nonetheless.

A rare smile crossed his lips. He pulled off a boot and dropped it onto the floor with a thud. "Here's some advice, Swanny. Never play poker. That angel face of yours gives away every single thought that runs through your mind."

He tugged off the other boot and began to peel off wet socks. "You're not going to bolt for the door when my back is turned. Know why? Because you're going to be in that shower with me. I'm not letting your sweet tush out of my sight."

Frozen, Taryn watched as the trench coat hit the floor. He reached for the zipper of the jumpsuit and any thought she might have had fled her mind as it slid downward. The bright orange material parted. With unwilling fascination, she watched as he shrugged it off his shoulders.

His chest was enough to make her mouth water. Muscles and sinew wove their way under smooth skin. She remembered his strength when he'd grabbed her, and her knees went a little weak. "Please, don't do this," she said softly. "If you leave now, I swear I won't tell anybody you were here."

"The moment I hit that door, you'd be on the phone."

She shook her head. "No, I wouldn't do that."

He stopped in the act of pushing the jumpsuit over his hips. The expression on his face was cold as he looked at her. "And why am I supposed to believe you'd be that generous? Because you like me?"

Her throat tightened. She'd like to think they'd been friends, but they both knew their relationship was more complicated than that. The stolen glances, the brushes of skin, the pounding heartbeats…She'd tried to keep things strictly professional between them, but something hot and wild had always lurked just below the surface. It had boiled over once…She pushed the heated memory from her mind. "I used to," she said quietly.

"Yeah? Well, I used to like you, too."

She looked at him closely, looking for any sign of the old Tucker—the whip-smart detective, the good-humored friend, the audacious flirt. She looked at the hard lines of his face and saw none of those people. All she saw was a big, angry man. A big, angry, *naked* man.

"Oh," she gasped.

Without a shred of modesty, he'd pushed the jumpsuit over his hips and taken the white briefs he wore beneath with it. He was naked and, suddenly, she realized that a towel was the only thing standing between them. Their forced proximity had abruptly become starker and more intimate.

Her gaze dropped to between his legs. Good Lord, he was hung like a racehorse. She couldn't look away as his penis swung heavily between his muscled thighs. It twitched, and something inside of her tightened in response.

"Keep staring, and you'll have to do something about it," he said in a low tone.

Shocked to the core, Taryn tore her gaze away. The mere thought of doing that big erection made her pussy clench and her nipples stiffen. The inappropriateness of her reactions horrified her. How could she be attracted to him when she knew what he'd done? What he was?

He reached past her to turn on the shower, and she bumped up against the wall. Hastily, she crossed her arms across her chest and tried in vain to concentrate on anything else in the room but him.

That was nearly impossible. He took up all the space.

"Get in the shower."

Her gaze snapped back to his. "No!"

He whipped back the shower curtain. "In. Now."

His tone brooked no argument, and she was once again reminded that he held all the power. She had to choose her battles, and this wasn't one she would win. She bit her lip, but stepped over the edge of the tub. She took the spot at the end, as far away from the shower head as she could get, but the confined space made her claustrophobic. The room closed in on her. Threatened and self-conscious, she clutched her towel to her chest like a security blanket.

Tucker had been imposing before, but naked? Forget about it.

He stepped in beside her. His gaze was hot, but she couldn't return it. Instead, she centered her stare on the middle of his broad chest. That wasn't such a great idea, either. Steam started to rise around them, and the effect was unnerving. Heavy moisture enveloped them, enhancing the intimate nature of their close quarters.

Taryn shifted nervously. Knowing that Tucker was an accused killer didn't reduce his sex appeal. She'd wanted him when they'd both been fully clothed, working across the table from each other. This? This was just unfair.

He reached for the soap and began to work up a lather. She watched as trails of water sluiced over his tight form. The uninhibited way he washed made it clear that he wasn't trying to entice her. He'd had a tough day. Lord knew what he'd gone through during the escape and the trek to her house. He was tired and dirty.

Oh, so very dirty...

His dark gaze connected with hers, and she realized that he *knew.* Appalled, she looked blankly at the shower curtain.

He grunted, but turned away to reach for the shampoo. He ran his hand through his wet hair, and white bubbles dripped down his neck. Mesmerized, she watched as they slid downwards. Her rational side kicked her out of her reverie. What was she doing ogling him? This was her chance! His back was turned, and his eyes were closed.

In a flash, she was out of the tub and lunging for the door. Her hand closed over the doorknob and gave it a quick twist.

It was as far as she got.

She yelped when Tucker caught her from behind. He jerked her back against him so firmly, her feet left the ground. She gave another cry and reached for the iron band circling her stomach, but his voice in her ear stopped her struggles.

"You just proved to me that I can't trust you, baby. Don't expect to get a chance like that again."

His body was hot and slick against her back. They were pressed together so tightly, she could feel his heart pounding. Skin to skin. The sensation made her toes curl.

Her eyes flew open. "My towel!"

The terrycloth had slipped during her brief sprint and was down to her waist. Frantically, she wrapped her forearm across her chest and reached for it. Without its protection, her vulnerability threatened to incapacitate her.

"Damn it, Tucker. Let me go!"

She was panting now. The towel was trapped beneath his arm and wouldn't budge. Whatever sense of calmness she'd achieved vaporized like the steam clouding the room. She couldn't stay logical and controlled when she was stripped bare. Not when he was touching her!

He lowered her feet to the ground, and she tried to scramble away.

"Not so fast." His strong arm kept her locked to his damp side. Bending down, he reached into the pocket of the trench coat.

Her eyes widened when he came up with a set of handcuffs. "What do you think you're going to do with those?"

"I'm going to try to take a shower in peace."

"Tucker?"

"Relax."

Relax? She was trapped in her own bathroom, naked as a jaybird, with a fugitive of the justice system. She couldn't relax! She was scared. Flat-out, pure terrified. Some of that panic slipped into her voice. "Please don't hurt me."

The words stopped him cold. He turned her in his arms, but she couldn't meet his gaze. The silence soon became deafening.

His voice was gruff when he finally spoke. "I'm not going to hurt you, Taryn. I just need a shower."

He gently pushed her backwards. One handcuff slid over her wrist, and she heard the ominous click. His hand settled on the forearm covering her breasts. She resisted, but he was insistent. She bit her lower lip as he lifted her arms above her head. The handcuffs went over the shower curtain rod before he locked them.

A low moan left Taryn's lips. The position left her mercilessly exposed. Her breasts jutted forward, their tips puckered into stiff little peaks. It was worse than it had been before when he'd caught her. Then, he'd been behind her. Now he was looking at her, studying her. She'd never felt so defenseless in her life. Or so submissive. She pressed her thighs tightly together and tried desperately to ignore the tingling between them.

"Taryn, look at me."

The calm tone was familiar. It was the Tucker she knew, the Tucker she'd trusted—justifiably or not. Hesitantly, she opened her eyes. She was surprised when his gaze settled on her face, not her body. Some of the tenseness left her muscles, but nothing could relax the wariness in her nerves.

He planted a hand on the wall beside her head and leaned in, crowding her. "Listen. I'm tired, I'm sore in places I didn't know I had, and I'm in a nasty mood. Yes, I'm a little peeved at you. What innocent man wouldn't be?"

Her shocked gaze collided with his even as her gut tightened. How dare he lie to her again? Especially like this.

"Don't give me that look. You heard me—*innocent*. I didn't sell those drugs to Justin Diaz any more than you…Well, any more than you slept with Marty Sheuster."

"What?" she gasped. The incongruity of his accusation threw her. "Marty? I never—"

"Exactly."

"But, but…Why would you say something like that?" she sputtered.

"To get my point across." He reached up and ran his wet finger over her cheek. "And to see how you'd react. I knew that scuzball was lying."

That one, slight touch sent a shiver through Taryn and effectively brought her back to her senses. What was she doing listening to him talk trash about one of her coworkers? He was an accused drug dealer. He'd lived a double life without anyone knowing. And he'd just taken her captive! Still, she couldn't help but ask. "Marty told you that we'd…slept together?"

"He was a little more descriptive than that. I wanted to rip his fucking head off."

She swallowed hard and tried to concentrate. She was in a bad situation; the last thing she needed to do was worry about Marty Sheuster. Still, she knew the A.D.A. well enough to know what he was capable of. The creep. They had a casual relationship, at best. She'd never even considered anything more. To hear that he'd spread rumors about her after she'd fought so hard to keep her reputation spotless angered her. "How did you know he was lying?"

One of Tucker's eyebrows lifted. Slowly, his hand moved from her face. His callused fingers trailed down her neck and stopped against her thundering pulse. He timed it, and a small smile touched his hard lips. His hand slid lower, and Taryn's breath came more quickly. His touch was confident and all too comfortable. She shouldn't be excited by it. She shouldn't enjoy it. She shouldn't…

"Ahhh." His fingers had settled over her naked breast.

"He said your nipples were brown." He leaned closer so he could whisper in her ear. "He was wrong. They're a light, pretty pink."

He trailed his thumbnail over the sensitive tip, and it popped up like a jack-in-the-box. Arousal unfurled in Taryn's stomach, and she tried to roll away. The handcuffs didn't let her get far. She couldn't escape. He could touch her as he wished. "Tucker," she groaned.

He cupped her breast, taking its weight, and she saw a flutter in the pulse at his temple.

"I'd never hurt you, Swanny," he said quietly. "I might be pissed and tired, but that's something I couldn't ever do."

Her hands formed fists as she fought the sensations that spiraled in her belly. His words lingered in her ear, and his touch burned. It felt so sinfully delicious. Her head dropped back against the bathroom wall. What was wrong with her? Why was she letting him get to her? She was smarter than this. She knew better than to trust him.

But she did trust him. At least when it came to her safety. He wouldn't hurt her physically; she knew that deep down inside. But emotionally? Emotionally, she was in jeopardy. "I know," she whispered.

His eyes flared. Slowly, his other hand trailed down her waist to cup her buttocks. She whimpered lightly when his fingers dipped into the crevice between them and squeezed.

"This thing between us—it feels good, doesn't it, baby?"

She squirmed against the intimate contact, ashamed to be wanting more. He loomed over her, so close that the air from his words brushed against her lips. She pressed them together to stop their sudden tingling. Her mind refused to let her be attracted to this man, but her body didn't seem to be listening.

"We could have been doing this for the past two years if you weren't so stubborn."

She flinched when he pinched her nipple. The sharp pain made her breast swell even more, and she rolled her head against the wall. The move stretched her arms tightly overhead, but it felt good. His touch felt so good.

His big, rough hands were sure and bold. They set off sparks everywhere they touched. And they touched everywhere. Her shoulders, her breasts, her quivering belly, the crease of her upper thighs...

Her mouth went dry as he traced the crease inward, approaching the part of her that craved his intimate strokes the most.

Suddenly, his touch was gone.

Her eyes flew open, and she saw him take a step back.

"Don't go anywhere," he said with a hard smile on his lips.

She watched in disbelief as he turned his back on her. A frustrated cry left her lips when he went back to his shower and pulled the curtain closed between them.

"Tucker! Don't you leave me here!" Angrily, she pulled at the handcuffs that held her in place. They refused to budge. Her body ached with wanting, and she realized that he'd brought her to that point on purpose. She'd been afraid he'd hurt her, but this form of revenge was even more cunning.

He'd made her want him.

A child killer.

"Arrrg!" she growled. She pulled harder against the handcuffs, but all that got her was the harsh sound of metal against metal. Her breasts jiggled as she fought the restraints, and the sensation angered her. All he'd had to do was touch her, and she'd forgotten her fear and her distrust. "That was low, Michael! Do you hear me? Low!"

Tucker hung his head under the spray of water. He listened to Taryn's struggles behind him, but for the moment, he just let the liquid heat soak his aching muscles. Why argue with her when she was right? He was fighting dirty. Why the hell not? Playing by the rules had gotten him nowhere.

The handcuffs scraped loudly against the metal shower curtain rod. "Damn you, Michael. I'm going to send you to prison so fast, your head's going to spin," she yelled.

"Not if I have anything to say about it," he muttered under his breath.

They were going to do things his way now. He'd come here for one reason and one reason only—to clear his name. And he had a definite, if unusual, plan on how to get her to help him do that.

He knew he could have just run. When the opportunity had presented itself, he could have hit the road and disappeared. He knew the system well enough; he could avoid it if he wanted. That wouldn't have solved anything, though. He'd be looking over his shoulder for the rest of his life, and he'd have to stomach the fact that everyone thought he was guilty of causing a kid's death.

Everyone. Including Taryn.

Of all the things he'd had to endure since the charges had been brought against him, her betrayal had hurt the most.

She was at least going to listen to him, by God.

The sound of her fighting the handcuffs roused him enough to glance over his shoulder. The silhouette of her body played against the opaque plastic of the shower curtain like an x-rated black and white movie.

"Perfect," he breathed. She was perfect. Her breasts swayed as she struggled with the handcuffs, and his gaze zeroed in on the voluptuous globes. They were full and firm, with nipples that practically begged for the rasp of his tongue.

His cock sprang to attention, but he couldn't move. He stood frozen as his gaze slid down the outline of her form. Her ass didn't rank far behind her tits when it came to rating points. The curves had fit his hand perfectly. It had been all he could do not to spread her legs open wide and thrust up into her.

He was about two milliseconds from pulling back the curtain and doing just that now.

But she was afraid he'd hurt her.

He wiped the water from his face and leaned back against the shower wall. "Damn."

That put a definite kink in his plans.

He wasn't here to scare her. It had just been a bitch of a day. He'd walked for miles through mud and muck. He was cold, hungry, and tired. She'd been a major player in getting him into this predicament, and he was hardly a saint. Knowing that she was the one leading the trial against him pissed him off royally.

Still, that gave him no right to scare her physically.

And it wouldn't help him get what he wanted.

"Stick to the plan," he muttered. Irritated with himself, he reached for the bar of soap and began to lather up again. His muscles protested when he reached to wash his back, and he knew that he'd be sore in the morning. Still, a night in bed with Taryn Swanson could do a lot towards curing his aches and pains.

He couldn't stop himself from glancing at her again.

The thought of crawling under the covers with her had his cock standing at full mast. Erotic thoughts pulled hard on him, and he clenched his teeth. Before he lost his senses, he shut off the water. He refused to jack off when she was only three feet away.

He threw aside the shower curtain, and she jumped. Her eyes rounded when she saw his stiff cock, and she renewed her struggles against the handcuffs.

"Just hold on," he said. "I'll only be a few more minutes."

"Get me out of these things," she demanded.

He ignored her and reached for a towel. She looked even better without the shower curtain between them. He rubbed the towel over his chest, but choked back a groan as he lowered it to his swollen cock.

He tossed the terrycloth aside. First things first. He needed to do something about his appearance. Half the state's law enforcement community was probably out there looking for him. He reached for the razor he'd seen in the shower. "Is this blade sharp?"

"Why?"

"I want to shave, that's why."

"I hope you cut your throat."

He lifted an eyebrow. "And then who would let you out of those things?"

She gave a growl of frustration. "The refills are in the medicine cabinet."

He found the new blades, but scowled when he saw the scented shaving cream in a lavender can. Great. That was all he needed—to smell like pretty flowers when the boys in blue finally caught up with him and carted him away. He made do with what she had and started scraping the growth of dark beard off his face. It felt good to finally stop the itching. The whiskers had been bothering him all day. Finally, he turned to the mustache he'd grown for his last case. The Ramirez case.

Damn, he hoped that wouldn't fall through the cracks without him.

He watched Taryn out of the corner of his eye as he worked. She stood quietly, but the glare she was throwing at him nearly seared his skin. And that body...It was frying his brain.

He decided to work slower.

Getting rid of the mustache helped, but it wasn't enough. He rubbed his chin as he looked at his reflection in the mirror. "I don't suppose you have any hair coloring around here."

She sniffed haughtily.

He looked pointedly at the tangle of hair between her legs. "No peroxide there."

She shifted uncomfortably, and he saw her glance again at his cock. It still stood at attention. Her look quickly darted away.

Good. He wanted her aware of him. Not scared. Aware.

She didn't have any aftershave. He picked up a bottle of lotion and glanced at the label. Good enough. "Has the media caught wind of my escape yet?" he asked as he squirted some into his palm.

The question brought her head up. "It was plastered on every network."

He clucked his tongue in disapproval. He'd always loved her spunkiness. "What did I tell you about that face, Counselor? If I had been on the news, you wouldn't have been so surprised to see me."

She glared at him. "Fine. I didn't see anything. Yet."

"That's good. It gives me more time." He smoothed the lotion onto his face and wiped away the white streaks.

"Time for what?"

He might as well tell her flat out. It would give her some time to get used to the idea. He watched her carefully as he turned and leaned back against the sink. "Time to screw you until you'll listen to me."

Her restless movements stopped, and her eyes went wide as a doe's. She stared at him for a heartbeat—and then ten.

"Don't you dare lay a finger on me, Tucker."

He knew that tone. He'd heard it often enough in court. Too bad the pulse fluttering at the base of her neck gave her away.

He looked her straight in those startled eyes. "I'll lay my fingers, my hands, my mouth, and my cock on you. Whatever it takes to break down that barrier you've erected against me."

She swallowed hard, and tension reverberated around the room.

"Don't take it personally," she said, her voice hardly above a whisper. "I hate all drug pushers. You should know that by now."

Enough. He'd heard enough of that crap to last him a lifetime. "And you should know that I'm innocent, damn it! We've worked side by side for too long. You know me better than this, Taryn."

"Stop it! Just stop with the lies." The handcuffs screeched against the curtain rod as she started struggling again. "I've been through the evidence. I've gone over it a hundred times."

Lies? He was the only one who'd been telling the truth. He was the victim of a frame-up, and he was sick of seeing that look in her eyes—the one she usually saved for drug runners, murderers, and pimps. He didn't deserve to be lumped in with that crowd.

"I've never lied to you, Taryn. No matter what else happens, before I leave here, you'll be convinced of that fact."

Her chin lifted, and her mouth took on a stubborn set. "Why? Because you're going to force me to have sex with you?"

"I won't have to force you," he said in a low voice. "We both know that."

Her cheeks turned pink. Her mouth worked for a moment, but she didn't have a comeback. She knew just as well as he what had happened the one and only time he'd touched her. The stain in her cheeks spread down to her chest, and her thighs clamped together. Almost desperately, she looked at the handcuffs overhead.

Tucker reached up to rub a kink in his neck. "I didn't have to use force to get that search warrant."

Her eyes flashed fire. "Don't."

He shrugged. "Sex got me what I wanted then. I figure, hell, why mess with success?"

Her hands fisted above her head, but he didn't go into the specifics. He didn't have to. They both knew well enough what had happened.

He'd been knee deep in the Rodriguez case when her buddy, Marty, had stalled on getting him the search warrant he'd needed. It had gone against protocol to bring in another ADA, but Tucker had had it with the idiot. They'd never bring the kingpin down at the rate Sheuster had been moving, so he'd called Taryn down to the station.

She hadn't been pleased about stepping on someone else's turf, but he'd pulled her into an interrogation room to explain. That had been the idea anyway—to talk to her.

Instead, he'd practically jumped her.

The warrant had soon been his. She would have been, too, if Sheuster hadn't been in the next room.

Sheuster wasn't here to stop them now.

Tucker watched Taryn's reactions closely. He'd been blunt about his intentions. Expediency was the name of the game now. People were coming for him. He needed her on his side, both for her brains and her power within the judicial system.

There was more, though. Most of all, he needed to regain her trust. He'd never have peace of mind if he didn't right things with her. He'd seen how she'd steeled her heart and her mind against him when he'd entered his plea. There was only one avenue left for him to take, and he wasn't above using it.

They'd been attracted to each other from the first day they'd met. He had to get her close to him. They'd start physically. The rest would follow.

He let out a long breath. Her eyes were still wide, but fear was no longer part of the equation. He saw uneasiness, though. That could be soothed...*with time*. It was one luxury he didn't have.

He had a good head start, though, and he was hiding in the best place possible—right under the authorities' noses. A familiar image of Taryn in a big, soft bed flitted into his weary mind and the decision was made.

He took a step towards her. "Let's go to bed, Swanny. It's been one hell of a long day."

Chapter Two

Taryn's head whirled. Bed. The word brought up muddled visions of sex. Heat. Betrayal. Deception. Justin!

No. She couldn't do this. She couldn't let it happen.

She watched as Tucker bent down to search the pockets of his trench coat. Her resolve strengthened when he emerged with a key. "I thought you escaped," she said. "How convenient for you to have the keys to your own set of handcuffs."

It had been impossible to avoid the controversy that surrounded the Tucker drug case. The media played up the sensationalism in every newscast. It was the hot topic in diners, barbershops, and churches everywhere. Even inside the police department, there were two distinct factions. There were those who believed that Detective Michael Tucker had gotten pulled under by the temptations associated with vice work. The people closest to him, though, couldn't even stomach the notion. It was possible that he'd found a sympathetic guard.

His eyes narrowed. "Don't even think it. Everybody did his job. We had an accident during my transport, and I managed to get loose. Unlike most people in that situation, I didn't just run. I knew I had to have the key, so I made sure I got it."

He lifted the key to her handcuffs, and Taryn's nerve endings went on the alert. He stood so close, her nipples brushed against his chest. Softness against hardness. Coolness against heat. Light, pretty pink against fading tanned flesh. Her concentration began to waver. "They'll find you," she blurted. "They'll use dogs to track your scent. They're probably outside right now."

He released the handcuffs from one wrist, and the freedom disconcerted her. She couldn't decide whether to rub the soreness or cover her body from his sight. With him this close, shielding herself seemed

to be the most prudent choice—especially since her body was reacting like a lit firecracker. She wrapped one arm about her chest and,
handcuffs jingling, used the other to cover the curls at her groin.

She jumped when he touched her.

"I know how things work, Swanny. Why do you think I was so
wet and grungy?"

He didn't try to move her hands to expose her. Instead, he lightly
circled her wrists and applied soft pressure to the joints. The flow of
fresh blood made her fingers tingle, but it was impossible to determine
if the circulation or he was the source of new heat.

His unexpected display of tenderness confused her. With his hands
placed as they were, his knuckles came into unavoidable contact with
her breast and belly. The twin points of contact zinged with electricity,
but he didn't push the intimacy to the next level. It left her on edge,
comforted by his touch, yet poised for something more.

"I ran through more than a few creeks on my way here," he said,
his voice a little gruff. "I even boarded a bus when I found some spare
change in that coat. There's no way a dog could track me."

Taryn bit her lower lip. Her hopes of a quick rescue were fading
fast. Nobody would think that Tucker would come here. The idea was
just too far fetched.

Maybe her neighbors... No, they wouldn't be any help. Her house
sat too far back from the road, and she had a large plot of land. Even
if she did scream, the seventy-year-old Parsons wouldn't hear her.
Nervously, she began clutching at straws. "My roommate will be
back any time now."

He actually chuckled. He moved his hands away from her wrists
and began massaging the stiff muscles at the base of her neck. "Nice
try. You don't have a roommate."

He turned her by the shoulders and directed her to the door. She
jumped in surprise when he gave her bare bottom a quick pat. "To
the bedroom."

Taryn's mind went blank. He wanted to go to bed.

She just couldn't think of a way to stop him. The idea of slipping
under the sheets with him turned her hot and cold at once. Her body
wanted to, but her mind rebelled. He was using her. She had to remember that.

His arm wrapped around her waist to steady her. The touch was gentle, but it felt unbearably hot against her skin. With a jolt, she realized that she wasn't scared so much as hypersensitive. It was a mind game now. He'd said he wouldn't hurt her, and she believed him. Still, he'd been blatant about his intentions. He'd come here to have sex with her.

And he'd already proven to her how readily her body gave in, no matter what her heart and her head told it to do.

He knew her weakness; she had to find his.

Tucker guided Taryn into the bedroom. The bathroom light spilled in from the doorway. When he saw the queen-sized bed, he knew he'd rebounded straight from hell into heaven. "Oh, yeah," he murmured.

He let out a shuddering breath. He'd been running on adrenaline for too long. He was at the end of his rope—mentally, physically, and emotionally. All he'd been able to think about as he'd slopped through ice-cold creeks and shuffled through dank alleyways was *this*—being with her. Taking comfort from her.

He gently pulled her back against him until they touched, skin against skin. Intense pleasure uncoiled inside his chest. Her skin was like raw silk. He spread his hand across her midriff and luxuriated in the feel of her. The sensation was doubly powerful where her soft backside cradled his erection, and he couldn't help but nudge his cock against her more firmly. A sensual haze began to overtake him, and he buried his face in her sweet-smelling hair.

"Taryn," he whispered.

Suddenly, the weight of the world settled on his shoulders. This wasn't how he'd wanted things to be between them. He'd wanted her to be with him willingly.

Of course, that had been before his world had turned upside down. And inside out. He'd always thought he'd have time to coax her into his bed. He'd thought things would evolve between them naturally.

There was nothing natural about this. Somehow everything had sprung out of control. How the hell had things come to this? A few weeks ago, he'd been a cop, and she'd been his sexy ADA. Now, he was an accused murderer on the run, and she was his hostage.

Fuckin' A.

He gave her a gentle squeeze. "Come on, baby. It's cold in here." Her feet didn't move. "I won't do this with you."

The stiffness had reentered her body. Tucker sighed. Damn it, he shouldn't have told her. All it had done was lift her defenses against him, and he really didn't have the energy to chip away at them. Not tonight. He brushed a kiss against her proud shoulder. For a hard-nosed attorney, her thoughts were pretty easy to read.

"Just get under the covers, Swanny. I swear we won't do anything you don't want to do."

"But I don't want to do anything with you," she said tightly. "I don't want to get in that bed with you."

Her gaze was focused hard across the room, not on the bed, but on the picture above it. His own stubbornness took hold. Like it or not, she was getting into that bed with him.

For one thing, he had to keep an eye on her. He had her at a disadvantage physically, but she was wickedly smart. If she saw another opportunity for escape, she'd take it. Keeping her plastered to his side limited those opportunities.

It also provided him with other, more obvious, benefits. If they slept together—just slept side by side—she'd get used to the weight of his body, the feel of his hands on her skin, the brush of his breath at the back of her neck...

Just picturing it made him rock hard.

"All right," he said smoothly. Before she could react, he opened one hand possessively across her breast. The other slid down her stomach as he spread her legs with his knee. "We'll get busy right here."

As expected, she bolted before he'd barely touched her.

But it wasn't soon enough. She'd been hot.

And slick.

He almost groaned out loud when she flew across the room and hopped into bed. She tore at the covers and pulled them up to her chin. Light from the doorway slashed across the bed, illuminating her nervousness.

Anticipation made Tucker's fists clench. His cock had been too hard for too long. There were things he wanted to do with her—and to her. Intimate things. Shocking things. This might be the one and only time they had a chance to be together.

Slowly, he crossed the room. He'd promised her that he wouldn't force her, and he'd hold true to that. It was just that combining a sexual seduction with a mental one was going to be tricky. He needed to find just the right approach, because in the end, he needed her help. She was the only person who could get him out of this godforsaken mess.

She was the only one who could save him.

Taryn watched Tucker as he came towards her. How many times had she fantasized about this? About him? Her rules about dating coworkers had kept them apart, but abstinence hadn't stopped her from daydreaming. Her fingernails curled into the soft comforter. Her simple dreams paled in comparison to the reality of him.

Light from the doorway silhouetted his shape. He was masculinity in its purest form. Tall, dark, and built. His muscles were sleek and powerful. His chest was wide, his hips were narrow, and his legs were long. The very heart of him was no exception; he was thick, hard, and ready.

For her.

It was enough to make a woman beg.

But she couldn't, and it made her want to scream. Why did it have to be this way? Why couldn't he be innocent like he claimed? She wanted to believe him—even now. Even after she'd pored over the evidence, the statements, and the rest of the case file looking for something to clear him. She'd been desperate to find even the tiniest detail that would cast the light of doubt on his guilt. In her obsession, she'd nearly gone blind.

But she'd come up empty-handed.

She shook her head. This wasn't how she'd wanted it to be—with them at odds, time running out, and the cold of winter slicing through the room. She pulled the covers around her more tightly as shivers wracked her body. Her mind raced. The drugs. The dead teenager. She had to resist him. She had to.

He came at her like a silent predator. Before she could react, he'd tugged her security blanket out of her hands and uncovered her. A combination of fear and excitement froze her in place. She watched breathlessly as he crawled onto the bed with her. Their gazes locked; his dark eyes were fathomless.

"Stop fighting it, baby," he whispered. He planted a hand on each side of her head, trapping her. Watching her reactions, he stretched out full-length on top of her and gradually lowered his weight. "Stop fighting us."

Taryn clutched his shoulders as he came down upon her, unable to make up her mind whether to push him away or pull him closer. She could feel his strength, his textures, and his desire as his body pressed her deep into the mattress.

Pleasure hummed through her. He was better than any blanket she'd ever owned.

"See?" he said, his nose brushing against hers. "See how good it is?"

Her resistance drained. Her hands came up hesitantly, and she heard the handcuff on her right wrist jingle. She hadn't had a chance to touch him before. He'd kept her restrained. Now, her fingers itched.

She spread her palms wide on his back. He felt so solid. So warm. She caressed the plateau of muscles and warm flesh and was delighted by the groan that rang in her ear.

"Don't stop," he whispered as his head came down.

His mouth pressed against hers, open and hungry. She moaned as her eyelids fluttered shut. Their lips sealed together. Textures and tastes filled her senses. Her grip on him tightened. The kiss was firm, coaxing, and determined. Desire smoldered deep in her belly as she met his tongue.

Why would she want to stop this?

Because of the drugs! Because of the dead teenager!

Her hands stiffened on his lower back.

What was wrong with her? *Was she insane?* She couldn't take Michael Tucker as her lover.

She tore her mouth away from his and gasped for air. "No," she said harshly.

He pulled his head back and looked at her in confusion. "What?"

Anxiety rolled in Taryn's stomach. What she wanted and what was right were two different things. She swallowed hard and looked into his face. "I'm saying 'no'."

The quiet words rang throughout the room. Tucker's body became rigid on top of hers, and the tension seemed to make him even heavier.

Anger and frustration flared in his eyes.

"You're already charged with possession of drugs with intent to distribute, providing drugs to a minor, and third degree murder," she said painstakingly. It was getting harder to talk with each word. "The list is only getting longer. You're holding me hostage. Do you really want to add—"

"Don't say it," he snarled.

With a harsh curse, he leveraged himself off of her and rolled onto his back. He covered his eyes with a forearm as his hands clenched into fists. The friction in the room heated as his harsh breaths echoed.

Taryn didn't dare move. She didn't dare speak. They both knew what her one little 'no' meant. He had to stop or he'd be charged with rape.

She felt miserable.

She'd done the right thing, she knew. Kissing him and touching him had felt incredible—but she would have regretted it in the morning. He wasn't the Michael Tucker she'd lusted after for the past two years. That man was a facade, but thank God he still had enough decency in him to stop him when she asked.

The tense seconds turned into tense minutes. The light that slashed across the bed didn't help. It glared in Taryn's eyes, refusing to let her hide. The rays lit Tucker's chest as it went up and down in strictly controlled breaths. His body was like a primed spring. She was afraid to set him off.

But he'd rolled right on top of the covers, and she was cold.

She curled into a ball to try to retain her body heat. She looked into the clock as the minutes clicked off one-by-one. When her teeth started to rattle, she couldn't stand it anymore.

"The heat," she said. Her soft words boomed in the darkness. "I was heading to turn it on when you...grabbed me. Do you...Would you mind if I went to adjust the thermostat?"

"Yeah. I'd mind."

His flat refusal made her look at him. His face was like granite. She couldn't read him at all.

He let out a long breath and sat up. "Give me your wrist. I'll go take care of it. I have to fix your window anyway."

Her wrist. He meant to handcuff her. She tucked her hand under her body. Not again. "What's wrong with my window?"

He ran a hand through his hair and actually looked embarrassed. "You have deadbolts on the doors. I had to break in."

Dread crawled down Taryn's spine. Intellectually, she'd known that he'd found a way into her house. Hearing how he'd done it was another thing entirely. Her guilt fizzled away. "One more for the list," she said bitterly.

He threw her an angry look, and suddenly they were right back to where they'd been when he'd first snatched her in the hallway. "I'll pay for repairs when this is all straightened out. Hell, I'll even come over and replace it myself."

"That will be a trick, considering how you'll be in prison."

"Give me your wrist."

She rolled onto the hand with the clunky bracelet. "No."

"Damn it, Swanny." He ran a hand over his face. "I've got to do something about that window before it attracts attention, but I can't trust you to stay put. This isn't easy on me, either, but I've got to look out for number one."

"You're not going to lock me up again. I won't let you."

One of his eyebrows rose at the challenge. When he moved, it was like a big cat pouncing on its prey. Taryn let out a screech and tried to pull away. His hands groped her as they wrestled for control.

She was quickly subdued.

"You know you're only making this more fun for me," he said. There wasn't even a glimmer of a smile on his face. He lifted her arm and locked the bracelet around one of the rods in the headboard.

Taryn grumbled at the sound of the click.

Shaking his head, Tucker ran a finger across her cheek. "You're the most obstinate woman I know, but you still look like one of my favorite teenage wet dreams."

She lunged at him, and the blankets fell to her waist. "If you don't go fix that window, the pipes in this house are going to freeze."

His chest rose and fell slowly as he stared at her nakedness.

"And your nipples will be hard enough to cut glass," he said in a voice like sandpaper. He reached out to test one with his index finger. "Oh yeah, wet dream material. Hard core."

"Get out!"

"Right. The window," he said as he stood. He was completely oblivious to his own nudity as he turned on his heel and displayed a tight backside. He plucked up the key to her restraints as he headed back into the light. "And I'll turn on the heat. What are you? A miser?"

Taryn slouched back against the pillow as he left the room. Damn the man! Not only were her nipples taut, her breasts felt heavy and engorged. She quickly pulled the sheet over herself, but gasped when a jolt shot straight down to her core. Even the touch of cotton was too much.

Double damn him! All it took was a word or a look from him, and she was aroused. But a touch? A touch made her delirious. She flopped onto her stomach to try to ease her discomfort.

She couldn't believe what she'd almost allowed him to do. It shouldn't have taken her so long to stop him. Where was her brain? More to the point, where was her backbone? He'd broken into her home. He'd taken her hostage and bound her to her own bed. How could her body betray her like this?

The hard press of the mattress against her breasts gave her some relief. Groaning, she dropped her head onto the pillow and tried to think. *What was she going to do?*

She knew that there had to be people out there looking for him, even if there hadn't been anything on the news. Her head snapped up. The Diazes! They were going to be panic-stricken when they heard about Tucker's escape. She thought again about little Benny. She had to do something.

Her gaze settled on the nightstand on the opposite side of the bed. The phone. The answer to her problems was staring her right in the face! Flinging her arm wide, she reached out for the receiver. The muscles in her shoulder pulled tight as she stretched across the bed.

"Taryn, where's your broom?"

The sudden question made her start, and she accidentally knocked a book off the nightstand. It fell to the floor with a thud, and she cringed. She quickly looked over her shoulder to the doorway. Had he heard?

"It's in the laundry room beside the dryer," she called loudly.

Her ears craned to hear his movements. For once, the squeak of the floor in the laundry room was welcome. She relaxed, and her concentration returned to her task. The phone was so close, yet so far. She stretched out and wiggled her fingers. They brushed against the corner, but she couldn't get a solid grip.

It was right there!

"Got any cardboard?"

She slumped against the pillows, but her mind raced. This might be the only chance she got. She needed to call for help—because for as much as she'd resisted him tonight, she knew she couldn't last much longer.

Right or wrong, she wanted him.

An idea occurred to her, and she rolled onto her back. Squirming around, she repositioned herself so her legs were pointed towards the phone.

"Taryn?" His voice was closer. "Cardboard?"

He couldn't come in here now!

"There might be some under the sink," she yelled.

She didn't wait to see if he followed her directions. She had to give it one more try. Her legs were longer than her arms. It took three attempts, but she finally managed to grasp the receiver between her toes. Gingerly, she pulled her knees to her chest.

A harsh gasp escaped her when she lost her grip. The phone and her hope nearly toppled onto the floor, before her quick reflexes saved her from disaster. She clamped the phone between her feet and paused to get her pulse under control.

She knew she didn't have much time. Contorting her body, she dropped the phone onto the bed where she could reach it. With one hand, she dialed 911 and lifted the receiver to her ear.

Silence greeted her.

Anxiety settled like a rock in the pit of her stomach.

"Flexible, aren't you?" The deep voice came from the doorway.

Her head snapped towards the sound. Tucker was standing with his arms propped overhead against the doorframe. The casual pose was at odds with the steel in his voice. He seemed totally unconcerned with his nudity, but she couldn't ignore it. Her gaze was drawn to his body like a magnet to steel. He was still blatantly aroused, but his good humor had vanished. The dangerous combination sent a sizzle down her spine.

"What did you do to the phones?" she asked, going on the offensive.

"I took the cords."

She looked at the wall jack and a discomforting thought made her pause. "How long have you been in my house?"

He hit the hallway light, and the room plunged into darkness. "Long enough to hear what a fumble fingers you are."

The back of Taryn's neck tingled when she heard him push himself away from the door. She'd dropped the soap in the shower— twice. She'd been thinking of him locked in that jail cell with nothing but a hard cot, a sink, and a toilet for company. But he hadn't been in a cell. He'd been here. How long had he stood in that hallway listening to her? How long had she had an intruder in her house while she'd been naked, vulnerable, and unaware?

She heard him moving across the room, and her heart began to thud in her chest. Her eyes adjusted to the moonlight that filtered through the crack between the curtains and she found him standing over her. He took the phone away from her and set it back in its cradle.

"Time's up, baby. Enough with the fake-outs and excuses. I'm tired."

His gaze ran over her intimately. His hot hand settled against her waist and lightly backtracked up her body. The light touch brushed against the side of her breast, tickled her armpit, and caressed the tender inside of her elbow. "Let's make you more comfortable," he said in a low voice.

Taryn lay still as he reached for her handcuffs. His behavior made her edgy. She'd angered him more than once tonight; she felt justified to be scared.

With the sound of a click, she was free. Hesitantly, she lifted her wrist to him. The handcuffs jingled, and the sound reached the four corners of the room.

There was a silent battle of wills as they stared at each other. She held her ground, but was somewhat surprised when he reached for the metal bracelets. Relief started to flow through her, but it faltered when he slipped the handcuff around his own wrist. "No!" she cried.

"Yes," he said firmly. He climbed over her and put the key on the far nightstand. Then he settled down as guard, pulled the blankets up, and adjusted his pillow. "I've had enough of your tricks, so I'm not even going to give you the opportunity to try to sneak out of this bed while I'm asleep. It's not going to happen. Deal with it."

She pulled hard on the handcuffs, but she was chained solidly to him. "Tucker, I'm tired of this. It isn't funny anymore."

"You're complaining to the wrong person, Counselor." He stopped her sharp tugs by grabbing her wrist and pressing it against the mattress. "I've spent a hell of a lot more time in cuffs than you have. Believe me, your experience has been a lot more pleasurable than mine."

She quieted when she heard the flare of temper in his voice. Stiffly, she lay down on her back. It was unsettling to stretch out beside him, especially with his anger still heating the room. He was a big man, and there wasn't much she could do to avoid touching him. Even the sound of his breathing seemed to press on her.

The darkness magnified her trepidation. She'd been warned about the dangers she could face in her line of work. Angry defendants seeking retribution were rare, but she'd always known it was a possibility. What was it that she'd been told to do to protect herself?

She couldn't remember.

Tucker sighed. "Come here."

With a tug, he pulled her across the sheets until her back was flush against his chest. Taryn tried to calm her thundering heart. His body cocooned hers, and the heat he exuded nearly made her faint. She waited anxiously in the darkness.

"Go to sleep, Swanny. You said 'no', and I heard you. Relax."

Relax? Her nerves were stretched like a tightrope.

Tucker didn't seem to have to same problem. She was amazed when, all too soon, the arm around her waist went slack and heavy. The handcuff loosened as his hand covered hers on her belly. She glanced over her shoulder, but his breathing was deep and steady.

He'd fallen asleep.

She waited, but the more time passed, the more she realized that he was dead to the world. Gradually, her wariness eased. She'd been on pins and needles ever since she'd stepped into that darkened hallway. Knowing he was asleep, she finally allowed her guard to drop.

This was better. With him sleeping, she didn't need to use all her energy battling wits with him. Now was the time to think. She had to find a way to escape. A way to call for help. A way to incapacitate him.

It was hard to plot out a strategy, though, with his body pressed so close to hers. She stretched luxuriously. She liked the feel of his big hand spread across her bare stomach even if the handcuff felt cold. She loved how his muscled chest rubbed against her back with every breath he took. And the intimate tangle of their legs... Nothing had ever felt so deliciously sinful.

The more she tried to think, the less the ideas came to her. Her body became heavy. The tightness in her neck loosened, and her head sunk into the pillow. Finally, her eyelids drifted shut.

Behind her, Tucker finally relaxed. Playing dead was damn near impossible with a hot babe in his arms. He lifted his head and looked down at her. The lines of worry on her forehead had smoothed. He brushed a kiss across her temple and settled back down behind her. As much as it rankled him, she'd outwitted him tonight. He had to give her credit for that.

But there was always tomorrow, and he was persistent type of guy. Tomorrow, he wasn't going to give her so much time to think. Tomorrow, she wouldn't be saying 'no'.

Chapter Three

Taryn awoke hours later as the pre-dawn light was beginning to erase the blackness of the night sky. Consciousness pulled at her, tugging her out of the depths of sleep, but she fought the urge to wake up. Her sleep had been too heavy, too satiating. She hadn't slept this well since Tucker had been arrested.

Tucker!

She nearly moaned out loud as she came fully awake. He wasn't in custody anymore; his big body was spooned against hers, warming her like a furnace. They were in her house. They were in her bed.

She'd spent the night in his arms.

She closed her eyes tightly as failure overwhelmed her. What had happened to her plan to escape? She was supposed to have plotted a strategy. Instead, she'd *cuddled.*

The bed suddenly shifted, and her pulse skipped a beat. Was he awake? His feet stretched outward, and his hand flexed on her stomach. She let herself go limp. She wasn't ready to start the battle again, not before she had a plan.

A jingling sound drifted softly through the morning air, but was quickly muffled. The key! Instinct told her to remain still.

She kept her breaths deep and low as Tucker leaned over her. His nearness made her want to tense, but when he lifted her wrist, she let him take its weight. The lock on the handcuffs clicked, and hope sprang forth in her chest.

He watched her closely; she could feel his concentration focused on her like a laser beam. With a murmur, she rolled away and pressed her face into the pillow.

Seconds stretched into an eternity before his hand ran gently down her side. She nearly cursed aloud when her traitorous body arched into the touch, but the bed shifted as he slid out from under the covers. He left the room silently, but she didn't allow herself to move until she heard the bathroom door close.

Then she kicked into high gear.

He hadn't chained her to the bed. She was free!

She had to move *now*, and she had to move fast. Flinging back the covers, she shot out of bed.

She'd made it three steps before she realized she had to be quieter. Tucker hadn't gone deaf. He was only a room away. Any unusual noise and he'd pounce.

To make matters even worse, she had to pass through the hallway by the bathroom door in order to get out of the house. Sweat broke out on her forehead, but she knew she didn't have time to worry about such things. If she thought too long, her chance would be gone.

So would her courage.

Her robe lie in a heap by the bed. She swooped it up and slid it over her shoulders.

She scurried by the bathroom on tiptoes. She didn't know how he didn't hear her. Her heart was pounding like a big bass drum. Luck was with her, though, and she made it to the living room without catching his attention.

Her immediate choice for a getaway was the back door. The front door was too far, and she needed to get outside as soon as possible. Once there, she could run. She could hide.

She flew to the kitchen. Her fingers shook as she unlocked the dead bolt. Flinging open the heavy wooden door, she reached for the screen.

A big hand came crashing down on hers as she gripped the latch.

"Going somewhere, Counselor?"

The growl in her ear made Taryn wince. If Tucker had been mad before, he was doubly ticked off now. Her fingers gripped the latch tighter. He pried her hand away and set the lock.

His body heat buffeted her as he stood behind her. Defeated and a little scared, she dropped her head against the glass window. Its chill nearly gave her a headache, and she reflexively backed away from the cold.

It was the wrong move to make. She collided solidly against him, and his steel-like arms wrapped around her.

"You shouldn't have done that, baby," he whispered into her ear. "Didn't you learn yesterday that when you run from me, there are consequences?"

A low moan slipped from Taryn's suddenly constricted throat. She didn't need to be told what the consequence would be this time. His hands were already working on the tie of her robe. She reached to stop him, but her efforts had little effect. He was too strong—too intent on his purposes.

His wildness sent a secret thrill through her.

The robe was pulled open, and she sucked in a gasp as the cold seeped through the screen door and onto her skin. She squirmed against him, trying to find relief, but instead, he pressed her forward.

She cried out when her nipples touched the frost-covered window.

"I'm tired of your teasing, baby—and I'm not talking about just last night. You've been teasing me for years with that stupid rule about not dating coworkers, with those sexy little suits, with your perfume...Do you know how many times you've gotten me all hot and bothered and then run away?"

"Tucker!" she gasped. The cold nipped at her, shocking her. "Please!"

"I've had it with your little 'look but don't touch' game. I've learned what happens when I touch, and I like it." He pulled the robe down her arms, and it pooled at their feet. He stepped forward and pressed her more fully against the glass. "Your running days are over, Swanny."

Taryn was in turmoil. Her belly and thigh muscles constricted from the cold, but the heat of her skin was enough to make the frost melt. Soon droplets of water were running down her legs. The icy sensation was as sharp as her anxiety—and as acute as her growing desire.

"Tucker, it's too cold," she begged.

"Don't worry. I'll warm you up."

Instead of backing away, he squeezed his hands between her body and the glass. His rough palms covered her breasts, and the resulting heat shocked her. He fondled her tender flesh, creating such a fervor she could hardly stand it.

The contrast was just too much. The door was a big sheet of ice, but her backside was bathed in heat. His chest rubbed against her shoulders and back, but it was her bottom that was on fire. He thrust himself suggestively in the cleavage of her buttocks, and the friction sent her need skyrocketing.

"It's too cold. Too hot." She couldn't think. "I can't take this."

"You can, and you will."

She shuddered. He wasn't talking about the cold.

"Do you know how pissed I was at you yesterday in that courtroom when you were strutting around in your little blue suit?"

He nipped at her earlobe and excitement shot through her veins.

"You think those outfits make you look professional, but I'll let you in on a secret. They get me hot. I always wonder what you're wearing underneath them."

He pinned her with the weight of his body as his hands roamed. To her breasts. Around her waist. Along her thighs. He spread his fingers across her stomach and stroked downwards until they tangled in her blonde curls. Her lungs shuddered as yearning poured through her.

"You were intent on putting me in prison, but all I could think about was the slit going up the back of your skirt."

"Tucker," she panted. Sensation was about to overwhelm her.

"You should have believed in me, baby. You owed me at least that much."

He slid one foot inside hers and bumped her leg outwards, widening her stance to give him better access. Taryn's muscles quivered as she waited for him. Finally, his hand covered her mound. His devious fingers snaked along the grooves of her pussy, making her legs go weak. She groaned from both the ecstasy and the torment. He was intentionally avoiding the tiny bud that would give her the most pleasure.

"We're going to deal with this little problem first." He gently squeezed his fingers together, and a jolt of energy made her jump. "Then we'll talk about the other."

Taryn rolled her forehead against the door, and water trickled down her face. The collision of hot and cold air had fogged over the glass everywhere except the places where she touched. Anybody looking in from the outside would have a clear view of her naked, undulating body. The thought only heightened her arousal.

"Are you ready for me, baby?" he whispered.

Ready? She was about to come unglued. He parted her lower lips and pushed two thick fingers up into her.

"Ahh," she cried out. Her need sharpened to a razor's edge.

"Christ, you're tight."

The strain in his voice nearly matched hers. His fingers plunged deep, hard, and fast. Little sounds left Taryn's throat. Her hips begged to move, but she couldn't. He had her trapped. Soon, more than condensation was running down her legs.

Tremors started radiating out from her belly. She spread her palms wide on the smooth surface of the glass and braced herself. Suddenly, Tucker spread her legs even wider apart. He bent his knees and positioned his throbbing cock. She was given no time to prepare before he surged straight up into her.

She cried out sharply, and he cursed.

It was almost too much to take—the shock, the amazingly full penetration. He pulled back and her pussy burned with friction. Before she could gather herself, he was pushing inexorably upwards, stretching her wider. He found a rhythm and was soon pounding into her with long, deep thrusts.

Taryn felt herself spiraling out of control. Oh, God, she'd needed this. She'd needed him.

She whimpered when he stopped and adjusted her stance so her body pressed flush against the pane of glass. The chill was almost welcome against her overheated flesh. Almost. One of his hands slid around to the front of her mound. His fingers opened her so her clit was subjected to the cold glass, and the concentrated sensation pushed her over the edge.

"Michael!" she cried.

He began stroking into her again; each hard thrust lifted her right up on her tiptoes.

The tension inside her sprang loose with a vengeance. Pleasure pumped through her body, and she let out a scream as the orgasm shook her.

Tucker rode Taryn hard as she climaxed. It had taken everything inside him to wait until she went first, but now, it was his turn. And he wanted more. Hell, he hadn't even kissed her yet.

"I can't get at you good enough," he growled.

Abruptly, he pulled out of her. She gasped at the loss, and a tight smile pulled at his lips. He turned her and lifted her in his arms. Unable to bear being apart from her for another moment, he plunged back into her.

"Better?" he snarled. His civility was quickly coming to an end.

"Uh," she whimpered. "So full."

Her back arched, and he took advantage of the access to her breast. He pulled her nipple into his mouth and sucked. Her skin was cold—like a big, delicious ice cream cone. He was more than happy to have a taste.

Her legs tightened around his waist, and he was lost. The way her muscles gripped him made the top of his head nearly come clean off. He worried that he might be too much for her from this angle, with thrusts this hard.

"More, Tucker. I need more."

The words sifted through the mists in his head and scattered his remaining coherent thoughts. With both hands, he grabbed her ass and rammed into her. It didn't take long before he was spurting like a volcano.

Weak with the aftershock, he sagged against the door with her securely in his arms. His body was mush; his brain was a complete blank. He felt her fingers run through his hair, and his knees nearly buckled.

Holy hell. He'd dreamt of screwing her for two years. Two long, frustrating years. He could have chosen better circumstances, but *damn*, even with the threat of capture hanging over his head, coming here had been worth the risk.

But did she feel the same way?

The thought caught him from out of the blue, and a zap of wariness shot down his spine.

Ah, shit. There wasn't much hope of that. She'd been running from him before he'd caught her and literally screwed her to the wall. He couldn't have planned a less romantic scenario.

The world began to right itself on its axis as they stood in silence.

Cool water dribbled down his hand, and he plucked Taryn away from the glass door. In a vain effort to warm her, he ran his palm up and down her spine.

She didn't respond. She was already withdrawing from him mentally; he could feel it. Her body began to stiffen, but he wouldn't allow it. He *couldn't* allow it—not after what had just happened.

He kissed her, coaxing her back into the moment. She went still at the touch of his lips, and he took it as a sign of encouragement. She felt so soft. So vulnerable. He wove his fingers into her hair, nearly desperate to bring back the closeness he'd felt only moments ago. Keeping it slow, he deepened the kiss. When his tongue touched hers, though, she trembled and pushed at his shoulders.

"You don't play fair, Tucker."

He was breathing hard. "Fair doesn't always win. I play for keeps."

She looked at him as if seeing him for the first time. "And you don't care who gets in your way, do you?"

The accusation stung, and he nearly lashed back before spotting the anguish that swirled in the depths of her blue eyes. "You've got it wrong. All wrong. I'm not a drug dealer," he said emphatically. He wanted to shake the truth into her, but instead he rubbed the base of her spine in soothing circles. She was looking at him so guardedly, it made him anxious. "You know me, baby. I'm a cop. I drink bad coffee, I type with two fingers, and I catch the bad guys."

"But you—"

He stopped her with a finger to her lips. "I didn't do anything wrong—other than to trust the system to clear me. I swear it, Taryn. I didn't come here to scare you or to hurt you. I came here for your help."

A shuttered look settled onto her face. "Put me down, Michael."

Frustration made him want to put his fist through the door, but he'd learned she was serious when she called him that. Carefully, he uncoupled their bodies. Her face turned red with embarrassment, and he hated that. He tried to make her look at him. "Taryn, I didn't give those drugs to Justin."

She wrapped her arms about her body and stared at a point somewhere over his shoulder. "Please let me go. I'm cold, and I need to clean up."

He wasn't going to let her do this. "No."

Her indignant gaze snapped to his. "No?"

He saw the shiver that ran across her skin, and a feeling of protectiveness hit him hard. "Shower? Yes. Let you go? Absolutely not."

Before she could protest, he leaned down and swept her up in his arms. She let out a sound of outrage, but he didn't care. She wanted to be stubborn? She'd just come up against the king of bull-headedness. "You've proven to me that I can't let you out of my sight. Until I've convinced you that I'm innocent, it isn't going to happen again."

He bumped the back door closed with his hip. "Lock that."

Amazingly, she complied. He carried her to the bathroom, her body stiff in his arms. It was a disappointing change. Only moments ago, she'd been warm and pliant. Aggravation made him clench his teeth together so tightly his jaw hurt.

What was it going to take for him to change her mind? He was innocent, damn it. Why couldn't she see that? Why didn't she just *know*?

Taryn stepped as far away from Tucker as she could when he stood her on her own two feet. A huge ball of fire mixed with regret and humiliation had settled somewhere just under her lungs. How could she have let that happen?

She'd just had mind-blowing sex with a drug dealer. A murderer. He might not have pulled a trigger or thrust a knife, but he'd killed that poor boy just the same. By supplying Justin Diaz with those drugs, Tucker had caused his overdose.

And she'd just let him touch her as he saw fit. She'd taken pleasure from his hands, his mouth, his... She lifted a hand to cover her face.

"Don't look like that," he growled. "You got off on it as much as I did."

"Are you taking the first shower, or am I?" She refused to talk about what had just happened. She was too ashamed of herself.

His lips thinned. "We're showering together."

"But..."

"I told you that I'm not going to let you out of my sight."

"Fine." Whipping back the shower curtain, Taryn stepped inside. She turned on the water, but flinched when it smacked against her. The heat was heavenly, but her body was still overly sensitized. Especially her breasts. When the water pellets sprayed against her nipples, it was all she could do not to whimper.

"Here," he said with a sigh. He stepped in behind her and settled his hands on her waist. "Body heat is better."

She resisted, but he turned her around. She batted at his shoulders in a late display of defiance, but he wrapped his arms around her. A soft "shhh" and a kiss to her temple made her go quiet. She stood in his embrace with her head hung low.

"Taryn, you know me," he said calmly. "I've never supplied drugs to minors—or to adults, for that matter. My job was to get the drugs off the streets. You saw me do it. You *helped* me do it."

The irony wasn't new to her. She'd spent many sleepless nights thinking about how and why he could have turned. "It was always a losing battle, though. We both saw how much money the pushers were making on the streets. The temptation obviously became too strong. You crossed the line."

His voice took on an edge. "No, I didn't."

She lifted her head. "Then prove it."

"Counselor, our justice system works on the presumption of *innocence*."

Her shoulders slumped in disappointment. She knew how the system worked better than anybody. She also knew how much evidence there was against him. All she'd been asking for was a bone—just one little bit of info she'd missed that would refute the charges against him.

Yet he couldn't give it to her.

"I'm warm," she said dejectedly. "Please, let me go."

His hands tightened on her, but after a moment, he let them drop. Turning around, Taryn reached for the soap. Her throat was tight as she fought back tears. When it came to the case, she didn't believe him. She'd seen the evidence. She'd been over it forwards, backwards, inside and out. She'd approached it from every angle, trying to find a flaw. There wasn't one.

She swallowed past the lump in her throat. She'd always thought so much of him. He was bright, funny, determined, and the best damn cop she'd ever seen. How could he have tossed all that by the wayside for dirty money?

The need to be clean was suddenly overwhelming. She kneaded the bar of soap between her hands and scrubbed her legs, her face, her chest…She halted abruptly when she realized that Tucker was watching her every move. "Stop it!" she hissed as she wrapped her arms around herself.

"Damn it, Taryn. Why are you so ready to believe the worst about me?"

"I'm not! Or I wasn't—until I saw the proof."

She gave him her back. The proof—it made her feel even filthier. She didn't want to touch herself in front of him, but the stickiness on her thighs reminded her what she'd done with him. Steeling her nerve, she reached for her sex. Her senses were still on overload down there, and she bit her lip to keep from groaning.

He grabbed her by the shoulders and spun her around. "Forget the so-called 'proof'. Evidence can be planted. I was framed."

She gaped at him. Hastily, she pulled her hand away from her crotch and slammed the bar of soap into its tray.

"Framed? I don't see how." She stepped around him and reached for a towel. "Your fingerprints were found all over the pack of heroin in Justin's pocket."

"I didn't give it to him."

"They were also covering most of the stash discovered in your gym bag at the Y."

"Anybody could have put that there."

"It was in your locker."

"The Y isn't known for its high security measures, Swanny. Besides, do you know how much heroin, cocaine, marijuana, and other crap I've handled in my career? How many bits of evidence I've seized? Shit, look how much stuff we found during the Rodriguez case."

He hit the faucet handle and stepped out of the shower after her. "Hell, that doesn't even have to be the explanation. My fingerprints were on the plastic baggies, not the drugs themselves. I've been known to pack a few lunches in my day."

Taryn wrapped the heavy weight towel around herself and relished the protection it provided. The war between her body and her mind was disconcerting. She tried to retreat to her role as prosecutor. "Fifty-thousand dollars was found in your house. Explain that one away, Detective."

That seemed to humble him. He stopped rubbing his towel across his chest, and the expression he gave her was pained. "I can't."

She felt her last flicker of hope die.

"You knew Justin Diaz," she said.

"Sure I did. He played on the basketball team I coach at the Y. He was a good kid."

"He was also a kid who'd had drug problems in the past. Most of the kids on that team have had similar problems. That kind of makes them good targets, good buyers, doesn't it?"

She didn't expect him to react so swiftly. His hand whipped out and caught her by the nape of her neck. His eyes shot sparks as he glared at her. "I've never put a kid in danger in my life. I coached that team to keep the kids off the streets. I can't believe you would accuse me of something like that."

"I can't believe you would do something like that," she shot back.

The look on his face changed.

"Then don't believe it," he growled. "Believe in *me*, Taryn."

Oh, God. Why was he making this so hard? She braced her hands against his chest.

"Stop it! Just stop," she said, losing her tenuous grip on her control. "You're trying to spin things. You're trying to twist everything around in my head so I have doubts."

He caught her chin. "As in 'beyond a shadow'? You bet your sweet ass, I am."

She was at a loss for words.

He took a deep breath and softly brushed his thumb over her trembling lips. "Think about it, Swanny. How would you feel if you sent an innocent man to jail? What if that man was me?"

Emotion clogged her throat. She didn't want to hear things like that. She knew her actions affected people's lives every day. That was why she was so careful. That was why she double and triple checked everything. She couldn't afford to make mistakes—especially mistakes like that. They would destroy her.

He saw her hesitation.

"Come on, baby," he said coaxingly. "Work with me, if for nothing but your own peace of mind. What have you got to lose?"

Chapter Four

Taryn tried to steel herself, but she couldn't stand to see him this way. Lying or not, he could be anywhere right now, running for his freedom, but he'd chosen to come to her. He'd covered miles just to talk to her.

And the possibility that he was telling the truth? Frankly, it terrified her. Putting away an innocent was one of her most secret, darkest fears.

But he knew that.

They'd talked about it many times before, on long nights, during confusing cases...

She rubbed her aching forehead. Her head was spinning out of control. He'd set her off-balance on purpose, but if there were even the slightest possibility, no matter how remote..."All right, I'll listen. I just don't see how you're going to change my mind. I've been over the evidence a million times, looking for something that would clear you."

An unidentifiable emotion flashed in his eyes. "You looked?"

She sighed. "I looked."

He kissed her again hard and quick—just enough to muddle her senses.

"Then let's talk," he said.

She pushed him away and clenched the towel to her chest. "I want to get dressed first."

He looked down at himself. He'd wrapped a towel around his waist, but the clothes that he'd worn the night before were lying in a heap on the floor. "That might not be such a bad idea. We need to think, and that's hard for me to do when you're naked. Hell, it's hard enough when you're twenty feet away and fully dressed."

Taryn felt herself begin to weaken, but she stiffened her back-bone. She refused to let him sweet-talk her. She'd listen to his side of the story, but she was good at her job. In all the years she'd been a prosecutor, she'd never come across a criminal who didn't claim to be innocent. Just because she wanted Tucker to be didn't mean that he was. "My dad left a sweat suit behind last time my parents visited. You can wear that."

As they dressed, she desperately tried to pull on her professional cloak. If she was going to listen to his side of the story, she needed to detach herself. She tried to put on one of her work outfits, but he tossed a pair of jeans and a T-shirt at her. An attempt to put her hair up was firmly vetoed, too.

"You're not going to hide behind your armor," he said as he followed her into the kitchen. "I won't let you."

She scowled when she saw the broken window, but opened a cup-board, pulled down a box of cereal, and grabbed a bowl. When she turned, he was blocking her way.

"I said I would listen to you," she said. "What more do you want?"

His arms bracketed her as he braced himself on the counter. He leaned down to her level, and his gaze seemed to pierce into her soul. "I want all of you—ADA Swanson, the soft woman who slept in my arms last night, and the fireball who just nearly burned off my cock. You've spent so much time trying to prove yourself as a lawyer, baby, I think you've forgotten that there are more sides to you."

She pushed the box of corn flakes against his chest. "Do you want to talk about the case or not?"

He gave her a hard look, but backed off. "Yes, I do."

She took her breakfast to the table. She turned to get the milk, but he was already standing there with the gallon out of the refrigerator and a bowl of his own. Veering in a different direction, she opened a drawer and returned with two spoons. Stiffly, she sat. "So talk."

He glanced at the small TV on the kitchen counter. "I think I'll check up on the posse first."

He clicked on the television and soon found a morning news program. By the time he got his bowl of cereal prepared, the news anchor was talking about his case.

"Authorities are still searching for Michael Tucker, the former po-lice detective charged with drug running," the blond Ken doll reported. "Yesterday, Tucker escaped when the police vehicle transporting him from his arraignment hearing was involved in a two-car collision at the intersection of Highway 16 and Maple Road. Armed guards in charge of watching Tucker were injured in the accident, but have subsequently been treated and released from a local hospital. Due to their injuries, neither guard witnessed Tucker's escape. The driver of the car, who is believed to have run a stop sign, remains in critical condition and has not regained consciousness."

The camera changed angles, and the anchor cocked his head ac-cordingly. "At this time, Tucker's whereabouts are unknown. He is not believed to be armed, but should be considered dangerous. If you have any information, you are encouraged to call the authorities at 555-4000."

Tucker shot her a look. "Don't even think about it."

Taryn dipped her spoon into her cornflakes. "Why would I? My phones don't even work."

The jab must have landed, because he scowled. "I'm sorry about that, babe. I know I must be acting like a crazy man, but you're my only hope."

"So you take me hostage." Milk sloshed over the side of her bowl. "That's always a good way to win over people."

"Swanny," he said shortly. "I'm the subject of a statewide hunt. They're coming after me, and I've got two choices—run or clear my name. I'd prefer to do the latter, but for that, I need your help. Unfor-tunately, you don't seem to be in a very helpful mood."

"Can you blame me?" She gave up on her breakfast, and her spoon came clattering down.

"Hey, I'm sorry, but I've got my reasons."

"Your reasons. Remind me again what they are."

He gave a short bark of laughter and ran a hand through his hair. "You got me into this mess. You're going to get me out."

She glared at him. How dare he turn this whole thing around on her! She slapped her hands on the table, stood from her chair, and advanced on him. "*I* got you into this mess? Sorry, but that doesn't compute, Detective. I've got file upon file of information that shows that *you* did just fine getting *yourself* into this bit of trouble."

Tucker caught Taryn's finger as it poked him in the chest, and his senses went on the alert. The tingle in the back of his neck had saved his butt too many times to count. He wasn't about to ignore his instincts now. "Where are those files?"

She hesitated, and her face went intentionally blank. "At the office."

The tingling intensified. "Liar," he said smoothly.

Her jaw dropped, and she jerked her hand back. "I'm the liar?"

"I warned you about that angel face." He reached out and caught her chin. He ran his thumb across her lower lip, and it quivered. "I know when you're bluffing, babe. Go get the damn files."

She pulled back so she was out of his reach, and her anger shimmered like a halo around her. "Fine," she ground out.

She spun around and headed out of the kitchen. He was right on her heels. He could hardly believe she had the files here. He'd wanted to get his hands on this information. If he could just go through it, he might find something that the investigators had missed. At this point, he would be grateful for anything, *anything* to go on.

The office was actually a small, second bedroom that had been converted into a workspace. With the desk, computer gear, and file cabinets, there wasn't a lot of empty room. He immediately headed to the desk. There, sitting right on the desktop were at least a dozen files marked with his name.

"Wow." For a moment, he was taken aback. He thumbed through the stack and shot her a quick look. "This is a lot. Do you have everything here?"

She shrugged and glared at him. "Maybe."

"But why would you keep it here? Why not at the office?"

"What else am I supposed to do in my spare time?" she snapped.

Tucker felt a surprising surge of satisfaction. So the ADA did have doubts. It made him more optimistic than he'd been in a long time.

In a swift move, he grabbed her and pulled her hard against him. "I can think of quite a few ways to pass the time," he murmured as his head dropped.

He caught her mouth in a steamy kiss. She resisted at first, but soon her body melted against his. He brushed his lips across her cheek and nipped her earlobe. "Go through them with me," he said.

"I can't," she said in a strained voice.

"Why not?"

"I've been over everything so many times, I've practically got it memorized. I can't look at it again."

He was beginning to understand. It wasn't that she didn't want to help him; it was that she couldn't find a way. The files were so dog-eared, she must have spent hours going through them. From her perspective, though, everything pointed to him being guilty.

"That's okay," he said. He gave her a comforting squeeze. "Help me carry them out to the living room, and I'll look at them."

"What's wrong with here?"

"The room's too small," he growled. "If we stay in here ten more seconds, I'm going to be banging you like a bull."

It took nine seconds for her to help him move things to the floor of the living room. Tucker didn't know whether to be amused or offended. The files were too tempting, though, and he dropped to the floor to read them. Taryn sat well across the room from him with her back leaning against the couch. It was just as well, he supposed. Any closer and he wouldn't have been able to concentrate.

He was soon immersed in the reports. After about twenty minutes, though, he felt a flare of annoyance. His head snapped up, and he glared at her. "You questioned my *mother*?"

Her cheeks flushed, and she toyed with the weave of the carpet. "I was looking for a second set of keys to your house. If somebody planted the money, they had to have gotten in somehow. There were no signs of tampering with the locks. I thought she might have had access."

"You thought my *mother* was involved? Swanny!"

"No, I didn't think your mother was involved," she snapped. "I was looking for keys. Somebody might have taken her set without her knowing."

"Oh, Mom would know." A smile pulled at Tucker's lips. "Did she give you a hard time?"

"She was... protective."

His smile turned into a full-out laugh. "That's a nice way of putting it. I know how she can get."

"She hates me," Taryn said quietly.

He winked at her. "She'll change her mind when you help clear me."

She shrugged uneasily and glanced around the room. "Mind if I open the shades? I'm getting claustrophobic sitting around in the dark."

"The light's good enough," he said. He looked back down at the file in his hand. His mind was already focusing on its contents. "Leave them closed."

"Fine," she sighed. She leaned her head back against the couch and closed her eyes.

Tucker dove into the files. Many of the pages were worn and crinkled, but he still felt he had a chance of finding something useful. After all, he had a unique perspective on this case. He should be able to see things his former coworkers hadn't. Reading through the notes was strange, though. These tidbits of info were all about *him*. It was almost like he was having an out of body experience, but he shrugged off the feeling. It needed to be done.

Half an hour later, he roused Taryn from her short nap. "Was this bag in my gym locker checked for prints other than my own?"

Groggily, she opened her eyes. "Hmm? Yes, the bag was analyzed."

"What about the locker, especially this area around the door latch?"

"What? Where?" She rubbed her eyes and leaned closer.

She gasped when he pulled her onto his lap. "This will work better if we go through them together," he explained.

Over time, the two of them had developed an uncanny method of communication when it came to casework. They played off each other's thoughts and often came up with answers that neither of them would have concluded alone. He'd never needed that calculating mind of hers more.

He quickly arranged them so that his back was against the couch and she was leaning against his chest. Her butt fit snugly between his outstretched legs. His cock automatically reacted to the contact, but he ignored the ache for the time being. Patiently, he held the picture in front of her. "How much of the locker was dusted?"

She sat stiffly in his arms. No doubt, his erection was as distracting to her as it was to him. "The whole thing," she said.

"The whole thing?" He looked at her sharply. "The floor? The roof?"

"Everything. Including the lock."

He felt a surge of irritation. "I told you before, that lock wasn't mine."

"Then why did it have your fingerprints on it?"

"Hell, I'd just come out of the shower. My clothes were in there. How was I supposed to know what was going on? I saw the lock and looked at the locker number. It didn't compute. It was stupid, I know, but I touched the damn thing."

She squirmed, so he adjusted her into a more relaxed position.

He grabbed another file. "It says here that you found metal shavings on the floor. That proves that somebody used a bolt cutter."

"The police unit did that. And before you say anything, they had a valid search warrant."

"Provided by that son-of-a-bitch Sheuster." Tucker ran a hand through his hair. "So compare the shavings. If they don't match the lock you have, I've got proof."

"The shavings aren't conclusive. I've already checked with a met-allurgist. The same type of steel is used in both the brand of lock we found and the one you claim to have used."

"All right," he said, his chin brushing against her hair. "All right."

They weren't getting very far, but it was clear that she had tried to find holes in the case. That, at least, made him feel a little better. Wrapping his arms around her again, he lifted the stack of pictures so they could both see them. "Let's look through the rest of these."

He flipped to the next picture, which was a shot of the tank of his toilet. The lid had been removed, and a plastic bag of money was stuffed inside. "Somebody's been watching too many bad movies. At least you haven't broadcast it on the news that I hide my valuables in the toilet."

"I still can."

"I'm serious," he said as he rubbed his chin against her temple.

As angry as he'd been with her, he had to admit that she'd behaved professionally. She'd even showed small signs of compassion. "You did me a big favor by not fighting the judge's ruling to bar cameras from the courtroom. I appreciate that."

"If I'd known you'd come to my house and hold me hostage, I might have acted differently."

"I don't think so." He brushed his lips against her hair and turned to the next shot in the stack.

Taryn felt Tucker's muscles freeze when he realized what he'd uncovered. It was a picture of Justin Diaz's body as it had been found in an empty alleyway downtown. The boy lay on his back with his empty eyes staring blindly at the sky. He wore workout clothes that were still sweaty, and his hand was draped limply over a basketball. She'd checked. The last time he'd been seen alive and well was earlier that evening at practice.

Tucker quickly put the picture aside and turned it facedown. The next one was nearly as upsetting. It was a picture of him with the teenager. Tucker was spinning a basketball on his finger, and Justin had his arm slung around his coach's shoulders.

Taryn struggled to find something to say. "It looks like you two were very close."

"We were." His voice was raspy with emotion.

Instinctively, she covered his hand on her stomach. She didn't know why, but she felt compelled to comfort him. Her brain told her that he'd killed this kid. It was probably unintentional, but still, he'd given Justin the drugs. Her brain knew all that, but her heart hated seeing him this distressed.

She rubbed her palm against the back of his hand. "I know you didn't mean to hurt him."

"I didn't hurt him, Counselor." He threw out the title like it was garbage, but sighed and settled his chin against her shoulder. "I was trying to help him off the streets. I know how the Diazes presented themselves in court yesterday, but his home life sucked. I was trying to show him there was a better way."

"Drugs are enticing to kids that age. If they can help them escape, they want them badly."

"You think I don't know that? I was trying to get him away from that crap. I would never have given him more."

She linked her fingers through his. She could feel his pain, and she did believe him. He might not have given the drugs directly to Justin, but somehow the kid had gotten his hands on them. "Did he know the combination to your locker?"

"Are you kidding me?" He turned his head to look at her. "I'm not stupid. Those were good kids I coached, but they're street kids. If I wanted to keep my wallet, I didn't give them the temptation."

She returned his look, and their noses almost brushed. "Then give me something, Tucker. Explain to me how this happened. I'm out of ideas."

Lines wrinkled his forehead, and his jaw hardened as he glanced at the files strewn across the floor. "What about the money?" he said. He reached for the photograph of his bathroom. "I never touched that."

She blinked. He was usually sharper than that. It proved how desperately he was grabbing at straws. "The money was found in a plastic bag inside your toilet tank. Water and fingerprints don't mix."

He grimaced and the photo fluttered to the ground. Tiredly, he reached up to rub the back of his neck.

"Who could have framed you, Tucker?" she asked quietly. "Who had the knowledge, the opportunity, and the motive?"

"Hell, I don't know." He rubbed his hand against her stomach and sighed. "But I like hearing you ask the question." He softly nuzzled her earlobe. "This is much better. I don't like fighting with you, Taryn."

They'd gotten nowhere. He'd done nothing to prove her wrong, but he was getting harder and harder to resist. "I don't like it, either," she admitted.

"Do you know how much I've enjoyed working with you over the past two years?" His tongue rimmed her earlobe, and the little hairs on the nape of her neck perked up. "I liked seeing your eyes light up as you put a case together."

Taryn felt goose bumps pop up on her skin. His lips and the hand on her belly were creating havoc with her system. "I like puzzles," she said, "And you always brought me all the right pieces."

"I wish I had them for you now."

So did she.

He tugged her white T-shirt out of the waistband of her jeans so he had access to her skin. He settled his palm on her abdomen and electricity shot through her nerve endings.

"Tucker," she groaned. Not again. She'd never be able to resist him.

His voice dropped to a whisper. "You made me wait a long time, Swanny."

She squirmed, but stopped when she realized she was only rubbing herself against his erection. "It wasn't appropriate for us to become involved."

"Why not?" he asked. He leaned over her shoulder so he could see her face. "You never told me why."

She bit her lip. She didn't like talking about that, but she didn't see what it could hurt now. And anything that would ease his anger towards her would be a bonus. "I dated another ADA at my last job. It ended...poorly."

"You got dumped?"

"I dumped him, but that wasn't the problem. After we broke up, everyone looked on me as the ex-girlfriend, not an ADA in my own right. I had seniority, but cases that should have come to me started going to him. I didn't get a pay raise that year. It finally got so bad, I had to leave. I transferred here and swore that I'd never let my personal life and work life cross again."

"Weren't you ever tempted? I tried my damnedest."

"Of course, I was t-tempted." Her voice hitched when he placed an open-mouthed kiss on the side of her neck.

"Temptation doesn't even begin to cover the feelings I had for you," he said. "Your perfume, your body... Hell, I could get a hard-on just by hearing your voice on the phone."

His hand slid up her stomach and began toying with the front clasp of her bra. Taryn knew she should push his hands away, but instead, her fingers sank into the muscles of his thighs.

He grunted with approval. "Did you ever cream your panties when we were talking on the telephone?"

Lust hit her hard. She moaned when her bra clasp let loose, and his hand slid under one of the cups.

"Did you?"

"Yes," she groaned.

His other hand slid under her T-shirt, and he cupped her posses-sively. "That still doesn't explain why you went out with Sheuster," he growled. "Why him, but not me?"

"I never went out with Marty." She hissed when his fingers pinched her nipples in rebuke. "I didn't. We might have had a working lunch or two, but it was all platonic."

"Not from the way he described it. The picture he painted was of the two of you humping like rabbits."

"I never... Tucker!" He'd pushed her breasts together and was simultaneously assaulting her nipples with his thumbnails.

"Mind if we get rid of this bra?"

His teeth nipped at her earlobe, and Taryn couldn't voice a protest. She didn't want to; desire had her wound too tight. She started to pull up her T-shirt.

"No, no. Leave that on. I like the way the material pulls tight over your tits."

She squeezed her thighs together. He could make her wet with only words, but she didn't stand a chance when he touched her and talked dirty at the same time.

With his help, she managed to shrug out of the bra. He pulled it though the arm sleeve of her shirt and tossed it to the side. He then settled his hands on the waistband of her jeans. With slow, intentional movements, he undid the button and slid down the zipper. Together, they watched as his hand glided under her panties to her moist sex.

"You needed this as much as I did."

"God, I've never been this horny before," she groaned.

"You've been screwing the wrong guys."

Unable to stop herself, Taryn lifted her hips to give him better access. He penetrated her with two fingers. As he ground the base of his palm against her pubic bone, he let out a soft laugh. "You need a slippery when wet sign, baby."

She was beyond conversation. She arched her neck back against Tucker's shoulder and pushed her mound hard against his hand. His fingers were scissoring inside of her, stretching her, preparing her for more.

His other hand was practically mauling her breasts, but she loved it. Her hips lifted completely off the ground. Soon, she was moaning in

delight and panting with exertion. She wanted more. She needed...
The doorbell rang.

They both froze. Taryn dropped to the floor and stared at the door in confusion. She was horrified when the bell began ringing non-stop and insistent pounding began.

Thank God he hadn't let her open the drapes!

"Who do you think it is?" she asked hoarsely.

"Nobody good, that's for sure," he said. He pulled his wet hand out of her panties and hurriedly zipped up her jeans. "You'd better go see who it is before they send for back-up."

She was disconcerted when he helped her to her feet and pushed her toward the door. Her head snapped toward him when she comprehended what he'd said. "You think it's the cops?"

"Probably," he said as he disappeared from the room.

The doorbell was still buzzing, and the knocking had intensified. Dazedly, Taryn headed towards it. With every step, she could feel the moisture that had collected in the crotch of her jeans. They'd be sopping wet within a few minutes. The seam of the denim was rubbing against her clit, keeping her arousal right on the edge.

There was nothing she could do about it now, though. Taking a deep breath, she pushed her disheveled hair over her shoulder and opened the door. A uniformed officer stood on her doorstep.

She went still.

It was the police. She hadn't thought about what that would mean.

This was it—her rescue.

But for Tucker, it was the end of the road.

Indecision jammed her thought processes.

"Ma'am?" the man said.

She looked at him blankly. "Officer," she said, the word awkward on her lips.

Tell him!

No, don't. You'll regret it for the rest of your life.

"Can I help you with something?" she asked.

She needed time to think; time to make a decision.

For a moment, the officer didn't respond. He simply stood there gaping at her with wide eyes. It was only then that Taryn realized that she hadn't put her bra back on. The T-shirt was close fitting, and her nipples were distended. A cold breeze swept into the house, and they promptly perked up higher.

Her face flared. The cop was getting quite the show, but he was distracted. She needed to use that to her advantage.

She needed to consider her options.

Steeling herself not to cover her exposure, she repeated her question. "Is something the matter, Officer?"

He licked his lips, but couldn't seem to tear his gaze away from her breasts. The attention only focused her awareness of her nipples. They itched under his concentration, and she felt the stickiness on her thighs. "Officer?" she said, her voice strained.

"Um, yes, ma'am. We're on the lookout for Michael Tucker. You haven't by chance seen him, have you?"

Seen him? She'd seen him, touched him, kissed him, screwed him...

Tell the cop he's in the next room...

The place he went when he let **you** *answer the door.*

Her fingers tightened on the doorjamb. Tucker had put his fate securely in her hands.

Would a guilty man do that?

A cunning guilty man might.

Stop it! Just stop it!

Circular thinking was getting her nowhere, but it all came down to one thing.

She couldn't turn him over. Not now. Not until she'd fully explored his side of the story. He seemed honestly intent on proving his innocence. She had to see that through, for better or for worse. He wouldn't hurt her; she knew that with every fiber of her being. She needed to play this out until the end.

At least then she'd know for certain whether or not he'd killed that poor kid.

And whether this attraction growing between them was real or a twisted, cruel ploy.

"No, sir, I haven't." Guilt hit her square in the chest, and she gripped the doorjamb tighter. "Why would you think he'd be here?"

"You're the one prosecuting the case, ma'am. He might have revenge on his mind."

She shifted her weight, and the officer's gaze followed the swaying motion of her breasts. By now, her nipples were two pink tent posts under the material, and he'd given up all pretense of not looking at them. "If I know Detective Tucker, he's in another state by now," she said.

"We haven't been able to pinpoint his whereabouts yet, ma'am." The officer pushed his hat back on his head and finally met her gaze. The lust in his eyes was unmistakable. "You should be careful. ADA Sheuster was concerned when he couldn't reach you by phone."

The policeman looked over her shoulder. Taryn realized that her files were still spread out all over the floor. And her bra! It was draped over the hassock in front of her chair! She took a quick sidestep to block his view. "I'm working on a new case. I unplugged my phone so I wouldn't be disturbed. I must have fallen asleep."

Playing the part, she ran her hand through her mussed hair. "Your knocking woke me up."

With her arm lifted the way it was, she was practically pushing her tits in the man's face. It didn't escape his notice. "Must have been quite the dream, ma'am."

Her face flamed, and she dropped her arm. She tugged at her T-shirt in embarrassment, but that only pulled the material tighter. The officer practically began drooling.

"You can tell ADA Sheuster that I'm fine," she said. "If there's nothing else, I really should get back to work."

The officer hooked his thumbs in his gun belt, but didn't move from her doorstep. Desire hardened his features, and Taryn felt an inappropriate shiver of response run down her spine. There was something about a man in uniform.

His voice went low. "Do you need any help with that work? Ma'am?"

The respectful term touched her like a caress, and Taryn flinched. Enough. She'd let things go too far as it was.

"Good-bye Officer..." She looked closely at his badge. "Denton."

She finally crossed her arms over her chest. The free show was over. "Good luck with your search."

He got the message. The glint in his eyes dimmed, but he took a step back and tipped his hat. "The best with your case, ADA Swanson."

He turned and walked down her steps, but moved gingerly. Taryn shut and locked the door behind him. Groaning, she leaned her forehead against it. She couldn't believe the extremes she was going to—all for Tucker, a man she didn't even know if she could trust.

"Swanny?"

She slowly turned around and leveled a look on him.

So help him, she'd better not regret this.

"I just broke my code of ethics for you."

His face was solemn. "You couldn't give me up."

Tucker took a step towards her. "You believe me."

Her hand whipped up, and she pointed at him to ward him off. "No, I don't. I don't know what to believe anymore, and you've twisted my thoughts into knots. I'm just giving myself time to straighten everything out."

He kept coming. "You *want* to believe me."

"That's beside the point."

"No, it's not." He walked right up to her and settled his hands at her waist. In a flash, he whipped down the zipper on her jeans. "To me, that's pretty much all I've got."

Taryn gasped in dismay. Her jeans hadn't even been buttoned! Heavens, she'd been parading in front of that dazed police officer with her breasts standing at attention and her jeans halfway undone. She batted at Tucker's hands. "Don't touch me," she snapped. "I swear I'll call him back here and have him arrest your ass."

"Who? Denton? He'd be too busy looking at yours."

"Damn it, Tucker!" She shoved at his shoulders, but he didn't budge. "I just crossed the line for you, and all you can think about is sex?"

"All I can think about is you." He pulled her into a hard kiss. "You're listening to me, and you're protecting me. You can't blame me for being excited about that."

She tried to slither away, but he slid his hands right under her panties and cupped her bottom. The intimate touch was shocking, and she had to fight the inclination to shimmy against it. "Well, I'm not excited," she said stubbornly.

"Liar. You don't want to send me back to that holding cell any-more than I want to go. What we both want is me right here, screwing the daylights out of you."

With a flick of his wrists, everything she was wearing below the waist dropped to her knees. Her clothes didn't stay there long, because he set his foot in the crotch of her panties and pushed down. He lifted her out of the pile and kicked it away. He took three steps and dropped her on the couch. "Stop denying it."

Chapter Five

"I can't believe you! You cocky bastard! I lied for you. I put my reputation on the line and, now, you expect me to put out?"

Taryn had never been more furious in her life. She tried to kick Tucker, but he just caught and held her legs. With a tug, he brought her hips to the very edge of the cushions. He tore off his borrowed sweats. When he dropped to his knees between her legs, her anger turned to acute self-consciousness.

She was still wearing the T-shirt, but it only came to her waist. Everything below was left exposed, and he wasn't being shy about looking. She could practically feel the heat of his laser-like stare. He'd spread her legs wide, and the position left the most private part of her defenseless. Unable to bear his intense examination, she covered herself with her hands.

"No, baby. Let me look at you." He gently gripped her wrists and moved her hands aside. He held them against the couch and renewed his inspection. "You're gorgeous."

Taryn squirmed on the cushions. "Manhandling me isn't going to change my mind," she hissed. "I'm still mad at you."

He gently held her in place. "I'm getting that fact loud and clear. If you'll just lie back and relax, I'll try to help you out of that grumpy mood."

For some reason, she felt more vulnerable half-clothed with him than she'd felt totally naked. Looking down, she saw her nipples rubbing against the white material of her T-shirt. If possible, they'd grown even redder and stiffer. Below, Tucker kneeled in the vee of her legs. He was only inches from the tangle of curls at its apex.

It was too much.

"Please, Tucker," she said. "This is making me uncomfortable."

His gaze shot up to her face. He read whatever emotion was in her eyes and gave her a soft smile. "We can't have that."

Reaching over, he grabbed a pillow from its place against the arm of the sofa. He tucked it in the hollow space between the curve of her spine and the couch cushions. She had to admit it eased some of her physical discomfort. Still... "That's not what I meant," she whispered.

"I know," he said in a low tone that rippled over her skin. He pushed himself up from his kneeling position and hovered over her. "You just put yourself in the line of fire for me, baby. Let me show you how grateful I am."

He kissed her softly before backing away. "Trust me, Taryn."

His gaze connected with hers and a shimmer of excitement shot through her system. He was waiting for her approval, and an emotion she didn't want to define gripped her. "All right," she said slowly.

She'd thought he'd smile again. He didn't.

Instead, his expression turned intense. His weight came down on her, and his open-mouthed kiss was hot, hard, and very personal. He kissed her forever, until her anger, her discomfort, and her uneasiness all vanished.

Taryn found herself clutching him as his lips left hers, but he wasn't through. He ran soft kisses across her closed eyelids, her cheekbones, and the point of her chin. His gentleness was driving her mad. She turned her head to give him access to the side of her neck. His tongue on her pulse made her wriggle, but this time she wasn't trying to get away.

His hot mouth dropped lower, and she gasped when his teeth closed on her nipple. Need spilled through her veins. "Tucker!"

"That cop wanted to do this. He couldn't take his eyes off your tits."

"You were watching us?" she gasped.

His tongue ran across her aching flesh, leaving a big wet spot on the T-shirt. "I saw the whole thing. Including your reaction. You liked having him watch you."

"I did not!" The words ended with a moan when he drew her breast, T-shirt and all, into his sucking mouth.

"Oh, yeah?" His hand suddenly pressed hard between her legs.

He dipped a finger inside her and tested her wetness. "Evidence is evidence, baby. You liked teasing that poor bastard. Admit it."

His touch made her all the more aware of how vulnerable she was. She bit her lip as he explored her, and the muscles at the small of her back clenched. She looked at his slick finger when he held it in front of her, and shivers coursed across her skin.

He was grinning at her again.

"Well... maybe I did," she confessed. Strutting around in front of the helpless policeman had made her feel naughty. But not as naughty as this. "It was all your fault though. You got me all worked up and then just left me there."

"If you remember our situation, babe, there was a cop at our door. I'm on the run from the law. Is any of this ringing a bell?"

"Excuses, excuses." Her eyes widened. Had she said that out loud?

He closed his teeth softly across her nipple. "I promise to finish the job this time," he said.

She gave in. Why fight it when she wanted it so much?

She trailed her fingers through his dark hair. "You'd better get back to work."

He smiled deviously. "Yes, ma'am," he drawled in a dead-on imitation of the police officer.

Taryn's belly clenched. If he'd been looking for an aphrodisiac, he'd just found one. She'd never been one for games, but combine Tucker and that leering cop, and *ohhhh*!

He dropped his head to her other breast, and she felt her pleasure mounting. The wet material abraded her nipples and made her want more. "Harder," she groaned. "Oh, please. Harder."

Tucker pulled back and looked at his handiwork. The front of Taryn's top was one big wet spot. She was breathing roughly, and her breasts shuddered with every breath she took. Her nipples were in plain view, and he liked the effect. "We're going to have to take you down to Flashers next Tuesday night, baby. You've got that wet T-shirt contest in the bag."

"Michael," she panted. Her impatience was beginning to show.

He loved it when she called him that. She only seemed to use it as a last resort whenever she was really mad or really horny. The really mad part could be fun, but the really horny part was better. Way better.

Using his thumbs and forefingers, he reached out and clamped down on her wet nipples. She nearly came off the couch.

He calmed her with a path of kisses down her stomach.

His own breaths were getting short. She did things for him…incredible things. He couldn't remember ever getting so hard so fast—not even when he'd been a sex-starved teenager.

Then again, at sixteen, he hadn't had a blonde bombshell laid out like a sacrifice before him.

He dipped his tongue into her belly button and felt her quiver. He could hardly believe that he was with her. Just when his life had been jerked out from under his feet, things between them had clicked.

Wasn't that just his luck? He'd finally gotten the girl, but he was most likely headed to prison for the next twenty-five years of his life.

He kicked the thought out of his head. Nothing was going to spoil this.

Nothing.

He determinedly ran his hands down her hips. Giving in to an impulse, he slid them under her buttocks and squeezed the round globes. Her low moan told him how much she liked the attention.

"I'm going to have to search you, ma'am," he drawled. He'd seen how sharply she'd responded to his imitation of Officer Denton, and he wasn't above using it to his advantage. If she got off on it, so did he.

His fingers nudged into the crevice of her ass, and her butt cheeks clenched. "But Officer, what did I do?" she said on a high note.

She was into it.

Looking down, Tucker saw the prize. Her legs were spread, and she offered no resistance. "You've been a very bad girl, Ms. Swanson."

He raked his hands from her buttocks down to the back of her thighs. Her breath caught when he lifted her and draped her legs over his shoulders. The position put her right into his face. He gave her one, long lick.

She gave a strangled cry, and he deliberately went in for more. Using his tongue, he sought out every crevice, every curve, and every sensitive nerve ending. She was thrashing on the couch by the time he found her opening. He pushed his tongue inside her as far as it would go, and she arched like a bow.

"Don't resist, ma'am," he said, his mouth moving against her.

"Officer," she panted. "It's too personal."

"Let me do my job."

Simulating the sex act, he thrust his tongue in and out of her. She gave a high-pitched whimper, and he increased his pace. He felt the flutters begin, and he quickly changed tactics. He slid his mouth up-wards until the bud of her clit popped inside. He gave the epicenter of nerve endings one hard suck, and she came undone.

"Ah, Michael!"

Her orgasm was hard and violent. She shuddered in his arms, but he continued working her with his mouth until the last palpitations drifted away. Only when she lay limp against the pillow did he give her a reprieve.

But not for long. His dick was as hard as the nightstick he'd carried as a beat cop. All he could think of was getting it inside of her and doing a different kind of beating.

"I'm nearly finished, ma'am," he said through heavy breaths. "But I'm afraid I'm going to have to do a more thorough body cavity search."

Her heavy-lidded eyes opened. "But, Officer, is it really necessary?"

"Oh yes, ma'am, it's *absolutely* necessary."

His control was unraveling at a frightening pace. He couldn't wait for her to catch up. His fingers dug into her hips as he lowered her to him. He let gravity help, and she slid right off the couch and onto his waiting cock.

"Oh!" she cried. Her sleepy eyes popped open, and her hands clutched at his shoulders. "Tucker?"

"You can do it, baby," he growled. "You're flexible enough."

She was nearly bent in two. Her legs had slid down the front of his chest and were now pointed straight up in the air, with her ankles somewhere around his ears. Wedged between his body and the couch, she had nowhere to move.

But he could move. He drew his hips back, slowly pulling himself out of her. At the very end of the stroke, he reversed directions and filled her again.

Her eyes glazed over, and her neck arched back. "Ah! You feel twice as big."

"Good, huh?"

"I... I don't know."

He did. The expression on her face was primal. Her hair was wild around her shoulders, and hunger burned in her eyes. What they were doing was beyond good, so much so it was almost frightening.

He gave another experimental stroke. "Too much, ma'am?"

He'd hit her trigger.

"No," she said slowly. Her breaths started pumping faster as her excitement returned. "I can... I can handle it, Officer."

"All right, ma'am. Take a deep breath and relax. Let me work, and it will all be over soon."

Tucker gave another thrust that made his head spin. She was so hot and wet. And tight. She gripped him like a vice. Carefully, he increased the speed of his thrusts to see how she would take it.

She took it well.

Suddenly, his gnawing arousal couldn't be held back any longer. The need for her overwhelmed him, and he began to buck against her. If anything, his cock seemed to grow bigger inside her tight passage.

She made a mewling noise and her toes went en-pointe. Her inability to move seemed to thrill her, because she was already making little sounds at the back of her throat.

He was beginning to love those little sounds.

"Michael," she whined in desperation.

His control snapped, and he slammed into her. Her mouth opened in a soundless cry, but he kept plunging. He shagged her until sweat was running down his back, and stars shimmered behind his eyelids. Finally, *finally* he felt his balls draw up tight.

With a roar, he exploded. She gripped his shoulders hard, and collapsing, he pulled her down to the floor with him. Her damp skin clung to his, and her hair spread across his shoulder. He wrapped his arms around her to keep her close.

"Holy hell, Swanny," he said when he could catch his breath. "You're going to be the death of me."

"I was only trying to cooperate, Officer," she said shakily.

Lifting an eyelid took supreme effort, but he managed to give her a look. "That guy's starting to piss me off."

"Why?"

"He makes you hot."

She glanced away shyly. "No, Michael. You make me hot."

Tucker lifted his head sharply. "Say that again."

Her cheeks turned pink. "I didn't mean...You also make me angry, frustrated, and—"

He caught her chin and made her look at him. "Come on," he prompted.

She sighed and looked at the ceiling. "You make me feel a lot of things, and it's all jumbled up inside my head. You've been charged with murder, and you've taken me hostage. Yet when a policeman shows up at my door, I cover for you. I'm not myself. I'm not thinking straight."

"So don't think. Go with your gut."

She ran a hand over her eyes. "I can't trust myself."

"Why not?"

Finally, she looked at him. "Because I want to believe you, but for *me*. I can't tell anymore if I'm being selfish, if you deserve it, or if it's because of...you know...the sex."

"Ah, baby," he sighed. "It's all of the above."

"How can I be sure?"

Her mistrust cut deeper than Tucker expected, but he pushed the hurt aside. He had to remember that Taryn Swanson was the whole package: beauty, personality, and brains. They'd already confronted the physical. Now, he had to appeal to her logic. "If you thought I was a cold-blooded killer, you would've rushed into Officer Denton's arms, half-naked or not."

She opened her mouth to say something, but he covered her lips with his finger.

"If you didn't have doubts about the case, you wouldn't have dog-eared copies of the files lying around your home. You wouldn't be having chats with metallurgists, for God's sake. Your gut is screaming at you, Taryn. Your brain just isn't letting you listen."

"It would be easier if there was a hole in the evidence."

"You're picking at details, Swanny. It shouldn't be that difficult for you to have faith in me. You *know* I wouldn't do what I'm accused of doing. You wouldn't let me touch you, kiss you, or screw the daylights out of you if you weren't sure."

A sharp pang of uncertainty suddenly caught him. "Would you?"

Time stood still as they hesitantly looked at each other, and panic flared up inside Tucker's chest. He'd never even considered that she might be screwing him because she was scared or biding her time. Or even worse, manipulating him.

The tension slipped from her face. "No," she whispered.

He went still.

"I couldn't be with you if I thought you were a murderer." Her body relaxed against his. She shook her head as she stared at him incredulously. "It doesn't make any sense. I've got nothing to back it up, but I don't think you did it."

"Swanny." He dropped his forehead against hers. Relief made him lightheaded. "God, it's good to hear you say that."

"Don't make me regret it," she warned.

"You won't," he promised.

He pressed his lips to hers and all the emotion that had built inside him over the past few days poured into the kiss. The anxiousness, the tension, the frustration, the anger—and the fear. This was why he'd come here. He'd needed her faith in him.

He'd needed her.

He tucked his head into the crook of her neck and breathed deeply. Her body felt warm and comfortable pressed against his, and he savored their closeness. All of it. He hadn't realized how much he'd had invested in his plan, but thank God it had worked. Knowing that she was in his corner made him feel stronger. Together, they could fight this.

Her fingers tightened in his hair. "We have to do something to fix things," she said anxiously, "And we can't get sidetracked again. The police have already been at my door."

He wasn't ready to let the rest of the world back in. "Let's just stay like this for a little while longer."

"No, Tucker," she said gently. "We need to make plans. Let me up."

She cupped his cheek, and the one, little touch turned him to putty in her hands. He gritted his teeth. "Ah, hell."

He slowly disconnected their bodies, rolled onto his back, and rubbed his eyes with the balls of his hands. It was damn hard to fall back into the role of Detective Michael Tucker, Super Cop, when she'd just given him everything he wanted.

Well, nearly everything.

"What's our next step?" he asked tiredly. "I thought the files would help, but nothing popped out at me."

"Get dressed," she said. "We need to think."

"Right." He ran a hand over her tangled hair. "Can't do that naked."

She reached over him and grabbed the remote. He looked at her in bemusement as she clicked on the TV and began intently flipping through channels. With a sigh, he sat up and stuffed his legs into his borrowed sweatpants. His head came up, though, when she hit a news report.

"Michael Tucker, accused drug dealer, remains on the run today," the reporter said. "Authorities have narrowed their search to the Wurthington Heights area. A man matching the escapee's description was seen getting off a bus at the corner of Wilmington and Neiman Avenue. Residents in the Heights area are encouraged to be on the lookout for a man matching this description."

"How far behind are they?" she asked as she gathered up her clothes.

"A ways."

"That's good, at least," she said. She headed for the bedroom to change.

Tucker watched her backside until she was out of view and then reined himself in. *Think, man. Think.*

He made himself mentally review his movements as a picture of his scruffy face filled the TV screen. After getting off that bus in the residential area of the Heights, he'd followed the creek bed down to the business district. He'd caught another bus there. So far, the police hadn't made that connection.

He picked the remote up off the floor and tossed it onto the end table with a clatter. Damn, but it pissed him off that his own friends and coworkers were hunting him down like a dog.

His picture was replaced by video of the Diaz family walking up the steps of the courtroom to his arraignment, and the anchor's voice spoke over the clip. "Tucker is at the center of a controversial murder case that has brought to light cracks in the city's law enforcement system. Sources say that—"

"Wait a minute!" Tucker blocked out the Ken doll's words as he watched the video behind the man's head.

Something wasn't right.

He dove for the remote and frantically searched the menu buttons. He jabbed the instant record button and prayed there was a tape in the VCR.

"What is it?" Taryn said as she poked her head out. Her eyebrows went up when she saw what he was doing. "My soaps!"

He waved her off and focused on Justin's younger brother, Benny. He couldn't have seen what he'd thought he'd seen.

But he had.

"Oh, shit," he breathed.

"What?" she asked. She pulled her robe on as she hurried back to the living room to look at the screen.

The news reporter had gone on to the next story. Tucker squinted at the remote and pressed stop. He rewound the tape and hit play. "How do you slow this down?" he asked.

She took a step closer and peered into his hand. She poked a button and the film slowed down to a frame-by-frame advance. "There. What is it?"

"Look at what's on Benny's feet."

Her eyes narrowed. She watched intently as the boy climbed the steps, but just shrugged. "They look like new tennis shoes."

"Exactly," Tucker said in a hard voice. "Those are Mercury Wings. They cost about two hundred and fifty dollars."

She looked at him in confusion. "I don't understand. Is that supposed to mean something to me?"

Tucker's gut turned, but he went back to the stack of photos he'd left next to the couch. A few had been crumpled by their sexual acrobatics, but he found the one at the bottom of the pile—the one he'd turned over so he wouldn't have to look at it.

He flipped it over and tried to be impartial, but he couldn't. This wasn't just evidence. He'd known the poor kid in the photograph. He'd known his quiet intensity, his dry sense of humor, and his quick move to the basket. Tucker swallowed hard. "Look at the body. Look at the shoes."

Taryn nibbled at her fingernails as she examined the photo. The teenager lay on his back with his feet pointing limply at the sky. "Is that duct tape?"

Tucker couldn't look at the picture anymore so he passed it to her. "The Diazes didn't have enough money to buy Justin a decent pair of cross trainers, and he was the basketball player in the family. Why the hell is Benny walking around with a shiny pair of Mercury Wings?"

Taryn's face was blank for a good ten seconds. When she finally put the pieces together, her breath hitched and her eyebrows rose to almost her hairline. "But he's only twelve!"

"Remember that case a year ago? The kid was ten."

"Oh, God." She raked her hand through her mussed hair and turned swiftly back to the television. The video was still running in slow motion. "Oh, God! I've been worried about him. He's gaunt and every time we start talking about the case, he looks like he's going to be sick."

She stared at the TV for a long time, and Tucker could practically hear the gears grinding inside her head. His were already spinning at high speed. Had Benny been around the evening that Justin had died? Was he strong enough to use bolt cutters?

Taryn's gaze suddenly turned to meet his. "He's been on your side the entire time. He kept saying 'Coach couldn't have done it.' I thought he was in denial, because he liked you."

Tucker wanted to punch his fist through a wall. Instead, he clasped his fingers at the back of his neck and started circling the room. "He was always hanging out around practice. He wanted to play. I told him when he was fourteen, he could try out."

Taryn slowly sank down onto the chair. Her gaze kept flicking between the television screen and the picture in her hand. "Why would he plant the drugs in your locker?"

Tucker let his hands drop. "Panic?"

She shook her head. "There's got to be more to it. He wouldn't have been calm enough or sophisticated enough to plant the evidence. Your fingerprints were on everything."

Tucker jerked when the answer came to him. "He's got to have a supplier. And if the guy knew I was a vice detective, it would be one helluva way to get me off his back."

Taryn's eyes widened. Abruptly, she pushed herself to her feet. "This is it," she declared.

He looked at her sharply. Raw determination had settled onto her features. She walked straight across the room towards him and laid a hand on his chest.

"This is the break we've been looking for," she said.

His pulse leapt, and he stared at her hard. He trapped her hand against his heart. "We?"

"Yes, *we.*"

Her eyes went soft as she looked up at him. Still, he was surprised as hell when she went up on tiptoe and covered his lips in a long, sexy kiss. Tucker's heart tumbled over itself. It was the first time that she'd kissed him, and the implications sent his mind reeling. He couldn't even try to stop her when she pulled back and looked at him solemnly.

"I'm sorry I've been such an idiot," she said.

He watched mutely as she disappeared into the bedroom. After a few minutes, he heard the bathroom door open and close. Water was running before he was functioning enough to sit down and stop the tape, which was now showing a muscle-bound bartender kissing the socks off a sultry brunette.

Oh, man. Was he in deep.

Absently, he began searching for another newscast, but he couldn't think straight. He didn't want to get his hopes up too high. A new pair of tennis shoes could mean nothing. But that kiss…That had felt like it meant something.

The door to the bathroom opened, and he glanced up from the television broadcast. Taryn stood in the doorway, dressed to the nines in one of her high-powered business suits.

She might as well have slammed a sledgehammer into his brain.

"What the hell do you think you're doing?" he barked.

She wasn't intimidated. Calmly, she took a stance he'd seen her perfect in the courtroom.

"I'm going to my office."

Chapter Six

Taryn forced herself to stand her ground when Tucker came out of his seat like a warrior springing into battle. It took him only three steps to cross the room.

"What did you say?" he asked in a low voice.

She brushed a speck of lint off her dark jacket. "I'm going to my office. Somebody needs to talk to Benny. There's obviously only one of us who can do that."

"Think again, baby. You're not going anywhere."

Her eyes narrowed at the tone of his voice. "Why? Are you afraid of losing your hostage?"

"Damn it, Swanny!" He took a step closer. "You know better than that."

Did she? She clicked her tongue against the back of her teeth. He'd sure expected a lot out of her. Now that the tables were turned, though, things weren't as easy. "You don't trust me," she said pointblank.

She sucked in a hard breath when his hands whipped out and closed about her waist. He jerked her to him, and his nose nearly brushed against hers as he stared into her eyes. "I don't want you to get caught in the middle of this," he bit out.

The intimidation tactics only made her more stubborn, and she met his stormy gaze in challenge. "You came here for that exact reason."

A muscle worked in his jaw. "That was then. This is now."

"So what's changed?"

Butterflies swirled in her stomach. She refused to let them show. There was something important going on here, and she had to hear his answer.

"Everything," he finally said in a raw voice. "It's too dangerous.

I didn't realize the scope of the frame-up, but if this guy will use kids, he'll do anything. If you somehow got hurt, I wouldn't be able to take it."

He cared. The tortured look in his dark eyes showed that it wasn't all lust for him either. Emotion clogged Taryn's chest, but it only strengthened her resolve. With an unsteady hand, she cupped his cheek. "I'll be fine, Tucker. I'm the ADA trying your case. It would look suspicious if I didn't go out there and make some kind of statement."

The muscle in his jaw only ticked faster. "At least let somebody else question Benny."

"Will your captain and your partner do?" She ran her thumb along his lower lip and smiled to lighten his mood. "Joe's been a royal pain in the butt ever since the charges were first brought against you. He'll jump at the chance to look at another suspect."

Tucker shook his head. "It's going to draw attention to you. You've got to look like you're taking part in the manhunt."

"I will. I plan on inviting the Diazes down under the guise of updating them on the progress of the search. I promise that nobody else will know what we're really doing."

He stared at her hard. "I don't like it."

"Trust me, Michael," she said softly. He'd asked her to put her faith in him. It was time to give a little in return.

She could see the war within him, but he didn't answer with words. Instead, his arms wrapped around her like bands of steel. He pulled her close and buried his face in her hair. She wrapped her arms around him and clung.

"I believe you, and I want to fix my mistake," she said in a choked voice. "I don't want you in prison. I want you right here, screwing the daylights out of me."

That got a rough laugh out of him. He gave her a hard squeeze and reluctantly let her go. Running a hand through his rumpled hair, and he shot her an amazingly shy look. "That's what I want, too."

He was vulnerable. The realization threw her. She'd seen his tough side when he was working, his caring side when he was coaching, and his passionate side when…. Well, that was obvious. But vulnerability? To her? It was disconcerting, and it sent her protective instincts surging. Suddenly, she wanted to lock him in her bedroom and barricade her home against anyone who tried to invade its sanctity.

"Then let's do something to make that happen," she said. "And fast. I'm sure the media will be knocking on my door next."

Purposefully, she reined in her emotions and headed to the kitchen. There was work to be done. She couldn't let her feelings overwhelm her, not when he needed her help so badly. She'd done a lot of thinking alone in the shower, and she had a plan. A good plan.

She could lock him in her bedroom later.

"I'm going to give you the keys to the Vallingers' car. They're snowbirds that live in the yellow house next door. They went to Florida last week and asked me to look after their things."

She picked up her purse and jumped when she sensed him right behind her. He moved so quietly, she didn't think she'd ever get used to it.

"You can use their Taurus if you need it," she continued. "I don't want you trapped here with no escape route."

He lifted an eyebrow, but took the keys she offered.

"Nobody will report you. That should give you some valuable lead-time."

He gave her a calculating look, but still didn't answer. His silence was beginning to make her uneasy. She'd thought he was through fighting her on this.

"I've thought of someplace you can go," she said stubbornly. "My parents have a cabin on Indian Horse Lake. Nobody's using it this late in the season."

She grabbed a pad and pencil out of her purse and leaned down to write the address. Her breath caught, though, when he suddenly grabbed the hem of her tailored skirt and pushed it up to her waist. "Tucker!" she gasped.

She quickly looked back over her shoulder, but he was already staring at what he'd uncovered.

"That's what you've been hiding," he said. His hand spread wide on her backside and rubbed in a slow circle. "Niiiice."

A delicious feeling of naughtiness caught Taryn unexpectedly. On impulse, she'd worn her good black lingerie. It was a sexy combination that she rarely wore. She'd just been thinking ahead to how they could celebrate when she returned with good news. She shivered when he ran his finger along the elastic band of her garter belt to the lace atop her stockings.

"So I take it you've got this all figured out," he said in a low voice.

His touch was decadent, but she'd warned him they couldn't get sidetracked again. She cleared her throat and looked at him from her bent-over position. "I got you into this mess. I'm getting you out."

To her surprise, his jaw went tight. "Listen, Taryn. When I said that, I was a little hot under the collar. I didn't really mean it."

She quivered as he slid his finger under the elastic and ran his knuckle over her buttocks. "Sure you did, but that's okay. I'd be a little put out if you did the same to me."

He shifted his weight uncomfortably, and his attention focused on her thong. "You just did what you thought was right. There were a lot of things that had to come together for this to happen. Somebody went to a lot of trouble to frame me."

The pad of his finger traced the triangle of material to the point where it disappeared into the cleavage of her buttocks, and Taryn fought desperately to clear her fogging brain. "And I was just a pawn?"

Tucker shrugged.

He hooked his forefinger under the triangle of material and gave a tug. Her thong popped out of its hiding place and the thin line of black silk rode atop the crevice of her buttocks.

She let out a soft cry, and her back arched. *Sidetracking.* They were sidetracking. "We're going to get the person responsible for this. I swear."

"Swanny?"

With his thumb, he pushed the thong back home. It slid in with a distinctive pop.

"What?" she groaned.

He jerked the material back out. "Do you always wear risqué panties underneath your starched suits?"

The soft question pushed her right past naughty. She felt absolutely wicked when he slowly tugged the thin line of material upwards again. Her head dropped to the table. Sidetracking be damned. Good God, she hadn't realized she was so sensitive back there. The action was so erotic, her toes were curling inside the cramped confines of her pumps. "No," she whispered.

"This is all for me?"

He could now flick the material in and out of the tight space using his thumb alone. Her butt cheeks clenched tight, and she couldn't relax them. With every move of that clever thumb, the thong brushed against the tightly pursed rose of her anus. The slight, rhythmic brush of silk was driving her crazy. "Yessssss."

"Then this is for you," he growled.

Unexpectedly, he changed the action of his hand. Instead of pulling the thong out from between her buttocks, he pulled the material straight up towards her waist. The silk rasped in her sensitive crack, directly over the bud that was causing her so much distress. The crotch pulled tight over her sex and her wetness flooded the cotton-lined panel.

"Michael," she said on a tight note.

"Oh, yeah," he growled. He reached around and anchored her with his palm against her pubic bone. The position left his fingers free to clench her underwear from the front.

Taryn's anticipation sharpened. "Please."

"Hold on, babe. I'm getting there."

Her entire body went rigid when he began to saw her panties forwards and backwards. The friction lit up every erogenous zone between her legs. Her clit, her pussy lips, and her anus burned with fire.

A high-pitched cry erupted from her lips. "Mi-chael!"

His front hand ground harder against her, and he increased the speed of the sawing motion.

It was too much.

The fire was going to eat her alive.

Taryn tried to shift her hips away, but he held her down. The rubbing became faster and hotter. Still, she couldn't reach her peak. It was right there—just out of reach. She was hovering below it, aroused beyond belief, but she couldn't quite get there.

She gave a cry of despair and lifted her hips higher. Suddenly, the hot motion of the material stopped. She nearly started crying at the loss, but her back bowed when she felt his hot hand take its place.

With his front hand still tightly cupping her mound, his back one burrowed into the crack of her ass.

He touched her anus with the pad of his thumb, and she came.

She screamed, and her body shook from head to toe. Through it all, he held her tightly. He held her as she reached the precipice, and he held her as she came back to earth. He even held her as lay like a puddle of protoplasm on the kitchen table.

"Oh, God," she gasped. She had to wait several seconds until her lungs functioned properly. "What did you just do to me?"

His voice was raspy in her ear. "That was hot."

"But you didn't even..."

"I know—and it was still fucking hot."

She pushed herself up onto her elbows. "Damn you, Tuck. Now I've got to take another shower."

He chuckled and dropped a kiss onto her temple. "You are such a fussbudget. Do you know you've spent half the time I've been here in the shower?"

"That's because you keep making me..."

"Cream?"

"Shut up."

He nipped her earlobe softly. "Stay where you are. I'll clean you up."

"You'll what?" Her palms dropped flat onto the table and she nearly pushed herself all the way to a standing position before he pressed her back down. His fingers began working on the clasps of her garter belt. They were undone with an efficiency that made her eyebrows lift, and her mushy muscles tensed again.

"Relax."

That was hard to do when he hooked his thumbs under her panties and pulled them down her legs.

"Step out of them."

She stared straight down at the tabletop as she followed his orders. To her amazement, he simply reattached her garter belt to her stockings.

"Don't move."

She stayed put as he left for the bathroom, but unsureness gripped her when she heard water running. He was busting through all her sexual hang-ups like a wrecking ball. There was just no stopping him.

And she didn't want to.

He returned, and she felt self-conscious when a warm washcloth settled between her legs. It began moving, and the intimacy alarmed her. She must have made some sound, because he quieted her with a soft "shhh" before continuing.

She flinched when his nimble fingers caught sensitive areas, but he calmly repeated the procedure until she began to crave his attentive touch. She went right up onto her toes, though, when he used his finger to push the washcloth deep into her.

"Got to get you clean," he said silkily.

His finger was twice as thick with the washcloth wrapped around it. The shocking fullness made Taryn clench the edge of the table until her knuckles turned white. Her hunger returned, sharp and voracious. He refused to feed it. He worked slowly and meticulously until he was satisfied he was done. He finished by wiping the stickiness off her thighs and, just as carefully, dried her.

"There you go," he said as he pulled her skirt back down over her hips.

She didn't know what to say. "Thank you" seemed so inappropriate. "More please," sounded downright greedy. "Well," she said.

She turned around and smoothed the skirt over her hips. She felt the lines of her garter belt and struggled to get herself under control. She was overwhelmed by his easy familiarity with her body—and her eager responses. It was going to take some time to get used to it all.

And time was something they held in very short supply.

"Yes, '*well*'," he mocked.

"Stop it," she said. Embarrassed, she settled her hands on his chest and pushed him away. "What am I supposed to say after something like that?"

He didn't stop laughing as he caught her by the waist and pulled her close. "Did you enjoy it?"

She felt herself flush. "Yes."

His grin stretched wider, and he dropped a kiss onto her forehead. "That's all I need to know."

She pushed him away again. She was onto him. "You're trying to stall me, but I'm still heading out that door."

"I expected as much." He finally backed away to lean against the kitchen counter. He crossed his arms over his chest and gave her a serious look. "You need to be careful."

"I will," she promised. Still feeling extremely self-conscious, she sought out the mirror on the refrigerator. She was stunned to see that her make-up and hair were still intact.

"Lawyer look still in place?" he asked cockily.

She caught his intimate look in the reflection of the tiny magnetic mirror and hesitated. There was something about the sparkle in his eyes....

Her suit! He'd told her that they made him horny, but she hadn't dreamed... How long had he been fantasizing about doing that to her? A year? Two?

Her pussy clenched, and his cleaning job turned out to be a waste of time.

She turned to head to her bedroom, but he moved in that smooth, lightning quick way of his and caught her about the waist. "Don't," he said softly.

"But I'm not wearing—"

"I know."

"You want me to go to work this way?"

"Yes."

"But why?"

"That way, I'll know you're thinking about me."

᠅᠁(ᢗᢩ)᠁᠅

Hours later, Taryn was pacing around her office like a tiger. Thinking about him? She was obsessed with wanting to get back to him! With each step she took, she was clearly reminded that under her conservative business suit, she was stripped bare.

She stopped pacing and pressed her thighs together to try to stop the ache. If something didn't break loose soon, she was going to have to go to the ladies room and take care of matters herself.

She glared at the clock for the hundredth time. The delays and hold-ups were driving her stark, raving mad!

She'd wanted to meet as soon as possible, but nobody was conforming to her schedule. Captain Holcomb was busy in a meeting. She didn't doubt that the main topic of discussion was the manhunt for Tucker. Joe Payne had headed out of town for the weekend, most likely to avoid the search for his partner, but she'd managed to catch him by cell phone. He was headed back, but it would take at least another forty-five minutes. And the Diazes. Justin's mother had sounded drunk when she'd answered the call, and his father hadn't been in much better shape. She'd finally convinced them to come down for a talk, but they'd groggily muttered that they needed to find Benny first.

They didn't know where he was.

Taryn's hands closed into fists as she turned to pace in the opposite direction. *They didn't know where he was!*

She let out a long breath. It was possible the boy had just gone out to shoot hoops or hang with his friends. Her fingernails pressed more sharply into her palms. It was also possible he'd heard about Tucker's breakout and had freaked.

She felt panic rising in her chest. Benny was their one link. He was their best hope in clearing Tucker's name. If he ran away, she didn't know what she'd do.

One step at a time, she told herself.

She forced herself to unclench her fists, but the clip-clop staccato of her heels echoed off the office walls. She needed to calm down. She was getting too far ahead of herself. She didn't know that Benny was gone. Heck, she didn't even know if he had a reason to run.

She swiveled around, but teetered unsteadily when she saw a familiar form in the hallway. Marty Sheuster was walking past her office with a cell phone plastered against his ear. She quickly ducked. He was the last person on earth she wanted to see right now.

The ADA walked by, but his footsteps stopped abruptly. He leaned back and looked through her open door. "Taryn?"

"Damn!" she hissed under her breath.

He clipped his cell phone onto his belt and strutted across her office. "Hey, beautiful. What are you doing here?"

She impatiently brushed back a tendril of hair that had fallen out of her French twist. She could barely look at the man after hearing all the lies he'd told about her. Just picturing the two of them together made her sick. He was at least two inches shorter than her, but twice as big around. His hairline was receding and those teeth... Ugh.

"Unless you've been living under a rock, you must have heard that Michael Tucker has escaped," she said. "I came in to find out what's being done."

Sheuster sidled up to her desk and propped a hip against it. "If you're nervous with him out there, I'd be happy to keep you company."

"I'm not scared, Marty. I'm mad." *At you*, she nearly added. You lying pig.

"No, really," he said in that sugar sweet way of his. "You shouldn't be alone. Why don't you come stay with me until things settle down?"

She took a deep breath and tried not to let her revulsion show. "Thank you for your concern, but I feel secure in the privacy of my own home."

"Are you sure?" He leaned towards her, and she fought not to shrink back. "The policeman I sent out to your house said you looked disheveled when he dropped by earlier today. Quite disheveled, I might add."

"He woke me up."

"I'm sorry. Were you in bed?" With the last insinuating word, he reached out and covered her hand.

"Marty!" She snatched her hand back, and fought for composure. She couldn't let him draw her into an argument. She had more important things to do. "Listen, I don't mean to be rude, but I really need to work right now."

"It's nothing to be embarrassed about." He threw her a wink. "I understand."

"The officer caught me at a bad time," she said flatly. "Let's just leave it at that."

He smiled, and her skin crawled.

"All right, but my invitation still stands." He absently picked up her favorite pen and began rolling it between his fingers. "I've got plenty of room and a nice, big, king-sized bed. I think we'd both sleep better if you were under my protection."

She snatched the pen away from him and threw it into the trash. No amount of disinfectant would ever make it clean enough for her to use again.

"We could invite Officer Denton to guard you, too, if that would make you feel safer." Sheuster's voice dropped to a conspiratorial tone. "I don't suppose you're into that sort of thing?"

Warning alarms sounded in Taryn's head. Officer Denton...Marty couldn't know. She and Tucker had been locked inside her house. How could he have picked up...? No, he didn't know. He was just taking a stab in the dark.

"Are you here for a reason, Marty?" she asked, ice dripping from her voice. "Other than to sexually harass me, that is?"

Sensing he'd pushed her too far, Sheuster stood up and stuffed his hands into his pockets. "Same as you. I came down here to get the scoop on Tucker."

"What do you care? It's not your case."

"No, but my Rodriguez case is crumbling because of that crooked cop's association with it. All the evidence is tainted now."

Taryn's stomach soured. "You think Rodriguez could walk?"

"There's no 'could' about it. He *will* walk."

"Oh, God." She hadn't even considered that. She reached up to rub her shoulder. Could things get any worse?

Marty watched her for a moment. Finally, he cocked his head and looked at her through slitted eyes. "So where do you think the bastard is?"

She stopped massaging the kink at the top of her shoulder blade. "Who? Tucker? How would I know?"

He shrugged. "I got the impression you two were tight."

The fax machine started to whir, and she gratefully turned towards the distraction. She walked over to look at the message, but found another interview request from a local news station. "I worked with the detective on quite a few cases," she said as she tossed the fax into the recycling bin, "But that all stopped when he was arrested for drug dealing."

"I wasn't talking about work, sweet cakes."

The hair on the back of Taryn's neck stood on end. "I don't know what you're implying, Marty," she said coolly, "But I don't date people from work. You know that probably better than anybody."

He shrugged. "Semantics."

She hesitated. She didn't like the look in his eye. "What are you talking about?"

"You might not 'date' them per se, but you are open to other... *propositions*. Say when a vice detective wants a search warrant. I could see you letting him stick his tongue halfway down your throat when you're in an empty interrogation room and you think nobody's watching."

She stopped breathing.

"Or allowing his hands to slither up under your skirt."

She felt like she was going to be sick.

"Or humping your hungry cunt against his leg."

She reached for the table to steady herself.

"Oh, wait a minute. I *did* see all that. You did realize the big mirror in that room was a two-way window, didn't you, sweet cakes?"

The implications sent Taryn's mind spinning. Marty had seen her and Tucker together! If he'd told anyone about their relationship, she would be suspect. For all she knew, he could already have attained a search warrant for her house.

Tucker was in danger. The police could be on their way. He'd be caught unaware.

And he'd think that she'd turned on him!

"I...I've got to get ready for a meeting," she said clumsily.

Marty stepped closer and whispered into her ear. "I've got some propositions of my own. Why don't we head down to the janitor's closet and I'll show you?"

His hand settled intimately on her backside. Revulsion rocked Taryn. Gut instinct sent her hand flying towards the man's ugly face, and she slapped him hard.

The sharp sound pierced the air like a thunderclap.

Air heaved in her lungs as she stepped back and watched him rub his jaw. She was stunned by her actions, but she refused to be sorry for them. The man had spread vicious rumors about her. He'd made filthy insinuations. She wouldn't let him paw her.

Unbelievably, he smiled. "You're a fiery one. I like that."

"Don't you ever come near me again," she hissed.

The slimy snake. His touch had been nauseating. Had he felt that she wasn't wearing any panties? The possibility made her nearly retch. Her gaze dropped unwillingly to the front of his pants. The bulge behind his zipper gave her the answer.

She straightened her shoulders. She couldn't show any signs of weakness before this pervert. "And if you ever question my commitment to my job, I will turn you in for sexual harassment."

Out of the corner of her eye, Taryn saw Captain Holcomb striding down the hallway. She'd never been more grateful to see anyone in her life. "Captain," she called. "Could you wait just one minute?"

She picked up her things with as much grace as she could muster. "Get out of my office, Marty."

"Touched a chord, did I?" he chuckled.

"Get out or I'll have the Captain make you get out."

"Fine, fine. Don't get your panties in a bunch."

His phone rang again as she swept up her purse. She maneuvered around him as he whipped the cell phone out of its holder like a gunslinger.

"Hit me," he said cockily.

She'd hit him, all right.

"Captain," she said efficiently as she stepped into the hallway. "Thank you for coming. Let's go to the conference room. I've got something I want you to take a look at."

❦

It was all Taryn could do not to run to her car when the meeting with the Diazes ended. It took supreme self-control, but she kept her pace to a quick walk as she headed down the hallway. She made sure to say good-bye to everyone she saw as she left the building and headed to her car. She let herself inside and locked the doors, but she couldn't tamp down the impulse to rev the engine.

She'd gotten it! She'd gotten what they needed!

Her fingers tightened around the steering wheel, but she reined herself in. She put the car in gear and drove sedately out of the parking lot. Okay, she'd gotten half of what they needed. There was just one more link that needed to be made.

Once things fell into place, though, Tucker wouldn't be the subject of a statewide manhunt. She couldn't wait to give him the good news. After the hell that he'd been through, he was going to have a hard time believing the tale she had to tell.

Benny Diaz had cracked like the Grand Canyon.

The weekend traffic was light, but she passed three patrol cars on the way home. They reminded her that the danger wasn't gone yet, and she eased up on the gas. The trip seemed to take forever and when she finally turned onto her street, she didn't even bother to pull her car into the driveway. Instead, she parked in front and bolted to the house. She took the front steps two at a time and unlocked the door. "Tucker?" she called as she stepped inside.

She dropped her briefcase onto the table by the couch and bumped the door shut with her hip. As an afterthought, she turned and locked the deadbolt. "Michael? You're not going to believe this."

She kicked off a shoe. "You were right. Benny's in this up to his neck."

The house was silent.

Eerily silent.

"Tucker?"

Her heart began a slow, dull throbbing. She slipped out of her other pump and, in stockinged feet, slowly walked to the bedroom. "Tucker?" she called again.

He wasn't there.

In a rush, she checked the second bedroom, the bathroom, the kitchen, and even the basement. She was frantic by the time she thought about the Vallingers' car. Unmindful of what would happen to her hosiery, she ran down the back steps and across the yard. She yanked open the side door to her neighbors' garage.

The car was gone.

So was Tucker.

Chapter Seven

He'd left.

Taryn's knees buckled, and she grabbed the doorframe for support. Had something happened? Had Marty sent Officer Denton back? Had reporters spooked Tucker into leaving? She'd told him to take the car if he needed it.

Another possibility sprang to mind, and pain rippled through her. Please God. Don't let him have run because he hadn't trusted her.

She clapped a hand over her mouth and choked back a sob. It was too strong a possibility to ignore. The house sat undisturbed, and reporters tended to hang around like vultures when they sensed a story.

If Tucker had left, it had been on his own volition.

And that meant one thing...He'd thought she was going to turn him in.

The hurt she felt was devastating, but she should have seen this coming. He hadn't wanted to let her go. He'd tried everything except strong-arming her to make her stay. Even when he'd finally relented, he hadn't been supportive.

Carefully, she closed the garage door. She turned and walked stiff-legged back to the house. Unshed tears made it swim in her vision, but she grabbed the metal railing and pulled herself up the steps.

Now she knew how he'd felt when she hadn't had faith in him.

The screen door slammed behind her, and she winced. The sound had such finality to it. She closed the wooden door more quietly and made it as far as a kitchen chair before she collapsed.

She'd made such a mess of things. This was all her fault. If only she'd listened to him before...

She took an unsteady breath, but she just couldn't find it in herself to be angry with him. His life was on the line. He had to be very careful about whom he trusted, and she'd been quick to believe the worst of him.

But things had changed. She'd thought that they'd made a connection. The sad thing was that if the situation were reversed, she would have trusted him to help her. She'd already trusted him with her body and her very life. A single tear trailed down her cheek, and she dropped her face into her hands.

She'd trusted him with her heart.

She closed her eyes and tried to think past the pain. Where could he have gone? Would he have headed to her parents' cabin? Maybe—if he'd been flushed from her house. There was no way she could know for certain. He'd never answer if she called.

She let out a shaky breath. She had to believe he was okay. Whether he trusted her or not was inconsequential, because she knew the truth. She had to help him. The only way she could do that now was to follow through on what she'd started.

She needed to stop this manhunt.

She leaned her elbows onto the table and let out a hysterical laugh. And how was she supposed to pull off that miracle?

A creak sounded from the back door. "Hey." Tucker eased into the house. His eyebrows drew together when he looked at her face. "What's wrong?"

Taryn stared at him in astonishment, but then nearly flew out of her chair. She launched herself at him, and he stumbled back a step as he caught her. The look of concern on his face grew stronger. Carefully, he wiped the dampness off her cheek.

"What happened? Did your talk with the Diazes go that badly?"

"Where were you?"

His eyebrows shot up when she grabbed him by the lapels of his jean jacket. She pushed him down into the chair she'd just vacated and surveyed him from head to toe. "Did you go out? Where did you get those clothes? Did you go shopping? *Are you crazy?*"

"Whoa! Ease up on the interrogation bit, babe."

"The car was gone!"

"Well, yeah. I moved it around to the alley in case I need to make a quick break for it. Driveways are easily blocked."

Taryn raked a hand through her hair and pulled loose the last pins that were holding her French twist in place. She couldn't believe he was sitting in front of her. She'd thought he'd left her. "I looked for you," she said. "Why weren't you here? You were supposed to be here."

"Settle down. I thought it would be safer to hide out at the Vallingers', and I borrowed some of the old guy's clothes. Your dad's red sweat suit made me stand out like a sore thumb."

Her adrenaline was rushing through her veins too fast to be stopped. Everything he said made sense, but she wasn't thinking with her head. "Why didn't you come back when I got home?"

His eyes narrowed. "I had to make sure you weren't followed first."

And there it was. He'd been watching her, testing her. He'd done everything he could to prepare for a fast getaway in case she failed.

His mistrust cut like a knife to the chest. She folded her arms to try to contain the pain. "Don't you mean you were watching to make sure I didn't bring a S.W.A.T. team with me?"

He went dangerously still. "What?"

"You hid because you didn't trust me to come back on my own," she said flatly. "You thought I'd turn you over to the authorities."

He moved fast. This time, it was he who grabbed her by the lapels. He pulled her forward until she was straddling him on the chair, and his nose bumped against hers as he glared into her eyes. "I thought no such thing."

"No?" she said challengingly.

"No," he growled. He yanked her to him and planted a hard, chastising kiss on her lips. "You're the only one I let myself count on, Swanny."

She watched him like a hawk. "Really?"

"Really."

With that one word, all of Taryn's hurt and fear seeped out of her like a pricked balloon. Weakly, she dropped onto his lap and wrapped her arms around his neck. Just minutes ago, she'd thought she'd never see him again. She couldn't remember ever being so scared—including when she'd stepped out of her bathroom and been grabbed by a dark stranger. "I was so afraid somebody had found you," she said.

He smoothed her hair away from her face. "I'm trying my best to make sure that doesn't happen. Or to at least hold it off for as long as I can."

"It might not be that much longer," she said. Her hysteria was subsiding, but her need for him was growing. She craved to touch him, make sure he was all right. Shifting in his lap, she settled more firmly against him. She sank her fingers into his hair and held him still for another hot kiss.

He pulled back. "Why do you say that? What happened?

Her patience had reached its end. She'd been tied up in knots for hours and hours—and she'd been naked under her skirt ever since she'd left him. She'd never gone so long without panties, and it made her feel sexy and reckless. She reached down between them for the tab of his jeans.

"Taryn," he said. He grabbed for her hand. "Tell me."

"You were right about Benny's tennis shoes," she said fiercely. Her concentration was on his zipper. It was difficult to work her hands between their tightly pressed bodies, but she managed. She undid the button and slid down the zipper, but she didn't have time for the niceties. She wrapped her fingers in his belt loops and yanked down on the denim. "Lift," she demanded.

He raised his hips but caught her face with both hands and made her look at him. "You're killing me here, babe."

Within seconds, she had his jeans and underwear down to his knees. For all his concern about the case, his body wasn't able to ignore her. His erection already stood like a flagpole. With hurried hands, Taryn pulled up her skirt. Her blonde curls brushed against the tip of his penis as she hovered over it, and he let out a curse.

"Benny has been dealing to make a fast buck," she said. "Justin got the drugs from him."

"He what? Damn it, Swanny. Justin overdosed on...*Christ*!"

She'd begun to slowly lower herself onto his erection. The broad tip pressed at her, and she felt her body stretch to accommodate him. She grabbed the chair behind his shoulders and braced herself. Every nerve ending inside her tingled. Using her body weight, she began to impale herself onto him.

"Wait," he gasped. "Talk first."

"I want you inside me." She was so wet and needy.

He gripped her waist. "No. It's too fast."

"It's not fast enough!" He'd started this hunger when he'd sent her out into the world bare. He had to finish it.

"Taryn!" His hand dropped between her legs, and his fingers found her bud. He began to pluck at it insistently. "Give me a minute."

She grabbed his wrist. "I can't," she moaned. "Deeper. Get in deeper."

"I don't... Ah, shit!"

She'd dropped another inch onto him, and pleasure seared them both. Taryn swayed in his lap. She was uncomfortable, but *Oh, God!* She wouldn't do anything to change this. He'd never felt this thick before.

"Baby, you're swollen," he hissed. "We've gone at each other too hard today."

"Touch me!"

He swore under his breath, but pushed off her suit jacket. The only thing she wore underneath it was the black bra that matched her thong. He yanked a strap off her shoulder and hungrily dropped his mouth to her breast. All of her concentration had been on the connection below her waist. To feel the tug of his mouth on her nipple nearly caused sensory overload.

"Michael!" With a cry, she let her muscles relax. Gravity pulled her solidly down until she was filled to the brim. She closed her eyes, and her head dropped back.

Tucker clenched her ass as if he was never going to let her move. She didn't know if she could. His fiery rod was standing straight up inside her—stretching her, inflaming her. If she moved, she might combust.

She moved.

Determinedly, she began to pump herself up and down on his erection. Her ripped stockings made her feet slippery on the kitchen floor, but she found what traction she could. Her thigh muscles burned as she lifted, sank, retreated, and surged forward. Gripping the chair hard, she ground herself onto him, needing him.

"Swanny!" he said desperately.

In unison, he pinched the bundle of nerve endings between her legs and bit down softly on her nipple. Taryn shuddered and felt the moisture gather inside of her. Her juices slathered his cock, and her thrusts became smoother.

"I'm not going to last," he warned.

"I don't want you to," she said on a hard breath.

Her excitement was out of control. Rising up, she let herself slam down onto him. She found a hard, fast rhythm, and the muscles in his jaw clenched.

He gave her a frantic look. Then his hand was between her legs again. He pressed firmly against her clit. With a yell, he spurted into her.

Taryn squeezed her eyes tight as her own orgasm gripped her. She rode him for as long as she could before she collapsed against him. His arms came up around her, and he held her tightly.

"Are you all right?" he asked between heavy breaths.

"Mm."

"You could have given me a little more warning."

She sagged against his shoulder. "I couldn't help it," she whispered. "You scared me."

He groaned and ran a hand down her spine. He slid it under her hitched up skirt and caressed her buttocks. "So fear does it for you, huh? I can't wait until Halloween."

The hand on her backside stilled, and she glanced up at him. "Don't even think it," she said firmly. "You'll be here."

He took a deep breath. "Tell me about Benny. And no more fooling around until you do."

Taryn's excitement came back in a rush and her head came up so sharply, she nearly clipped his chin. "He's been dealing on the streets for almost six months. You were right about the family. His mother hadn't even noticed that her youngest son was throwing around wads of cash. His father did, but instead of asking questions, he just borrowed from him."

Tucker's gaze was steady on hers. "Did Benny admit giving the heroin to Justin?"

"Yes. He was there when his brother started convulsing." She shook her head. "It only took Joe two questions about the Mercury Wings before the entire story gushed out of the kid. I couldn't help but feel sorry for him. He killed his own brother. The guilt has been eating him alive."

"Did he plant the stuff on me?"

"No. He swore he had nothing to do with that, and I believe him. He's sick about how everything got turned on you. He never expected that to happen, but he didn't know how to help you without admitting what he'd done."

Tucker's face remained detached. "Who's his supplier?"

She grimaced. "That's where the problem lies. The guy's slick. He networks by phone. He hooks up with kids through other pushers. Once they start working for him, he keeps in contact by voice only. If Benny were low on product, he'd call a number and schedule a drop-off. He never even saw the guy."

The impassive look on Tucker's face slipped. "So I'm still not in the clear."

"Not yet," she said quietly. "The stash inside your gym locker was the same grade as that found in Justin's system during the autopsy."

His head dropped back, and he stared at the ceiling. "When am I going to catch a break?"

"Easy," she said. She rubbed the tight muscles at the back of his neck. "Let me finish."

His dark eyes narrowed.

"The night that Justin collapsed, Benny panicked. He didn't know what to do, so he called his supplier. The man said he would 'take care of it'."

"He didn't mean Justin."

"He meant the situation. We're dealing with a professional."

Tucker's hands bit into her hips. "We're dealing with a heartless psychopath. A kid was dying in an alleyway, and all the guy thought about was pinning the rap on me."

"Listen." She caught his face with both hands. "We have the phone number."

He looked at her blankly. "You're kidding."

Goose bumps popped up on Taryn's skin. They were so close to clearing him, she could practically taste it. "The guy told Benny to destroy it, but the kid's been carrying it around in his back pocket. Joe checked it. It's a secure cell phone, one of those kinds that you buy with minutes on it and then throw away."

Tucker sat up a little straighter. "But they could get the phone company to pull up the calls made to and from the number."

"Exactly. Joe's already on it. He's hoping he can cross reference the information and figure out who Benny's contact is."

"Has anybody thought about just dialing the number and seeing who answers?"

"Your captain's putting together a trace right now."

"Fuck the trace."

Taryn gasped when Tucker lifted her off of him. Their bodies disconnected, and she felt gapingly empty. Her legs wobbled when he set her on her feet. She smoothed her skirt over her hips as he stood and zipped up.

"Give me the number, Counselor."

She didn't like the reckless look on his face. "I don't have it."

"Bullshit. I know you. Give me the damn number."

She understood his impatience; she felt it with every cell of her being. Still, there was a right way and a wrong way to handle this. She didn't want him to lose his freedom because they couldn't contain themselves.

"We can't jeopardize the investigation," she said firmly. Her head snapped up when she remembered something. "Besides, my phones are dead. You can't call from here."

By way of answer, he strode into the living room and picked up her phone. Turning it over, he slid off the bottom panel. Her eyes rounded when she saw he'd just wrapped up the cords inside.

"Hide in plain sight," he said. "That's my motto."

He held out his hand. She glared at it.

"The number, baby."

"Oh, all right!" she snapped. She stomped over to her briefcase. "The guy's probably ditched it already anyway."

"These aren't brain surgeons we're dealing with," Tucker muttered. He looked at her notes and punched the numbers she'd written down. "Whatever's between me and this guy is personal. I might be able to recognize him."

She gave it one last shot. "Wait! My name will show up on Caller ID."

His lips curled up in a smile that held no humor. "Nice try, but you've got an unlisted number. It doesn't come through. I know. You've called me from home before."

"Fine," Taryn muttered.

She went to stand next to him. If he was going to do this, she was going to help. She had nearly as much experience with the lowlifes in the city as he did. He tilted the receiver and leaned down so she could press her ear against it.

They both tensed when they heard ringing on the other end of the line. Taryn tried to quiet her breathing. It was all she could hear, and she knew she'd only get one chance at this. She wiped her damp palms on her skirt and bit her lip. The phone rang three times before it connected.

"Hit me."

Her breathing stopped, and she looked, wide-eyed, at Tucker.

"Hello? Is anybody there?"

Her heart lodged in her throat. She knew that voice. Tucker's eyebrows drew together, but she wrenched the phone out of his hands. It would arouse suspicion if they hung up, and she didn't want to leave any sort of forewarning. Not if she was right about the person on the other end of the call. "Is this A-n-A Dry Cleaning?" she asked in breathy voice.

"Wrong number, sweetheart."

"Sorry," she said before disconnecting.

"Was that –"

The telephone bell jingled when she slammed down the phone. "Marty!"

"Sheuster? Why, that son-of-a-bitch!"

The pressure built inside Tucker's head until he thought it would explode. He couldn't believe it! That fat little slime ball had set him up! He jammed his hand into his pocket and pulled out the keys to the Vallingers' car.

Taryn saw the keys in his hand, and her blue eyes turned flinty. "Don't even think about leaving now."

The tension was so strong, electrical sparks nearly flew across the room.

Tucker took a step towards the door. Marty Sheuster. The bastard was playing God with kids' lives, and he'd tried to frame him for murder. The guy was going to pay.

Taryn stepped into his path and pointed a threatening finger at him. "Don't."

His muscles strained towards the door. "I can make him talk."

"So can I!"

A tight band wrapped around Tucker's chest. God, this was exactly what he hadn't wanted to happen. His sweet Taryn was planted smack dab in the middle of all this. That slimy Sheuster had cost them both.

"We need to reason this out," she said.

He dragged a hand through his hair. He didn't want to reason it out. He wanted to take a more proactive approach—like pounding the truth out of the doughboy. It would be much more satisfying.

She stomped over and waved a hand in his face.

"Work with me," she snapped. "Marty. He has access to the drugs in evidence lock-up. Has any of that come up missing?"

Tucker planted his hands on his hips. "No. At least not up to the time I left."

"But he had access to things such as the plastic bags with your fingerprints on them. And your keys! They booked you on the basis of what was found in your gym locker. He could have gotten into your personal effects."

"And with the keys to my house, he could have planted the money before the forensics unit got permission to search it." Tucker let out a curse. She was right. They did need to go through it step-by-step. He couldn't afford to miss anything. Not now.

"Why you, though?" she continued. She began to nibble on her fingernails out of nervous habit. "Why would he try to frame you? Were you onto him?"

Oh, that one hurt. Tucker hadn't seen this thing coming at all, and it killed him that Sheuster had been working the streets right under his nose. "I didn't have a clue," he admitted. "I don't know why he chose me, other than out of spite. I can't think of anything else that might have been in it for him."

A funny look crossed her face. "What about me?" she asked hesitantly.

The question was like a kick in the gut. Suddenly, Sheuster's raunchy talk about her seemed even more lurid. Tucker had never tried to hide his attraction to the pretty ADA. If Marty had seen him as a competitor…"But you weren't mine to take. Not then."

"He saw us," she said quietly.

"What do you mean?"

"He saw us in the interrogation room."

Tucker took a step back. That had been private. The idea of that creep watching them...watching *her*...

He was going to kill him.

The keys bit into his palm as he made a move to the back door. Taryn stopped him by grabbing his arm and throwing herself fearlessly between him and the exit.

"Could he be working for somebody?" she asked.

Tucker stopped in his tracks. Red-hot anger filled his brain, but she'd just tapped something in the recesses of his mind...Something he was missing...A connection of some sort.

He tried to pull in his wandering thoughts. Sheuster a patsy? It made more sense. The idiot wasn't smart enough to plan something as elaborate as this. Somebody was pulling his strings, but who? Who could have that much against a vice detective?

The answer lit up his brain like fireworks on the Fourth of July.

He rubbed a tired hand across his forehead. Why hadn't he thought of this before? "Who would have the most to gain by getting me off the streets?" he said wearily.

"I...I don't know."

"Think about it, Swanny. We're talking about drugs and money."

Her face paled. "Oh, my God. He's working for Rodriguez!"

Tucker nodded slowly. The rage building inside his chest was nearing its boiling point. "It explains why Sheuster was dragging his feet on that case. He did everything he could to get in my way."

"The search warrant," she hissed.

He gritted his teeth. "Marty's the operation's inside guy, and I got too close. Rodriguez wanted me off the streets, but coming after me directly would have caused too many problems."

"Killing you would have resulted in an investigation."

"Framing me and sending me to prison would be easier and more gratifying. I don't know if they planned what happened to Justin, but the opportunity certainly fell into their lap."

She pressed a hand to her temple, and he could see the gears turning in her brain. "Marty was just saying today that his case was falling apart due to your involvement."

It was all coming together. Sheuster and Rodriguez had turned his life upside down, and there'd been nothing he could do to stop it. He rubbed a hand over his burning stomach. "They got two birds with one stone. I'm locked up and Rodriguez gets turned loose."

"Damn him!" Taryn swore.

Tucker spun away. Thoughts were screaming through his brain, and his heart was pumping like a steam engine. Fury colored everything, but hope and excitement tinged the edges.

Freedom was at his fingertips. He'd never thought he'd get this close again.

"It's all speculation," he said with a tinge of desperation. He knew with everything inside him that they were on the right track, but they didn't have hardcore proof. "We still don't have enough on them."

"But we'll get it," she said determinedly. She picked up the phone again, but her fingers shook as she dialed. "All we have to do is put Joe on it."

He hadn't expected her to call his partner. Uneasiness rocked his already unsettled stomach, and he grabbed for the phone. "No! You'll have to tell him what we did, and it could be considered interfering with the investigation. I don't want you to get in trouble."

"I'm not interfering. It's *my* case." She spun away. "Hello, Joe? This is ADA Swanson. I know who has that cell phone."

Tucker reached around her and made another grab, but she scooted away.

"How?" she said. "Well, you're not going to be happy with me, but I dialed the number. I recognized the voice on the other end."

He backed her up against the wall, but she straight-armed him like a NFL receiver.

"It's Sheuster, Joe. Go get him."

Tucker suddenly heard his partner's voice booming over the line. Taryn grimaced and held the phone away from her ear until the tirade ended.

"Yes. ADA Marty Sheuster," she said, bringing the phone closer with care. "Bring him in for questioning and check the cell phone he has on him. The number should match the one Benny gave us."

Tucker planted his hands on the wall on either side of her and hung his head. There was nothing he could do to stop her when she got like this. He knew from experience. He just hoped to God they hadn't made a mistake and jumped the gun. They should have let the department trace the call first. Joe or somebody else probably would have recognized Sheuster's voice.

Taryn hung up and lowered the phone to her side. There was empathy in her eyes when she looked at him. "It will be okay," she said softly.

"They're going to find a way to slip through the cracks." He knew how the system worked. So did Sheuster and Rodriguez.

She dropped the phone. It fell noisily onto the floor as she wrapped her arms about his neck. Her hair was wild, and her breasts hung heavily in the little black bra. "We'll make it stick," she said in a tone that brooked no argument. "Joe will drag Marty down to the station and go one-on-one with him. He doesn't stand a chance. You know that better than anyone. Payne will be all over him. Marty will give it up."

Hope flickered again. She could be right. He'd take his partner over Sheuster any day. "How long do you think it will be before he tracks him down?"

"Marty was at the office when I left. He's either still there or at home. It shouldn't take long."

"Damn." Needing to hold onto something, he slid his hands down her back and cupped her bottom. "I don't think I can take any more waiting," he admitted.

"No?" She sidled up closer. "Would you like me to distract you?"

He didn't know if it would work, but he wasn't going to turn her away. He jerked her up to him, and she wrapped her legs around his waist like a vice. Flinging her hair over one shoulder, she leaned down and began kissing the side of his neck. His toes curled when her tongue flicked against his pulse.

It would work.

He started for the bedroom, but his steps slowed. He didn't know how all of this was going to work out, and the boys in blue were still out there looking for him. A lot of things could go wrong. "Swanny," he said hesitantly. "I just need to tell you…in case something happens…I never should have come here and put you in danger. I'm sorry for intimidating you. Manhandling you. I just didn't know what else to do or where to go. You were my only hope."

"It's all right," she whispered into his ear. "I understand."

"No, it's not all right. I should have found another way."

"I'm glad you came to me. I wouldn't have wanted it any differently." She pulled back slowly. "I love you, Michael."

He jolted so hard, he nearly dropped her. She met his stunned gaze shyly, but then glanced away.

"I love you," she whispered again.

He hadn't realized it, but that was what he'd needed to hear all along. He tightened his arms around her and buried his face into the crook of her neck. "Ah, baby, I'm head over heels about you, too. I'm so crazy about you, I can't think straight."

"So don't think," she said, repeating the words he'd told her. "Go with your gut."

All of a sudden, Tucker knew everything was going to be okay. *Everything.* With a sigh of relief and a refreshed sense of purpose, he headed to the bedroom. He felt an unexpected need to celebrate.

⁂

The phone rang just before midnight. Taryn dove for it over Tucker's prone body and had it to her ear before the second ring. "Hello?"

"ADA? This is Joe Payne."

"Yes?" she said breathlessly.

"The captain's called off the manhunt for Tucker. Sheuster confessed."

Epilogue

Eight months later....

Tucker sucked in air and tried not to let his weight crush Taryn. She was bent over a desk in the custodian's room at the courthouse with her legs spread wide. He'd just taken her from behind, and the aftermath of the orgasm had left him powerless. They were both breathing as if they'd just completed a marathon.

"Now that's the way to celebrate," he said into her ear.

"I'll say." She fought hard for oxygen, and he could still see the pulse pounding in her throat. "Do you think anybody heard us?"

He nuzzled the soft hair at her temple. "I don't give a rip if they did. We deserved this. It took us eight months of hard work to put that bastard away."

She reached up and cupped the side of his face, coaxing him into a slow kiss. "We got him, didn't we?"

Her grin was contagious.

"Alejandro Rodriguez isn't going to be dealing drugs to anybody for a long, long time."

"Do you think they could put him in a cell with Marty?" Her eyes sparkled with mischief. "I think they'd make a cute couple."

Tucker let out a laugh. He gave her another hard kiss and slipped his hand under her belly. He was already hard inside her again. He gave a soft push, and she groaned. With a smile, he stood upright. Another smooth, deep stroke made him clench his teeth.

"Not as cute as us, baby," he growled. "Not as cute as us."

About the Author:

Kimberly Dean also writes for Black Lace Books out of the U.K. When not slaving over a keyboard, she enjoys reading, sports, movies, and loud rock-n-roll.

Wake Me

❧⟨❦⟩❧

by Angela Knight

To My Reader:

To me, there's nothing as much fun as taking a standard plot and turning it sideways and inside out. Fairy tales are perfect for that. *Wake Me* is my take on *Sleeping Beauty*— only in this one, the guy is the one asleep. And I can assure you, Walt Disney will not be making a movie out of this version any time soon...

Chapter One

Chloe Hart eyed the newspaper with all the enthusiasm of a woman surveying a dentist's chair before a root canal. "Don't be a wuss, Chlo'," she muttered to herself, and picked the paper up.

Gripping it like a club, she marched back into the house to the kitchen table, where a bracing cup of coffee and a Danish waited to fortify her for the coming ordeal. She tossed the paper on the table, plopped down in her chair and picked up the mug. An incautious sip scalded the tip of her tongue.

At Chloe's lisped obscenity, Rhett Butler looked up from his Tender Vittles with an inquiring "Meow?"

"Ignore me, Rhett," she managed around her boiled tongue tip as she unfolded the newspaper with a series of grim snaps. "Just having a bad morning."

Happy to comply, the muscular black tom settled back down over his bowl. Like his namesake, he frankly didn't give a damn. But as she'd told her dog-loving buddy, Amanda Rice, there was something to be said for blunt feline honesty.

Chloe paged past a murder, a house fire, and a really spectacular pileup on I-26 to reach the account of her personal Waterloo. She found it on page four in section C.

The bride smiled her familiar grin from a dozen yards of tulle and seed pearls, clutching a bouquet of white roses that cascaded to her silk-covered knees. Chloe could almost hear her mother sniff that a woman with three kids had no business in that much white. From a professional standpoint, she herself thought the composition was a little off; the tilt of the bride's veiled head and the position of her flowers didn't quite lead the eye in the proper flow.

"That's what you get for using a cheap photographer, you backstabbing bitch," she muttered at the photo. "Then again, if I'd shot you, I wouldn't have used a camera."

Without bothering to read the description of the wedding—she wasn't that big a masochist, thank you—she closed the newspaper and looked at Rhett. "As God is my witness," she drawled in her best mock-Scarlett O'Hara growl, "I'll never be a sucker again."

Knuckles rattled the storm door. Chloe looked up in surprise. Amanda wouldn't bother to knock, and she wasn't expecting anybody else. "If that's Debbie and Chris, stopping by to beg for forgiveness on the way to the honeymoon," she told the cat as she got up to answer it, "You have my permission to attack."

Rhett yawned and twisted around to lick his furry backside.

She looked back at him. "Or you can do that. Does express the general sentiment pretty well."

Chloe opened the door to find a man in a familiar brown uniform, a huge box tucked awkwardly under one arm. "Delivery," he said, and juggled his electronic clipboard into her hands.

She took it and signed her name in the window, eying the package. "Wonder who that's from?"

He shrugged, supremely indifferent. "Looks like a picture to me."

It did have the right dimensions—four feet across and more than a yard wide, but only three or four inches thick. Curiosity piqued, Chloe accepted the heavy parcel and hauled it inside as the delivery truck roared off. Putting it down on the kitchen table, she went in search of a pair of scissors to attack the packing tape. "If it's a portrait of the bride and groom," she told Rhett as she dug through the kitchen drawer, "your litter box is gonna get filled with little bits of photo paper."

Ripping off a strip of the heavy brown cardboard, Chloe lifted her brows at the intriguing sight of bare, tanned chest and a tight male nipple. "I take it back, Rhett," she murmured. "Somehow I don't think this is going in the litter box."

Ten minutes later, the box lay ruthlessly demolished on the floor, and the oil painting it had contained stood propped on the kitchen table.

Chloe stared reverently.

The knight sprawled in sleep across a tumble of rich sable fur, one hand resting on the jeweled hilt of a sword. It looked as if he'd stripped and fallen asleep after a battle.

He was a big, blond Viking of a man, his hair cropped short, a neat beard framing his lush sinner's mouth. His starkly handsome face looked as though it had been carved by God's own chisel, but if so, He'd been in a hurry. There was something a bit crude and brutal in the angles of the knight's cheekbones and big, square chin. Luckily, those features were balanced out by a regal Roman nose and thick blond brows. The whole effect was intensely masculine—and just a little intimidating.

So was the rest of him. He had the build of a man who'd spent his entire life swinging a blade in an era when losing could cost you your life. He'd cut it close a time or two; his brawny body was slashed here and there with scars that reminded Chloe of a tiger's stripes.

"Really big hands, too," she purred under her breath, eying his long fingers and broad palms. Unfortunately, one of the pelts lay across his hips in a pool of sable, preventing her from determining if the interesting bits lived up to those hands. Chloe sighed, wishing the artist had been less coy.

Coy or not, though, he'd had a firm grasp of history. Artists too often painted knights in the full Germanic plate mail that was only worn in the sixteenth century, when knighthood was actually breathing its last. But the conical helm by the warrior's elbow looked thirteenth century, as did the chain mail coat that lay on the floor, its hammered links gleaming with a muted shimmer.

Emphasizing all that barbaric splendor, the knight's sword glittered with rubies and gold, engraved with intricate symbols she couldn't quite make out. Similar runes were worked into the heavy gold frame.

Chloe stepped close and bent to examine the ancient designs. But the longer she stared, the more they made her think of witches dancing in the firelight, chanting ancient spells. She felt the hair rise on the nape of her neck.

And instantly felt a little silly. *Don't be ridiculous, Chloe,* she told herself, impatient. *There's no such thing as magic.*

Chloe was still staring at the painting in awed fascination fifteen minutes later when Amanda walked in, a fencing bag looped over her shoulder.

"Ready to get your ass kicked?" her friend asked, pushing the kitchen door open with her usual blithe disregard for the custom of knocking.

"As if," Chloe retorted absently before nodding at her gift. "Was this your idea of a distraction? Because it's doing one heck of a job."

"Whoa." Amanda joined her at the table to gape. "Where did you get that? And do they have any more?"

Momentarily distracted, Chloe glanced at her friend. Amanda was dressed in her usual Saturday morning workout togs—a red T-shirt and sweat pants with a pair of white Nikes. She wore her blond hair scraped back into a curling pony tail that emphasized the clean contours of her pleasantly angular face.

They'd met in the fencing class Chris Jennings taught at the local Y, back when they'd all attended the same college. Since Chloe, Amanda and Debbie Mayes had been the only females in the class, the three women had started practicing together. Before long, they'd fallen into such an easy, close friendship, everybody called them the Three Musketeers.

Chris, for his part, quickly took up the role of their seductive young D'Artagnan. He'd set his sights on Chloe, and it hadn't taken him long to get her. She'd moved in with him a year later, about the time Amanda fell head over heels for a budding young housing contractor named Richard Rice.

Debbie, for her part, wed her high-school sweetheart, who morphed into an abusive son of a bitch even before she gave birth to their three kids. She divorced him a year ago, but he already owed her twenty thousand in child support.

Debbie's solution to being flat broke was to seduce Chris. When Chloe finally caught them at it, Debbie had whined, "But I need him more than you do!" True, but hardly the point.

Amanda had come down firmly on Chloe's side in the resulting ugly brawl. Which was a good thing, considering that by then, she and Chloe had been business partners in H&R Graphics for three years.

Their unswerving friendship was the reason Chloe had been so sure the painting was a gift from Amanda. Only…"You mean you didn't send it?"

Amanda was gazing at the knight's naked glory with glazed eyes. "Chlo', I love you like a sister, but if I'd found *him* anywhere, I wouldn't have given him away."

Chloe snorted. "Yeah, right. Richard would just love coming home to find a naked man hanging over the couch."

Ignoring that entirely likely prediction of her husband's reaction, Amanda asked, "So where'd it come from?" She took a step back and cocked her head to one side, the better to ogle.

"Delivery guy just brought it. You ever heard of a company called Evanesce?"

"Nope. I think there's a rock band with that name, though."

Chloe shot her a dry look. "Somehow I doubt it's them."

They contemplated the painting in reverent silence a moment before Amanda suggested, "Maybe your mom and dad—?"

"Yeah, right. Can you imagine Emily Hart sending her unmarried daughter a picture of a nekkid man? I don't think so."

"It's not a nekkid man. It's art. With a capital A."

She was right. Now that the bass throb of Chloe's libido had subsided to a thrum, she realized the painting did look like the work of some Renaissance Old Master. There was obvious skill in the composition, in the warm golden glow of candlelight falling on bare skin, in the juxtaposition of colors, even in the angle of the brush strokes.

Not exactly Elvis on black velvet.

Yet at the same time, there was a carnal sensuality to the painting that was starkly modern. Classical painters had dared that level of eroticism only when painting martyrs.

"Damn," Amanda said. "Wouldn't you love to kiss *him* awake?"

"Yep." Chloe shot her a wicked grin. "But failing that, I'm gonna hang him on the wall. And I know just where."

Her friend rolled her eyes. "Honey, I'd bet money he's already hung."

Five minutes later, the two women manhandled the heavy painting as they tried to catch the wall hook in Chloe's bedroom. Finally the hook snagged the wire strung taut across the painting's back, and they settled it into place.

Chloe nodded in satisfaction as she surveyed the new addition. It

fit right in with her heavy walnut furniture, while the colors compli-
mented the warm gold of her drapes and carpet. "Much better."

Amanda gave her a look. "Certainly more so than asshole's photo,
anyway."

"Hey, I thought that was one of my better pieces."

"Yeah, you almost made the skinny little bastard look sexy."

The artistic nude she'd shot of Chris had hung in that spot for the
past five years. Chloe had taken it down six months ago—in order
to sling it at him like a Frisbee as he rolled off Debbie. One corner
had caught him right in the nuts. The memory of his howl still made
her grin.

Reading her mind as usual, Amanda laughed. "I would have paid
money to see you nail that particular target."

"Just as well you didn't. It wasn't one of my finer moments." She
squared her shoulders. "Let's go fence. Suddenly I'm in the mood to
kick some ass."

"Dream on."

꧁⬥🝁⬥꧂

"Don't you think it's time you started dating again?" Amanda asked,
holding her foil in an efficient guard that protected her right side.

"No." Chloe bounced on the balls of her feet, letting the point of
her practice weapon dip in hopes of luring her friend into an attack.

It was a beautiful spring day. The new-cut grass felt thick and fragrant under her Nike-shod feet, and there was just enough breeze to keep
her from sweating too much in her thick protective fencing jacket.

Chloe and Amanda had been getting together to fence every
Saturday since they'd discovered the sport. Days like this were the
reason why.

"No?" Amanda glared at her through the thick black mesh of her
fencing mask. "Do you want to give that bastard the satisfaction of
knowing he hurt you?"

"The only male I want in my life right now is Rhett." Chloe
launched herself into a blurring lunge, pushing off with her left foot,
her long body uncoiling like a spring as she feinted toward her friend's
shoulder. Amanda retreated smoothly, angling her blade to parry the
attack. Chloe dropped the point of her foil beneath it and popped her

in the ribs. "At least I expect him to tomcat around."

Amanda held up one finger, acknowledging the hit. "You need to get back on the horse, Chlo'. You're never gonna find a guy like Richard if you don't."

"There are no more guys like Richard. Face it, kid, you hit the jackpot in the hubbie lotto."

Amanda sprang at her, and she scrambled into a retreat, parrying, the two blades scraping. "Well, yeah. But Richard knows this gorgeous carpenter…"

"Forget it." Chloe's lunge was so hard and fast, her blade bent as the buttoned tip dug into Amanda's chest. "I'm not going on another blind date."

"Touché, dammit! Would you quit aiming for the tits?"

"I'm not aiming for the tits. And anyway, you're wearing breast protectors." The metal cups were tucked into pockets sewn in the lining of their jackets.

"I don't understand why you won't go out."

"He said I'm a sex addict, okay?" Suddenly unable to tolerate another second of the conversation, Chloe stopped dead and tore off her mask, the better to glare. "I'm *not* a sex addict."

"Who said that? Dickless?" Amanda dropped her own point.

Chloe threw down her mask and tugged off the fencing glove that covered her right hand. "He said that's why he started doing Debbie. He said she's *normal*."

Her friend curled a lip in a sneer. "Only Chris would complain about having a woman who wants sex. Let me guess—he's impotent."

"Not with her." She jerked down the zipper on the side of her jacket, letting it hang open. A cooling breeze instantly swirled in to reach her sweat-damp T-shirt. "I told him once I wanted him to tie me up. He said I was a pervert."

"And he's a congenital liar with the morals of a mink." Amanda tore her own mask off and slung it across the yard. "Asshole."

Now that she'd brought it up, the story came pouring out of her in a bitter flood. "I just thought we could try it. You know how I love those old historicals—you know, the ones where the hero ties the heroine up and seduces her? The idea struck me as hot, and God knows our love life sucked. I thought maybe he'd get into it, and we'd both have a nice little climax for once. Instead he just got all pissed and offended and said I was disgusting."

Amanda snorted. "Probably because you were the only one who wasn't getting any."

"Yeah, it's occurred to me to wonder if he was doing Debbie by then. But still…"

"You're not a pervert, Clo'. It was an excuse."

Needing to move, to do something, anything, Chloe walked across the yard and picked up Amanda's mask. "Doesn't look like you dented it," she said, examining the thick black wire mesh. "You really need to watch that kind of thing. Screw up your mask, and somebody'll drive a point through it in competition. I did that to a guy once. Scared the crap out of me."

Amanda stomped over to take the mask out of her hands. "Quit trying to change the subject. I can't believe you swallowed Chris's bullshit."

She smiled slightly. "Well, he always gave such good bullshit. I just got in the habit."

"Let me set you up with…"

"Not now." Chloe took a deep breath. "Look, you're right. I need to start dating again, but I'm not ready yet. I just…don't feel like trusting anybody right now. Later. Later I'll be ready."

Much, much later.

Chloe lay sleeping in her big bed, a shaft of moonlight falling pale and bright across her face.

She was the first thing Radolf saw when he stepped from the painting.

He walked soundlessly to the foot of the bed, then strode through the thick oak footboard and the mattresses beyond them like a man strolling through mist.

Pausing at her pillow, he stood looking down at her clean profile. Thin red brows arched over her closed eyes, matching the cap of auburn curls that framed her face. He wished her hair was longer. He loved wrapping his fist in long, silken strands while he rode a woman hard.

As if sensing his attention, she turned over on her back, a faint frown gathering between those soft brows. Contemplating her oval face, Radolf decided he liked its sweet, subtle elegance. Her lips were particularly pleasing, seductively full and pink.

He wanted to watch her suck him. It had been a very long time since a woman had pleasured him with her mouth.

"At least this one is passably pretty," Radolf murmured. Chloe didn't even stir, of course; his voice made no sound. Holding out a hand, he ran it the length of her sheet-covered body. "Decent breasts."

"Did I not tell you that you would like her?" Belisarda said, striking a pose in a patch of moonlight. Radolf did not look around, though her dark, seductive beauty was enough to steal a man's breath. He had known her too long to be fooled. Besides, he no longer breathed. At least, not in this form.

"Look at her," the demon witch continued, her voice a suggestive purr. Her great, oval eyes flickered with crimson reflections as her mouth curled into a smile. It had taken Radolf years to notice how thin Belisarda's lips really were. "All lush promise, just waiting for your touch. Surely she will love you."

He shot her a shimmering glare. "The last one loved me."

"Not enough." The witch pushed off with one bare foot, drifting toward him wrapped in her glittering diaphanous robes. "None of them loved you enough to come for you. None has even attempted to give you the kiss of freedom, no matter how you seduced and tempted."

Radolf curled his lips back from his teeth. "I know how that grieves you, witch. You feed from what I make them feel."

"Well, of course." Even as he'd spin his dreams, she'd float above the girl's sleeping body, drinking the mortal's pleasure to sustain her own magical life. "It would be a sin to let such glorious effort go to waste." Belisarda extended pale, slender fingers toward his naked shoulder. He flinched away, and her eyes chilled. "Since you fail at all else."

He looked down at Chloe. "Not with her. This one will love me." The glare he threw Belisarda shimmered with hate. "By God, I'll see to it. And then I'll be free of you."

Radolf turned and bent over the girl buried under a mound of covers. Lifting a big, translucent hand, he touched her forehead and sank into her with a last soft, low growl for his enemy. "This one will break the spell."

The witch's smile was small and catlike. "I do hope so, my lord Radolf," she whispered as he vanished into his prey. "I do indeed."

"The conqueror comes!"

Chloe jolted and looked around. She stood in the great hall of a medieval castle. All around her, people in the garb of thirteenth century knights and ladies milled under the vaulting stone ceiling, faces pale and eyes wide.

"Whoa," she muttered. "What the heck is going on?"

"See where thy willfulness has brought us!" Gnarled hands clamped around her forearm, spinning her around. A tiny, bird-like woman in blue wool glared up at her, faded periwinkle eyes accusing. "He has taken the castle," the woman continued, "and his anger is terrible to behold!"

Chloe blinked. "Who?"

"Lord Radolf of Varik, of course. Who do you think? Now, heed thy old nurse, milady. I know you are but a maid…"

"A virgin? Me?" She snorted. "What medieval mushrooms have you been smoking?"

"…But 'tis as I told you. Lord Radolf hungers for you. You must curb your willfulness, set yourself to please him, or 'twill go badly for us all!"

"Who the hell is Lord Radolf?"

"As if you don't know!" The old woman threw up both hands. "The King's Champion. The man you swore you'd not marry, king's command or no."

Damn, this sounded just like one of her favorite romances. *Dreaming*, Chloe realized suddenly. *I'm dreaming.*

Of course. The portrait had triggered something in her fertile little subconscious, and it had spit out a scenario from one of those used bookstore historicals she loved so much.

Though, she thought, gazing down at the woman's liver spots, she'd never had a dream quite this *real*.

"My lord Radolf!" someone called in ringing tones.

The old lady shot a hunted glance over her shoulder before turning back to her. "Heed me well, girl!" She shook an arthritic finger under Chloe's befuddled nose. "None of your sharp tongue! Make him happy, or..."

"Wait a minute," Chloe interrupted in growing outrage. "Let me get this straight. You expect me to play hide the broadsword with this guy so he'll make things easier on everybody else? Forget that. No way am I..."

The man from the painting walked through the castle's great doors, his chain mail ringing with every long stride. He looked even more stunningly gorgeous in person.

As Chloe gaped, he headed straight for her. His eyes burned hot and hungry, green as emeralds in sunlight, and his smile was raw, distilled sex.

Aimed right at her.

Chloe licked suddenly dry lips and squeaked, "On the other hand, what's a little self-sacrifice between friends?"

When Radolf of Varik finally stopped to loom over her, her knees went weak. Damn, he was big. His green gaze flicked down to her cleavage in blatant anticipation, then up to her face again. Something in his expression put her in mind of Rhett stalking a particularly fat chipmunk. "Well met, milady."

She gave him a dazed blink. "Right back atch..."

He snatched her off her feet before she could even get the rest of the sentence out of her mouth.

The kiss was not even remotely foreplay. It was a sex act all by itself, conducted with lips and tongue and teeth as Radolf's big hands cupped her head and turned it here and there for his leisurely conquest. He bit, he licked, he suckled. He claimed every last millimeter of her mouth.

And while he was at it, he made all kinds of feral promises about what he'd do to the rest of her, without ever saying a word beyond soft male growls. He made her feel more thoroughly plundered in five minutes than Chris had managed in six years. By the time he finally put her back down again, she was swaying.

It took her a full thirty seconds to realize she was also trussed like a turkey on a cooking show.

Chloe blinked down at herself in astonishment. Her wrists were tied behind her back and lashed tightly against her body with multiple turns of rope that circled her torso just under her bust. The pose thrust out her breasts, making the hard peaks of her nipples doubly obvious under the thin blue silk of her kirtle. "How the heck did you do that?" she demanded, too surprised for anger.

Radolf gave her a lazy grin. "Magic."

Glancing wildly around, she realized they were no longer in the great hall. Somehow he'd transported her to a medieval bed chamber, complete with massive oak bed and roaring fire. A thick pile of furs lay beneath her bare feet, as if just waiting for all kinds of illicit activities. But how had...

Oh, yeah, Chloe remembered again. *This is a dream.*

Damned if it felt like one, though. She'd certainly never gotten a kiss that hot in any dream before.

Glancing up at him, she drew in a startled breath. Radolf's armor had disappeared since the last time she'd looked, leaving him gloriously nude, his big body tanned and muscular and dusted in golden hair. Half hypnotized, she scanned down all that mouth-watering male anatomy....

Yep. His cock definitely lived up to the promise of his big, sinewy hands. He was darn near as thick as her wrist, smooth and massive and uncircumcised, with heavy balls already tight with lust.

"Now, this is more like it," Chloe said, unable to drag her eyes away from that luscious erection. "I usually dream about knife-wielding psychos with serious anger management issues. You are definitely an improvement."

"On that, we are in agreement," Radolf rumbled, doing a hungry scan of his own. "'Ere this, Belisarda has given me naught but mincing virgins who expect me to compose sonnets to their eyelashes, or bitter wives who wish to punish me for their straying husbands' sins." He curled his upper lip. "I've spent more time on my knees than a scullery maid."

Not quite sure what to make of that, Chloe ventured, "You don't strike me as the kind of guy to crawl well."

"Indeed, milady," he purred, curling big hands in either shoulder of her kirtle, "I am not."

"Hey...!" Chloe began.

Too late. He did it anyway, shredding the fabric of the thin gown like tissue paper, leaving her breasts bare and quivering.

"You know, the whole bodice-ripping thing is *so* politically incorrect," she told him, her heart pounding as a smile of dark anticipation spread over his face.

Radolf cupped one breast in a big, callused hand. "At the moment," he said, lowering his head, "I am not remotely interested in politics."

His mouth closed over her, surrounding the tight flesh in such heat and hunger that she gasped. "Now that you mention...AH! ... it, neither am I." The gasp became a whimper as his teeth gently raked the little peak. Damn, but he was good at that.

Finally Radolf drew back to give her that predator's smile again. "Perhaps I'll go to my knees for you after all."

Then he did just that—the better to attack her nipples with his wickedly skilled mouth. While she was reeling from that luscious assault, he slid one big hand under the remains of her skirt. His palm felt deliciously warm against her thighs as he sent it questing upward.

Her arms bound helplessly behind her, Chloe could do nothing but stand there and moan. "This is really kinky," she managed at last, as his pointed tongue swirled around one hard peak.

"Oh, aye." He sucked her nipple into his mouth, bit gently. "Sinful, too."

She eased her legs apart. "A good feminist would never let a guy treat her this way."

"Absolutely not." One long finger traced the creaming opening between the swollen lips of her sex.

"I think you're missing the point."

"No." Radolf strummed his thumb over her clit. "I know exactly where your point is."

Chloe caught her breath. "Ohhhh, yeah. Yes, you certainly do."

He licked her nipples slowly, carefully, like a starving man forcing himself to take his time with some luscious dessert. As if that wasn't enough to drive her insane all by itself, one thick finger parted her labia, then gently screwed its way deep. She closed her eyes and moaned.

Radolf lifted his head to watch her as he added a second finger. "Wet and responsive," he said, his voice a rasping murmur. "And so deliciously snug. I can't wait to sink into you. I'll ride you hard, sweet one. Ride you like none of your bloodless lovers ever has."

For a long, delicious moment, there was no sound but her breathy sighs as the knight tormented her, twisting his fingers, scissoring them apart, then pushing in right up to the knuckles. Pleasure swirled and danced up her spine with every magical caress until she writhed, mindless and teetering on the brink.

"Now," he breathed, and abruptly thrust inside her, simultaneously circling his thumb over her clit. "Fly for me."

She convulsed, crying out in maddened joy as the heat rose in a sweet, burning flood.

His breath caught, then released in a growl. "Yes, that's it—tighten. Let me feel you pulse...."

The climax surged on and on, lifting her into a keening arch, arms bound, helpless in the face of the searing pleasure. She lost her balance, but even as she started to fall backward, he caught her and lowered her gently.

Dazed and panting, Chloe watched Radolf rise to his feet. She could feel sweat rolling down her back as her thigh muscles trembled deliciously.

Towering over her, he threaded those big fingers into her curls, his expression fierce. "Open your mouth."

She looked at his massive cock inches from her lips. With a shudder of arousal, she leaned over and took the thick, round head of his cock into her mouth.

"Yes!" he groaned, the powerful muscles of his abdomen lacing as Chloe engulfed as much of his shaft as she could. "Jesu, it's been so long..."

She'd never found giving a blow job all that hot, but there was something about the feeling of Radolf's big body trembling against hers that was unspeakably erotic.

Listening to his gasps, Chloe drew away to swirl her tongue over the flushed, nubby head of his cock. He shuddered.

She smiled.

Slowly, carefully, she licked along the shaft and each of its snaking veins. When she swooped in again to suck, his rasping groan sent a sense of sensual power rolling over her.

He might be six inches taller, and she might be trussed so tightly she could barely wiggle her fingers, but at that moment he was all hers.

Suddenly he arched his back, his hand fisting involuntarily in her curls as he pulsed against her tongue. "Ah, sweet Christ!" he gasped. "Yes!"

Smiling around his thick shaft, she swallowed.

When she drew away from him at last, she found him staring down at her, his gaze curiously desperate for a man who'd just come in a woman's mouth. "Wake me." Both big hands cupped the sides of her face, stroked just beneath her cheekbones. "Wake me. Wake me, and I'll show you such pleasure every night."

A slight, puzzled frown still curved Chloe's mouth as she slid gently into a deeper sleep. Radolf echoed it as he rose from her. Though he had not had a physical body in a very long time, he felt shaken. "That," he murmured soundlessly, "did not go at all as I planned."

Chapter Two

Radolf stood in Belisarda's palace in the realm of Evanesce, gazing down at his own helplessly sleeping body. "Wake, curse you," he muttered, but of course, his enchanted self did not so much as stir. He lay as he had for the past eight hundred years in this magical prison of his, his mail and his sword around him, unaging and eternal.

And asleep.

Only his spirit was free. Free to enter the dreams of women and try to seduce them into lifting the spell that held him. He could read their thoughts, their secret dreams. He could become any fantasy lover they wished, speak the language they spoke, create any world they wanted. Sorcerer, seducer and slave in one desperate man.

Yes, his spirit was free, if you could call it freedom. If you could call whoring for a demonic witch "freedom."

He, the greatest knight in Christendom. The man his brothers in the Order of Varik had called The Champion of God. How appalled they'd be to see him now, a failure and a slave, vows broken, plying his dick in woman after woman. Pursuing the lying hope his enemy dangled in front of him because it was all he had left.

He was surely damned.

"You arrogant dog."

On the bed, his body twitched, reacting to the terror pouring through him at the rage in the witch's voice. Radolf wheeled to defend himself, knowing it would do him no good.

Belisarda strode toward him, her face twisted and malevolent, her eyes burning with a cold glow. She was flesh here in her kingdom of Evanesce. Flesh as he was not.

And she had power.

Automatically, he tried to knock her hand away as it flashed toward his heart, but her arm punched right through his ghostly fingers. And kept going, plunging deep into his chest to wrap around the core of his soul.

He tried to brace himself, but it did him no good. Waves of black energy poured from the witch's deceptively slender fingers. Energy that tore into his spirit like a cat sharpening its claws on silk.

Radolf believed this must be what it was like to be drawn and quartered—gutted alive and ripped apart by horses whipped in opposite directions. He doubted such a death could be any worse.

"Scream for me," Belisarda sneered.

He clenched his insubstantial teeth. She'd broken him, aye, but he was not so bent beneath her boot that he'd give her a casual victory.

He did not scream.

He would not scream.

Radolf fought to cling to that last bit of dignity in the ruins of his miserable existence. He knew he could outlast her. She would grow tired or bored or drained if he could only hold on a little longer. If he could only lock his psychic shriek between his teeth another second, oh dear sweet Jesu...

Belisarda tore her hand from him and watched him swirl in glowing wisps, unable to maintain even the illusion of a physical form. "I am displeased with you."

Radolf wanted to use the phrase he'd just learned from Chloe's mind: *No shit.* It was probably fortunate he was not yet capable of speech.

"She could have taken more pleasure from her own right hand than that pitiful climax you gave her," the witch raged. "And then you dared—dared!—order her to suck you, as if you were master rather than crawling slave!"

When she started to reach for him again, Radolf somehow managed to re-form. "A master...is what she wants," he told her in the silent communication that was all he was capable of. "At least in...bedroom fantasy. She wants no man to crawl to her."

"She's a twenty-first century woman who's been tricked and cheated, fool! Of course she wants you to crawl."

"No." He felt himself growing more cohesive in his certainty. "I've seduced enough women to know my quarry. She does not want protection, but she does want a lover strong enough to give it. Even if all she needs protection from is the lover himself." He hesitated, thinking of the pain he'd sensed in her. "Mayhap especially then."

"Huh." Belisarda curled her lip. "Well, if it's strength she wants, you'd better play lord and master to the hilt." Whirling, she strode away down the dark stone corridor, the heavy gown she wore now whipping around her long legs.

Just before she vanished around a corner, she paused and glowered over her shoulder at him. "Because if she ever discovers what a weakling you are, she'll not waste her time with you."

"You're thinking about that dream again," Amanda said, dropping into the chair beside Chloe.

Startled out of her haze, she hastily clicked her mouse. "Nope. Sorting through candids."

Dammit, she needed to finish weeding out the clunkers from the wedding she'd shot this morning. If she didn't get the digital shots uploaded to the lab in time, the photos wouldn't be back by the time the clients returned from their honeymoon. *Wake up, Chloe.*

"You know, when you're sorting, I hear busy little click-clicky sounds," Amanda drawled. "Since I haven't heard a click in ten minutes, I can only conclude you're thinking about that dream. Again."

Chloe felt heat flood her cheekbones. She and Amanda had been partners in H&R Graphics for the past three years. They'd set up shop in an office in this converted warehouse, with her friend contributing the business know-how and Chloe handling the photography and graphics creation. She rarely felt as if she wasn't pulling her weight. She did now.

Sighing, Chloe rubbed her temples. "I don't know what's wrong with me."

Amanda hooked an arm over her shoulder. "You had a rough weekend, sweetheart. It's not really surprising your mind's wandering."

"It's just..." She stopped.

"What?"

"I've never had a dream like the one last night. Ever. It was so...detailed."

Amanda smirked. Chloe had already entertained her with a

play-by-play. "You mean, beyond giving the blow job to Sir Lottalance?"

She grinned reluctantly. "Beyond that. I never...Look, I almost
always dream in color, but I never dream in smells. Or tastes."

Her friend pursed her lips, considering. "You know, I don't think
I have either." She slanted Chloe a look. "What kind of tastes are we
talking about here?"

"*That* taste. And...him. I could smell him. He smelled...exotic.
Like leather and spices and iron."

"You know, they didn't bathe a whole lot back then...."

Chloe grinned. "Well, no, but evidently this dream wasn't going
for that much accuracy. Or else he'd just bathed. Anyway, he smelled
really good." She sighed, her eyes falling half shut in pleasure at the
memory. "And his hands. He had these calluses, like you'd expect
from a guy that swings a broadsword all day. They were just a little
bit rough on my skin."

Amanda gave a salacious shiver. "Damn, girl. You keep this up,
and I'm going to have to go home and attack Richard. My dreams
are never that good."

Chloe frowned, drumming her fingers on the mouse pad. "That's
what I'm saying—mine aren't either. I mean, I dream a lot. Weird stuff
that doesn't make much sense, based on what little I can remember
about it the next day. But I can remember this, down to the last little
detail. And other than the time he transported me into another room
with a kiss, it all made sense."

Amanda lifted a brow. "Did it ever occur to you that maybe this
is just your body's way of telling you it's time to get laid?"

Chloe glowered. "If you're about to offer to fix me up with that
friend of Richard's again, forget it."

"Well, it is pretty obvious that you could seriously use some,
babe. Why else are you dreaming yourself into a medieval porno
movie?"

"Maybe because somebody sent me a really hot painting that totally
caught my imagination?"

"Which reminds me," Amanda said. "Just who did send you that
painting, anyway? Have you figured that out?"

She frowned and pushed the mouse around, watching the cursor skitter across the screen. "No. I've been wracking my brain, but I haven't got a clue. I made half a dozen phone calls, but all my female friends plead ignorance."

"And somehow, this just isn't the kind of thing a guy would send," Amanda agreed.

"Yep. Heck, I even asked Mom and Dad. Neither of them knew anything about it either. I'm planning to call the shipping company on Monday."

"Maybe somebody was just trying to cheer you up."

Chloe clicked on an out-of-focus shot of the bride's face and deleted it. "Except I've got a feeling this was a damned expensive gift. Too expensive, maybe."

Amanda frowned. "What do you mean?"

"Well, that frame." Frowning, she scanned absently through the rest of the images, deleting those that didn't meet her standards. "I took a look at the frame this morning. It's not just gilded wood, it's actual metal. And it looks like real gold."

"Oh, Chlo', it can't be." Amanda sat back in her chair. "That frame's got to weigh thirty pounds. If it was gold, it'd be worth…"

"Thousands. Or even more, if the painting's as old as it looks. And another thing, I was looking at the designs engraved into the frame. They look like runes."

Amanda digested that for a long moment. "Okay, now you're beginning to freak me out."

"Yeah, well, I'm freaking me out too."

"Maybe you ought to get rid of it," Amanda suggested.

Chloe's blue eyes narrowed. "Oh, no. Oh, hell no. What if it really is gold? What if it's as old and valuable as it looks?"

"And what if it's freakin' cursed, Chlo'? What if it's hot?"

"You mean, what if some international art thief shipped a stolen painting to me just for giggles?"

"You got a better explanation?" Amanda nibbled on her manicured thumbnail, visibly worried. "People don't just send strangers fantastic pieces of art in solid gold frames for no reason. There's a catch, Chlo'. We may not know what it is yet, but there's got to be a catch."

Chloe lay in her bed, staring at the muted golden glow of the painting's frame as a shaft of moonlight fell across it.

Would she dream of him again tonight?

Did she want to?

Well, yeah. Which meant that she probably would. But with her luck, Radolf would morph into Ted Bundy, and she'd spend the whole damn night running from him. Her dreams were never that happy. Certainly not for long.

But wouldn't it be nice if tonight's was an exception?

Out in the hall, she heard her big grandfather clock chime in long, rolling bongs.

Midnight.

Who was she trying to kid? As wound up as she was, she'd never get to sleep to *have* the dream. She'd toss and turn all night, staring at that stupid picture, unable to sleep a...

A rich female voice said, "This grows tiresome."

Hey, wha...?

It was her last conscious thought until morning.

The floor pitched, almost tossing her completely off her feet. Chloe flailed a hand, grabbed something taut and prickly, and steadied herself. Shooting a look at what she held, she realized it was a taut hemp rope, more cable than anything else. Something boomed overhead, and she glanced up to see enormous sheets billowing overhead.

No, not sheets. Sails.

She was on a boat.

And not a sailboat either, Chloe realized, squinting up at the blinding blue sky that framed an intricate web of rigging, spars and flapping canvas. This was a tall ship, a...

BOOM!

Somebody bellowed a curse. Steel clashed on steel.

Chloe jolted, staring wildly around. Now men surrounded her in surging, thrashing knots of combat, hacking at one another with cutlasses or trying to bash each other's brains out with belaying pins. Blood was everywhere, rolling across the wooden deck, pooling around the corpses until men slipped and cursed in it.

Across the pitching deck of the ship, another massive warship bucked alongside. A flag flapped from its mast. The wind dragged the black fabric straight out to reveal a grinning skull, a rose between its teeth.

"Well," Chloe muttered, "I always did have a thing for pirate romances." She glanced down and wasn't even remotely surprised to see all the cleavage revealed by her tight laced bodice.

But as she contemplated the miles of blue silk hugging her body, she spotted something else. "Now that's convenient."

Just past one slippered foot, a rapier lay abandoned on the deck.

Chloe picked it up, smiling in appreciation at the way its cleanly balanced weight rode her hand. Giving the crowded deck a scan, she muttered, "So where is Captain Hardcock, anyway? Isn't it time he…"

High overhead, a powerful male figure stepped off one of the pirate ship's spars.

"Cue sex god," Chloe muttered, "swooping stage left."

She watched Radolf swing toward her, one big hand wrapped around a length of rope, the other holding a sword. At just the right instant, he let go of the line and dropped ten feet to land lightly on the deck. His grin lit his tanned face with a broad slash of white. "Ho, wench!" he called.

Chloe grinned back, ridiculously happy to see him. "You do realize you just violated half a dozen laws of physics?"

"Oh, aye," he said, swaggering toward her. "I just don't care."

Tonight Radolf wore a flowing white shirt open to the waist and a pair of black pants so tight she could tell he dressed to the left. A rapier swung from the leather baldric that draped his impressive chest, and a pair of black leather boots sheathed his muscled legs to the thigh. Though his blond hair had been cropped short in the previous dream, now it tumbled to his shoulders. Only the goatee framing his rakish grin was the same.

With a sigh of pleasure, Chloe admired his lazy, long-legged stride as he approached. His path was oddly free of inconvenient corpses. Looking around, she realized everybody else had disappeared from the ship, taking the blood and assorted body parts with them.

She and the pirate were alone.

A little quiver of lust snaked up her spine. Ignoring it, she said, "I'm beginning to think you've got a thing for dramatic entrances."

"No, milady. You do."

Chloe thought about it. "Now that you mention it, yeah." Bracing the point of her rapier on the deck, she let her eyes skim down to contemplate those skin-tight trousers. Judging from the bulge, she wasn't the only one who approved of the scenery. "So what's on the menu for tonight?"

"Actually," Radolf drawled, "I thought I'd bend my pretty captive over a cannon and see how many times I can make her beg for mercy before she starts begging for more."

He did that pirate grin extremely well.

Her heart started pounding. "Tacky, Radolf. Very tacky."

"Very." His green eyes crinkled at the corners. "And yet it made you cream."

"Did not," she lied.

"It certainly did." One big hand dropped to his sword. He drew it with a slither of steel.

She licked her lips and tightened her grip on her own rapier. "Now, what are you going to do with that?"

"Not much." The ends of his mustache twitched up like Rhett's whiskers. "Just find out how many laces I'll have to cut before your breasts spill out of that bodice." His point flicked toward her.

"Nuh-uh." Her rapier snapped up into an automatic parry, knocking his aside. "Not gonna be that easy, Captain Radolf of the good ship *Raging Hardon.*"

He straightened, breaking into a delighted grin. "Oh, surely you jest."

Chloe awkwardly gathered a mile or so of skirt in her left hand and fell into guard. "What, you think I watched all those Errol Flynn flicks in film class because I liked his dimples?"

He lifted a golden brow as he surveyed her. "The concept of your fighting me at all is ludicrous, but it's particularly laughable given those skirts."

"Hey, I'll have you know I was state fencing champ…" She broke off at his feral grin broadened.

When Chloe glanced down, her gown had disappeared. In its place was a white corset that pushed her breasts up and together until they strained to spill free. A tiny pair of thoroughly modern thong panties made very little pretense at modesty, while a white garter belt held up delicate lace stockings. A pair of stiletto heels rounded off the whole Victoria's Secret effect.

She glowered. "This is not even remotely period."

His grin widened. "I know."

"And if I try to fence in these heels, I'm going to break both ankles."

"Actually, you won't, but I suppose they do push credibility rather far."

The shoes instantly became delicate dancing slippers. Not mollified in the least, Chloe demanded, "I thought you were a medieval knight. How do you know so much about modern lingerie, anyway? Or seventeenth century piracy, for that matter? Or, hell, twenty-first century grammar?"

Radolf shrugged broad shoulders. "Actually, I know very little about any of that. You, however, know a great deal, and since you're the one having the dream, that's enough." He began stalking her, moving as lightly as a panther over the swaying deck. "The question is, what do you know about using that sword?"

"That's a..." Very good question. It suddenly occurred to Chloe that neither of their weapons were buttoned fencing foils. If one of them actually hit the other, the phrase "agony of defeat" could have real meaning.

She scuttled back from his advance, wondering what the hell to do now.

"Probably lose," he told her, as if reading her mind.

Then he launched into a long, slow, lazy lunge.

He was so big, Chloe had plenty of time to see him coming. Retreating hastily, she flicked her blade for the parry, but his weapon did an intricate dance around hers and kept right on coming. Panicking—this was going to hurt—she tried for the parry again, missed and...

Pop. Chloe cringed as she looked down, half expecting blood.

The top lace of her corset was neatly cut. "Hey!"

Radolf straightened as he regarded her cleavage like a connoisseur. He let his rapier dip, but the weapon between his brawny thighs strained at full attention. "As I said," he purred, "the concept of fighting you is ludicrous, but I find myself willing to indulge your fantasies." He grinned wickedly. "Whatever they may be."

Chloe had a redhead's temper, and now it flared into full, glorious roar. This wasn't the first time she'd encountered blatant sexism in the men she fenced, but somehow—God knew why—she'd expected better of Radolf. "I," she growled, "am going to kick your arrogant ass."

"Actually, you're going to get stripped naked and bent over a cannon while I impale your tight, creamy little..."

With a snarl, she went after him with teeth bared.

Chloe often fenced with men. She was feared on the tournament circuit, because though most of her opponents were bigger and stronger, she made up for her weaknesses with skill. Too, she excelled at the kind of strategic play that turned fencing into highly physical chess.

None of which did her a bit of good against Radolf.

Nobody that big should be that fast. He parried her most nimble attacks with flicks of his blade that looked deceptively gentle. At least until he connected and damn near tore the rapier from her hand.

Radolf's offense was even more murderous. Trying to block his attacks was like trying to parry a 747. It should have taken him about five minutes to turn Chloe into sushi. Luckily, all he was interested in cutting were the strings on her corset. It wasn't long until the garment gaped wide enough to reveal the areolas of her nipples. And worse, encumber her arms.

"Hell with it," she growled, and started jerking at the corset with her left hand, trying to pull it off and maintain her guard at the same time.

But though the three remaining laces did nothing to hold the corset closed, they were snarled tight. She couldn't seem to get them untied, especially with one eye on her opponent. Frustrated, she looked down....

A rapier point danced in, flicked. All three laces popped, and the corset slid down around her hips.

Chloe shot Radolf a glare. Spreading his free hand, he attempted a guileless smile that wasn't even remotely convincing. "I was simply trying to help."

"Yeah, you're a real gentleman." As she jerked the garment off and threw it aside, his green eyes lit at the sight of her bare, bouncing breasts.

Enough's enough, she thought with a snarl, and launched right into an attack.

Radolf was so busy admiring the sweat gleaming on Chloe's chest that he missed the parry. He had to scramble back out of range of her lunge.

"Ha!" she crowed, throwing herself into another combination. Pressing ruthlessly, her blade beating against his, she managed to back him into one of the twelve-pounder cannons that stood on the deck.

Radolf leaped away from her assault, landing on top of the big gun as lightly as Rhett jumping on the kitchen counter. "Not fair," he told her. "I was distracted by those hard little nipples."

"I'll show you distracted," Chloe growled. "I'll distract you with a sucking chest wound." She slashed her sword in a ruthless cut right for his muscled calves.

He bounced over her stroke to hit the deck on the opposite side of the cannon. "That doesn't sound at all pleasant."

"Oh, it won't be." She thrust at the muscled V exposed by his open shirt.

A big brown hand flashed out and locked around her sword wrist. One hard jerk dragged her halfway across the gun.

"Now, look at that." Radolf tossed his own rapier aside and casually plucked her weapon from her hand. "Half naked and draped across a cannon." His grin was pure lupine threat. "Whatever will I do with you now?"

I'm screwed now. Literally, Chloe thought in dismay, staring into his wickedly hungry gaze. Rallying, she managed a glare. "Forget it," she growled, fighting to jerk out of his hold. "I wouldn't have you if you were the last romance hero in publishing."

"Of course not," Radolf said, cupping the back of her head to lean in for a quick kiss. He pulled back just before her teeth could snap down on his lower lip. While she glowered, he gave her another one of those Red-Riding-Hood-eating grins. "Assuming I gave you a choice."

Realization dawned. "Dammit, you've done it to me again, haven't you?"

He grinned. "Oh, aye."

Sure enough, her wrists were tied together behind her back, while her wide-spread ankles had been tethered to rings set to the deck.

"Have I mentioned," Radolf purred, tracing a big finger along the naked contours of one hard nipple, "how much I adore your breasts?"

Both the nipples in question tingled and hardened. Chloe licked her lips. "Cut that out."

He smiled slowly. "No."

Callused fingers stroked and teased until curls of pleasure swirled through her breasts. "I don't want this," she managed.

"Liar."

"Rapist."

He dropped to one knee. "I'll make you a bargain, my sweet one. If you still want me to stop in five minutes, I'll stop."

He tilted his blond head so that one of her hard little peaks pouted just above his lips. Then, ever so slowly, he licked. Chloe gasped at the silken pleasure that cascaded through her body with the first pass of his clever tongue.

And knew she wouldn't be telling him to stop.

Chapter Three

Radolf had a great mouth.

And he knew how to use it too. He swirled just the tip of his tongue over and around Chloe's breasts in tiny little circles that made her jerk against her bonds.

"Sweet," he whispered. Green eyes flashed up to meet hers roguishly. "And so helpless."

His sinner's lips opened just a bit wider so he could rake his teeth over a tight, pouting point. One big hand came up to cup the other breast. His callused thumb rasped over its peak.

She squirmed.

"Your little pussy is next," Radolf told her, his voice a velvety male purr. "I'm going to lick and suck…" He paused to demonstrate. "And bite…" A quick nip made her gasp. "Do you know why?"

"You want to drive me crazy?"

He smiled slowly. "Yes. And I need you very, very wet. Because my cock is thick and hard, and you're so exquisitely tiiight." He squeezed both breasts with those big hands of his, gently milking pleasure from her flesh. "It's going to take a long time to work my entire shaft in up to the balls."

She swallowed and managed, "Oh, now you're just bragging."

"No." He gave her an exquisitely slow, careful bite. "I'm not."

Remembering what it had been like to suck him the night before, Chloe knew he was right. Imagining her slow impalement on that big shaft, she shivered.

God, this was going to be good.

Radolf's long fingers ceased their seductive stroking. "Unless you tell me no, of course." Blond lashes veiled knowing green eyes. "I wouldn't want to force you."

She snorted. "Except on days ending in Y."

He widened both green eyes, as if trying for an innocence he missed by a mile. "You malign me, milady." Gently he twisted her nipples, sending twin streams of pleasure streaking right for her sex. "Do you think me such a barbarian I'd rape some poor lass, simply because she was foolish enough to think she could best me in combat?"

"After you'd stripped her naked and tied her over a cannon? Gee, let me think—Yes."

"I'm wounded, lady. Truly I am." The laughter rumbling in Radolf's seductive voice made heat well deep inside her. "I'm the very soul of chivalry."

She snorted. "In the words of the Big Bad Wolf, '*What* Three Little Pigs?' You'd be more convincing without the bacon on your breath."

"Oh, sweet, nobody could ever mistake you for a pig of any sort." He flicked an auburn curl with one big finger. "Now, Red Riding Hood…"

"As long as you don't try to dress up as my grandma. The concept of you in drag…" She gave a mock shudder.

Radolf lifted a blond brow. "Oh, you have nothing to fear on that score." A sly smile quirked his mustache. "Though now that you mention it, I am interested in your basket of goodies."

When he rose to his feet, she got a crotch level view of his own goodies. "My, Grandma," she muttered, *sotto voce.* "You're hung like a Clydesdale."

His laugh as he walked around behind her was wicked enough to make her quiver in her bonds.

She quivered even harder when he caught the fragile waistband of her lace thong and ripped it off her body. "Now," he purred, "That's better."

"Yeah," she managed. "I'd say so."

A big finger stroked down the crack of her bare backside to find her sex. His fingertips traced between the swollen lips. "Ah," Radolf rumbled, "a creamy little tart. My favorite dish."

Chloe tried to crane her head around to see what he was doing, but the cannon blocked her view.

Which didn't keep her from feeling every glorious sensation. Like the tickle of his beard against her ass. Or the hot, masculine tongue that licked the length of her, catching her clit and the opening of her vagina in one pass.

As she gasped and squirmed, he did it again. And again, back and forth, slowly, in long, teasing laps.

In minutes, he had her on the edge of shameless begging. She wanted him to circle his tongue around her clit the way he had her nipples, but he was too intent on driving her out of her mind. Every stroke of that clever tongue sent pleasure sizzling up her spine. She could feel her body tightening, on the verge of a hard, pulsing climax. If only he'd circle her clit just once....

"Radolf," Chloe gasped at last, unable to stand any more. "Please!"

"Please what?" he drawled.

She felt no shame at all. "Let me come!"

Another deliciously torturous lick. "Do you deserve to come?"

"God, yes!"

"But you've been wicked." One big finger explored her. Entered slowly. "You drew a weapon on me. And you lost." Slid out again. His thumb brushed her clit, just enough to make pleasure jolt through her, but not enough to trigger that pulsing climax. "I won. So now..." Another mind-blowing entry. "...I get to punish you."

"Radolf!" It was a whimper.

"You're so tight and swollen and wet, Chloe." She heard the jangle of a belt, the rustle of clothing. "I think you're ready for your punishment."

She closed her eyes as hot lust roared through her. "Be my guest."

"Sweet, do you really think I need permission?" Radolf laughed as the head of his massive cock brushed her creamy flesh. While she caught her breath in an agony of erotic anticipation, he began to work his way inside.

He was much, much bigger than Chris.

Then he stopped and pulled out. "No, on second thought, you're not ready yet."

"Radolf!"

"I can't do it too soon, sweet." He stroked the big head between the lips of her sex, teasing her opening but carefully avoiding her clit. "I'd hate to take you before you're completely ready."

"You know how ready I am!" Frustrated, Chloe rolled her hips, trying to capture the taunting shaft.

A big hand landed lightly on her ass in a gentle swat. "None of that, sweet. You lost, remember?"

"Take me already, you big jerk!"

He slid inside a bare inch. "Now, is that any way to talk to your lord and master?"

Her inner feminist rebelled, but her inner hedonist promptly strangled it into submission. Chloe didn't care what delusions he cherished, as long as he gave her more of that magnificent cock.

Radolf obliged her, slowly feeding her a little more of the broad shaft. And then still more. Damn, he made Chris feel like a toothpick by comparison. Slick, sliding heat, stretching and filling her. More. And more.

And more.

She could feel her climax gathering power, like a tidal wave roaring toward shore.

"Aye," he gritted, when he was seated to the balls, "Oh, aye. You're ready…."

And then he began to thrust. He started slowly, gently rocking against her, teasing her with delicious little strokes down in her hot depths. His big hands rested on her ass with blatant possession. As he lengthened his thrusts, she felt him lean back and part her, as though to watch his cock delving between her lips.

"I love the way you grip me, sweet," he said softly. "Wet and snug." He drove in a deep stroke and groaned in pleasure. "And good. Sweet Jesu, you're good."

"You're not—AH!—so bad yourself," she gasped.

He started riding harder, faster. She could feel her climax building, gathering, the tidal wave whipped higher by his masculine storm.

Radolf was lunging hard now, his hips slapping her ass. He reached beneath her with one hand, found her clit. Stroked.

Chloe screamed as the white hot explosion rolled over her, ecstasy jolting through her entire nervous system like a lightning blast. "Radolf! Oh, God!"

"Aye!" He jammed to his full length and froze, coming, his roar blending with her cry.

It went on and on, blazing, creamy spasms of it jarring her body. Until finally, she collapsed, only dimly aware of the cool metal of the cannon under her and the heat of Radolf's hands.

He was softening inside her when at last he spoke, his voice hoarse. "Wake me."

A furry weight thumped onto Chloe's chest, jolting her ruthlessly awake. Green, glowing eyes stared into hers. Her heart gave a startled slam.

"Mrroooow?"

Her head fell back on the pillow in relief. "Jesus, Rhett, you scared the stuffings out of me!"

The cat turned to stare into a darkened corner beside the bed, ears folding flat to his head. He hissed—the long, distinctively vicious get-the-hell-away hiss he normally reserved for the neighbor's Great Dane.

Gooseflesh popped up along Chloe's skin in a cold wave. She flailed out with one hand, found the bedside lamp. Designed to turn on at a touch, it instantly blazed light into the room.

Chloe's wide eyes searched the corner Rhett stared into with such malevolent feline hostility. It was empty. She relaxed.

"There's nothing there, Rhett." She looked at the cat.

He was still staring at the corner, ears flattened, lips pulled back from his fangs. He hissed like something out of a horror movie.

"Oh, hell, Rhett, don't do this to me!" Chloe scooped the cat into the curve of one arm and threw back the covers with her free hand. "I just had a really good dream, and you're breaking the mood. Big time."

Rolling to her feet, she gave the corner another wary look. Still empty. She looked down at Rhett.

The cat seemed to be watching something move across the room.

Toward the painting.

And was the knight lying in a different position than he had the last time she looked?

"Okay, this is just toooo creepy." Chloe trotted toward the door, eying the painting warily. "Let's go watch CNN."

Probably for the rest of the night.

※⟨�◡⟩⟆※

In Evanesce, Radolf lay sated on the pile of furs next to his sleeping body.

"Thrice-cursed cat," Belisarda snarled. "I was not finished."

"I was," he said lazily.

She hissed at him, sounding remarkably like Chloe's tom.

※⟨�◡⟩⟆※

After watching an entire CNN headline cycle and drinking a mug of cocoa, the cat incident began to seem like a bad dream. Chloe went back to bed, hoping for another delicious encounter with Radolf.

She didn't get one.

But when she fell asleep Monday night, he returned as an Arab sheik with an English mother and a taste for redheaded Scottish travelers. On Tuesday, he became an adopted Apache warrior who captured a pretty settler.

On Wednesday, she played Confederate spy to his ruthless Union major. He was a Viking warrior on Thursday, making off with a lovely Celtic lass. On Friday, he became an English lord who won the virtue of a wastrel's daughter in a card game.

And each and every night, he taught Chloe more about pleasure than any flesh and blood man ever had.

※⟨ᴏ⟩⟆※

She saw the attack coming in plenty of time to parry. Chloe dropped her blade...but not in time. Her opponent's weapon struck home between her ribs.

"Touché, dammit." Sighing in disgust, she dragged off her fencing mask and wiped her sweating face with the back of her wrist.

"Which makes it five-oh, my favor." Amanda frowned as she took off her own mask. "I have never beaten you five-oh in my life. What's wrong?"

Chloe reeled over to the porch and collapsed on the top step. A muscle was jerking spasmodically in her thigh. She rubbed it absently. "Just tired, that's all. Haven't been sleeping well."

"You look like shit."

Chloe looked up at her friend and lifted a brow. "Thank you."

"You've got dark circles under your eyes, and you're paler than even a redhead has any business being." Amanda walked over to crouch on the grass in front of her, concern in her eyes. "And you were fencing at half speed. You anemic or something?"

"Maybe." Sighing, she leaned back to brace her elbows on the edge of the porch. "I don't know. I've felt rough for the past couple of days now. Guess I'm coming down with something."

"Better see a doctor."

"I will."

As if relieved, Amanda smiled and changed the subject. "So," she said, in a teasing voice, "had any more dreams about Sir Lottalance?"

"Not since the last one." Chloe told herself it wasn't really a lie. She couldn't help it if Amanda drew the wrong conclusion about which one the last one had been.

Her friend grinned impishly. "Too bad. After that Union major/spy thing, I was looking forward to finding out what romance novel you'd dreamed yourself into this time. I was kinda hoping for a western."

"Yeah," Chloe said. "That does sound like fun."

∗∾⟅ᗑ⟆∾∗

That night, she leaned against the kitchen counter, watching a frozen dinner turn lazy circles in her microwave. It dinged at last, and she pulled the plate out, hissing at its heat.

Peeling the plastic off, Chloe watched steam roll up without much interest. She dug her fork in with a grimace and scooped up a bite of Thai chicken. This particular dinner was one of her favorites, but tonight it tasted like sawdust. She forced herself to eat it anyway.

She'd lost seven pounds since Saturday. Seven pounds she'd always wanted to lose, true, but not by being unable to eat.

Too bad last night's dream didn't count. Radolf had fed her a deliciously exotic meal of roast pheasant before ravishing her on his endless dining table. It had tasted a lot more real than the Thai she was choking down now.

"Bllrtt?" Rhett reared onto his haunches and threw himself against her calf in a butting rub designed to get her attention. As if unconvinced he had it, he leaped up onto the counter.

"Hey." She shoved his furry muzzle away from her plate. "You already had two cans of cat food, not to mention my lunch. Keep this up, and you'll be too fat to terrorize the neighbor's dog."

"Mmrr." He rolled over on his back, presenting his fluffy black belly.

Too wise to fall for that trap, Chloe scratched him under one ear instead. If she'd tried for the tummy, he'd have gone after her hand with all four sets of claws. "What is it with you guys?" she asked as he started purring like a Jag after a tune up. "You beg for love, and then you go all Ginsu when a girl tries to give it to you. It's no wonder I prefer dream men."

Talking about Radolf reminded her she'd lied to Amanda. Chloe frowned guiltily as she gave the cat's ears another scratch. She'd always been able to tell her friend anything, and yet somehow this particular secret had grown too delicate to share.

"He's not even real," she grumbled to Rhett as the cat nosed her plate. "And yet, he is. Or this little voice in my head insists he is, anyway. How weird is that?"

"Blrtttt?" The animal looked up at her, green eyes intent.

"You think I'm nuts, don't you? You're probably right." Chloe sighed. "It's just—Chris never made me feel the way Radolf does." Absently, she poked at her dinner. "And I'm not just talking about the fantastic orgasms, either. In the entire six years of our relationship, Chris never once gave me the look Radolf gives me every damn night. As if I mean something to him. As if he needs me."

"Nrrrrr?"

She tossed down her fork and raked both hands through her hair as she turned to pace. "'Wake me.' What the heck does that mean? Radolf says that at the end of every dream. But how do you wake a dream?"

She stopped in the middle of the kitchen, head down, both hands laced behind her neck. "But it doesn't feel like a dream. That's the problem. His touch, his kiss, his body—it all feels so real."

Taking a deep breath, Chloe admitted, "And every morning, I hate waking up even more."

❧ ⚭ ☙

The moment she slept, Radolf stepped from the painting, eager to be with her again. He was only vaguely aware of Belisarda floating after him, as insubstantial in this plane as he was.

All day, he had waited impatiently for Chloe to sleep again. He had come to crave her company in a way he'd never craved any of the other women he'd known over the centuries.

Chloe was different.

Beautiful, yes, sensual, yes. But she was just as intelligent as she was lovely, and her wit was a match for both. Which was ironic, really, since he'd never considered either a prerequisite in a lover.

Just one more of his assumptions Chloe had turned on its head. Before, he'd had more frustration than pleasure with the women whose dreams he inhabited. Yet he enjoyed being with Chloe for its own sake. Something about her made even his eternal captivity bearable. He....

Something was wrong with her.

Radolf stopped dead in the mattress, staring into her sleeping face. She lay huddled beneath a pile of blankets as if cold, though he could tell the night was pleasant. Illuminated by a pool of silver moonlight, her face looked thin, drawn, and there were shadows under her eyes.

"What's wrong with her?" he demanded, glancing at Belisarda. "She looks ill."

The witch's eyes widened in startled interest. Then her expression smoothed. "She's well. The moon casts strange shadows, 'tis all."

Radolf studied his lover's face anxiously. "Nay, I think not. Could it be something we've done? I have...visited her longer than the others."

Belisarda nodded. "Most of your past lovers would have blocked you out by now." She shrugged. "They seem to sense ... something. But she is unusually obsessed with you."

"Yes. Obsessed. She's not getting enough sleep," he decided, turning reluctantly back toward the painting. "Best let her rest tonight."

As he strode past, Belisarda gaped at him in dismay. "But she's so close! This very night, she might break the spell." The witch hurried after him. "And then the two of you can sleep all you wish."

"No," Radolf said shortly. "I want to be free, but not enough to risk her."

The witch stopped in her tracks. "You've fallen for her!" Her burble of malicious laughter dragged him to a stop. "Radolf of Varik has finally fallen in love!"

A wave of ice rolled over Radolf's skin. He knew he didn't dare let Belisarda know how much Chloe had come to mean to him. "Don't be ridiculous," he snapped. "She's just another girl, no different from the others."

"Aye, Black Lord? Then why are you so willing to spend the night alone?"

He shrugged, fighting to keep his expression cool and unconcerned. "It may be some time yet before I convince her to free me. If she sickens, I could loose this chance."

The witch studied him, her eyes shimmering with that hellfire glow he'd come to fear. Then, slowly, she smiled. "The child is fine. Look." She gestured, and a cool, glowing orb appeared over Chloe's sleeping face, illuminating her features.

The shadows he'd thought he'd seen were gone. She was as beautiful and healthy as ever.

"You see?" Belisarda purred. "It's as I said. It was but a trick of the light. Go to her."

Sweet Christ, he wanted to. And yet…"I know you feed from the heat of her passion. Have you taken too much?"

The demon witch flicked long fingers in dismissal. "What I take, she'll not miss."

He frowned, his instincts clamoring.

"Unless your lover's heart fears to take even so small a chance as this," Belisarda said, her voice soft with mock sympathy.

Radolf shot the witch a glare and strode back toward Chloe. "Fine. Mayhap tonight she'll break the spell, and you and I will be quits."

"Oh, milord," Belisarda said as he sank into Chloe, "I look forward to the day."

"Not as much as I," he growled, and disappeared into his lover's dream.

※ঙ৩৮※

Chloe smelled woodsmoke, leather, and horse.

She frowned, suddenly, uncomfortably aware that she was lying on something coarse and prickly spread out over something hard and lumpy. Like a wool blanket on sandy ground.

If this was one of those dreams, it wasn't getting off to a very enticing...

A loud CLICK interrupted her train of thought. Her frown deepened as she struggled sleepily to place the noise. It sounded like...

A revolver being cocked.

Her eyes popped open.

Radolf stood over her, straddling her body, in a pair of Levi's that did amazing things for his long, muscular legs. A white shirt hugged his powerful chest, unbuttoned halfway down his washboard belly. Over the shirt, he wore a leather vest, a silver sheriff's star glittering against the rough, dark hide.

The gun in his hand was pointed right between her eyes.

"What a purty little thing you are," he drawled. "'Specially for a murderin' outlaw."

Chapter Four

Chloe stifled a snicker. "Did you actually say, 'purty'?"

He swooped into a crouch, almost sitting on her chest, the Colt an inch from her nose. "Yeah," he snarled. "And I cocked this here *gun*, too."

This was going to be fun. She banished her grin and batted her lashes. "Oh, please don't shoot me, mister!"

His eyes narrowed to deadly green slits. "You got a lot of gall beggin' for mercy, lady, after the way you stabbed that poor son of a bitch you were married to."

If she knew this particular kind of plot, the dearly departed had probably been trying to kill her at the time. If this was a novel, he'd turn up alive in chapter nineteen, just in time for his comeuppance. "It was self defense!"

"Tell it to the judge, lady." Radolf was really getting into this.

Probably because he intended to get into her.

Which sounded like a pretty good idea to Chloe. She widened her eyes, hoping she looked seductively helpless rather than goofy. "Please, Sheriff—I'll never get a fair trial! His daddy bought off the judge." They always did.

"Too bad," Radolf said, cold and implacable. "You're goin' back."

Chloe laid an artistically trembling hand on his bent knee. "I'll do *anything*!" God, what cheesy dialog. Good thing she wasn't a romance novelist.

He stood, six feet plus of luscious male slowly unfolding. Chloe hoped she wasn't visibly drooling.

He aimed the Colt between her breasts and sneered, "Now you're bein' insulting. You think you can seduce me dressed in those dusty boy's clothes?"

Now, there was a cue if ever she heard one. Chloe bit her lip and toyed with the top button of her cambric shirt. "I could ... take them off."

Radolf didn't move a muscle, but heat leaped in his gaze. She unbuttoned the button, then, slowly, the next.

Green eyes narrowed, burning hotter in his expressionless face.

Her heart began to pound. She slid the next button free, then paused to pull the edges of her shirt open a little more, revealing a V of cleavage. Daring a glance up at him through the screen of her lashes, she saw his poker face had not softened one bit.

But the erection straining his jeans would have made a stallion weep with jealousy.

She opened another button.

"Faster, sweetheart," he growled, gesturing with the Colt. "I'm gettin' bored." Apparently he wasn't in the mood to magically strip her naked this time.

Chloe opened her eyes wide and then gently bit her lip. His gaze flicked to her mouth. She could have sworn that massive erection got bigger.

She unbuttoned another button.

By the time all the buttons were free, she was as wet as he was hard. Se let her hands fall away, leaving her shirt open only enough to expose an inch-wide strip of bare flesh.

"That's not good enough," he growled. "Take it off."

She lifted her chin in mock defiance. "Make me."

His grin was every kinky fantasy she'd ever had. "Oh, it'll be my pleasure."

Radolf went to one knee, the other straddling her, as oiled-silk smooth as a cat. Deliberately, he touched her breastbone with the muzzle of the Colt. The metal felt cool against her heated skin.

"Now, wait a minute." Chloe caught her breath. "I don't think..."

"You don't need to." Slowly, he dragged the barrel of the gun over the swell of one breast, pushing her shirt aside until he raked the Colt right over her nipple. The little nub instantly drew into a hard, pointed peak. She whimpered.

He reversed his stroke, pushing back the other side of her shirt, baring the full swell of the other breast, again teasing her nipple with the gun.

"You've got real pretty breasts," he said, his voice hoarse and raw with need.

Then he raised the Colt until its muzzle pointed at the sky. "Play with 'em."

"Radolf..."

"Now."

Sweet Lord, this was getting hotter than the time he'd banged her over the cannon. Feigning reluctance, her heart pounding, Chloe reached for one breast and cupped it shyly.

"Squeeze it," Radolf ordered. "Offer it to me."

Licking her lips, she shifted her grip on the soft, full mound, kneading gently. The peak popped out at him, hard and insolent.

He looked at it, his eyes darkening into shadowed emerald. "That's a sweet little nipple. Nice and pink and tight." He contemplated it a long, burning moment. "Flick it with your thumb," he ordered finally. Bracing the elbow of his gun hand on one knee, he rested the other hand on his thigh, drawing her attention to the horse-choking bulge behind the tough denim. "Get it good and hard."

From the looks of it, it's already good and hard, Chloe thought, but obediently stroked her thumb over the little peak. The curl of pleasure made her gasp.

He smiled at her, slow and feral. "You like this, don't you? You like gettin' me hot. You like gettin' *you* hot." Gesturing with the Colt, he purred, "So let's get you hotter. Twist that nipple."

She hesitated.

He leveled the gun at her again. "That wasn't a request."

Biting her lip, Chloe obeyed, intensely conscious of his glittering gaze. "You really are a very bad man, aren't you?"

"Yeah, well, at least I'm not a killer." His beard twitched around his wicked grin. "Well, not lately. Both hands, sweetheart. Tug 'em for me."

Her heart was pounding a heavy metal drum solo as she tugged and twisted the swollen pink peaks under his gun.

As she milked both of the hard points, he reached back with a big hand and cupped her sex through the fabric of her jeans. She caught her breath, freezing like a rabbit. He pressed two fingers against the seam that lay between her thighs, rasping the coarse, thick fabric over slick, delicate flesh.

"Radolf!" she gasped, squirming.

"Keep milkin' those pretty tits, girl." He stroked, pressed, never taking those glittering green eyes off her. "You know," he said, lifting his hand away, "maybe what you need is something harder."

Chloe almost sobbed in gratitude. "Yes. Oh, yes. I want you so…" She broke off in alarm as he reached back with the gun and ran the muzzle along the seam of her jeans. "Radolf!"

"You know," he said, ignoring her yelp, "you're wearin' too many clothes. Take off these britches."

"Now, look…"

Like a rattler striking, he whipped the gun around. Chloe knew perfectly well the weapon wasn't real, any more than he was, but her blood chilled in her veins. "You'd rather hang?" he snapped.

"No." Her voice actually shook.

"Didn't think so." He stood, unfolding to his full, menacing height, and took a step back. "I want you naked, Chloe."

Something about the silken note in his voice sent heat pumping in to replace her fear. She licked her lips and decided to throw in the obligatory protest. "I'm not…like that."

"Yeah." He gave her a cynical Clint Eastwood smile. "You are." He gestured with the Colt. "Take 'em off." When she started to sit up, he growled, "No. Laying down. I want a good look."

This felt way too real. So why was she creaming inside her Levi's? Swallowing, she reached for her fly.

As she fumbled the buttons open, Radolf settled on the ground to watch, crossing those booted feet and propping up on one elbow. His biceps strained the sleeves. He put the gun down, but she knew just how fast it could be back in his hand.

"Strip 'em off," he ordered, his voice rough and dark.

Time for another obligatory virginal protest. "Radolf…"

"If I have to do it for you, I'm gonna paddle that little ass once I get it bare."

Her heart leaped in her chest. For a moment she was tempted to goad him into doing just that—but decided she'd much rather get that horse-choking erection where it would do her the most good.

Slowly, spinning it out, Chloe wiggled free of the jeans, knowing every little squirm made her breasts bounce.

Radolf really, *really* liked the view. She only wished he was naked, so she could see the source of that intimidating bulge without his jeans in the way.

When she finally lay on the bedroll in nothing but her open shirt, Radolf looked at her for a long, long time while she grew steadily wetter. "Damn, you really are a redhead, aren't you? Touch yourself. Deep." His lowered his lids, his mocking smile a white slash within the blond frame of his beard. "I want to make sure you're good and ready when I start working my cock in past those pretty copper curls."

Oh, she was ready. God, was she ready. But masturbating in front of him felt so damn kinky...

Still, she knew better than to refuse, so she reached shyly between her thighs and ran her fingers over the slick, swollen flesh.

"I want a better view," he rasped. "Spread 'em."

With an inward shudder of arousal, Chloe raised her knees and opened her thighs.

"Yeah, you're wet," he said, and started unbuttoning his Levi's. "Finger yourself."

She eyed his cock as his tanned fingers worked to free it from his fly. "Wouldn't you rather...?"

"Not yet. Do it."

She slipped a middle finger inside the tight entrance as he liberated his massive shaft. Radolf purred approval and told her to add another finger as he lazily began to stroke himself.

Arousal flowed through Chloe's veins like heated honey as she watched him caress his own hard shaft while rumbling erotic orders at her.

Shuddering in pleasure, she stroked her clit and pumped her fingers in and out of her swollen flesh. He watched her like a cougar picking its moment to pounce, naked lust in his eyes, triumph in his smile. All the while, one big hand pumped lazily at his big, straining cock. The other held his gun trained on her in silent threat.

She didn't think she'd ever done anything so kinky in her life. She could feel her climax simmering, just about to boil over..."God, Radolf, I'm coming..."

"On your feet!"

The rough bark froze her fingers. "But…"

He pointed the Colt right between her eyes. The long fingers of the other hand were still wrapped around his thick rod. "You come when I say you can come. On your feet!"

"Go to…"

"Finish that sentence, and you're goin' over my knee. And you won't like what I'll do to that pretty little ass when you get there." He bared his teeth. "On… your… feet."

Glaring at him, she stood.

Radolf gestured with the gun. "Turn around and bend over. I want a good look at that luscious butt." Brazenly, he cupped his heavy balls with his free hand and watched her like a wolf.

Another squirt of heat shot through Chloe at the stark eroticism of his pose. Which still didn't mean she liked what he was doing to her. Reluctantly, she turned around, set her feet apart, and bent.

"Finger your pussy," he growled.

Chloe threw him a simmering glare over her shoulder. His cock looked about a yard long. She imagined what it would feel like as he drove it hard into her.

"Aren't you going to do anything with that?" she demanded.

"Not yet. Now I want you to…"

She straightened and spun on him, furious. "And you can kiss my pink, puckered…!"

"Finish that sentence and you'll get that spanking—among other things. Now turn back around and bend over."

"Creep!" Snarling in frustration, she whirled—and spotted two saddled horses that stood at the edge of the campfire's light.

Chloe didn't think twice. She didn't think about being naked, or wonder where the hell she was going to go. She just sprang for the nearest horse, shoved a bare foot into the stirrup, boosted herself into the saddle, and banged both heels into the mare's silken white sides. The big animal leaped under her and tore off into the night.

Behind her, Radolf roared in fury.

She grinned and leaned over the horse's whipping mane. He'd catch her, of course. And when he did…

Well, he wouldn't be in the mood to tease.

The night wind whipped into her face, carrying the smell of

sagebrush and sand. *Damn,* Chloe thought, for what had to be the hundredth time that week, *this all seems so real.*

Hearing hoofbeats drumming behind her, she grinned at the full moon floating high in the night sky. She couldn't wait for him to catch her.

Radolf plunged after her on the big black stallion, enjoying the hot wind in his face. None of this was real, of course; he'd created it in her dreaming mind out of her own fantasies, aided by details he'd picked up over the centuries from other women's thoughts. Yet illusion or not, it seemed as real to him as it did to her.

Though her pale, luscious ass bobbing in that saddle looked more like something out of his own dreams than hers.

His stallion ran hard, its long strides gaining rapidly on the little mare's lead. Radolf licked his lips in anticipation, his heart pounding. Tonight might be the night she freed him, but even if it wasn't, he'd soon know the lush pleasure of Chloe's glorious body. And for now, that was enough.

It had to be.

One minute she was tearing through the night with the rolling thunder of hoofbeats in her ears.

The next, a hard male body slammed into hers, knocking her right off her horse.

Chloe had time to think, *This is going to hurt,* just before she tumbled onto a thick feather mattress and cool satin sheets. "Oof!" she gasped.

They both should have somersaulted right off the bed, as fast as they were going, but once again, the laws of physics gave them a break. They bounced just once and fell back into the slick, cool sheets, safe but shaken.

Winded, Chloe didn't even bother to struggle as Radolf settled on top of her and caught her wrists in both big hands. She was too busy surveying the brass bed that had somehow materialized in the middle of the Texas plains. "Well now, this is convenient."

"Definitely more so than breaking your neck," he agreed, lowering his head to sample one of her nipples.

"Got me there."

"I certainly do." He grinned sidelong at her and gave the hard peak an erotic rake with his teeth.

Chloe caught her breath and wiggled under him. He tightened his grip on her wrists, silently warning her she wasn't going anywhere. "So, Sheriff Radolf," she purred, "what are you planning to do with li'l ole me?"

He lifted his head, heat and humor in his gaze. He'd evidently decided to drop the big, bad sheriff act. "Ride you until you beg me to stop."

Chloe grinned. "That's what I thought."

"Clever wench." Returning his attention to her breasts, he settled down to suck one with a wicked skill and devoted attention that soon had her gasping.

Craving the feeling of his strong, naked body under her hands—his clothes had vanished—she tried to pull her wrists free. "I want to touch you."

"Not yet." He transferred both wrists to the grip of one hand as his gaze flashed up to meet hers. "You're my captive, sweet. I'm the one who does the touching."

Gently, ravenously, he moved over her, stopping here and there to nip and nibble and suckle, stroke and squeeze. In no time at all, he had her writhing mindlessly in the sheets, begging for his cock.

"No," he whispered the fourth time she pleaded with him. Then he lowered his head between her spread thighs to circle her clit. Almost bringing her to climax. Almost.

She could feel it shivering there, like a huge soap bubble filled with magical fireworks, just waiting for one tiny thrust.

Desperate for release, she ground against him. "Please, Radolf! God, you're driving me insane!"

"Only because I want company," he murmured, sliding one big finger slowly into her core. "I'm mad for you."

"Radolf!" Chloe cried, rolling her hips desperately.

He laughed softly and sat up, moving into the eager cradle of her thighs. "I can't resist you when you beg."

She caught her breath as he aimed his thick cock for her silken opening and slid inside in one long, hard thrust.

"Ahhhh, Christ," he whispered when he was in to the balls, his tone oddly reverent. "You're so sweet."

Chloe tossed her head on the pillow in pleasure as he settled over her in a delicious blanket of muscular strength. "God, your cock --!" There were no word for the glory as the hot satin shaft drew out of her, then thrust back inside in a searing lunge.

Lost, half-blind, she stared up at his face, silvered in moonlight. The muscles in his powerful shoulders worked as he braced himself, stroking slowly, his eyes half closed with the delight of being so deep within her.

Realizing he'd finally released her hands, Chloe wrapped both arms around his brawny torso and held on as his thrusts jarred her body. The glittering bubble of her climax swelled impossibly, trembling on the verge of breaking.

Mindless, she ground her pelvis against him, her breath sobbing in her throat as she stared up into his lost green eyes.

Radolf shuddered at the feeling of her silken calves riding his working ass as her nails dug into his back. He'd learned to make it real for his partners, but it had never been so real to him.

Then he felt her slick, tight walls pulse around him, and she threw her head back as she came, writhing against him.

He'd never in all his centuries seen anything as beautiful as Chloe's face, transported in hot joy.

As he stared into her eyes, he felt his own climax roll up his spine in a ferocious wave. Throwing back his head, Radolf bellowed his pleasure at the moon.

They lay together when it was over, tangled in the satin sheets like ordinary lovers.

Radolf lay still, listening to her heart as it slowed its desperate beat. She felt impossibly soft and precious in his arms.

He'd seduced so many women so many times over the past eight hundred years that he'd long since lost count. Yet none of them had ever touched him the way Chloe had. None had ever surprised him, aroused him, reached him the way she had.

Would she be the one to finally set him free? Would she believe him?

Would she pass the test?

If, pray God, she did, he'd stay with her. If she'd let him. If she loved him in truth as much as she seemed to in these delicious dreams. As much as he...He cut off the thought, unwilling to admit it to himself.

Feeling too much for her was dangerous. And not just because of what Belisarda might do to them both.

He tightened his grip on her narrow waist at the thought. "Wench, you've destroyed me." He'd intended the words as a joke, but they sounded all too fervent.

Chloe smiled at his words, looking up at the moon as she traced designs over his forearm with her nails. She could feel tendon and muscle ridged beneath his smooth skin. Golden hair dusted his flesh like threads of silk under her fingertips. "This isn't a dream." The words popped out of her mouth, without any conscious premeditation at all. They still rang with truth. "Somehow it's real." She turned her head to gaze into his face in wonder. "You're real."

His smile was a little sad. "You're only half right, I'm afraid." He swept a hand in a gesture at the brass bed sitting in the middle of the desert under a breathtaking night sky. "All this is a dream. But aye, I'm real."

It was impossible. Ridiculous.

Yet Chloe didn't doubt him. She knew he existed, felt the truth of it on some level that went beyond reason and logic.

Somewhere all the way down in her soul.

"How are you here, Radolf? How did you get inside my mind?"

He looked away, staring around across the darkened landscape. A muscle worked in his jaw. "Magic."

Chloe nodded. What other explanation was there? "Are you some kind of..." She searched for a word. "Wizard?"

He flashed her a cool look. She realized she'd somehow offended him. "I'm a knight. I belonged to the order of the Knights of Varik."

She digested that. "That sounds...medieval. Like one of the Holy

Orders, like the Templars."

"Very like, but we were an order even more secret. Some called us heretics, which is why the Church eventually wiped my brothers out. Ironic, that, for we were formed to defend her." He shrugged. "But we used magic, and most churchmen believed the source of all magic is the Devil."

Chloe looked at him. "Just how old are you, Radolf?"

"I was born in the Year of Our Lord, 1232."

She found she wasn't at all surprised. "So you're immortal."

"No." A muscle worked in his jaw. "Bespelled."

And from the sound of it, it wasn't a spell he enjoyed. "By whom?"

"Belisarda. A...I know not what she is. I call her witch, but I do not believe she's human. Demon, perhaps, or Sidhe. Or succubus, most like." He shrugged. His speech had slipped back into its medieval cadences again, as though that was most natural for him.

Chloe rolled on her side so she could drape an arm across his waist and prop her chin on his chest. "So how did you get on her bad side?"

"I was sent to kill her."

"That would do it."

He smiled slightly. "Indeed. At the time, it was possible for her to live in corporal form on Earth. Your science, your beliefs, have made that impossible today."

"A lot of people believe in magic," Chloe objected. "I'm not one of them, but still..."

"It's more than that. There are beams in the air..." He paused, frustrated.

She lifted her head, interested. "You mean radio waves? Electrical fields, that kind of thing?"

"Aye, those. They block Belisarda, disrupt her magic. 'Tis like breathing acid to her." He shrugged. "But when I was sent for her these eight centuries past, she could come and go as she pleased. And she pleased to live in a castle in England and feast on wayward young knights."

"She *ate* them?"

"Not the meat of them. But their pain, their pleasure. And eventually, when she slew them, their souls."

Chloe curled her lip. "Eeeww."

"Exactly. My order had been formed to fight such creatures. When we heard rumors of what she did, I was sent to investigate, since sometimes such tales were born of nothing more than malice."

"Wait a minute." She frowned, outraged on his behalf. "They sent you to fight her *alone*?"

Radolf shrugged his brawny shoulders against the silk pillow. "I had battled such creatures before and won. My sword was bespelled, worked with runes that made it possible for me to slay them. So I was confident." His expression turned bleak. "Too confident."

He fell silent so long she finally felt driven to prod him. "What happened?"

"I had been taught to shield my mind from magical invaders, so Belisarda could not read my thoughts—she would certainly have slain me if she had. She was wary of me on that account, so I set out to win her trust, the better to learn if the accusations were true." His green gaze turned brooding. "There were many knights around her who seemed bewitched, right enough, but she was beautiful, so that alone was no evidence of dark power."

Feeling a little prick of jealousy, Chloe asked, "How beautiful?"

"Enough that I grew to love her a little, until I learned of the evil in her." He stared up at the sky, his expression going grim. "I tarried with her longer than I should have, trying to decide if she was the demon the rumors said. Enough that she grew confident in me, and slipped back to her old ways."

"What happened?"

"One of her young knights grew jealous and challenged me. Fool that I was, I drew my sword, prepared to fight him—but she struck him down with a bolt of magic. I could only watch in horror as she moved to stand over him and drink down his soul. I could see it pouring from him in glowing streamers."

Chloe winced. "That must have been an ugly surprise."

His nod was short and grim. "Very. I knew I'd been duped. Here was no lovely innocent, but the very demon we'd been told. I lifted the blade I held, spitting curses on her. She turned, raging, and with the life force she'd stolen from that lad, she struck me down."

Chloe lifted her head and stared at him in horror. "Oh, God. You're a ghost!"

He stroked her cheek soothingly with a big, warm hand. "Nay, milady. I but sleep. I have slept for all the centuries since."

"'Wake me,'" she whispered in a burst of realization. "That's what you meant! But if you're asleep, how are you here? And why didn't she kill you when she had the chance?"

"As to that, I know not. But I believe Belisarda was frightened by how close I came to killing her. She decided she no longer wished to stay on mortal Earth to run such risks. Instead she returned to her own realm, somewhere in a world beyond this, taking my sleeping body with her."

Chloe frowned. "Why? I mean, why keep you?"

His expression grew even more grim. "I was provisions."

A sense of chill horror grew in her belly. "What do you mean?"

"Belisarda prefers to devour souls, but she can subsist well enough on the emotions mortals feel. Passion. Pleasure. But what she enjoys most is suffering."

The chill deepened. "But if you were asleep..."

"Only my body sleeps. My spirit walks like the ghost you named me, aware and feeling. So she used her powers to torture me for two hundred years until I agreed to be her whore."

Her horror took on a cast of sick understanding. Unable to lie against him any longer, Chloe sat up, staring down at him. "You go into women's dreams, and you seduce them. And Belisarda feeds on the pleasure they feel." Anger began to simmer in her blood. "The pleasure *I've* felt!"

"Aye, but..."

She ignored him, rolling the bed to pace. "That's why I've felt so damn weak. That's why I can't eat. You *fed* me to her, you bastard!"

Radolf stared at her. "You've been unable to eat? I thought you looked drawn. Damn the witch! She told me she did no harm!"

Chloe wheeled on him, shaking with hurt outrage. "You *used* me. Just like Chris! Get out!"

"No!" In an eye blink, he was in front of her, gripping her shoulders in both big hands. "It's not like that. Chloe, I love you. Yes, I need you to come into the painting, to give me the kiss that will wake me. But that does not change what I…"

"What are you, Sleeping Beauty?" She sneered at him, so angry and sick she wanted to throw up. "Find some other sucker, Radolf."

Anger ignited in his eyes. "I used the other women, aye. As they used me to live their secret dreams. But you are not like them. You *are* my dream, Chloe!" His voice dropped, going warm and deep. "You are my love."

She wanted to believe him so badly, she clenched her fists and seriously considered punching him in his beautiful, lying face. "What kind of idiot do you think I am? Get out of my head, Radolf. And don't come back."

His eyes widened as he realized she meant it. For an instant, raw desolation filled his face.

Then it was gone, and he drew himself to his full height. "It will be as you say. In forty-eight hours, the painting will disappear, and me with it. If you change your mind ere then, touch the heart and come to me. If not…" Bitterness darkened his eyes. "I will still love you the rest of my days, whether I will it or not. Now, wake you."

With a gasp, Chloe sat up. Staring wildly around, she realized she lay in her own bed.

A patch of darkness lay on the pillow next to her. Her heart gave a violent thump, and she rolled onto the floor with a yelp.

Then she realized the black shape was Rhett. The cat was staring at the painting, his green eyes unblinking.

Chloe's chill deepened. Licking her dry lips, she walked toward the moonlit canvas.

Before, Radolf's painted face had worn an expression of sleeping serenity. Now there was sadness in the line of his mouth, grief in the set of his thick brows.

She braced a hand against the wall beside the painting and bowed her head. "Radolf," she whispered, her voice choked. "What have you done to me?"

Her shoulders shook as she began to cry.

Chapter Five

Chloe sat staring numbly at the computer screen with eyes gritty from lack of sleep. She'd spent all day Sunday pacing the floor in front of the painting, trying to convince herself the events of the night before had been nothing more than a dream.

Her heart insisted differently.

She finally dropped off around four in the morning, but even then, Radolf had kept his promise to stay out of her dreams.

Now it was Monday. The painting would disappear at midnight.

And Chloe had no doubt at all it would disappear. Illogical or not, she believed what Radolf had told her in the dream. He really was a thirteenth century knight under a mystical spell cast by some kind of succubus, or witch, or whatever Belisarda was.

Suddenly a hand clamped over the back of her chair and spun her around. Chloe yelped.

And met Amanda's hot glare. "Dammit," her friend growled, "why are you letting them do this to you? They're not worth it!"

But he is, her heart whispered. *He is*. "Amanda..."

"For God's sake, it's been six months since you caught them in the sack! I thought you were over this!"

Chloe blinked. "This has nothing to do with Chris and Debbie. I'm not in love with him anymore." Thoughtfully, she added, "I'm not sure I ever really was." She'd felt hurt and humiliated when she'd realized what was going on between her lover and her friend, but she hadn't felt anything like the kind of desolation Radolf's betrayal had caused.

"What?" Glowering, Amanda fell into the chair next to hers. "So what the hell is going on?" Her blue eyes widened in sudden fear. "Did you get a bad report from the doctor?"

Chloe shook her head. "I haven't even been to the doctor. No, this is about something else. Somebody else."

"Gotta be a man," Amanda decided. "Nothing else would depress you this bad. So who is this guy, and why don't I know about him?"

Chloe glanced away helplessly, knowing her friend would never believe the truth. "It's...somebody I just met. I've only known him a week."

"You've gotten this flipped in a week? Must be a hell of a guy."

For once she could reply honestly. "He's like nobody I've ever met. He really puts Chris in perspective, you know? He's so damn hot, and he does things to me that..."

Amanda's jaw dropped. Then, thoughtfully, she closed it. "It's not just infatuation, is it?" she said slowly. "You're really in love with this guy! You've known him a week, and you've still fallen for him like a ton of bricks. So what's the problem?"

"He's...leaving tonight."

"So stop him. Or go with him. Or something."

Chloe sighed and rubbed her aching temples. "It's complicated, 'Manda."

"He's married."

"No, nothing like that. But I found out there've been...others."

Storm clouds gathered in Amanda's loyal eyes. "He's fooling around on you already? Hell, you're well rid of the creep."

"No. The others were from before he met me."

"Oh, God, he's HIV positive!"

"Of course not. That's not even a possibility. He's just...had a lot of women."

"So we're restricting ourselves to virgins now?" She snorted. "Girl-friend, unless you're only going to date fourteen-year-old boys—and I think there's a law against that—every guy on the planet is going to have some kind of romantic past."

Unable to sit still any longer, Chloe rose to pace. "But he says he loves me, Amanda! How do I know he's not just using me? It was bad enough when Chris did it. I don't think I could survive if I found out this man was just playing me for what he could get."

Amanda stood and caught her shoulders, halting her nervous strides. "Listen to me, sweetheart. You can't go through the rest of your life wearing body armor. For one thing, Kevlar and Victoria's Secret do not match."

Chloe slumped, thinking of Radolf and Belisarda, of demons and enchanted knights. So much could go wrong. "I just don't want to get hurt again."

"Baby, that's the thing about the Lover Lotto. You gotta play to win."

Chloe stood staring at the painting.

From the hall outside her room, the grandfather clock began a series of sonorous bongs, one after another as it chimed eleven.

You're running out of time, she thought. *Make up your mind, dammit.*

Her heart was pounding violently, even as her gritty eyes burned. She could almost feel Radolf's lips on her skin, his hands on her breasts, his thick cock surging into her sex. She could almost hear his whisper: *I will still love you the rest of my days, whether I will it or not.*

"You have to play to win," Chloe whispered.

She straightened her shoulders. Her heart began to pound even harder. "All right. Look out, Bitch Witch, here I come."

Chloe reached for Radolf's sleeping face—and touched canvas. Frowning, she ran her fingertips over the painting, but it remained stubbornly solid. "Dammit, I thought he said I was supposed to come through the painting. How do I get in?"

There had to be a way. And she'd better figure out what it was, because midnight was growing closer by the second.

Radolf stood on the other side of the painting, watching Chloe's beloved face as she frowned in concentration. "She's going to do it," he whispered, hardly daring to believe. "She forgave me. She's coming for me!"

"It does look like it," Belisarda whispered in his ear.

Something about the dark pleasure in the she-demon's voice made his heart clutch. He glared at her over his shoulder. "Will you go back on your word to free me, then?"

Belisarda gave him a chilling, catlike smile. "I would not dream of it, Lord Radolf. The moment her sweet lips touch yours, you'll be free." The smile widened into a cold, triumphant grin. "And I'll have my revenge."

Radolf's stomach sank as he spun to face her. This was it. The trap he'd always suspected was hidden somewhere within the rotten heart of her offer. "What treachery do you plan, bitch?"

Her eyes glittered with malicious pleasure. "You never asked what would happen to the girl, Radolf."

Sweet Jesu, it was worse than he thought. "No. Belisarda, I've whored for you. I've endured your torture and screamed for your pleasure for eight endless centuries. Surely that's enough revenge to sate even a devil's appetite!"

"It's not." Her inhumanly beautiful face twisted with hate. "Not for what you did to me."

"I did nothing!" Radolf roared. "You stopped me before I could strike!"

Her hand flashed out, drove into his ghostly chest and closed around the core of his soul. "You made me love you, cur! You made me ache for your touch. I, who was worshiped as a goddess, blinded by a mortal's pretty lies!"

Agony tore at him as her fingers tightened. He ached to spit defiance into her face, but in his pain he couldn't speak.

Belisarda raged on. "I should have slain you then, knowing what you were, but no. I kept you by me these eight hundred years, thinking that perhaps, one day, you would come to love me as I deserve. Instead you give your heart to one of those puling whores who feed me with their lust!"

Now outrage gave him strength. "You tormented me without cease! How could you imagine I'd ever care for you, you black hell bitch?"

"I am a goddess!" she shrieked in his face. "But if you won't give me what I deserve, I'll take what pleasure I can. When that slut's lips touch yours, you'll return to her world to live out your mortal life, just as I've sworn. But she will take your place in sleep!"

"No!" he bellowed.

"Yes! And she will suffer such torment as to make your time with me seem a pretty spring day. I will whore her, my lord Radolf, whore her as I have you, to every twisted thing whose polluted male mind I can force her into. They'll rape her in their dreams as she curses your memory. While you live out your mortal days, tortured by the thought of her torment."

His fury drained away, stolen by sick horror. "No. Belisarda, don't." He knew he begged, but for once, he didn't care. If the demon wanted him to crawl, he'd crawl. Anything to save Chloe. "I will serve you however you want, but don't do this to her! Keep me and I will…"

A malicious cat smile curled her mouth. "No."

And she was gone, leaving him to float in thin, sick wisps, cold with despair.

"Touch the heart," Chloe murmured, suddenly remembering what Radolf had said the moment before he'd disappeared. "He said 'touch the heart.' What heart?"

She scanned the painting desperately, conscious of the minutes ticking past.

Then she saw it. There, at the bottom of the painting, in the very center of the frame. A tiny heart shape. Her heart gave a nervous thump.

Chloe hesitated a moment, saying a silent prayer. Then, carefully, she reached out and pressed her fingers against the inlay.

Nothing happened.

She frowned, then reached to touch the surface of the canvas again. Her hand sank into the painting as if sliding into water. "That's it!" A broad grin spread over her face. "That's it! Oh, Radolf, I did it! I'm coming!"

Except…Chloe hesitated, remembering his description of Belisarda's powers. She really didn't like the idea of just popping into the painting. No way was the witch going to let her simply kiss Radolf and waltz off with him.

It couldn't be that easy.

But—what kind of weapon could Chloe use against somebody with that kind of power…?

An idea popped into her head. She smiled in savage pleasure. "Oh, yeah!" But would it work?

There was only one way to find out.

Chloe spun away from the painting and ran to the night table beside her bed. Finding what she was looking for, she stuffed it into a pocket of her jeans and hurried back to the painting.

To her relief, when she touched the canvas, she found it was still liquid.

"Question is," Chloe muttered, taking a step back, "how am I supposed to get in there?" She threw a quick glance at her bedside clock.

11:45 p.m.

"Screw it," she muttered.

And, taking a running step forward, Chloe leaped up and threw herself through the canvas in a long, flat dive.

Fire danced over her skin, lifting every hair on her body. She heard wild laughter and sobbing screams as a flare of cold blue light blinded her.

Then she hit cold stone hard enough to jar her teeth. Tucking into a ball, she rolled with a fencer's agility across the marble floor, tumbling to absorb the momentum of her fall.

When Chloe bounced to her feet again and glanced around, she immediately recognized her surroundings. The gleaming stone walls were splashed with the same golden light she'd seen in the painting.

On the bed before her lay Radolf, lying asleep in all his glorious blond nudity, his hand on his sword, his armor around him, a sable pelt spread across his bare hips.

"Real," Chloe whispered in wonder. "Oh, he is *real.*"

As a giddy grin broke over her face, she stepped toward him. She'd never wanted to kiss a man so badly in her life.

Stop.

Radolf's voice, faint, ghostly. It made the hair rise on the back of her neck. Chloe turned, heart pounding.

He stood behind her, a glowing, insubstantial presence. *It's a trap,* he said, though she didn't hear his voice with her ears. *Belisarda has lied to me all these years. If you kiss me, you'll wake me—and you'll take my place in this hell.*

Chloe nodded, not at all surprised. "Yeah, I figured it was something like that. But if I kiss you, you will wake, right?"

Aye, but 'tis not worth it, Chloe. The expression on his ghostly face was grim and urgent. *"You'll be imprisoned here as I have been, hers to torture for centuries. You must go back. The painting will vanish in minutes, and you'll be trapped.*

"And leave you here? I don't think so." She reached into her pocket and pulled out her weapon. He watched, uncomprehending, as she prepared it with a flick of her thumb. "That magic sword still work?"

Aye, but she'll give me no chance to use it. His eyes blazed with urgency. *Chloe, you must leave. Now. I have no wish to be free if it means you'll sleep an eternity in torture!*

"Yeah, well, I guess you'll just have to wake me, then." She held up her secret weapon and tapped it with her thumb. "When the time comes, press this button."

Chloe, for the sake of all the saints...

She turned away and crouched to tucked the object in the left hand of his sleeping body. Her heart was pounding a wild adrenalin beat, but she felt no fear as she looked down into his familiar, roughly handsome face.

"I love you," Chloe whispered, and pressed her lips to his.

Radolf's eyes flew open for the first time in eight centuries to meet her gaze in horror.

Then her lovely blue eyes rolled back in her head, and she dropped in a heap beside the bed.

"Chloe!" he roared, flinging himself from the bed. "No!"

"Yesssss!" Belisarda purred, appearing beside him as he dropped to one knee. "Time to leave, my lord. I want to be alone with your pretty lover." The demon witch lifted her hands to cast her spell. He knew he'd never be able to stop her in time.

Then he felt the small, cool object in his left hand.

He didn't even take the time to feel hope. Desperately, Radolf lifted Chloe's weapon, pointed it at the witch, and hit the button his lover had pointed out.

The one marked SEND.

Belisarda staggered as the cell phone sent out its pulse of radio waves, dialing the number to Chloe's house in a series of cheerful beeps, just as she'd set it to do.

"Bastard!" the witch shrieked as the phone's radiation ripped into her magical body. "I'll tear out your cursed heart while she..."

"You'd do nothing but die, bitch." Radolf snatched up his sword and drove it hard into her chest. She staggered, but reached for her power, obviously determined to destroy him even as she died.

Not this time, Belisarda, he thought, and flung all his mental strength into the spell he'd memorized eight centuries before. Even as the witch's clawed, glowing hands reached for him, Radolf drove the burst of magic down the blade and into her black heart.

She shrieked in agony as a wave of pure white light rolled up her torso from the enchanted blade. For an instant, he saw the twisted, demonic thing that was her true nature.

A soundless explosion flung him back. He hit the ground hard and rolled to his feet, turning his eyes toward the spot where the witch had stood.

She was gone, the blade with her.

But before he could feel any sense of relief, Radolf heard the first rolling bong of Chloe's grandfather clock.

The painting! The gate was about to close!

He scooped Chloe's unconscious form into his arms. Whispering a silent prayer, Radolf turned and raced for the painting that, on this side, showed a view of her empty bedroom.

BONG!

He threw himself in a flat dive into the frame, Chloe clutched against his chest. The two of them surged through the gold framed opening...

BONG!

Something snagged his left foot just before they hit the carpeted floor of Chloe's bedroom. Canvas tore. Radolf twisted, taking the brunt of the impact, as they tumbled together.

BONG!

They fetched up against the bed. Heart pounding, he looked back at the painting.

BONG!

Now the canvas showed only the empty castle chamber, though there was a torn place in the center. He remembered the sensation of something catching on his foot and winced. It had been too cursed close.

BONG! The last chime.

Tiny shimmering flames raced across the canvas. The painting vanished with a sullen hiss.

"Thank God," Radolf whispered, then looked down into Chloe's face. He caught his breath.

She still slept.

Oh, sweet Christ, what if Belisarda's death meant the spell could no longer be broken? "No," he whispered. "Sweet one, wake. Please wake..."

Taking her chin in his hand, he tilted her face upward and pressed his lips to hers.

Radolf gave the kiss everything he had, lips and tongue and teeth as he plastered her slim body desperately against his own.

Until...

"Mmmmm," she purred into his mouth, "promise me you'll always wake me up this way."

Hope expanding in his chest, Radolf lifted his head to gaze down into her face. She smiled up at him sleepily. He grinned back, suddenly drunk with pure happiness. "Oh, aye! Every single morning!"

"I knew you'd save me," Chloe murmured, turning her face sleepily against his throat.

"No, lass." He closed his eyes in relief. "You're the one who saved me."

"Witch dead?"

"Oh, aye."

"Good." She settled against him with a sigh. "'Cause I've been up for two days straight, and I really need some sleep."

Carefully, he got to his feet, holding her cradled in his arms. "You go ahead, sweet. I've had all the sleep I need."

A soft snore was her only answer.

He smiled and crawled in the bed with her, wanting only to hold her for the rest of the night.

❦

Chloe awoke to a warm male mouth moving over hers, coaxing, suckling. The hot, liquid stroke of a tongue, the gentle nip of teeth on her lower lip. She opened her eyes and lifted her head.

Radolf looked down at her as the morning sunlight ignited his blond hair into a golden blaze. Stretching in his arms, Chloe smiled sleepily up at him. "Mmm. Tell me this isn't a dream."

He cupped her bare breast, thumbed her nipple until it tightened, pouting pink. "No, sweet, this is definitely real."

"Good." She slipped both arms around his torso, feeling solid muscle and bone working under her hands. "'Cause if it's not, I never want to wake up."

The arm around her waist tightened. "Never say that, sweet. It came too close to coming true."

"Well, it didn't." Chloe threaded one hand through his hair, enjoying the silken slide of the strands against her fingers. "We beat the bitch."

"Aye," he breathed, his eyes closing in relief. "Oh, aye, that we did."

She frowned slightly. "I only wish I'd seen it. What happened?"

He lowered his head to her breast. "Your gambit with the cell phone worked. It disrupted her magic long enough for me to kill her." Radolf's gaze flicked up to meet Chloe's. "And no, I don't want to talk about the details. I have other pastimes in mind."

As satin masculine lips closed over her nipple, Chloe arched into the mattress and lost all interest in anything else.

Finally, finally, she could touch him, kiss him, however she wanted.

As his teeth raked the taunt peak of her breast, she indulged herself, stroking her hands over the fine, hard muscle of his broad shoulders, exploring tendon and bone that lay under his smooth, tanned flesh.

It was so hard to believe. This amazing man—this literal knight in shining armor—had fought for her. Had been willing to sacrifice himself for her.

And she'd almost lost him.

So when he started to nibble and lick his way down her torso, obviously intent on even more erotic kisses, Chloe stopped him. "No," she whispered. "I want to pleasure you, too."

He gave her a hot sidelong look as he traced her navel with his tongue. "This does pleasure me, sweet."

She knew her own grin was equally wicked. "But we can make it even better."

So with a little coaxing, Radolf rolled over on his back, allowing her to straddle his face as she bent over him to pay loving attention to his bobbing cock.

"Well," Chloe purred, as she ran her tongue down the violently hard shaft, "I'm glad to see my dreams didn't exaggerate."

He gave a mock growl and closed his mouth over her clit in retaliation, sending pleasure shooting up her spine like a Roman Candle.

Humming in delight, she licked the tight plum head, enjoying the salty taste of his pleasure almost as much as the delicately erotic sensations his tongue created.

Radolf reached down and caught the tip of one breast, squeezing and rolling the little peak as he circled her clit with his tongue. She shivered at the heated honey pleasure and nibbled the head of his cock.

He growled and slipped one big finger into the slick opening of her sex. Stroking in and out, he caught one of her labia between his teeth and gave it a gently maddening tug.

"You're not a nice man," Chloe moaned.

"Oh, I'm a very nice man," Radolf rumbled, and proved it when he added a second finger to the next deep stroke.

In gratitude, she angled his cock upward and engulfed it in one long swoop that had him gasping against her sex. He felt lusciously smooth and tight against her lips as she suckled him.

She'd never tasted anything as erotic as Radolf's hot, taut shaft. The smell of him made her feel dizzy with a breathless combination of joy and lust. Moaning—half from the sensual pleasure of taking him, half from what he was doing to her with his own talented tongue—she swallowed around his massive shaft.

The feeling of her mouth on him made Radolf moan against her sweetly astringent pussy. Her sweet, full breast filled his palm with silk as he squeezed each of her tight little nipples in turn.

Radolf had never felt like this in his life. Despite the hundreds of women he'd seduced, he'd never known the delicious sense of having found the other half of himself. He wanted to tell Chloe how he felt, but he had no words for the sheer dimensions of the thing. He, the erotic sorcerer of so many female dreams, felt as overwhelmed as a virgin.

So he said nothing, instead trying to show her with his body even as she drove him mad with her hot, silken mouth.

"That's enough!" Chloe gasped at last, pulling suddenly away from him.

Radolf growled a protest, but before he could snatch her back, she took his cock in one cool, small hand, and guided it to the opening of her sex.

Then she sank down over him, impaling herself one glorious inch at a time.

"God!" Chloe moaned at the sweet, burning heat of taking him to the very heart. "Radolf, you feel so good!"

"Oh, aye, sweet," he groaned, as her silken little ass settled across his hips. He clenched his teeth desperately, fearing that he'd lose control and spill in her before she even made her first thrust.

Somehow he held on as she rose again, wet and slick and tight around his aching cock. Then, slowly, she began to move up and down, bare breasts quivering, her little hands braced on his chest.

He'd never seen anything as beautiful as her face, blue eyes wide and dazed, full mouth open as she panted.

Joy swelled in him, as hot and savage as the pleasure of her slow strokes. Finally, after so many centuries, he was free. Free to love the exquisite woman who'd freed him.

Suddenly he found the words for what he felt. "I love you!" he gasped.

"Yes!" she cried out, arching her back, grinding down hard. "Oh, God, Radolf, I love you too!"

It was that glorious admission that shot him over the edge. He came, roaring her name.

As Radolf arched hard under her, driving to his full length, Chloe felt her own climax fountain up through her body in an burning electric surge. She threw back her head and screamed out her ecstasy.

They ground together, writhing, for endless, exquisite moments before she collapsed, panting and spent, across his powerful chest.

It took her two tries to manage speech. "I do love you."

"And it's a lucky man I am." She felt his strong arms wrap around her sweating ribs. "For I'd hate to love like this alone."

Epilogue

One Year Later

Chloe watched as the two masked, white-garbed figures faced each other across the fencing strip. Each held a fencing saber in a gloved hand as four judges watched, two on either side of the strip.

The state championship rode on this particular bout, and she knew neither man was in any mood to lose.

Suddenly, with a blood-chilling roar, the taller of the two sprang forward. His opponent parried and scuttled aside from his charge.

The big man shot past, twisted, and slashed backward with his saber, catching the other squarely across the buttocks. The thinner man yowled as all four judges threw up a hand, indicating they'd seen the hit.

"Yes!" Chloe, Amanda and Richard howled in joyful chorus from the gym bleachers, applauding wildly.

Radolf pulled off his fencing mask, tucked it under one arm, and stepped toward the man he'd beaten so thoroughly, offering his hand in the traditional fencer's gesture.

Chris Jennings ripped off his own mask and shot the bigger man's hand a fulminating glare before limping off the strip. Debbie hurried out to meet him, stepping back when he snarled.

Chloe stifled a snicker. The thin, flexible sabers, unlike the stiffer fencing foil, were designed to be used in cutting strokes, like cavalry swords. Though too dull to break the skin, a saber blade could whip viciously in the hands of a fencer as skilled and strong as Radolf.

She didn't envy Chris his bruises. Especially since Radolf had caught him twice across the ass and once over the hips, along with a couple of good solid blows to the mask that had probably rung his chimes.

"That was mean," Chloe told her husband as he pulled open his jacket flap and collapsed on the bleachers beside her.

"Don't listen to the little hypocrite," Amanda said. "She loved every minute of it."

"So did I," added Amanda's husband, Richard, slapping Radolf on the shoulder. "That bastard has needed an ass-beating for years. Good to see him finally get one."

Radolf grinned and wiped his sweating face with the back of his hand. "Well, my loving wife wouldn't let me jump him in an alley, so it was the best I could do."

"Civilized people," Chloe told him firmly, "do not jump their wives' ex-boyfriends in alleys."

"Don't bet on it," Richard drawled. Amanda smacked him on the arm, and he ducked, smirking. "I mean, *of course* we'd never do anything like that. Really."

"Hardly ever," Radolf agreed, deadpan.

The two men had become fast friends over the past year as Radolf struggled to adjust to life in the twenty-first century. He wasn't completely ignorant, having picked up a great deal from the minds of the women he'd pleasured, but he still had broad gaps in his knowledge.

There'd also been his complete lack of identification, but he and Chloe had managed to solve that problem with Richard's help. Apparently not all the skilled brick masons and carpenters the contractor used were legal aliens; among his contacts was someone who knew how to produce the needed documentation.

Neither Chloe or Radolf was inclined to look a gift horse in the mouth.

After that, the former Dark Lord enrolled in an adult ed program while she taught him to drive. Meanwhile, he'd gone to work for Richard, whose thriving business had almost grown too big to manage alone.

Though Radolf started out doing grunt work, he proved to have a real talent for carpentry, as well as an eye for construction. Add to that his natural leadership skills and taste for hard work, and Richard quickly decided he was an obvious choice for foreman.

The two men now split the job of overseeing Richard's various residential building projects. They were seriously discussing a partnership, since they'd be able to build twice as many houses as Richard could alone.

Still, sometimes Chloe wondered if Richard suspected the truth—that Radolf was far more than he seemed. But if he did, he never asked.

"Hey, Chloe Varik!" one of the judges called, dragging her back to the present. "You're up!"

Grabbing her foil, she jumped to her feet, then caught her husband's bearded face and swooped down for a kiss. He gave back in kind, putting so much tongue and enthusiasm into it, somebody started applauding.

When they finally came up for air, Radolf grinned at her. "What was that for?"

"My happily ever after," Chloe said, and sauntered off to meet her next opponent—who just happened to be Debbie.

Radolf watched her go, a hot glitter in his eyes. "No," he murmured, "Thank *you*."

About the Author:

Angela Knight's *first book was written in pencil and illustrated in crayon; she was nine years old at the time. But her mother was enthralled, and Angela was hooked.*

In the years that followed, Angela managed to figure out a way to make a living—more or less—at what she loved best: writing. After a short career as a comic book writer, she became a newspaper reporter for the Spartanburg Herald Journal, among other newspapers. She covered everything from school board meetings to murders. Several of her stories won South Carolina Press Association awards under her real name, Julie Woodcock.

Along the way, she found herself playing Lois Lane to her detective husband's Superman. He'd go off to solve murders, and she'd sneak around after him trying to find out what was going on. The only time things got really uncomfortable was the day she watched him hunt pipe bombs, an experience she never wants to repeat.

But her first writing love has always been romance. She read The Wolf and The Dove *at 15, at least until her mother caught her at it.*

In 1996, she discovered the small press publisher Red Sage, and realized her dream of romance publication in the company's **Secrets 2** *anthology. Since then, her work has appeared in four* **Secrets** *anthologies. She's tremendously grateful to publisher Alexandria Kendall for the opportunity to make her dreams come true.*

Angela enjoys hearing from readers. You may email her at angelanight2002@bellsouth.net. *Check out her website at* www. angelasknights.com.

If you enjoyed *Secrets Volume 11* but haven't read other volumes, you should see what you're missing!

Secrets Volume 1:

In *A Lady's Quest*, author Bonnie Hamre brings you a London historical where Lady Antonia Blair-Sutworth searches for a lover in a most shocking and pleasing way.

Alice Gaines' *The Spinner's Dream* weaves a seductive fantasy that will leave every woman wishing for her own private love slave, desperate and running for his life.

Ivy Landon takes you for a wild ride. *The Proposal* will taunt you, tease you, even shock you. A contemporary erotica for the adventurous woman's ultimate fantasy.

With *The Gift* by Jeanie LeGendre, you're immersed in the historic tale of exotic seduction and bondage. Read about a concubine's delicious surrender to her Sultan.

Secrets Volume 2:

Surrogate Lover, by Doreen DeSalvo, is a contemporary tale of lust and love in the 90's. A surrogate sex therapist thought he had all the answers until he met Sarah.

Bonnie Hamre's regency tale *Snowbound* delights as the Earl of Howden is teased and tortured by his own desires—finally a woman who equals his overpowering sensuality.

In *Roarke's Prisoner*, by Angela Knight, starship captain Elise remembers the eager animal submission she'd known before at her captor's hands and refuses to be his toy again.

Susan Paul's *Savage Garden* tells the story of Raine's capture by a mysterious revolutionary in Mexico. She quickly finds lush erotic nights in her captor's arms.

Secrets Volume 3:

In Jeanie Cesarini's *The Spy Who Loved Me*, FBI agents Paige Ellison and Christopher Sharp discover excitement and passion in some unusual undercover work.

Warning: This story is only for the most adventurous of readers. Ann Jacobs tells the story of *The Barbarian*. Giles has a sexual arsenal designed to break down proud Lady Brianna's defenses — erotic pleasures learned in a harem.

Wild, sexual hunger is unleashed in this futuristic vampire tale with a twist. In Angela Knight's *Blood and Kisses*, find out just who is seducing whom?

B.J. McCall takes you into the erotic world of strip joints in *Love Undercover*. On assignment, Lt. Amanda Forbes and Det. "Cowboy" Cooper find temptation hard to resist.

Secrets Volume 4:

An Act of Love is Jeanie Cesarini's sequel. Shelby's terrified of sex. Film star Jason Gage must coach her in the ways of love. He wants her to feel true passion in his arms.

The Love Slave, by Emma Holly, is a woman's ultimate fantasy. For one year, Princess Lily will be attended to by three delicious men. She delights in playing with the first two, but it's the reluctant Grae that stirs her desires.

Lady Crystal is in turmoil in *Enslaved*, by Desirée Lindsey. Lord Nicholas' dark passions and irresistible charm have brought her long-hidden desires to the surface.

Betsy Morgan and Susan Paul bring you Kaki York's story in *The Bodyguard*. Watching the wild, erotic romps of her client's sexual conquests on the security cameras is getting to her—and her partner, the ruggedly handsome James Kulick.

Secrets Volume 5:

B.J. McCall is back with *Alias Smith and Jones*. Meredith Collins is stranded overnight at the airport. A handsome stranger named Smith offers her sanctuary for the evening—how can she resist those mesmerizing green-flecked eyes?

Strictly Business, by Shannon Hollis, tells of Elizabeth Forrester's desire to climb the corporate ladder on her merits, not her looks. But the gorgeous Garrett Hill has come along and stirred her wildest fantasies.

Chevon Gael's *Insatiable* is the tale of a man's obsession. After corporate exec Ashlyn Fraser's glamour shot session, photographer Marcus Remington can't get her off his mind. Forget the beautiful models, he must have her —but where did she go?

Sandy Fraser's *Beneath Two Moons* is a futuristic wild ride. Conor is rough and tough like frontiermen of old, and he's on the prowl for a new conquest. Dr. Eva Kelsey got away once before, but this time he'll make sure she begs for more.

Secrets Volume 6:

Sandy Fraser is back with *Flint's Fuse*. Dana Madison's father has her "kidnapped" for her own safety. Flint, the tall, dark and dangerousmercenary, is hired for the job. But just which one is the prisoner—Dana will try *anything* to get away.

In *Love's Prisoner*, by MaryJanice Davidson, Jeannie Lawrence experienced unwilling rapture at Michael Windham's hands. She never expected the devilishly handsome man to show back up in her life—or turn out to be a werewolf!

Alice Gaines' *The Education of Miss Felicity Wells* finds a pupil needing to learn how to satisfy her soon-to-be husband. Dr. Marcus Slade, an experienced lover, agrees to take her on as a student, but can he stop short of taking her completely?

Angela Knight tells another spicy tale. On the trail of a story, reporter Dana Ivory stumbles onto a secret—a sexy, secret agent who happens to be a vampire.She wants her story but Gabriel Archer believes she's *A Candidate for the Kiss*.

Secrets Volume 7:

In *Amelia's Innocence* by Julia Welles, Amelia didn't know her father bet her in a card game with Captain Quentin Hawke, so honor demands a compromise—three days of erotic foreplay, leaving her virginity and future intact.

Jade Lawless brings *The Woman of His Dreams* to life. Artist Gray Avonaco moved in next door to Joanna Morgan and now is plagued by provocative dreams. Is it unrequited lust or Gray's chance to be with the woman he loves?

Surrender by Kathryn Anne Dubois tells of Lady Johanna. She wants no part of the binding strictures of marriage to the powerful Duke. But she doesn't realize he wants sensual adventure, and sexual satisfaction.

Angela Knight's *Kissing the Hunter* finds Navy Seal Logan McLean hunting the vampires who murdered his wife. Virginia Hart is a sexy vampire searching for her lost soul-mate only to find him in a man determined to kill her.

Secrets Volume 8:

In Jeanie Cesarini's latest tale, we meet Kathryn Roman as she inherits a legal brothel. She refuses to trade her Manhattan high-powered career for a life in the wild west. But the town of Love, Nevada has recruited Trey Holliday, one very dominant cowboy, with *Taming Kate*.

In *Jared's Wolf* by MaryJanice Davidson, Jared Rocke will do anything to avenge his sister's death, but he wasn't expecting to fall for Moira Wolfbauer, the she-wolf sworn to protect her werewolf pack. The two enemies must stop a killer while learning that love defies all boundaries.

My Champion, My Love, by Alice Gaines, tells the tale of Celeste Broder, a woman committed for a sexy appetite that is tolerated in men, but not women. Mayor Robert Albright may be her salvation—*if* she can convince him her freedom will mean a chance to indulge their appetites together.

Liz Maverick takes you to a post-apocalyptic world in *Kiss or Kill*. Camille Kazinsky's military career rides on her decision—whether the robo called Meat should live or die. Meat's future depends on proving he's human enough to live, *man* enough, to make her feel like a woman.

Secrets Volume 9:

Kimberly Dean brings you *Wanted*. FBI Special Agent Jeff Reno wants Danielle Carver. There's her body, brains—and that charge of treason on her head. Unable to clear her name, Dani goes on the run, but the sexy Fed is hot on her trail. What will he do once he catches her? And why is the idea so tempting?

In *Wild for You*. by Kathryn Anne Dubois, college intern Georgie gets lost and captured by a wildman of the Congo. She soon discovers this terrifying specimen of male virility has never seen a woman. The research possibilities are endless! Until he shows her he has research ideas of his own.

Bonnie Hamre is back with *Flights of Fantasy*. Chloe has taught others to see the realities of life but she's never shared the intimate world of her sensual yearnings. Given the chance, will she be woman enough to fulfill her most secret erotic fantasy? Join her as she ventures into her Flights of Fantasy.

Lisa Marie Rice's story, *Secluded*, is a wild one. Nicholas Lee had to claw his way to the top. His wealth and power come with a price—his enemies will kill anyone he loves. When Isabelle Summerby steals his heart, Nicholas secludes her in his underground palace to live a lifetime of desire in only a few days.

Secrets Volume 10:

In Dominique Sinclair's *Private Eyes*, top private investigator Niccola Black is used to tracking down adulterous spouses, but when a mystery man captures her absolute attention during a stakeout, she discovers her "no seduction" rule is bending under the pressure of the long denied passion.

Bonnie Hamre's *The Ruination of Lady Jane* brings you Lady Jane Ponsonby-Maitland's story. With an upcoming marriage to a man more than twice her age, she disappears. Havyn Attercliffe was sent to retrieve his brother's ward, but when she begs him to ruin her rather than turn her over to her odious fiancé, how can he refuse?

Jeanie Cesarini is back with *Code Name: Kiss*. Agent Lily Justiss would do anything to defend her country against terrorists, including giving her virginity away on an undercover mission as a sex slave. But even as her master takes possession, it's fantasies of her commanding officer, Seth Blackthorn, that fuels her desire.

Kathryn Anne Dubois' *The Sacrifice* tells a story about Lady Anastasia Bedovier who's three days away from taking her vows as a nun, but decadent, sensual dreams force her to consider that her sacrifice of chastity might mean little until she has experienced the passion she will deny. She goes to Count Maxwell, the infamous Lord of Pleasure, and in one erotic night, she learns the heights of sensual pleasure, then flees. Maxwell thought he was immune from love, but the nameless novice that warmed his bed has proved his undoing, and despite his desperate search, he can't reach her.

Men you've been dreaming about!

Secrets

Satisfy your desire for more.

*F*eel the wild adventure, fierce passion and the power of love in every *Secrets* Collection story. Red Sage Publishing's romance authors create richly crafted, sexy, sensual, novella-length stories. Each one is just the right length for reading after a long and hectic day.

Each volume in the *Secrets* Collection has four diverse, ultra-sexy, romantic novellas brimming with adventure, passion and love. More adventurous tales for the adventurous reader. The *Secrets* Collection are a glorious mix of romance genre; numerous historical settings, contemporary, paranormal, science fiction and suspense. We are always looking for new adventures.

Reader response to the *Secrets* volumes has been great! Here's just a small sample:

> *"I loved the variety of settings. Four completely wonderful time periods, give you four completely wonderful reads."*

> *"Each story was a page-turning tale I hated to put down."*

> *"I love Secrets! When is the next volume coming out? This one was Hot! Loved the heroes!"*

Secrets have won raves and awards. We could go on, but why don't you find out for yourself—order your set of *Secrets* today! See the back for details.

Secrets, Volume 1

Listen to what reviewers say:

"These stories take you beyond romance into the realm of erotica. I found *Secrets* absolutely delicious."

—Virginia Henley,
New York Times Best Selling Author

"*Secrets* is a collection of novellas for the daring, adventurous woman who's not afraid to give her fantasies free reign."
—Kathe Robin, *Romantic Times* Magazine

"…In fact, the men featured in all the stories are terrific, they all want to please and pleasure their women. If you like erotic romance you will love *Secrets*."
—*Romantic Readers* Review

In *Secrets, Volume 1* you'll find:

A Lady's Quest by Bonnie Hamre
Widowed Lady Antonia Blair-Sutworth searches for a lover to save her from the handsome Duke of Sutherland. The "auditions" may be shocking but utterly tantalizing.

The Spinner's Dream by Alice Gaines
A seductive fantasy that leaves every woman wishing for her own private love slave, desperate and running for his life.

The Proposal by Ivy Landon
This tale is a walk on the wild side of love. *The Proposal* will taunt you, tease you, and shock you. A contemporary erotica for the adventurous woman.

The Gift by Jeanie LeGendre
Immerse yourself in this historic tale of exotic seduction, bondage and a concubine's surrender to the Sultan's desire. Can Alessandra live the life and give the gift the Sultan demands of her?

Secrets, Volume 2

Listen to what reviewers say:

"*Secrets* offers four novellas of sensual delight; each beautifully written with intense feeling and dedication to character development. For those seeking stories with heightened intimacy, look no further."

—Kathee Card, *Romancing the Web*

"Such a welcome diversity in styles and genres. Rich characterization in sensual tales. An exciting read that's sure to titillate the senses."

—Cheryl Ann Porter

"*Secrets 2* left me breathless. Sensual satisfaction guaranteed…times four!"

—Virginia Henley, *New York Times* Best Selling Author

In *Secrets, Volume 2* you'll find:

Surrogate Lover by Doreen DeSalvo

Adrian Ross is a surrogate sex therapist who has all the answers and control. He thought he'd seen and done it all, but he'd never met Sarah.

Snowbound by Bonnie Hamre

A delicious, sensuous regency tale. The marriage-shy Earl of Howden is teased and tortured by his own desires and finds there is a woman who can equal his overpowering sensuality.

Roarke's Prisoner by Angela Knight

Elise, a starship captain, remembers the eager animal submission she'd known before at her captor's hands and refuses to become his toy again. However, she has no idea of the delights he's planned for her this time.

Savage Garden by Susan Paul

Raine's been captured by a mysterious and dangerous revolutionary leader in Mexico. At first her only concern is survival, but she quickly finds lush erotic nights in her captor's arms.

Winner of the Fallot Literary Award for Fiction!

Secrets, Volume 3

Listen to what reviewers say:

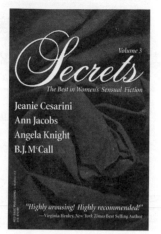

"*Secrets, Volume 3*, leaves the reader breathless. A delicious confection of sensuous treats awaits the reader on each turn of the page!"
—Kathee Card, *Romancing the Web*

"From the FBI to Police Dectective to Vampires to a Medieval Warlord home from the Crusade—*Secrets 3* is simply the best!"
—Susan Paul, award winning author

"An unabashed celebration of sex. Highly arousing! Highly recommended!"
—Virginia Henley, *New York Times* Best Selling Author

In *Secrets, Volume 3* you'll find:

The Spy Who Loved Me by Jeanie Cesarini

Undercover FBI agent Paige Ellison's sexual appetites rise to new levels when she works with leading man Christopher Sharp, the cunning agent who uses all his training to capture her body and heart.

The Barbarian by Ann Jacobs

Lady Brianna vows not to surrender to the barbaric Giles, Earl of Harrow. He must use sexual arts learned in the infidels' harem to conquer his bride. A word of caution—this is not for the faint of heart.

Blood and Kisses by Angela Knight

A vampire assassin is after Beryl St. Cloud. Her only hope lies with Decker, another vampire and ex-mercenary. Broke, she offers herself as payment for his services. Will his seductive powers take her very soul?

Love Undercover by B.J. McCall

Amanda Forbes is the bait in a strip joint sting operation. While she performs, fellow detective "Cowboy" Cooper gets to watch. Though he excites her, she must fight the temptation to surrender to the passion.

Winner of the 1997 Under the Covers Readers Favorite Award

Secrets, Volume 4

Listen to what reviewers say:

"Provocative...seductive...a must read!"
—*Romantic Times* Magazine

"These are the kind of stories that romance readers that 'want a little more' have been looking for all their lives...."
—*Affaire de Coeur* Magazine

"*Secrets, Volume 4*, has something to satisfy every erotic fantasy... simply sexational!"
—Virginia Henley, *New York Times* Best Selling Author

In *Secrets, Volume 4* you'll find:

An Act of Love by Jeanie Cesarini
Shelby Moran's past left her terrified of sex. International film star Jason Gage must gently coach the young starlet in the ways of love. He wants more than an act—he wants Shelby to feel true passion in his arms.

Enslaved by Desirée Lindsey
Lord Nicholas Summer's air of danger, dark passions, and irresistible charm have brought Lady Crystal's long-hidden desires to the surface. Will he be able to give her the one thing she desires before it's too late?

The Bodyguard by Betsy Morgan and Susan Paul
Kaki York is a bodyguard, but watching the wild, erotic romps of her client's sexual conquests on the security cameras is getting to her—and her partner, the ruggedly handsome James Kulick. Can she resist his insistent desire to have her?

The Love Slave by Emma Holly
A woman's ultimate fantasy. For one year, Princess Lily will be attended to by three delicious men of her choice. While she delights in playing with the first two, it's the reluctant Grae, with his powerful chest, black eyes and hair, that stirs her desires.

Secrets, Volume 5

Listen to what reviewers say:

"Hot, hot, hot! Not for the faint-hearted!"

—Romantic Times Magazine

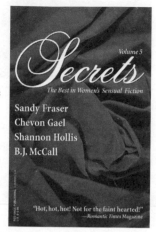

"As you make your way through the stories, you will find yourself becoming hotter and hotter. *Secrets* just keeps getting better and better."

—Affaire de Coeur Magazine

"*Secrets 5* is a collage of lucious sensuality. Any woman who reads *Secrets* is in for an awakening!"

—Virginia Henley, *New York Times* Best Selling Author

In *Secrets, Volume 5* you'll find:

Beneath Two Moons by Sandy Fraser

Ready for a very wild romp? Step into the future and find Conor, rough and masculine like frontiermen of old, on the prowl for a new conquest. In his sights, Dr. Eva Kelsey. She got away once before, but this time Conor makes sure she begs for more.

Insatiable by Chevon Gael

Marcus Remington photographs beautiful models for a living, but it's Ashlyn Fraser, a young corporate exec having some glamour shots done, who has stolen his heart. It's up to Marcus to help her discover her inner sexual self.

Strictly Business by Shannon Hollis

Elizabeth Forrester knows it's tough enough for a woman to make it to the top in the corporate world. Garrett Hill, the most beautiful man in Silicon Valley, has to come along to stir up her wildest fantasies. Dare she give in to both their desires?

Alias Smith and Jones by B.J. McCall

Meredith Collins finds herself stranded overnight at the airport. A handsome stranger by the name of Smith offers her sanctuaty for the evening and she finds those mesmerizing, green-flecked eyes hard to resist. Are they to be just two ships passing in the night?

Secrets, Volume 6

Listen to what reviewers say:

"Red Sage was the first and remains the leader of Women's Erotic Romance Fiction Collections!"

—*Romantic Times* Magazine

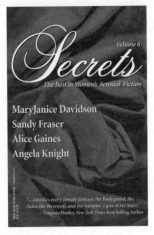

"*Secrets, Volume 6*, is the best of *Secrets* yet. ...four of the most erotic stories in one volume than this reader has yet to see anywhere else. ...These stories are full of erotica at its best and you'll definitely want to keep it handy for lots of re-reading!"

—*Affaire de Coeur* Magazine

"*Secrets 6* satisfies every female fantasy: the Bodyguard, the Tutor, the Werewolf, and the Vampire. I give it Six Stars!"

—Virginia Henley, *New York Times* Best Selling Author

In *Secrets, Volume 6* you'll find:

Flint's Fuse by Sandy Fraser
Dana Madison's father has her "kidnapped" for her own safety. Flint, the tall, dark and dangerous mercenary, is hired for the job. But just which one is the prisoner—Dana will try *anything* to get away.

Love's Prisoner by MaryJanice Davidson
Trapped in an elevator, Jeannie Lawrence experienced unwilling rapture at Michael Windham's hands. She never expected the devilishly handsome man to show back up in her life—or turn out to be a werewolf!

The Education of Miss Felicity Wells by Alice Gaines
Felicity Wells wants to be sure she'll satisfy her soon-to-be husband but she needs a teacher. Dr. Marcus Slade, an experienced lover, agrees to take her on as a student, but can he stop short of taking her completely?

A Candidate for the Kiss by Angela Knight
Working on a story, reporter Dana Ivory stumbles onto a more amazing one—a sexy, secret agent who happens to be a vampire. She wants her story but Gabriel Archer wants more from her than just sex and blood.

Secrets, Volume 7

Listen to what reviewers say:

"Get out your asbestos gloves — *Secrets Volume 7* is…extremely hot, true erotic romance…passionate and titillating. There's nothing quite like baring your secrets!"

—*Romantic Times* Magazine

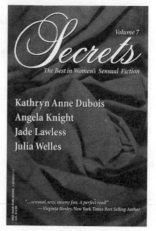

"…sensual, sexy, steamy fun. A perfect read!"

—Virginia Henley,
New York Times Best Selling Author

"Intensely provocative and disarmingly romantic, **Secrets, Volume 7,** is a romance reader's paradise that will take you beyond your wildest dreams!"

—Ballston Book House Review

In **Secrets, Volume 7** you'll find:

Amelia's Innocence by Julia Welles

Amelia didn't know her father bet her in a card game with Captain Quentin Hawke, so honor demands a compromise—three days of erotic foreplay, leaving her virginity and future intact.

The Woman of His Dreams by Jade Lawless

From the day artist Gray Avonaco moves in next door, Joanna Morgan is plagued by provocative dreams. But what she believes is unrequited lust, Gray sees as another chance to be with the woman he loves. He must persuade her that even death can't stop true love.

Surrender by Kathryn Anne Dubois

Free-spirited Lady Johanna wants no part of the binding strictures society imposes with her marriage to the powerful Duke. She doesn't know the dark Duke wants sensual adventure, and sexual satisfaction.

Kissing the Hunter by Angela Knight

Navy Seal Logan McLean hunts the vampires who murdered his wife. Virginia Hart is a sexy vampire searching for her lost soul-mate only to find him in a man determined to kill her. She must convince him all vampires aren't created equally.

Winner of the Venus Book Club Best Book of the Year

Secrets, Volume 8

Listen to what reviewers say:

"*Secrets, Volume 8*, is an amazing compilation of sexy stories covering a wide range of subjects, all designed to titillate the senses. ...you'll find something for everybody in this latest version of *Secrets*."

—*Affaire de Coeur* Magazine

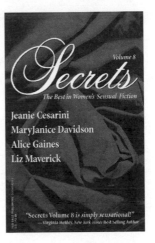

"*Secrets Volume 8*, is simply sensational!"

—Virginia Henley, *New York Times* Best Selling Author

"These delectable stories will have you turning the pages long into the night. Passionate, provocative and perfect for setting the mood...."

—*Escape to Romance* Reviews

In *Secrets, Volume 8* you'll find:

Taming Kate by Jeanie Cesarini

Kathryn Roman inherits a legal brothel. Little does this city girl know the town of Love, Nevada wants her to be their new madam so they've charged Trey Holliday, one very dominant cowboy, with taming her.

Jared's Wolf by MaryJanice Davidson

Jared Rocke will do anything to avenge his sister's death, but ends up attracted to Moira Wolfbauer, the she-wolf sworn to protect her pack. Joining forces to stop a killer, they learn love defies all boundaries.

My Champion, My Lover by Alice Gaines

Celeste Broder is a woman committed for having a sexy appetite. Mayor Robert Albright may be her champion—if she can convince him her freedom will mean a chance to indulge their appetites together.

Kiss or Kill by Liz Maverick

In this post-apocalyptic world, Camille Kazinsky's military career rides on her ability to make a choice—whether the robo called Meat should live or die. Meat's future depends on proving he's human enough to live, man enough...to makes her feel like a woman.

Winner of the Venus Book Club
Best Book of the Year

Secrets, Volume 9

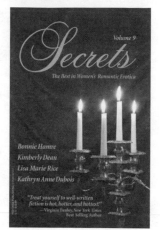

Listen to what reviewers say:

In *Secrets, Volume 9* you'll find:

Wild For You by Kathryn Anne Dubois

When college intern, Georgie, gets captured by a Congo wildman, she discovers this specimen of male virility has never seen a woman. The research possibilities are endless!

Wanted by Kimberly Dean

FBI Special Agent Jeff Reno wants Danielle Carver. There's her body, brains—and that charge of treason on her head. Dani goes on the run, but the sexy Fed is hot on her trail.

Secluded by Lisa Marie Rice

Nicholas Lee's wealth and power came with a price—his enemies will kill anyone he loves. When Isabelle steals his heart, Nicholas secludes her in his palace for a lifetime of desire in only a few days.

Flights of Fantasy by Bonnie Hamre

Chloe taught others to see the realities of life but she's never shared the intimate world of her sensual yearnings. Given the chance, will she be woman enough to fulfill her most secret erotic fantasy?

Secrets, Volume 10

Listen to what reviewers say:

"*Secrets Volume 10*, an erotic dance through medieval castles, sultan's palaces, the English countryside and expensive hotel suites, explodes with passion-filled pages."

—*Romantic Times BOOKclub*

"Having read the previous nine volumes, this one fulfills the expectations of what is expected in a *Secrets* book: romance and eroticism at its best!!"

—*Fallen Angel Reviews*

"All are hot steamy romances so if you enjoy erotica romance, you are sure to enjoy *Secrets, Volume 10*. All this reviewer can say is WOW!!"

—*The Best Reviews*

In *Secrets, Volume 10* you'll find:

Private Eyes by Dominique Sinclair

When a mystery man captivates P.I. Nicolla Black during a stakeout, she discovers her no-seduction rule bending under the pressure of long denied passion. She agrees to the seduction, but he demands her total surrender.

The Ruination of Lady Jane by Bonnie Hamre

To avoid her upcoming marriage, Lady Jane Ponsonby-Maitland flees into the arms of Havyn Attercliffe. She begs him to ruin her rather than turn her over to her odious fiancé.

Code Name: Kiss by Jeanie Cesarini

Agent Lily Justiss is on a mission to defend her country against terrorists that requires giving up her virginity as a sex slave. As her master takes her body, desire for her commanding officer Seth Blackthorn fuels her mind.

The Sacrifice by Kathryn Anne Dubois

Lady Anastasia Bedovier is days from taking her vows as a Nun. Before she denies her sensuality forever, she wants to experience pleasure. Count Maxwell is the perfect man to initiate her into erotic delight.

Secrets, Volume 11

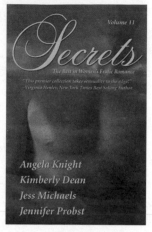

Listen to what reviewers say:

"*Secrets Volume 11* delivers once again with storylines that include erotic masquerades, ancient curses, modern-day betrayal and a prince charming looking for a kiss. ★★★★"

—*Romantic Times BOOKclub*

"Indulge yourself with this erotic treat and join the thousands of readers who just can't get enough. Be forewarned that *Secrets 11* will wet your appetite for more, but will offer you the ultimate in pleasurable erotic literature."

—*Ballston Book House Review*

"*Secrets 11* quite honestly is my favorite anthology from Red Sage so far"

—*The Best Reviews*

In *Secrets, Volume 11* you'll find:

Masquerade by Jennifer Probst

Hailey Ashton is determined to free herself from her sexual restrictions. Four nights of erotic pleasures without revealing her identity. A chance to explore her secret desires without the fear of unmasking.

Ancient Pleasures by Jess Michaels

Isabella Winslow is obsessed with finding out what caused her late husband's death, but trapped in an Egyptian concubine's tomb with a sexy American raider, succumbing to the mummy's sensual curse takes over.

Manhunt by Kimberly Dean

Framed for murder, Michael Tucker takes Taryn Swanson hostage—the one woman who can clear him. Despite the evidence against him, the attraction between them is strong. Tucker resorts to unconventional, yet effective methods of persuasion to change the sexy ADA's mind.

Wake Me by Angela Knight

Chloe Hart received a sexy painting of a sleeping knight. Radolf of Varik has been trapped for centuries in the painting since, cursed by a witch. His only hope is to visit the dreams of women and make one of them fall in love with him so she can free him with a kiss.

The Forever Kiss
by Angela Knight

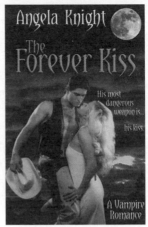

Listen to what reviewers say:

"*The Forever Kiss* flows well with good characters and an interesting plot. ... If you enjoy vampires and a lot of hot sex, you are sure to enjoy *The Forever Kiss*."

—*The Best Reviews*

"Battling vampires, a protective ghost and the ever present battle of good and evil keep excellent pace with the erotic delights in Angela Knight's *The Forever Kiss*—a book that absolutely bites with refreshing paranormal humor." **4½ Stars, Top Pick**

—*Romantic Times BOOKclub*

"I found *The Forever Kiss* to be an exceptionally written, refreshing book. ... I really enjoyed this book by Angela Knight. ... 5 angels!"

—*Fallen Angel Reviews*

"*The Forever Kiss* is the first single title released from Red Sage and if this is any indication of what we can expect, it won't be the last. ... The love scenes are hot enough to give a vampire a sunburn and the fight scenes will have you cheering for the good guys."

—*Really Bad Barb Reviews*

In *The Forever Kiss*:

For years, Valerie Chase has been haunted by dreams of a Texas Ranger she knows only as "Cowboy." As a child, he rescued her from the nightmare vampires who murdered her parents. As an adult, she still dreams of him—but now he's her seductive lover in nights of erotic pleasure.

Yet "Cowboy" is more than a dream—he's the real Cade McKinnon—and a vampire! For years, he's protected Valerie from Edward Ridgemont, the sadistic vampire who turned him. Now, Ridgmont wants Valerie for his own and Cade is the only one who can protect her.

When Val finds herself abducted by her handsome dream man, she's appalled to discover he's one of the vampires she fears. Now, caught in a web of fear and passion, she and Cade must learn to trust each other, even as an immortal monster stalks their every move.

Their only hope of survival is...*The Forever Kiss*.

It's not just reviewers raving about *Secrets*. See what readers have to say:

"When are you coming out with a new Volume? I want a new one next month!" via email from a reader.

"I loved the hot, wet sex without vulgar words being used to make it exciting." after *Volume 1*

"I loved the blend of sensuality and sexual intensity—HOT!" after *Volume 2*

"The best thing about *Secrets* is they're hot and brief! The least thing is you do not have enough of them!" after *Volume 3*

"I have been extreamly satisfied with *Secrets*, keep up the good writing." after *Volume 4*

"I love the sensuality and sex that is not normally written about or explored in a really romantic context" after *Volume 4*

"Loved it all!!!" after *Volume 5*

"I love the tastful, hot way that *Secrets* pushes the edge. The genre mix is cool, too." after *Volume 5*

"Stories have plot and characters to support the erotica. They would be good strong stories without the heat." after *Volume 5*

"*Secrets* really knows how to push the envelop better than anyone else." after *Volume 6*

"*Secrets*, there is nothing not to like. This is the top banana, so to speak." after *Volume 6*

"'Would you buy *Volume 7*?' YES!!! Inform me ASAP and I am so there!!" after *Volume 6*

"Can I please, please, please pre-order *Volume 7*? I want to be the first to get it of my friends. They don't have email so they can't write you! I can!" after *Volume 6*

Finally, the men you've been dreaming about!
Give the Gift of Spicy Romantic Fiction

Don't want to wait? You can place a retail price ($12.99) order for any of the *Secrets* volumes from the following:

① **Waldenbooks and Borders Stores**

② **Amazon.com** or **BarnesandNoble.com**

③ **Book Clearinghouse (800-431-1579)**

④ **Romantic Times Magazine**
Books by Mail (718-237-1097)

⑤ Special order at other bookstores.
Bookstores: Please contact Baker & Taylor Distributors or Red Sage Publishing for bookstore sales.

Order by title or ISBN #:

Vol. 1: 0-9648942-0-3

Vol. 2: 0-9648942-1-1

Vol. 3: 0-9648942-2-X

Vol. 4: 0-9648942-4-6

Vol. 5: 0-9648942-5-4

Vol. 6: 0-9648942-6-2

Vol. 7: 0-9648942-7-0

Vol. 8: 0-9648942-8-9

Vol. 9: 0-9648942-9-7

Vol. 10: 0-9754516-0-X

Vol. 11: 0-9754516-1-8

The Forever Kiss: 0-9648942-3-8 ($14.00)

Red Sage Publishing Mail Order Form:

(Orders shipped in two to three days of receipt.)

	Quantity	Mail Order Price	Total
Secrets **Volume 1** *(Retail $12.99)*	——————	$ 9.99	——————
Secrets **Volume 2** *(Retail $12.99)*	——————	$ 9.99	——————
Secrets **Volume 3** *(Retail $12.99)*	——————	$ 9.99	——————
Secrets **Volume 4** *(Retail $12.99)*	——————	$ 9.99	——————
Secrets **Volume 5** *(Retail $12.99)*	——————	$ 9.99	——————
Secrets **Volume 6** *(Retail $12.99)*	——————	$ 9.99	——————
Secrets **Volume 7** *(Retail $12.99)*	——————	$ 9.99	——————
Secrets **Volume 8** *(Retail $12.99)*	——————	$ 9.99	——————
Secrets **Volume 9** *(Retail $12.99)*	——————	$ 9.99	——————
Secrets **Volume 10** *(Retail $12.99)*	——————	$ 9.99	——————
Secrets **Volume 11** *(Retail $12.99)*	——————	$ 9.99	——————
The Forever Kiss *(Retail $14.00)*	——————	$11.00	——————

Shipping & handling (in the U.S.)

US Priority Mail:
1–2 books .... $ 5.50
3–5 books $11.50
6–9 books $14.50
10–11 books $19.00

UPS insured:
1–4 books $16.00
5–9 books $25.00
10–11 books $29.00

—————————

SUBTOTAL —————————

Florida 6% sales tax (if delivered in FL) —————————

TOTAL AMOUNT ENCLOSED —————————

Your personal information is kept private and not shared with anyone.

Name: (please print) —————————————————————————

Address: (no P.O. Boxes) —————————————————————————

City/State/Zip: —————————————————————————

Phone or email: (only regarding order if necessary) —————————————————

Please make check payable to **Red Sage Publishing**. Check must be drawn on a U.S. bank in U.S. dollars. Mail your check and order form to:

Red Sage Publishing, Inc.   Department S11   P.O. Box 4844   Seminole, FL 33775

Or use the order form on our website: www.redsagepub.com